Sweet Christine

by

C. C. Colee

PublishAmerica

Baltimore

First printing

ISBN: 1-4137-2472-8
PUBLISHED BY PUBLISHAMERICA, LLLP
www.publishamerica.com
Baltimore

Printed in the United States of America

~ Dedication ~

For my daughter, Heather, who loves stories about Old England and 18th century English nobility.

A big thanks to Cody for letting me 'play' with this idea.
~ Chris

To Joan,
Happy Reading!
C. C. Cole
Chris Cole
&
Cody Lee

Chapter 1
London, Winter 1728

Lady Elizabeth Hunnicutt smiled at her guests as she walked across the large room toward her husband. Dressed in a pale green velvet gown that complemented her auburn hair and hazel eyes, Elizabeth looked at the sea of faces and still did not see the one person she hoped would be attending her small gathering.

"Oh Lady Elizabeth! Your decorations are absolutely lovely," a woman said, stopping her. "I am sure the children are simply excited about the season, what with all the gift-giving."

"Why yes, Lady Harriet. Chelsea knows what the season is all about while Jonathon is still wide-eyed over the whole affair."

"Well, he is so young. How old is he now? Two years?" another woman asked.

"Yes, Lady Beatrice, and into everything we set down," Elizabeth told them.

With a warm hostess smile, she listened to the women chatter over her decorations. Vines of ivy and holly were strung across the mantel and outlined the entrances to each room. Hiding the nails that held the vines in place were sprigs of red holly berries. On the tables, the vines were formed into circles and dotted with more red berries to accent the larger platters of meats and bowls of stew, soup, and other mouth-watering dishes.

Around the house, Elizabeth placed red taffeta ribbons tied in large bows on mirrors and tables. The red bows also covered each place the vines were tacked onto the banister of the grand staircase leading up to the second floor. She had red berries and greenery hanging from chandeliers and other light fixtures.

Finding a pause in their comments, Elizabeth broke in with an apologetic tone, "If you will excuse me, I must catch Peter before he disappears on me once again."

Silently congratulating herself, she thought of the ease in which she extracted herself from the two women. She had done so all evening with other ladies who offered their wisdom and tales of their family traditions. Such prattling at any garden party would have given her a headache in a short period of time. Reaching her husband, she touched his arm and smiled at the tall slim man talking with Peter.

"Hello, Andrew. Somehow I missed seeing you come in," she greeted.

"You seemed to be in an enthralling discussion with Lady Fields and Lady Wells," Andrew replied with a smile, his eyes sparkling with humor.

Dressed in fawn colored britches, white shirt with a fashionably tied cravat, a green vest and matching waistcoat, Andrew Chandler, Duke of Kenilworth, caught many furtive glances from single and married women alike. His thick coal black hair was neatly tied back with a matching green ribbon to reveal a cleanly shaven chiseled face and emerald green eyes.

Looking at the auburn haired woman before him, Andrew bent his tall frame slightly towards her to whisper, "I dare say, anything those two had to tell you could not possibly be ignored. Such a wealth of knowledge, such insight into the—"

Elizabeth laughed and slapped at his arm. "You are still incorrigible, Andrew. If you must know, Meredith and Hazel were explaining the delicacies of raising a young boy."

"Ah, there you see!" Andrew continued playfully. "Such knowledge and intelligence. Having raised only daughters, they would know how to care and nurture a young boy's mind."

Peter chuckled behind his hand then quickly cleared his throat when his wife's hazel eyes shifted to him. Raising his glass in a silent toast to his friend, he sipped his drink to remain out of the conversation.

"Oh do be quiet, you rogue," Elizabeth playfully chided.

"Someone talking about me again?" came a man's voice from behind Elizabeth.

Turning her head, she found Lord Richard Pittman stepping around her. He was dressed in his usual dark blue colors that showed off his blue eyes and dark wavy hair. He placed a gentle kiss on her cheek and said, "Good evening, cousin."

"Richard, you are late," she grumbled.

"Have I missed dinner?" he asked with a frown.

"Well, no."

"Then I am not yet late," Richard said cheerfully. "Abby sends her regrets. Her father had not made it home this evening as planned, undoubtedly due to the snow, and her mother is still fighting a cough."

"Oh, too bad. I will miss her this evening. I was hoping to reunite her with Christine and Caroline. It has been almost two years since we were all together last." Looking around the room searchingly, she added, "Then again it would be difficult to reunite them if the other party does not arrive."

"Are you sure Christine will come tonight?" Peter asked. "She is, after all, still in mourning."

"And no doubt still blaming herself for Lord Christopher's death," Elizabeth muttered.

"What were they arguing about?" Richard asked.

"I have no idea," Peter replied.

"Nor do I," Elizabeth put in.

"Lady Christine Lockhart?" Andrew questioned.

"Yes, she and her mother returned from Vienna earlier this week and Christine assured me that she would come tonight," Elizabeth replied.

Peter turned to look at the new arrivals standing at the doorway and smiled. "Well, she did not disappoint you, my dear."

Elizabeth turned quickly in the direction of his nod and found Christine Lockhart standing in the doorway with two other women and a man. Patting her husband's arm, she hurried away to greet her newly arrived guests. The three men smiled at one another then looked in appreciation at the vision dressed in black.

Lady Christine Lockhart stood unsmiling as she looked around the room while her mother spoke with their companions, Lady Caroline Huntington and her husband, David. All four were dressed in black as they observed the mourning period at the death of Lord Christopher Lockhart, Christine's stepfather.

"Does she not smile?" Richard asked Peter.

"Yes, she does and has a beautiful smile if memory serves me correctly," Andrew replied, not taking his eyes from the new arrivals. When two pairs of eyes shifted to him, he smiled and added, "I would have to be dead not to notice such beauty, gentlemen."

The three men laughed in good humor. They continued to look on as Elizabeth happily greeted the newcomers. Catching sight of her friend, the young Lady Lockhart smiled.

"You see," Andrew said smugly and smiled.

"Good, now I can tell Abby I have confirmation that I am not dead," Richard said slapping his friend on the back. Andrew chuckled at his play as

Richard looked around and said to Peter, "However, a man could die of thirst because his own cousin did not offer a drink."

"Your legs look sturdy enough and you know where the drinks are served. Good God, how often have you been in my house, Richard?" Peter grumbled through a smile.

Richard laughed and headed into the small crowd to get his choice of liquors.

"Her presence should give the Ton something to talk about for the next several weeks," Andrew said to Peter while gesturing towards Christine.

"The Ton always talks about Christine Lockhart. Nothing she does is good enough for them but then she does not try to appease them either, which I fully applaud. If they bothered to know and understand her, they would truly be surprised at the woman they would find beneath that so-called heartless shell," Peter told him then let out a snort of disapproval.

Defending Christine when some lady or gentleman would purposefully alter her statements in hopes of stirring up gossip had become a weekly ritual if not daily in some instances. With a show of his irritation, Peter downed a good portion of his drink before lifting his gaze to Andrew. He found the Duke's green eyes watching him with amusement.

"Sorry, Andrew. You have heard me grumble too often of late," Peter apologized.

"She is your wife's friend. It is understandable," Andrew replied with a shrug.

"At least Christine is intelligent enough to carry on a conversation that is worth carrying on. Too bad most of these well-born ladies who think so highly of themselves cannot seem to—" Peter stopped abruptly and smiled at Andrew. "You can just tell me to be quiet, you know."

"Oh no, you are providing me with a great deal of entertainment, my friend," Andrew said with a chuckle.

The two men turned their attention to Elizabeth who now rejoined them with the Lockharts following her.

"I am not sure if you have been introduced in the past, but let me do so now. Christine, Maggie, this is the Duke of Kenilworth, Andrew Chandler. Andrew, this is Lady Christine Lockhart and her mother, Lady Margaret. Lord David Huntington married Christine's cousin, Caroline, whose mother was Maggie's twin sister, Lady Katherine Pinckney."

Andrew found himself looking into the deepest blue eyes he had ever seen. Christine smiled up at him and said, "We have met before, Your Grace, though it had been some years ago."

"Yes, I remember. Lord Christopher brought you along one day to observe the boring proceedings at the House of Lords."

"Not boring," she said with smiling blue eyes before she corrected, "informative."

Andrew looked up for an instant as if contemplating the statement then smiled and said with a nod, "Interesting word."

Peter chuckled lightly. "Only you would think a day of proceedings was interesting."

With Christine's attention on Peter, Andrew's gaze took in the beauty before him. Although dressed in black, the only other color she wore was a ruby red rose-shaped broach.

Giving both Lockhart women a rueful smile, Andrew said, "I must confess that I saw you last year—at Lord Lockhart's funeral. I apologize for not speaking with you that day, or to you, Lady Margaret. There were so many people in line to speak with you both that I slipped away to another appointment."

Christine's smile faltered slightly as she remembered the large number of people who attended the funeral and the reason why she and her family wore black now.

"Thank you, Your Grace. I do remember receiving your note of condolences," Lady Margaret told him.

"There you are, Andrew. I have been searching all over for you," a woman's purring voice rang out nearby.

The Duke's attention was sharply drawn away from Christine Lockhart as a beautiful woman dressed in a deep sapphire colored gown stepped into the small group. Her light brown hair was piled high upon her head and soft brown eyes looked up at him in a provocative manner as she slipped her arm possessively into his. Looking down at her, Andrew's gaze went immediately to the deep cut of the bodice that almost shamefully revealed the ample breasts. Catching the direction of his gaze, the woman smiled in pleasure at capturing his attention.

Ignoring her smile and looking briefly to the faces nearby as he lifted his gaze from his companion, Andrew announced in an almost bored tone, "May I present Lady Marian Sanders." When his gaze met Christine's eyes, he was struck with the thought that the sapphire gown Marian was wearing would better compliment Christine Lockhart as her eyes were of the same rich color.

No one noticed his extended attention to Christine's eyes as she offered a small smile in greeting to Lady Sanders. After a few moments of small talk, Elizabeth whisked the Lockharts to another group of people.

"Well, always against tradition, I suppose," Marian said scornfully. "After all, they are still in mourning. This is the last place either one of them should be attending."

She sipped her drink, watching over the rim of her glass as the women moved away. Andrew looked at Peter and was in time to see the man roll his eyes in vexation.

Chapter 2

Christine sat in bed with pillows propped up behind her as she ate breakfast. Her mind went back to the night before at Elizabeth's dinner and the introduction to Andrew Chandler. His green eyes were just as she remembered them, the color of emeralds and still with the gentleness reflecting from them. So many times she had seen eyes that were once kind and friendly turn cold and unyielding. *'Time plays against us, Christine.'* Christopher Lockhart told her once. *'Time and circumstance makes one impatient, bitter, and even unforgiving. Do not let those attitudes overtake you, dear girl.'*

She thought back to the first time she saw Andrew Chandler. It was in 1723 during the reign of King George I of the Hanover line. Sir Robert Walpole was England's first prime minister, having taken the officious title in 1721. Obtaining Walpole's permission, Christopher Lockhart had been allowed to have his young stepdaughter accompany him to a day's session of the House of Lords. Her presence, however, caused a fervor by several lords but it was a young Andrew Chandler who spoke up in her defense. Given the responsibilities of dukedom from his father, who stepped down a few months before, Andrew was learning for himself whom to trust and not to trust through experience.

It was his green eyes, however, that stayed with her through the years. A certain shade of green would conjure the sparkling humor she saw in his eyes when one of the lords tried to challenge him that day. *So much has happened since then yet it has barely been six years*, Christine mused as she stared at the music box on her bed.

The soft tinkling music of a waltz emitted from it and circling the top was a pair of dancers. Christopher Lockhart had given her the music box on her tenth birthday and she never parted with it until her first year of finishing school when she sent it home for safekeeping because a spoiled arrogant young titled lady tried to smash it in an argument.

Anne Lucas was very much like her mother with the constant reminders that Christine was not truly Lady Lockhart since she was not born to the title. That topic had been a favorite of Anne's but the disparaging remarks never received the reaction from Christine that the spoiled young lady had hoped.

With an irritated sigh, Christine pushed the thoughts of her days from school aside. Those days held very few memories that she deemed pleasant and worth remembering. That she came away with as many friends than she thought she would gain was the greatest memory she held from those years of school.

The door opened and her maid came in to assist Christine with her bath. Looking at the nearly untouched breakfast and the faraway look in the sapphire eyes, the young maid put her hands on her hips and teased with a knowing smile, "Now yer Ladyship, dreamin' of that man from last eve's dinner will not feed ye this mornin'."

Christine lifted her gaze to her maid and grinned. "What makes you think I have someone on my mind?"

"Because I know that look and I said 'man' not 'someone'," the young girl corrected.

"And how would you know that look, Roberta? You are barely my age," Christine scoffed playfully. The girl laughed lightly and waved away a response.

They both knew that the young girl was always more than friendly with the new stableboys that came to work for the head groomsman. Inexperienced herself, Christine learned a great deal of the intimacy between a man and a woman from her maid as they whispered between themselves.

"Very well, Rob, I suppose I should get myself out of here," Christine said with a resigned sigh.

"Tis no sense in layin' about all day in bed, my lady," Roberta said. Looking over her shoulder to make sure that they were still alone, the young maid leaned forward and whispered, "Unless there be a good lookin' man in there with ye."

Christine burst into laughter while Roberta turned to set about her chores as she was supposed to be doing. Suddenly, a fluffy pillow struck Roberta from behind and the two laughed.

* * *

The snow fell beautifully upon the city of London, leaving a soft blanket of white. Undaunted by the weather, people ventured out into the brisk

December morning to carry their prized gifts to friends and loved ones as they celebrated the season and prepared for the coming of the new year.

It had been a sennight since her party and Elizabeth was now entertaining a small group of friends in her parlor for tea. Sitting by the fire, her two small children were entertaining themselves. Her stepdaughter, Chelsea, and her younger half-brother, Jonathon, played with their new toys given to them by Caroline and David.

"I love this time of year," Caroline said to no one in particular.

"All the fuss over decorating—" David began but left the rest of his statement unsaid with a smile when Caroline turned a look on him.

Richard and Andrew chuckled lightly. Not letting David off so easily, Richard chided, "Decorating and buying that special gift for the woman in your life is all you need to worry over."

"Oh really?" Elizabeth exclaimed in feigned indignation.

"Ask him this next year. I am sure he will tell you a different story," replied Lady Abigail Winter. A petite blonde with light blue colored eyes, Abigail was a year younger than Caroline and two years younger than Elizabeth.

"Very well put, Abby," Caroline said to her friend.

"Now you have done it," Andrew said to Richard. "You know that what we say at the club is never repeated in front of the ladies."

"Whenever some unsuspecting young lady has the misfortune of snaring you and dragging you to the altar, Andrew Chandler, you will learn that husbands know what battles are best left untouched," Elizabeth said to the grinning Duke.

"Indeed, Andrew," Abby said with a sweet smile. "Richard will learn quick enough how cold a room can become and it would have nothing to do with the fire in the fireplace or the weather outside."

"See what you have done, Richard," Andrew scolded through a small smile. "I am in trouble with the women all because of you."

"Me?" Richard exclaimed. He pointed at David and whined in a childlike tone, "He started it!"

The men chuckled at the play. Elizabeth rolled her eyes as Abby let out an exasperated sigh. Caroline waved her hand in a dismissive gesture and said, "Oh Abby, Elizabeth and I can give you other tidbits to an almost frigid home."

"No!" Richard exclaimed emphatically.

Abby burst into a giggle and said, "Oh, I do believe you scared him,

Caroline."

"You know who would really scare him? Though she has had no firsthand experience with husbands, Christine has given me such grand ideas," Caroline replied in loud whisper to Elizabeth and Abby.

The women laughed as David shook his head and said to Richard and Andrew, "One must keep a wary eye on that cousin of hers. Christine is far too unruly even on her best behavior."

Trying to collect herself, Elizabeth asked Caroline, "Is she feeling any better?"

"Yes, thank goodness," Caroline replied with a smile.

"How awful to have the saddle slide off the horse. Christine was lucky that she was not riding across the fields at that fast pace she likes so much but to fall into the creek in such cold temperatures," Abby said.

"Thankfully she only caught a cold and was not seriously injured," Elizabeth put in.

"Having the strap snap in two only frightened her. Since returning from the Meadows these last several days, Christine was having such a time trying to catch her breath from the cough she developed that Aunt Maggie would not even let her set a foot on the floor. Knowing how stubborn Christine can be, if she could not walk around her own room, then she stayed in the bed and firmly refused to be carried anywhere in the house," Caroline replied.

"Stubborn? Is that not your cousin's middle name?" David asked teasingly.

"I would rather have that than some of the others I have heard," came a hoarsely sounding feminine voice from the doorway.

Everyone turned to find Christine being assisted out of her heavy cloak. One of the footmen stood beside her and waited patiently while holding her packages in his arms.

"Christine, you are infinitely stubborn," Elizabeth scolded as she stood up. "Coming out in weather like this while you are ill."

Chelsea stood up, ran by her stepmother and nearly toppled Christine to the floor when she slammed against her legs in a fierce hug.

"Oh Chelsea, do be careful. You know Tee has not been feeling well," Elizabeth scolded her stepdaughter.

Christine waved away the admonishment with one hand as she bent down to hug the child with her other hand. Chelsea beamed up at her and said with childish excitement, "I have to show you what Papa gave me this morning." She darted away and Christine straightened slowly.

Standing tall, Christine inhaled deeply to catch her breath. Elizabeth shook her head as David stood up and escorted Christine into the room. "You really should not be out in this weather, cousin," he scolded.

Christine clicked her tongue and rolled her eyes. "This day comes but once a year and I have the gifts for the children," she told him with a stifled cough.

"You could have sent someone else over with them," Elizabeth fussed.

"It would not be the same. The best part of giving is seeing their faces," Christine retorted. It was Elizabeth's turn to click her tongue and roll her eyes.

"Please, take this seat. No sense in going further than you need," Andrew stated as he stood from his seat. "You really should have waited until you were better."

"There! Even the Duke is scolding you. You are right, David, her middle name is stubborn," Abby said.

Looking up in surprise, Christine saw her sitting next to Lord Richard. Abby's blue eyes twinkled with humor and she laughed softly at her friend's stunned expression.

"Abby!" Christine exclaimed.

With a chuckle as he passed her, Andrew patted Abby's shoulder when she stood up and walked over to Christine who was trying to stifle another cough.

Crouching down, Abby hugged her then leaned back to give Christine a critical look. "You look pale."

Smiling, Christine said with exaggerated pleasantness, "Why yes, it has been quite some time. I have felt better but look at you." With a mischievous look, Christine glanced around the room as laughter rang out at her not so subtle ploy.

"Oh, you are still so silly," Abby said with a soft laugh. Holding out her left hand, she said happily, "Look at what Richard gave me this morning. We are going to be married this summer."

Christine looked down at the sapphire and diamond ring then looked at Richard in pleasant surprise. She smiled at him then turned her smile to Abby. Suddenly a look of feigned suspicion replaced the smile as Christine asked her, "Are you sure you want to do this?"

"Now do not give her reasons to change her mind," Caroline scolded but her smile belied her tone.

"She could not change my mind. Richard is soundly trapped now," Abby replied with a smile to her betrothed.

"Do you feel trapped, Lord Pittman?" Christine asked, a mischievous gleam appearing in her blue eyes.

"No," Richard answered smiling.

"Not yet anyway," David put in.

"David!" Caroline exclaimed making Christine laugh that turned into a short coughing spell. Chelsea stepped forward as Abby made to stand.

Putting out her hand to halt the child, Christine said gently, "Careful with Lady—Abigail's gown, Chelsea." The sudden pause in her statement as Christine took a quick deep breath quickly replaced the gaiety with concern. She knew the adventure would be taxing to her physically but she had to venture out in the weather.

Abby bent over her with a look of anxiety on her face while Elizabeth called her daughter to her and Caroline stood to aid her cousin. Christine halted all movement by holding up her hand then grabbed Chelsea's arm with the other hand.

"I am fine," she told them. Turning to the child, she asked, "Now what did your father give you?"

"Tee, are you really feeling better?" Chelsea asked in concern as Christine lifted her up onto her lap.

"I am breathing. We are considering that an improvement," Christine replied with a smile. Chelsea returned the smile that soon erupted into giggles as Christine wrinkled up her nose and touched it to the child's.

Proudly, Chelsea held out a box. Taking it, Christine opened it to find a multitude of ribbons in all shades of colors. Making appreciative noises that pleased the child and made the adults laugh silently, Christine played up her role of being overwhelmed by the prized gift.

"Now see that big box over there?" Christine asked pointing to the package on a table near the doorway.

"Yes, you brought it," Chelsea told her.

Christine smiled at her blatant reply and nodded. "Well so I did, but you probably are not interested in it now that I see these."

She smiled as the young girl looked at the large box then back up at Christine. "I would still like to open it," Chelsea said shyly.

With a look of feigned surprise, Christine asked, "Really?"

Chelsea nodded then waited with ill-disguised eagerness while Christine seemed to contemplate the worth of her gift in comparison to the ribbons. Releasing a sigh of feigned disbelief, Christine said, "Well, if that will please you."

Chelsea fairly flew from her lap and ran to open the box.

"You are spoiling my children, Christine," Elizabeth said quietly.

Smiling, Christine looked at her friend and said, "Indeed, and the best part after spoiling them is giving them back to you."

"Thank you so much."

Wrinkling her nose and waving her hand, Christine said, "My pleasure."

More laughter filled the room at their playful banter. Chelsea let out a shriek that frightened her younger brother. Jonathon stood up and hurried to his mother for protection.

"Mama! Look at this!" Chelsea exclaimed excitedly. She ran across the room holding up her new gown of pale pink with wide white ribbons. She proudly displayed it for her mother and the other guests. "And look!" the child went on. She touched the flower made from the same pink material that was sewn in place on the bodice. She whirled around in pleasure of her gown as Elizabeth looked over her daughter's head to Christine.

"You *are* spoiling my children."

Christine only smiled before she ordered the child to try on the gown in case it needed alterations. Chelsea ran out of the room and stomped up the staircase to her bedchambers. Meeting Elizabeth's gaze, Christine gave her friend a smile then called for Jonathon. The boy would not come to her so she asked a maid to hand over one of the boxes. Holding the smaller package out for the boy, Christine watched as he hesitantly slipped from his mother's lap then slowly made his way to the waiting present. Coaxing the boy to sit on her lap, Christine helped him open his gift. His eyes lit up as he reached inside the box and pulled out a wooden carving of a horse.

"Hold it up so your mama can see it," Christine whispered then smiled as the boy's arm shot up in the air to proudly display his new toy.

"Horsey!" he called out.

Letting him slide down from her lap, Christine's smile faltered slightly as she remembered another small boy call out '*horsey.*' Her sadness reflected in her blue eyes for only an instant.

From where he stood, Andrew seemed to be the only one to notice it. He had not been able to stop staring at this woman who was nothing like the indifferent unsmiling person the Ton gossiped over. '*If they bothered to know and understand her...*' Peter had said the week before.

Suddenly, the front door slammed and soon Peter stormed into the parlor. He halted in mid-stride when he saw Christine and stared down at her for a moment.

"What the hell are you doing out in weather like this?" he growled. The room went still and quiet at the anger in his voice.

Christine frowned at the tone and replied spitefully, "Well, good afternoon to you too, Peter. I am doing much better, thank you for asking."

Hearing the hoarseness in her voice, Peter muttered a curse then walked over to a small table and poured himself a drink from the crystal decanter on the tray. At that moment, Chelsea ran back into the room. Catching sight of her father, she ran over to him and flung out her arms to proudly display her new gown. Her long blonde hair was tied back with one of her father's ribbons.

"Papa, look at my new gown. Tee gave it to me," the child announced happily.

Peter drank the contents of his glass in one swallow then looked down at his daughter. Slamming his empty glass on the table, he walked half the distance to where Christine sat. Throwing his arm back to point at Chelsea, he told Christine angrily, "I am quite capable of buying my children clothes!"

"Peter!" Elizabeth exclaimed in astonishment.

Feeling the heat of embarrassment flush her cheeks, Christine could sense all eyes on her as she and Peter stared at one another. Looking away first, she smiled and slowly got to her feet. Glancing at Elizabeth, Christine said softly, "It is getting late and I should be going. Good afternoon, Elizabeth." Then giving Peter a cursory glance, she nodded once. "Peter."

Elizabeth angrily got to her feet and hurried to Christine's side as she glared at her husband. "She has not been well, Peter."

"Precisely! All the more reason for her to have stayed home," he argued. He then stormed out the room and up the stairs while grumbling something about bad weather and common sense.

Everyone stared in disbelief at his behavior. Feeling shamed by his outburst, Elizabeth opened her mouth to say something to Christine but the words failed her. With a smile of understanding, Christine said reassuringly, "Whatever it is, he will explain later. Let me know what I need to do for my part."

A footman assisted Christine with her cloak and, after her farewells to the others, she left the group still stunned over Peter's abrupt arrival.

Chapter 3

On this, the first night of the brand new year, the snow had stopped to be replaced with a cold chilling rain. Andrew was ushered into the drawing room of a modest townhouse near Hyde Park. Dismissing the butler, he poured himself a snifter of brandy then sat on the plush sofa. As he waited to escort Marian to the play, Andrew looked about the room and noted that she had done little to add her own touch.

He had known Lord Hayden Sanders and his wife, Lady Marian Sanders, for a number of years as merely friends. However, it was not until Hayden's death in a carriage accident, which also left Marian incapable of having children, before she sought Andrew out. After the appropriate period of mourning, Marian dropped many signs of wanting a more intimate relationship with the young duke. After a few months into the affair, Andrew bought the townhouse for her.

Now entering the third season of the affair, Andrew was becoming bored with her and the not-so-subtle hints of what she would do if she had the title of duchess. She seemed to demand a great deal of his attention of late that left him with little time to do things he enjoyed. With a sigh, Andrew thought back to a few months before when he announced that he would leave London for a few weeks to attend business at his estate in the country. She had all but insisted on going with him causing him to change his plans and remain in London.

As he sat waiting, he wondered why he was continuing with the relationship. Nearly a score and seven years, Andrew Chandler assumed his title and the responsibilities it carried nearly six years before when his father relinquished the title of Duke after the death of his wife, Andrew's mother. He buried his father nearly three months later with what Andrew was certain had been a broken heart.

His parents were married under the most rarest of circumstances. Theirs was a love match. The old Duke doted on his Duchess in public and in private. Andrew had been fortunate to be raised in such surroundings yet love had managed to elude him, the one and only child of their union. The Duchess had nearly died giving birth to her son and the doctor declared her incapable of ever carrying another child.

Andrew wondered if he would find someone who cared less about his title and money than the hopeful young women who tried to attract his attention. The swish of shirts pulled him from his musings as Marian stepped into the room wearing a blue velvet gown with long tight sleeves. She adorned the gown with the diamonds he had given her over the summer for her birthday.

"Well, shall we go now? I do not want to miss the first act," Marian said without looking up.

Andrew's gaze flickered over her dispassionately and the only thought that came to mind was her game of trying to outshine the other women. Assisting Marian with her cloak, another woman slipped into his mind with sapphire blue eyes and a mass of midnight black wavy hair. For a brief instant, Andrew wondered if Christine Lockhart's cough was better.

With Caroline on his arm, David led the way to the Lockhart box seats with Christine and Maggie following behind. Seeing that Christine and Maggie sat in the front two seats while he and Caroline took the back seats, he asked if any of them desired a glass of wine.

"Except for you, my dear," he said sternly to Caroline.

"One glass will not harm the baby," Caroline countered.

"Oh let her have just one, David," Christine told him with a smile. "It is the new year, you two are going to have another child, and you somehow managed to talk me into this silly outing. My goodness but you have been busy."

David laughed and nodded in agreement. "Very well," he said. "I leave you in charge of making sure she does not drink it down so quickly."

"Pace yourself," Christine said in a firm tone to her cousin. Looking up at David, she said confidently, "There, my work is done. I truly enjoy the easy chores, cousin."

Caroline swatted at her cousin's antics while David left them for a few moments. Maggie tapped her daughter's arm lightly and lifted the shawl snugly around Christine's shoulders.

"Remember, Christine, that you are just getting over your illness. This outing was David's idea and I just did not have the heart to tell him no, but you must keep yourself warm," she told her.

"I will be fine, Mother."

Maggie huffed and said reproachfully, "Fine? Sneaking off to give Chelsea and Jonathon gifts last week in the worst snowstorm I can remember. Sometimes, Christine, I wonder why you do such things."

"Mother, please, not tonight. I have stayed in the bed since then," Christine said with a sigh.

"Aunt Maggie, you know how Christine dotes on Chelsea and it was—" Caroline began.

"I thought I saw you come in," Abby greeted from behind them.

The three turned to greet Abby and Richard. After exchanging pleasantries, Christine hinted of Caroline's condition and Abby squealed in delight when Caroline confirmed the news.

"Another child, I think that is so wonderful. Oh, where is David? I must congratulate him," Abby said excitedly.

"He will be back soon," Caroline replied.

"How is your cough? Did the weather this past week hinder your recovery?" Richard asked Christine.

"Although the weather tried to deter my recuperation, my cough is much better, thank you. Changed your mind on marrying her yet?" Christine teased.

"Christine!" Maggie admonished.

"Oh, Maggie, you know how absolutely naughty Christine can be and I think Richard is just now learning," Abby defended then patted Richard's arm.

Seeing the impish grin and the gleam of mischief in Christine's blue eyes, Richard shook his head and chuckled lightly.

As the small group talked, Andrew watched from his seat across the span of the theatre. He could not believe that in thinking of Christine and her cough, he would see her out again.

"Who do you see, Andrew?" Marian asked and leaned towards him.

"Richard and Abby are over there with the Lockharts," he replied leaning slightly away from her.

"The Lockharts? What on earth are they doing out?" she said scornfully.

"Perhaps they want to see the play as well, Marian."

"They are still in mourning, for pity's sake. Just another example of Christine Lockhart's disdain for proper decorum," Marian scoffed.

Andrew turned slowly to face his companion and asked tightly, "Christine Lockhart's disdain? What of Lady Margaret and Lady Caroline Huntington?"

"I am sure Lady Margaret has had her hands full with trying to instill any proper behavior in that child. I mean, what can one expect from a daughter of sea captain?" Marian replied in obvious condemnation.

Andrew stared at her for a long moment that Marian glanced at him uneasily. "Why do you ladies detest her so?" he asked.

"Detest her? Andrew, that is such a distasteful word," Marian cooed.

"Very well, shall we try criticize?" he asked in a tone that made Marian look at him for a long moment.

"Really Andrew, how can one expect proper etiquette and grace from a homely country maid?"

Andrew's laugh was harsh to Marian's ears and she bristled at the subtle rebuke. "You cannot seriously believe that she could become a lady of high fashion and delicate grace?" she asked in marked disbelief.

"That is not something a woman is born with, Marian. It is taught," Andrew replied, matching her haughty tone.

"I attended the most highly recommended finishing school for girls of my status," she replied indignantly.

Andrew chuckled again and shrugged, saying, "Indeed, I believe Abigail attended the same school."

"She did," Marian replied with pride. She did not care for the smile on his face and said as she angrily smoothed an imaginary wrinkle from her gown, "Lady Abigail is from a highly respected and revered family in England."

Andrew again looked across the huge span of the theatre to watch Abby interact companionably with Christine and Caroline for a moment before facing Marian to remind her, "Abby was one year behind Lady Christine and Lady Caroline at that same school."

"Which was an absolute travesty to the reputation of the school to have Christine Lockhart stroll those halls," Marian hissed. She turned to face him and asked resentfully, "Why are you defending that woman?"

"Because I had not truly noticed until now that," Andrew was saying before he leaned closer to her slightly. Dropping his voice to a deceptively pleasant tone, he finished, "you are a snobbish and arrogant aristocrat, Lady Sanders."

Marian's indignant gasp turned into a cough as she fairly choked on her own resentment. She stared at him in disbelief as he merely presented her with a smile that bore no warmth. His unsympathetic gaze drifted from her flushed face to the diamonds she wore then to the blue velvet gown.

Feeling his condemnation and not understanding why, Marian made to stand. "Take me home, Andrew," she told him.

Anticipating her move, he caught her arm in a firm grasp that held her to her seat and said harshly, "Stay seated, Marian. I paid for us to attend this performance on your insistence so you will sit and watch it until the intermission."

With a long and irritated exhale, Marian jerked her arm free and, in a huff, turned her back slightly to him. Andrew looked at the stiff-backed attitude and smiled in amusement as he thought of who was now being the ill-mannered lady.

His emerald eyes drifted back to the Lockhart box. The woman he had the chance to glimpse last week was a very different Christine Lockhart from the stories told of her. She was kind and gentle to the children, playful and mischievous with her friends, then calm and graceful in her departure amid Peter's surprising attitude.

The musical prelude began that meant the curtains were about to open and he watched Abby and Richard bid their farewells. He thought again of Christine's quiet retreat when Peter lashed out unceremoniously. Though Peter had later apologized for his behavior to all his guests, Andrew could only applaud the reaction this so-called ill-mannered daughter of the sea captain had portrayed. Indeed, for all of Christine Lockhart's cool reserve, she could certainly teach Marian a thing or two of proper decorum.

Several days after the incident at the theatre, Andrew received a note from Marian stating that she was leaving London for an extended visit with friends who lived in Vienna. Unconcerned with her departure and, actually quite relieved, he decided that he would also leave London for a time and pay a visit to his home in Kenilworth. He would spend the day clearing up some business before leaving the city and called for his coach to begin his rounds.

Walking briskly by several shops, Andrew nearly collided with Chelsea Hunnicutt as the child suddenly shot out of one of them. Startled, the young girl spun around and dropped her package.

"Chelsea, please be careful when stepping out. I am sorry, Your Grace," came the soft feminine voice.

His green eyes lifted to meet blue ones for a moment before she reached out and pulled the girl protectively to her. "She was excited."

"Quite all right, Lady Lockhart," he replied with a smile then bent down to pick up the fallen package.

"I broke it," Chelsea said forlornly.

Looking at the package, Andrew shifted his gaze to Christine as he handed it to her.

"A music box," Christine said in answer to his questioning look. Then turning to the child, she added in a soothing tone, "Now let us see for ourselves, shall we?"

Chelsea nodded as her hazel eyes filled with tears. Christine smiled at the girl sympathetically then opened the package. Andrew offered his assistance as he reached for the object and turned the key. Soft tinkling music played while the small horse turned in the carousel.

"Well now, I think it is safe from damage, my lady," he said gently to the young girl. Chelsea lifted watery eyes from the carousel to Andrew's smiling face.

"Thank you, Your Grace. You are very kind," Christine said as Chelsea carefully took the music box and watched the horse turn the small circle.

"Tee let me pick it out for my birthday. I will be seven next week," the girl told the Duke proudly.

"Chelsea?" The girl looked at Christine and saw the expectant look toward the Duke.

Realizing what the gesture meant, Chelsea gave a quick curtsey and said to Andrew, "Thank you for your assistance, Your Grace."

"You are very welcome," Andrew replied gallantly having seen Christine's silent command. "May I escort you ladies to your next stop?"

"Tee is taking me to the bakery so I can pick out *two* of whatever I want because I did not wander off. We have been shopping all morning," Chelsea said proudly.

"Indeed," Andrew replied with a smile as he glanced at Christine. She was looking at the child with gentle affection.

"May I escort you?" Andrew repeated when he caught Christine's eye.

"I appreciate your offer, Your Grace, but my coach is just over there."

Andrew turned and noticed the Lockhart coach waiting behind them. He nodded then waved a hand for them to precede him. He assisted Chelsea into the coach then turned to offer his hand to Christine. He thought her smile was somewhat reserved before he remembered that Christine Lockhart rarely smiled in public. He stood for a moment, watching them ride away before he continued on his errands.

Stepping into the club several hours later, Andrew found Richard in conversation with Peter. Sitting down, he listened to their conversation.

When the conversation slowed down to a silence, Andrew told Peter, "I happened upon your daughter doing some shopping with Lady Christine earlier today."

"How much did Chelsea manage to coax out of her during this outing today?" Peter asked Andrew.

Chuckling, the Duke replied, "Only a music box that I had been privileged to see and that was because I literally bumped into Chelsea as she hurried out of the store with the package in her hands." Putting his drink on the table before them, Andrew smiled and added, "Christine promised her that she could pick out two treats from the bakery and that was their next stop."

"Sweets," Peter grumbled and rolled his eyes. "If she manages to keep Chelsea away from a nap this afternoon, we may be able to put her to bed within an hour of her usual bedtime." He took a sip of his drink then added, "Since Jonathon has not been feeling well for the past several days, Christine thought that Elizabeth needed some relief from the children so she offered to take Chelsea out for the day. She certainly has a way with that child. Do you know it was Christine that finally had Chelsea accept Elizabeth as her mother?"

"Chelsea could not possibly remember her mother. She was barely three when Claudia died," Richard reflected.

"I know, I could not understand it either. She would not even look at Elizabeth no matter what I did or said to try to make her understand. She was so young and Elizabeth would not force the issue. Then on the day we married, Christine and Caroline attended the ceremony and watched over Chelsea while Elizabeth and I made the rounds with our guests. Christine took Chelsea for an outing at the park. When they came back, Chelsea's entire attitude had turned completely around," Peter told them.

"What did this paragon do or say?" Andrew asked with a smile.

Richard laughed and held up his glass of bourbon as if to give a toast. "No one knows. Christine always manages to change the subject just when it would turn in that direction and Chelsea's responses made absolutely no sense."

Peter grinned and leaned forward in his seat to Andrew, saying, "I have given up asking myself. I no longer care and neither does Elizabeth. Chelsea now calls her mother, seeks Elizabeth out for comfort, all the wonders of being a mother. We thought that with Jonathon's birth, Chelsea would revert back but as you can see that never came to pass."

"Have they been friends for a long time?" Andrew asked.

"Christine and Elizabeth? Oh no. Elizabeth had thought like everyone else that Christine's title was undeserved, having only attained the higher status of it through Lord Christopher's adoption. Then something happened at school in Elizabeth's last year that changed all that," Peter replied. "I am not sure what exactly happened. All I know is that Christine took the blame for something that saved Elizabeth from being expelled just months before graduation."

"Christine Lockhart made some type of sacrifice for a stranger? Elizabeth was not truly guilty, was she?" Andrew asked.

"No," Peter replied shaking his head. "To hear Elizabeth tell it, she thought for several weeks after the incident that Christine was the one who tried to have her expelled." Seeing more questions rising from the conversation, Peter lifted a well-manicured hand and added, "I am confused over it, Andrew. I think I have yet to hear the whole story."

Andrew grinned at him and said as he raised his brandy to his lips, "Adds to the mystery of one Lady Christine Lockhart."

"I doubt anyone would ever truly understand that one. Not even Lady Caroline understands her cousin and they are practically inseparable," Richard said in observation.

"Why does Chelsea call her Tee?" Andrew asked.

Richard nodded and swallowed his mouthful of drink before saying, "I have meaning to ask you that as well. Abby asked me the other day. You know the day when you came in like a—"

"Be quiet, Richard. I apologized to everyone for that and twice to Christine," Peter growled. Turning to Andrew, he said, "At first, Christine told Chelsea that she could call her Teen because Chelsea was having trouble saying some of the sounds. Over time, Chelsea grew lazy in her speech and now it is as though Chelsea is only saying the one letter." Peter shrugged and smiled. "It could very well be."

As Peter and Richard moved to other topics, Andrew sat back and stared at the fire. The more information he learned of Lady Christine Lockhart, the more intriguing she became to him. He thought of all that he knew of her thus far and realized that there were far too many pieces still missing in understanding the beautiful young woman.

Chapter 4

Over the next few weeks, winter held its icy fingers around the city and blanketed it with another snowfall. Andrew stood at the French doors of his study with a snifter of brandy in his hand and stared out at the snow-covered ground. He had just returned to his townhouse after staying the fortnight at Kenilworth. He enjoyed the time to himself. It had only reinforced his suspicions that he was bored with Marian. Her prattling of what someone did or said or should have done and so on had grated on his nerves that he could barely tolerate being with her.

Sipping his drink, he wondered when was the last time they had actually enjoyed each other in bed. With a frown knitting his brows, Andrew could not remember. Certainly there was the need for release but that was not enjoying each other. Even in bed, he felt burdened with her nearby. The last time he had seen Marian was on the first evening of the new year when he attended the play with her. She had been so judgmental and his eyes narrowed as he tried to remember how Marian put it, '*Just another example of Christine Lockhart's disdain for proper decorum.*'

Andrew shook his head at Marian's prejudice. In thinking of Marian's dislike for Christine Lockhart, the sapphire blue eyes and dark wavy hair came to mind. Andrew was amazed that each time he encountered a certain shade of blue, his mind would bring up Christine Lockhart and wondered how was it that he had never paid attention to her before.

The clock on the mantel chimed the hour and Andrew glanced up. Finishing his drink, he headed out of his study.

"Your coach is waiting, Your Grace," his butler told him.

"Thank you, Parker. I will be having dinner with Lord Batson if you should need to locate me," Andrew told the man before stepping out into the cold wintry evening.

Lady Constance Batson sat on the sofa and squirmed slightly to get comfortable. Nearly at the end of her pregnancy, she almost groaned aloud at the loss of finding a comfortable position whether it was sitting or laying down. Christine offered her a pillow for her back but Constance waved it away in an irritated fashion.

"I had forgotten how hard it was to be still for more than one minute at the end of my time. Connie, would you rather sit in this seat?" Caroline offered.

"No thank you, I am not comfortable anywhere. In another two weeks, this baby will be born and the first thing I am going to do is lie on my stomach," Connie told them.

Caroline and Elizabeth laughed and told of how they had done the very same thing.

"How far along are you now, Caroline?" Connie asked.

"I am about to end my fourth month. I have to order new gowns because my clothes from Stephen were for the cold season and I will be far too warm in them for this baby," Caroline answered.

"Tell me again when is the baby due?" Abby asked.

"In July," Caroline said with a smile.

"Oh, you will miss my wedding," Abby said in disappointment.

"Christine will be there and she will give me a report to the very second," Caroline replied with a soft laugh.

"Maybe," Christine teased.

The butler stood at the doorway of the room and announced Andrew's arrival. Stepping into the drawing room, Andrew noticed Christine immediately as he greeted everyone. Moving to Connie, he presented her with a wrapped package.

"Just a little something for the baby," he said with a shrug then kissed her cheek.

"Oh Andrew, you are such a dear," Connie replied and opened the package.

She made appreciative noises as she pulled out several small blankets. Beaming up at Andrew, she thanked him again.

He shrugged and said, "I remembered that Henry's parents were saving everything but all was lost in the fire. Besides with days like this and the baby only a few weeks away, you will need the warm blankets."

"Oh we will," Connie told him, her hazel eyes twinkling with amusement. "Thank you, Andrew."

"So how have you been feeling lately?" he asked as he stepped back to smile down at her.

"Just fine. Lately I feel like a duck waddling around," Connie replied and everyone laughed at her quip.

"That is how it feels near the end sometimes," Elizabeth told him, "I felt like everyone saw this huge belly a long time before I entered the room." Andrew chuckled lightly, making Elizabeth add, "And all the men go about their usual business. For them, nothing has changed."

Groaning and shifting in her seat once again, Connie arched her back and nearly tossed the pillow Christine offered her back in her face. "I do not want the pillow, Christine," she growled.

"You do not have to yell, I can hear you just fine," Christine said patiently, "but you just looked so uncomfortable that I—"

"You what? You are concerned over my welfare?" Connie posed the question with such skepticism that Christine frowned at her.

"Of course, I am. Why would I not be concerned?" Christine asked somewhat taken aback at her tone.

"Perhaps the longer I am in this condition, the longer you can enjoy my husband's company," Connie grumbled as she shifted in her seat once again.

Christine stared at her in surprise, her mouth dropping open. Feeling all eyes on her, she asked in disbelief, "What is that supposed to mean?"

"Dear God, do not look so innocent! I heard the talk about you and other men but I never believed them until now."

"Connie, you—" Caroline began.

Christine turned to her cousin and said, "No, I can handle my own." Looking back at Connie, she asked bitterly, "So what has London decided I have done now?"

"I was told that you were with Henry and the two of you went into a house together, staying inside for quite sometime. How could you, Christine? How could you go behind my back and with me in this condition?" Connie told her angrily.

Christine stared at her for a moment then started to say, "Are you trying to say that—"

"You are having an affair with my husband! You who is always saying how much our friendship means to you then you do something like that," Connie wailed.

The room was silent over the outburst. Christine stared at her friend in disbelief, rendered momentarily speechless.

"Connie, I am sure you heard incorrectly," David began.

"Nothing happens to the man while the woman grows so big and grotesque. You can go about without nary a problem, bed the slimmer women while it was your doing that we," Connie pointed to herself and Caroline in her tirade, "we are trapped in these misshapened bodies." Turning to the stunned Christine, Connie added, "And the one that I thought was my friend—"

"I would never—" Christine tried to say but Connie interrupted her again.

"Well there are not many young women in London who wear black. All black."

"Connie, this—I mean, it is not—" Christine stammered in stunned surprise at the accusation. "I would never do something like that."

"Oh really? Then tell me why you were with my husband for more than hour in that house if not for that?" Connie asked angrily. Christine opened her mouth but she did not offer explanations.

"There must be some explanation for this," Abby said looking imploringly at Christine to say something.

"Connie, you can trust me to—" Christine began softly.

Angrily, Connie pointed to the door and said, "Get out! Get out of my house and never speak to me again, *Lady* Lockhart."

"Connie, calm down. This is not good for your baby," Caroline tried to soothe.

"I am certain it is just a misunderstanding," Elizabeth said.

"Oh? Then why can she not explain what she was doing with my husband?" Connie asked looking pointedly at Christine.

Christine felt all eyes on her as she looked at Connie. She dropped her gaze down to the protruding belly before looking to the floor with bowed head. In a voice so soft yet filled with regret, she said, "I cannot tell you, Connie."

Everyone stared at Christine in stunned surprise. With tears brimming in her eyes, Connie hissed through clenched teeth, "I called you friend when so few cared enough to bother. Get out of my house."

Christine flinched and all color drained from her face at the tone. She lifted her gaze, the well-known carefully guarded look, and met Connie's hazel eyes. Without another word, Christine got to her feet, turned away, and left the room.

Silence enveloped the room. Richard and Abby looked at one another somewhat stunned over what just happened. Peter patted Elizabeth's shoulder. David put his arm around Caroline who was shaking her head. Andrew sat back and took in all the reactions curiously.

"My God, this cannot be true," Caroline whispered.

"Christine would never do something like that, Connie. It has to be something else," Elizabeth said empathetically.

"She did not speak up in her own defense." Connie pointed out.

There were voices in foyer then Henry stepped into the room, looking over his shoulder. "Why is Christine leaving already?" he asked as he turned to face the others in the room.

"How dare you have your mistress in my house?" Connie growled and turned her head away when he tried to kiss her cheek.

Henry stopped and stared at his wife as if she were a ghost. "My *what*?"

"Do not bother denying it, Henry. Christine has already confessed going into that house with you near Eaton Square," Connie told him.

"House in—" Henry started to repeat. The light of understanding shone on his face and turned to the foyer quickly, calling out for Christine.

"I will not have her in this house!" Connie screamed.

"Stop uttering nonsense!" Henry shouted back from the foyer. He returned, pulling a reluctant Christine back into the drawing room. "Yes, we were at that house together," he told them and received a glare from Christine.

"Henry! This is not the time nor the place to discuss this," Elizabeth rebuked trying to stay calm herself.

After giving Henry the baleful glare, Christine would not look up but kept her gaze fixed on the floor. Henry was pulling her along until they stood before Connie while talking all the while.

"You remember the fire at my father's home a few years ago? It destroyed everything, even all of the furniture I had used as a baby. All was lost." Now he yanked Christine to stand between them and added, "Christine remembered how you marveled over some baby furniture one day when the two of you had gone shopping. When she went to the shop to investigate further, the shopkeeper told her that he put it on display in his sister's house since his store was too crowded. His sister had moved to the country so the house here was nearly empty. The house is near Eaton Square."

Henry paused and in that silence, Christine sighed audibly. "Connie, Christine met me there so I could take a look at it," he said in exasperation. "She told me how much you liked it but you thought that I would not want the whole set. I bought it only because Christine was able to barter the price down with the man. You know how good she is at bartering."

"You purchased the entire set?" Connie asked quietly.

"Yes, and as an added bonus to the shopkeeper, she told him that he would not have to deliver it. She would take care of that."

The room was so silent and so still that Christine slowly lifted her gaze to look around. Everyone was staring at her with a mixture of relief and surprise.

"My God, Christine. Why did you not say something?" Connie asked in amazement.

Christine shrugged and, not looking at her, said in a flat tone, "Because it was Henry's surprise and he wanted to make the presentation. I would never dream of taking this surprise from him."

Connie's eyes watered and her hand went to cover her mouth as her bottom lip trembled. With her voice shaking from the impending tears, Connie said in horror, "You let me say all those horrid things."

Again Christine shrugged, still not looking at anyone, said, "I have been called worse."

"Not from those who are supposed to be your friends!" Connie exclaimed.

Christine looked up then and the hurt was evident in the blue-eyed gaze. Connie let out a mournful wail and Henry was at his wife's side in an instant. "Shh, Connie, it is all right now. Shh," he was saying soothingly.

Connie pushed him away making Henry frown down at her. Before he could ask, Connie was putting her arms out for Christine. "Please, Christine. I said so many awful things. Please."

With a single tear rolling down her cheek, Christine knelt down and hugged her friend, saying, "It is only because you are going to have a baby. You may say whatever you want."

"But I—" Connie began but could not finish as she cried against Christine's shoulder.

Henry looked around the room to see that the other women were in tears and were dabbing them away with their handkerchiefs while the other husbands watched the scene with sideways glances and trying to soothe their wives. Andrew was sipping his drink while watching Christine and Connie covertly. Henry turned his attention back to his wife and Christine. The two women were huddled together with Connie crying and Christine whispering softly into her ear.

After a time, Christine moved from Connie then Henry was beside his wife with a handkerchief. He smiled at Christine and said apologetically, "Sorry, my lady, I only have the one."

Smiling back at him, Christine held up her hand to show that she held her own. A moment later, the butler announced that dinner was ready. Henry nodded and said, "Let us give the women some time to regain their beautiful faces then we will go in for dinner."

The butler nodded and left. When the women had left the room, Henry shook his head and said, "It simply amazes me that Christine would allow such talk like that. My mistress? Even Connie knows better than that. Christine is her friend."

"How many times has Christine said that people will believe what they want to believe no matter what common sense dictates?" David asked. "I know I have heard it many times."

"Just remember that Connie is in a delicate condition and she could say some of the most outlandish things. Trust me, I know," Peter said with a knowing smile.

"Ah, something for me to look forward to, Peter?" Richard said with a chuckle.

"Oh most certainly. There will be days when nothing you do will be enough, or right, or warm, or—" Peter drawled on.

"Yes, yes, I understand, Peter," Richard was saying amid his chuckles. Andrew and Henry were laughing. Looking at Andrew, Richard pointed out, "And why are you laughing? You have not experienced the realm of fatherhood or have you?"

Andrew shook his head and gave his friend a big grin, "No, I have not, Richard, but that is not to say that I should make note of what to expect for future use."

"Planning on getting married soon, Andrew?" Henry asked with a twinkle in his eyes. "Lady Sanders, perhaps?"

"No, on both questions," Andrew replied. "I personally have no plans to marry although the many mothers of the Ton have envisioned me standing at the other end of the aisle while their daughters walk toward me with a veil covering their faces."

"Well, why not Lady Sanders? She is a beautiful woman," Henry put in.

Puffing up his chest and tucking his thumbs into the small pockets of his vest, Richard spoke in a deeper and arrogant aristocratic style of his father, "As the Duke of Kenilworth, there is a responsibility to the title that necessitates the presence of heirs, my good man."

The men laughed again and Andrew made a playful swat at Richard who easily dodged the hit. Henry went to pour himself a drink and said at the same time, "Ah yes, the carriage accident. So Lady Sanders is your mistress and you find someone else to be your wife."

Andrew gave a non-committal shrug and said, "At the moment, I am in no hurry to marry."

Suddenly, their attention was drawn to the commotion in the foyer. The housekeeper was hurrying up the stairs as maids hurried past her in both directions. Henry slowly set down his glass and walked to the double doors.

"What is it?" he asked a passing maid.

"Her Ladyship," the maid said as she curtsied respectfully. "She—"

"Will you stop saying that?" came Elizabeth's scolding voice at the top of the stairs. She had drawn the men's attention from the maid who rushed away.

"You are so stubborn and thick-headed, Christine, that sometimes I just want to scream," Abby was saying as they reached the bottom of the stairs.

Looking up, the women met the men at the double doors to the drawing room. Andrew and Henry noticed that Christine looked away quickly, almost guiltily.

"What is happening with Connie?" Henry asked in concern.

"The baby has decided to join us this evening," Abby said softly.

"What?" Henry exclaimed. Then shaking his head, he added, "That cannot be. It is not due for another two weeks."

Andrew was watching Christine as she moved to stand by the window and away from everyone else. Her shoulders slumped and she bowed her head to look down at the floor, making him wonder what had happened this time.

"Babies have their own time schedules, Henry. Your child has decided that now is the time to meet his mother and father," Caroline was saying.

The butler stepped in and asked in a quiet and monotone voice, "What shall we do with dinner, my lord?"

Henry looked around at his guests not sure of what to do next. Elizabeth answered as she looked to Henry, "We should go ahead with dinner, Henry. It may be hours yet before your child arrives and we need to keep you calm."

"I am calm," Henry countered.

"You are now but as the evening wears on, you will grow impatient," David told him with a knowing grin as he put an arm around Caroline's shoulders and patted her rounding belly. Her response was to push his hand away and turn bright red.

Everyone grinned at them except Andrew who was still watching Christine. Peter glanced up, noticing Christine away from them and asked, "What are you doing over there, Tee?"

Elizabeth and Abby let out an exasperated sigh in unison. It was Caroline who said quietly, "Christine, you are not to blame for this."

"Blame for what?" Henry wanted to know.

"If you do not stop with your self-incrimination, I will turn you over my knee this minute," Elizabeth said with a stomp of her foot showing her aggravation.

Abby took a step towards her friend and, putting her hands on her hips, said in a slow and firm tone, "Now you listen to me, Lady Christine *Stubborn* Lockhart."

The middle name brought out smiles except from Christine who turned slowly to face her. Abby continued, "It is beyond me why you do not defend yourself more often than you do but we all understood why you did not this evening. Even Connie agreed when we were upstairs."

Christine rolled her eyes and turned to face the window again but Abby spoke more firmly, "Do not turn away from me, Christine Lockhart." Everyone, including Christine, turned to stare at the petite blonde in her stance with blue eyes flashing in anger. "You act so strong and indifferent when other people are around that are not your friends. I know that what they say about you hurts you. I can see it in your face."

Christine sighed in annoyance and said as if speaking to a child, "I will not give those like Lady Lucas the satisfaction of knowing that."

"We know, Christine," Elizabeth said then waved her arm around to include those in the drawing room. "We all know but it does not stop the hurt you feel."

"That is not the reason for how I feel now. Connie is giving birth earlier than she should because I upset her," Christine told them calmly.

"Utter nonsense!" Henry exclaimed. "If you think that to be true, then I will put you over Elizabeth's knee myself."

Everyone smiled as he used Elizabeth's comment. His grin gave away his ploy as he added, "When my older sister, Priscilla, was born, I was told that she was nearly three weeks early making my mother think that she was dying because she did not understand. Utter nonsense."

Caroline stepped forward and said softly, "Cousin, you know from my experience, Elizabeth's and several other of our friends who have gone through childbirth that no one can truly predict a birth. Elizabeth was in the middle of a small tea party when Jonathon made his announcement to join us. He was one week early. My little Stephen was also a week early, waking me in the middle of the night. Now stop blaming yourself. This baby decided to make his or her appearance before you arrived tonight."

Abby and Elizabeth were nodding in agreement as Caroline spoke. Turning to stand next to David, Caroline added in the same soft tone, "Now if you wish to continue blaming yourself then I will aid Henry in putting you over Elizabeth's knee. Shall we go to dinner?"

David laughed at her bantering as he took his wife's arm to escort her to the dining room. Peter took Elizabeth while Richard escorted Abby.

"Sorry, Andrew." Henry took Christine's arm with a wink to Andrew. "I believe I would like to take my mistress to dinner." Henry grunted as Christine jabbed him with her elbow.

Taking up the end of the line, Andrew's eyes roamed over the woman before him on Henry's arm. The look in his green eyes and the grin on his face turned appreciative.

After dinner, Henry decided to forego the usual separation from the women for some drinking and smoking with the men. Instead, everyone gathered together in the parlor. It was nearly midnight before the housekeeper entered the parlor and introduced the small group to the newest Lord Batson. Henry beamed with pride as he gazed down at his newborn son.

After seeing the newborn, Christine quietly slipped out of the room and hurried up the stairs.

"Connie?" she called from the doorway of the bedchambers.

"Hello, Christine. Did you see him?" her friend asked tiredly.

"Yes, he is beautiful, Connie. Young Lord Batson will break many hearts as I am sure his father did in his youth."

"Stop that. You hated literature class like the rest of us," Connie said with a tired laugh.

"I only pretended to hate it," Christine shot back playfully. "I just wanted to say that I did not mean to upset you earlier."

"I know I am tired and just spent the evening giving birth," Connie said, "but I was sure that we had this conversation before."

"You sound like Elizabeth and Abby," Christine grumbled.

"Good, then maybe you will listen to one of us," Connie replied in a low voice as she closed her eyes.

"I will visit you later. You will need all the sleep you can now that the baby is here. Sleep well, Connie."

"I will for now."

Christine kissed her cheek then turned to leave. Connie's call stopped her and she turned back, "Christine? I made the wrong conclusions and I nearly lost a friend—"

"No, never lost. I can understand how the scene could have been misconstrued," Christine told her.

"Be careful of those we do call friends. Emma and Gwynth chose not only to believe the gossip but to also help spread it. I did not want to believe them but they sounded very convincing."

Christine sat down on the bed and smiled at her friend, "I remember Caroline telling me that she could not understand how David could look at her with such love and affection when she was near her time with Stephen. She thought of herself as fat and ugly. When you are told that your husband is with someone who is unburdened as you are and you have thoughts as Caroline had, then it is understandable that you would believe the lie."

"Beware of Emma and Gwynth in the future, Christine," Connie warned.

"Do not worry yourself of that, Connie. I will deal with them when the time comes. Now go to sleep, Lady Batson, and get some much needed rest. Your son will demand your attention all too soon," Christine said with a smile.

Connie smiled at her as Christine got up and left the room. Alone, Connie had to wonder why people had to be so vicious in their attitudes to others who dared to be different. She remembered a time at school when Christine disregarded her own class schedule to fit in time to tutor her in the finer points of playing the piano. The day of her recital, Connie played the third movement of Mozart's *Sonata in A Minor* to perfection and Christine was there to lend support.

In the parlor, Andrew waited at the door and watched for Christine's return. When she had reached the bottom step, he was there with a smile.

"How is Connie?" he asked as they slowly walked back to the parlor.

"How did you know I—" she started to ask but he only shrugged. "She is doing well. Tired but well," Christine told him with a smile.

"Good." He paused before asking, "I know I may be prying but could I ask you a question?"

"That would depend on the question," Christine replied.

Andrew chuckled lightly. "I hope that you consider me a friend."

Christine stopped and turned to look up at him. Andrew went on before she made any comment. "I see before me a young woman who cares for her friends and feels blame when there is none to feel." He raised a hand to stop when she opened her mouth to speak. "So I wonder why you let Connie believe and say those things to you? Why did you not speak up for yourself?"

Christine looked into his eyes and inhaled deeply before she answered him. "I could not tell her why I was with Henry because it was his surprise to her and I was not going to ruin it. Yet at the same time, nothing came to mind I could tell her that could have otherwise explained why I went into a house with him."

He looked at her for a moment then said quietly, "You could have made up some lie."

"Why lie?" Christine asked. "Even if Henry had not come home just at the right moment, I would have talked with Connie later. Though I cannot fathom how malicious certain people can be to come and tell Connie in her condition, I am now concerned with whom it was that saw me with Henry and is now spreading all over London that I am whoring about."

She blushed at her own frankness and Andrew discreetly looked away from her reddening face to her ruby broach.

"Any significance to this pin? It seems that you are rarely without it," he said changing the subject.

"My father gave it to me as a graduation gift a few years ago," she replied softly.

Nodding in understanding, Andrew slowly lifted his gaze to meet her eyes once again. He looked at her thoughtfully before he changed the subject yet again by saying, "I remember a time in my early days of carrying the burden of my title when my father passed it down to me that everyone thought I would fail, but as you can see I am still here." His head lowered slightly toward her as he smiled encouragingly and added, "And you, too, will do well in time."

It was silent for several moments before Christine said in a tone of quiet surprise, "Thank you, Your Grace. I appreciate your confidence in me."

"My friends call me Andrew," he said still smiling.

She nodded and said with a small genuine smile of her own, "And mine call me Christine or Tee."

Chapter 5

Several days later, Christine sat in the library with a book open but she was looking out the window, her mind drifting. Christopher Lockhart was proud of his collection of books. Even though he provided Christine with a governess, Lord Lockhart had taught her many things that fathers usually passed on to their sons. He had told her once that he did not want her to be fully dependent on her husband.

'*Someday, you will be left behind because your husband will pass away before you. You should know and understand what it is you will be left with and responsible for, Christine girl. Trust no one if your head and heart tells you so. You will be a woman and most men take advantage of the fact that women are not properly schooled in the affairs of business. Always seek out Alfred for assistance. Yet even in that, you need to know what questions to ask,*' he had told her. With a smile, he leaned forward and made a funny face that brought out a girlish giggle from the young girl barely ten and two years. '*Know and understand but keep it a secret. Do not let the men know that you know. Let them think that they are superior. You will know when the time comes to let them see just how intelligent you really are.*'

Fingering her red rose broach, Christine looked down at the black gown she would be wearing for a few more weeks. The year was nearly over and it had been a long and lonely time. She missed Christopher Lockhart. He had taught her how to analyze, how to question, and how to argue a point. He had taught her to put away the games most women played using certain tactics such as tears and pouts. '*Use the games of the mind instead, Christine. Give them just a taste of your knowledge but only enough to leave them wondering. Most times, a man cannot resist the opportunity to expound on what he feels he is the master. We men are very arrogant creatures.*'

Her thoughts were broken by the loud boisterous calls from the foyer. Christine groaned as a bellow seemed to reverberate off the walls.

"Come out, niece," the man called out. "Show yourself to your uncle. We have to tend to business!"

Christine stepped out of the library and watched as her uncle stumbled to the double doors of the study.

Lord John Hanson was the eldest child with two younger twin sisters, Margaret and Katherine. Known as Jack since he was a boy, he inherited half of the family wealth while his sisters had to share half between them. It had taken Jack Hanson a mere dozen years to squander nearly all of his inheritance to drinking and women.

Christine had never known her grandparents who were killed by highwaymen as they journeyed back to London from visiting friends in Devonshire. She knew that because Jack Hanson was their brother-in-law, Christopher Lockhart and Michael Pinckney, Caroline's father, helped in her uncle's financial affairs. Now that both men were dead, Christine took up the responsibility of subsidizing her uncle's spending habits.

Seeing the tall lanky man with her uncle, Christine inwardly groaned. He was the banker in charge of advising her in financial matters. She did not want to deal either one of them today and most definitely not both of them together. Worst yet, her uncle was far too inebriated to *'tend to business'*.

"Damn it, niece, where do you hide?" the drunken man called out. He turned and saw her approaching in slow and quiet steps. His sapphire eyes, so much like the color of Christine's, were glassy and unfocused. His dark hair seemed plastered to his head and looked like it was in great need of a cleaning. His face usually clean-shaven showed a day's growth of dark stumble. His mouth turned to a sneer when he could make out the form coming towards him.

"Ah, there you are. Thomas and I need to discuss some important—"

"Come along, Jack. You are about to fall over again," the lanky banker said condescendingly.

"Did he break anything in the last fall?" Christine asked in a disinterested tone.

"Only his pride whenever he is sober enough to realize it," the banker replied with a smile.

Christine did not return the smile as she looked at her uncle with disdain. Without a word, she turned into the study and headed for the desk. The banker's brown eyes glared at her back as he and the butler, Taylor, helped the drunken man into the room.

"I am certainly glad that my mother is not here to see you in this condition, Uncle," Christine admonished.

"My sister has seen me during worse times," Jack rumbled.

Christine did not reply but maintained her look of disdain on her uncle. After a moment, she looked to the banker and turned the direction to business by asking, "How much do I need to pay this time for his debts?"

Over an hour later, Christine sat alone in the study behind the big desk. It was strange that she thought of her father and his teachings just before her uncle appeared wanting to *'tend to business'*. Glancing at the bills sitting in a small stack on the desk, Christine wondered how she could curtail her uncle's spending. He was buying whatever he wanted without regard to the cost.

Then there was Thomas Lakely who was of no help. He merely collected the bills and presented them with promises of more to come. *Blast that banker*, she thought irritably. He was supposed to be her advisor but the only advice she had ever heard him tell her was to just pay the bills since there was plenty of money to cover them.

"Plenty of *my* money, he means," Christine growled under her breath as she angrily stood up.

* * *

Lady Marian Sanders returned the day following the birth of Connie's son. Andrew was able to decline invitations to see her for several days claiming pressing business. On the third afternoon after her return, Andrew was sitting with Richard and Peter at the club.

"I should be going. I have a few things to do before I have dinner with Marian this evening," Andrew told them.

Richard grinned and said in torment, "You do not sound pleased."

Andrew shrugged and replied with a grin, "She will only prattle on about the climate and how she had managed to get so much accomplished without my constant attention."

"Constant attention?" Peter questioned with a chuckle. "If I did not know better, and I do know the signs, I would say that are you becoming bored with Marian, Andrew."

His comment was met with only a smile from Andrew. Peter returned the smile and nodded his head knowingly. "Since Marian has returned, do you want Elizabeth to include her for tomorrow night's dinner party?"

Andrew considered this. Personally, he did not want to take Marian. He found the evening was more enjoyable without her by his side. On the other hand, if he did not take her and she found out, then what? Andrew knew that she coveted being the new duchess but could not dismiss the thought that she would discredit him in some way. After all, he had heard much of the disdain concerning Christine Lockhart. Just the thought of the blue-eyed young woman made him smile.

"Ah, he is smiling. But what does that mean?" Richard teased.

Giving his friend a look of feigned annoyance that only made Richard chuckle, Andrew answered Peter, "I think that I would not want to put Elizabeth out with rearranging her plans. We will leave everything as they are. Thank you for asking, Peter."

"Oh well, that should please Elizabeth," Peter told him, waving a hand dismissively. "She does not care for Marian. It is not meant in ill will, Andrew."

"I understand," the Duke said with a grin. He then leaned closer making Richard and Peter do the same as if to keep a secret. "I would like to enjoy the evening and not wish to subject anyone else to Marian's overbearing attitude."

Richard sat back and roared with laughter. Peter looked at him and wondered at his sensitivity. Grinning, Andrew put Peter at ease by explaining, "He does not care for Marian either."

That evening, Andrew joined Marian at her townhouse. He was quiet throughout dinner but he doubted that Marian even noticed as she talked almost incessantly.

"I suppose I was just spoiled with the warmer climate in Italy," she was saying. "Why, the Contessa just had to show me off to all her friends. I cannot remember the last time I slept days and attended balls all night. Andrew, you must come with me the next time I visit her. You would be such a sensation."

Andrew murmured something noncommittal but Marian was not listening as she continued on, "Well, I did manage to do some shopping on occasion. The Contessa simply adores shopping as I do. I had to buy another valise just for all the gowns I bought while I was there. You never seem to want to go with me shopping but I have some gowns that will make you notice no one else save me, darling," Marian cooed. Placing a hand on his arm just as he was about to lift his drink to his lips, she added in a coquettish fashion, "No other man has ever been able to make me think of anything else but him. I have missed you, Andrew darling."

He smiled at her and raised a brow. "Not even Hayden? I cannot believe that, Marian."

She laughed at his quip and waved a bejeweled hand. She missed the look of disinterest on his face as well as the tedious sigh. "Oh really, Andrew. Hayden was my husband. That is entirely different."

"Really?"

He looked at her in a way that made Marian snatch her napkin from her lap and toss it on the table angrily. "What is the matter, Andrew? You have hardly said more than two words all evening."

"And when have I had the opportunity?" Andrew replied with a mocking laugh.

Marian glared at him and hissed, "Did you even miss me?"

He hated the direct question. He sighed and dabbed the sides of his mouth as he thought of his reply. Choosing his words carefully, he said calmly, "Marian, I have kept myself very busy so I could not think beyond the matters at hand. In truth, there were many times over the last weeks that I noticed your absence."

He knew that she would misunderstand him as he watched her face brighten instantly and she smiled at him. Taking his hand into both of hers, she asked in a low seductive voice, "Would you like to take this conversation upstairs?"

Gently pulling his hand free from hers, he replied as he stood up, "I must beg off this time. I had intended on an early evening with you. Tomorrow evening, Elizabeth is giving Abby and Richard a dinner party with only a few close friends."

Seeing that she was about to protest, Andrew added with a shrug, "Sorry Marian, but the arrangements were made before I knew of your return. How would it look for me to ask Peter or Elizabeth to add another person? I am only a guest myself."

Though she did not like the thought of Andrew going without her, Marian huffed and let out a sigh before agreeing, "Well, if you think so."

Andrew nearly smiled for she was not very graceful in her agreement, but he had managed to forestall any possible slips of the invitation. With a quick kiss on her cheek, he straightened and said with a smile, "Good, I knew you would understand. I must go now, Marian. Thank you for dinner. I am glad you enjoyed your holiday."

Once he was inside his coach, Andrew released a long sigh of relief. He had avoided another kiss like the one she bestowed upon him when she first greeted him. Her kiss was full of passion but it had left him empty. He wondered if he ever loved Marian. In the dark seclusion of his coach, Andrew shook his head. He had never felt for Marian in the way he had seen his father show his feelings for his mother. Andrew knew there was much more than the body and Marian no longer seemed to fill that void for him either. With a certainty, he knew that his relationship with Marian was at an end. Though he was relieved in knowing for sure, he was now faced with explaining it to her. It was not going to be easy.

* * *

Christine arrived early to help Elizabeth prepare for her dinner party. "I will keep the children out from under your feet while you dress."

"We hired a nanny to do that, Christine," Elizabeth grumbled as Christine made a face at Jonathon making the toddler laugh.

"Well, she has the next hour or two to clear her head before it is time for your guests to appear," Christine replied without stopping her play with the boy.

While Elizabeth and Peter dressed in peace, Christine kept Chelsea and Jonathon in the sitting room laughing and playing. Their merriment carried through into the bedchambers making their parents smile.

Elizabeth stepped out into the sitting room wearing a silver gray gown and a diamond tiara adorning her auburn tresses. Christine looked at the gown with an appreciative eye and said with a shake of her head, "I will be so happy when I can stop wearing black and wear my other gowns. I miss my colors."

"Just another week, Christine, then you can bedazzle all the worthless lords to your heart's content," Peter said coming from his room.

"With the children present, I cannot tell you what I would rather do to those lords, worthless or not," Christine replied with a smile.

Peter laughed as he bent to pick up his son. "Such a lady you are, Christine."

Within hours the Hunnicutt townhouse was filled with guests. Elizabeth smiled at the dancers who met her gaze as they whirled by on the dance floor. Christine was dancing with David and, as she went by, she made a face when she caught Elizabeth's eye.

"I must say, Christine's appearance here will set the gossips to talking on the morrow," Lady Mary Holden said to Elizabeth as they watched Christine and David.

"Actually, she was going to stay home but Abby and I talked her into coming tonight," Elizabeth told her and the other women in the small group.

"Christine was told that this dinner party is given in honor of Abby's engagement to Richard and since Christine is her friend, Abby wanted her here to celebrate the occasion."

"But Elizabeth, the period of mourning is to remember the loved one who passed away," Lady Holden said. "The Ton is—"

"I know very well the reason behind the period, Mary," Elizabeth cut in. "If anyone thinks that Christine does not remember her stepfather just because she is taking a turn on the dance floor, then that one is sadly mistaken. She remembers him in every move she makes. He taught her to dance, to play the piano, to ride a horse. Goodness, there are so many other things. She knows that she should be home but it was the persuasion of others – me, Abby, David, Caroline, and Peter – that brings her out."

Looking at each one, Elizabeth finished her tirade as she said, "Though we were one or two years ahead of her at Lady Bellows School, I am sure that in some way, you can remember a time when Christine stepped out of our orderly society and did something bold. In most cases, it was to break curfew so that she could help one of the girls in her studies and not fail. Now which would have been more of a disgrace?"

"Elizabeth, we did not mean to criticize," Lady Gertrude Perkins said softly.

Elizabeth let out a long sigh and smiled ruefully. "No Gert, I should apologize. It is just that I am so tired of hearing the awful things said about Christine. We all know how giving she can be."

"But she has changed since those days at school," Lady Holden pointed out. "She does not smile or laugh like she used to and she has even lost some of the mischievous gleam in her eyes. It is almost as if she mistrusts everyone."

"And if the Ton was talking behind your back in the way they talk about Christine, what would you find so amusing?" Abby questioned as she joined the group.

The women looked sheepishly at her then back to Elizabeth. Abby smiled at them and said, "Do not worry, your voices did not carry. I have to admit, I have thought the same thing myself. I know it goes beyond Lord Lockhart's death and the gossip mongers. Something happened in her last year at school. None of you were there, but something happened I know it. Even Caroline and Maggie noticed it, but trying to find out from Christine is like trying to say that tomorrow will be the darkest day of the year."

The women smiled at the remark. With Abby's urgings, the conversation turned to a lighter topic. Elizabeth looked up and smiled when she saw Christine dancing with Andrew Chandler. Watching them, she thought that they made an attractive pair. Though Christine was still wearing black, she radiated a beauty that even the black could not diminish.

Peter pulled on her arm and Elizabeth excused herself from the group. Putting an arm around her waist as they walked slowly away, he pressed his lips to her temple then whispered, "Am I seeing a glimmer of matchmaking in your beautiful eyes, my love?"

She laughed lightly as she playfully pushed against his chest making him chuckle. "Really, Peter."

"Well, did I?"

"I was just watching Andrew with Christine. They make a lovely pair."

Peter glanced to the dance floor and watched them for a moment. He smiled for his assessment was the same. "Christine will not forgive you if you pressed the issue. She will be in black for one more week. After that, you can dress her up, put into the path of any deserving young buck, and see if the fire lights up between them."

"Not any young buck, you rascal. That one," Elizabeth said nodding her head toward Andrew who was smiling at something Christine had said.

"May I make a suggestion, Liz?" Peter offered. She looked up at him without protest and he continued, "Perhaps you should rearrange the seating so that Andrew is near Christine at the table."

Elizabeth's eyes lit up at the thought. "Oh Peter, you are genius," she said and left his side immediately to make the changes. Peter only laughed at her obvious attempts to play out her game.

During dinner, Elizabeth watched as inconspicuously as she could down the table. Peter was hard pressed to keep the amusement of his wife's actions to himself. Glancing down the table, he was pleased to see that Andrew was indeed noticing the young Lady Lockhart. The green eyes seemed to be riveted to her throughout dinner.

Listening to the latest political matters facing those in the House of Lords, Christine was able to present her ideas in the form of questions. This cunning tactic was a favorite of Christopher Lockhart's whenever he wanted to make a point known without coming right out with it. *'Discretion, Christine. Always use discretion when venturing into the realm of men,'* he had told her. When the discussion bent to her so-called wondering, she merely shrugged and acted disinterested.

46

A small smile played on Andrew's handsome face as he watched her. Sitting across from her, he was given a prime seat to see and hear her tactical manipulations. *She is definitely clever in her subtle moves to turn their thinking,* he thought.

Realizing that he had drifted away in his thoughts, Andrew tried to focus on the topic of conversation as he ate his dinner.

"Well, you did not know Anne Lucas in school. She was an absolute terror," Lady Holden was saying a few seats from Christine's right.

"Agnes had taught the girl well in being superior over others but she met her match when she tried to intimidate Christine," Lady Perkins said from Andrew's right. Leaning towards Christine, she asked, "Do you remember the time Anne accused you of taking her favorite dress?"

"Until Christine pointed out that she had a gown just like it and found Anne's gown hidden in the valise," another woman said laughing. Christine tried to hide her smile as she drank from her glass of wine.

"Now Janey, it is not polite to speak of the dead in such a way," Lord Holden said, making the laughter slowly quiet down.

A man sitting to Christine's right asked softly, "I always thought you were innocent of the accusations that Agnes claimed."

"Thank you, Lord Perkins," Christine said with a small smile.

"I never understood how Anne could have been so careless. She prided herself in mastering horseback riding," Lord Perkins went on to say.

"She was angry," Christine said quietly. All eyes turned to her as she added, "From the argument we just had."

"What was it she accused you of doing then? Something about her horse, was it not?" Lady Holden asked.

"Perhaps it is best to leave it be," Perkins said eyeing Christine.

"No, I am fine to talk about it," Christine told Lord Perkins. Then turning to Mary Holden, she said, "Yes, it was about her horse. She complained that her horse was acting strange but when the doctor finally came by to look at the animal, Anne could not be found. All I did was show the doctor which horse needed attention. The next thing we all knew, the horse was taken away and was later put down. Anne claimed that I overstated the ailment and made the doctor think that her horse was suffering from some disease."

"I cannot remember what it was. Do you remember it, Christine?" Gertrude Perkins asked from Andrew's left.

"No, I never heard the name of the disease," Christine replied then sipped her wine without looking up at anyone.

Gertrude took up the tale as Christine looked as though she was not going to finish it. "Anne was angry with Christine. She did not sound much like a lady that day what with the language she used." She looked at Christine and said with a smile, "I think that was the first time I had actually heard you yell at someone."

"Gert, will you stay with the story," Janey exclaimed, eliciting soft laughter from those listening.

Waving her hand, Gertrude said, "Knowing that it would infuriate Christine, Anne saddled Midnight, Christine's horse, and took off into the woods. Within a half an hour, Midnight returned without Anne. A search of the woods was made and Anne was finally found. She must have gone under a low branch, breaking her neck."

"Agnes tried to implicate you?" the man next to Gertrude Perkins asked Christine.

She nodded but Lady Perkins continued, "She came to the school causing such an uproar over the whole incident. I had to give witness along with a dozen other girls that Christine never left the school grounds."

"That whole affair must have been quite upsetting to you, my dear," Perkins said patting Christine's right hand that rested on the table. "As I have said, I knew the accusations were wrong. My Gertie would never bear false witness." He turned to his wife and gave her a warm smile.

"Agnes still has not forgiven you nor has she forgotten," Janey said. "It would not surprise me if she is instrumental in all the vicious gossip about—"

"Janey, please," Lord Holden complained.

Slightly embarrassed, Janey gave Christine an apologetic smile and said softly, "Well, enough of such talk. What are Abby's colors going to be for the wedding? Do you know, Christine?"

Christine was grateful for the change of topics and related some of the ideas Abby had already mentioned.

Andrew had watched her throughout the tale of Lady Anne Lucas' death. He had also heard the tales and the implications. Christopher Lockhart had hurried to his stepdaughter's side and soundly crushed the vicious rumors that she was instrumental in Anne's death. But now watching her face, he saw fleeting glimpses of the hurt and pain in those beautiful blue eyes.

Dancing resumed after dinner for a while with the promise of Abby cutting into her cake. As everyone found their dance partners when the music started up again, Christine slowly made her way to the French doors leading out to the gardens. Seeing that she was not watched, she opened a door just a crack and slipped outside.

The cold February night air hit her immediately and took her breath away. Hurrying away from the doors so that no one would see her through the glass, she moved to a corner of the garden. The talk of Anne Lucas during dinner brought back some terrible memories from school. There were too many memories of her time at school that she tried desperately to keep locked away. The telling of Anne's death brought it all back like water rushing forth from the bursting of a dam.

She looked down longingly at the bench but it was covered with snow. Using some twigs, she brushed it off.

"Why are you out here in the cold and snow?" came Andrew's voice from behind her.

Christine whirled around startled that she was no longer alone. Seeing his smile, she narrowed her eyes and asked in playful accusation, "Do you delight in frightening people, Your Grace?"

He laughed at her tone. "No, my lady. I was unaware that I was being silent in my steps." Looking around at the gardens barren of color in comparison to the lush spring flowers yet to bloom, Andrew asked, "And what do you find so interesting in the gardens? Have you come across the elusive snow flower?"

Christine's blue eyes twinkled in amusement as she laughed lightly to his quip. Andrew felt his heart flip in his chest at the sound of her soft laughter. His green eyes turned to look at her as she shook her head.

"Sorry, Andrew, there are no snow flowers in this garden, I fear. Only this weed before you that is trying to catch her breath from the festivities within."

A burst of laughter coming from inside the house greeted her statement. Christine laughed again and looked at the Duke as her point was made. He grinned, having followed her thought.

Her laughter was taken away as a gust of wind stole her breath with its chill. Christine gasped and turned her head sideways. Without realizing it, she had moved her foot. Letting out a startled gasp as her foot slipped on a small icy patch, she reached for something to catch herself. Strong arms grabbed her and pulled her forward.

Standing on a more stable surface, Christine looked up at Andrew. He had turned them so that his body blocked the chilling wind and was now looking down into the sapphire eyes that had been invading his thoughts of late. In a slow yet unconscious move, he lowered his head and pressed his lips on hers. The kiss was light at first then he pressed further, opening her mouth with the slight pressure and tasting the sweet wine she had with dinner.

He felt her lean into him slightly and her fingers spread over his chest. Then he felt the subtle pressure as she pushed at him. Lifting his head slowly, he looked into her eyes and saw that the blue had become darker with the emotion he invoked from the kiss. The sight of her innocent arousal made his own desire surge within him.

"Andrew, I—" she whispered but did not know what to say.

With a tender smile, Andrew took a step back and released his hold of her.

"You should go back inside, Christine," he told her in a quiet tone. Seeing the anxiety on her face and the crimson cheeks that had nothing to do with the icy wind, he gently ran the tips of his fingers down the line of her jaw and whispered, "Go now before I forget myself and steal another kiss from you."

Her gaze dropped from his and she nodded almost imperceptibly. Holding her arm gently as she stepped by him, Andrew then released her and watched her return to the house. He stayed outside to cool his body and his mind. He had not meant to kiss her but the moment he held her close, a wave of heat and desire rushed through him. He had never felt such a force of wanting with any woman in his arms as he had felt the instant he held her close to him. *What is the matter with me?*

Christine could not believe that she let him kiss her. Just because she had been infatuated with those beautiful green eyes of his, she would throw herself at him.

"I was falling," she mumbled as she made her way to the French doors. Realizing that she actually spoke the words aloud, she glanced around but no one was outside. *No one but the Duke.*

She looked back but Andrew was not behind her. Instead he was standing where she had left him just moments before. Christine let out a loud sigh of annoyance that she would be so foolhardy.

"God, what does he think of me now?" she whispered to the wind.

He stood in the shadows of the house where the wind was not as icy or as strong. He had seen Christine step out and was about to approach her when he caught sight of movement in the garden. He froze and watched as the Duke of Kenilworth walked towards her. He muttered a curse that she was no longer alone and waited in the shadows. His impatience was beginning to wear thin then he noticed the Duke turn with Christine close to him. With eyes wide in amazement, he witnessed what he was sure were two lovers sharing a stolen moment together.

"An affair between the Duke and Lady Christine?" he muttered softly. His mind churned with the possibilities. *The pristine Lady Christine is having an affair with the most eligible and wealthiest bachelor in London? And if that small bit of information were to become public knowledge, what then?*

A smile crept over his face as he observed the Duke watching Christine go back to the house. *Interesting little tidbit,* he thought as he watched the couple. After several long moments, he was relieved when the Duke turned and returned to the house as well. He nearly laughed out loud when he noticed the Duke go through a different door when he entered the house. The smile stayed on his lips as his mind raced with ideas.

"It is something to consider," the man muttered.

Nodding his head as the debate raged on in his mind, he turned and headed back into the house.

Andrew walked through Peter's study instead of the ballroom doors as Christine had done. No one else would have ventured out in the cold and it certainly would not take much imagination for someone to reach the wrong conclusion.

As he headed for the ballroom, he heard the soft music of the piano and a small child singing. Curious, Andrew turned to the parlor. The door was left open a few inches and, peering inside, he saw several people sitting around facing the piano. Slipping inside quietly, Andrew was surprised to see Christine playing the piano as Chelsea shyly sang a song.

The little girl was looking at the ceiling as she sang and fidgeted while she stood before her audience but her voice was clear in her childlike soprano. Christine would smile radiantly at her whenever the large hazel eyes drifted in her direction.

Applause greeted Chelsea as she finished singing. She hurried to sit on the bench beside Christine and the dark haired beauty whispered in Chelsea's ear. Suddenly the child jumped off the bench and dropped into a curtsy that brought out a soft round of laughter.

"Chelsea would like to also perform for you a duet on the piano. It is a song that we have been practicing together," Christine announced to the small group.

Sapphire eyes met emerald green ones for a moment and Andrew smiled at her from his place against the wall. As the two played the duet, his eyes lingered on Christine. She was truly a beautiful woman who cared a great deal for her friends as he had witnessed on several occasions. His gaze roamed over the profile of her face and her body. He could still feel her body against his as he held her, smell the soft scent of roses, and taste her mouth when he kissed her.

He felt his body reacting to his thoughts. Willing himself to stay calm, Andrew tried to turn his focus on the piano duet instead of Christine. He was successful for only a few moments before his attention was drawn again to the beauty smiling down at the child.

The door opened and Peter stepped in. Seeing the impromptu recital, he looked around and saw Andrew leaning against the wall with arms crossed over his chest. Moving to stand beside him, Peter watched the performance with pride evident on his face.

When the song was over and everyone applauded, Peter leaned close to Andrew and whispered, "Someday, Christine Lockhart will make a wonderful mother."

Andrew did not reply as he watched Peter make his way to the front and announce with a smile, "Elizabeth will have Abby cut the cake in a few moments."

"Can I have a piece a cake, Papa?" Chelsea asked hopefully.

"I think that would be appropriate after entertaining our guests," Peter replied.

Chelsea's delighted leap for joy and clapping hands made those who were still in the room laugh.

"Come along, little one," Christine said to the child as she took her hand. Looking at Peter, she added, "I will see that she gets a small piece of cake."

He nodded in thanks and slowly followed everyone from the room. Getting to the end of the line beside Peter, Andrew complimented quietly, "Chelsea played well."

"Who would have known that just last summer, Chelsea refused to go near the piano. But between Christine and Elizabeth playing children rhymes, they made her interested in learning so that she could play the songs when she was alone. Subtle tactics, Andrew, without twisting her arm or holding desserts as hostage," Peter replied, making the Duke chuckle.

"I have to admit, Peter. I see what you mean about Christine Lockhart. She is not at all what the Ton makes her out to be."

"She is a very nice lady, Andrew. Though do be careful when she wants something. She knows how to talk you into giving it while the whole time you would swear it was your idea all along," Peter told him with a mischievous grin.

"I will keep that in mind," Andrew replied, clapping his hand on Peter's shoulder.

Chapter 6

Sitting at the club with a drink in his hand, Andrew stared into the fire. It had been nearly a fortnight since that kiss in the garden and he still had not been able to get Christine Lockhart out of his mind. Whenever he was with Marian, he found himself comparing her to Christine. Although Christine was younger than Marian by a half dozen years, the young Lady Lockhart seemed to come out to be the winner in many ways.

The younger woman seemed more attuned to business. Andrew was surprised on several occasions when Christine made small contributions to conversations dealing with business matters. She seemed more mature than Marian. He was growing tired of the pouts and resentful looks when Marian wanted something he thought was too frivolous. Given his present state of mind of his affair with Marian, he was finding her taste too expensive. The gowns she bought while in Italy had been billed to him. That discovery had led to another argument between them.

The latest comparison was the tolerance with servants that Christine seemed to show a great deal of patience whereas Marian held an air of disdain towards them. During a visit with Marian at the townhouse a few days before, one of the servants loudly clattered the china pot onto the silver tray. Marian's reaction was to berate the girl in front of him and inform her that a portion of her wages would be withheld. Since nothing was broken, Andrew had argued with Marian.

"She will remember her mistakes through such punishment, Andrew," Marian had fairly hissed.

"Not by subtracting from her pay, Marian," Andrew told her firmly.

The next day, Andrew noticed a bruise on the girl's arm that the servant was trying to conceal. When he had asked Marian about it, she merely shrugged and said, "She is just clumsy."

Trying to contain his anger, Andrew ordered the girl to pack her things. The servant was moved to his townhouse and was placed under the charge of his housekeeper, Bailey. When he had asked about the girl's abilities, Bailey informed him that the girl was quite efficient and conscientious of her work yet suffered from other bruises.

"I will groom young Mary to attend the new Duchess," his housekeeper had told him with a mischievous grin. "That is. whenever you decide to bring her home."

In comparison to Marian's reaction, Andrew thought back to Elizabeth's dinner party when a maid dropped an empty tray and it clattered loudly in the foyer. He and Richard were talking with Elizabeth and Abby at the time when the noise startled quite a few people nearby. Elizabeth took a few steps toward the maid but Christine appeared and waved her away, seeing to the matter instead. Watching Christine with the maid, he saw that she had managed to bring out a smile from the girl before the maid disappeared towards the kitchen.

"What happened?" Elizabeth asked when Christine joined them.

"One of your gentleman lords was looking to where he had been instead of watching where he was going. He stepped into her path, caused the accident, and then he blamed her," Christine told her as she looked around the room. Looking pointedly at Elizabeth and rolling her eyes, she added, "And they call themselves gentlemen. Loosely defined I assure you."

Andrew smiled at the fire crackling in the fireplace as he remembered the laugh they had all shared from her remark.

His musings were interrupted when Richard dropped into the chair across from him. "Now what has you smiling?" he asked.

"Just thinking," Andrew replied.

"Hmm, really? And would you be thinking of that new mistress you have taken on? I am rather put out that you mentioned nothing to me about her," Richard told him with a grin.

Andrew frowned while his smile turned suspicious. "What are you talking about? What new mistress?"

"Word is out, my friend, that you have a new and younger plaything. So have you finally severed the ties with Marian?" Richard asked.

"A new plaything? What are you talking about?"

Richard let out a mocking sigh and rolled his eyes. He moved to sit in the chair next to Andrew and said in quieter tone, "Come now, Andrew, you can tell me who she is. I do not plan on running to Marian and letting the surprise out, though I would love to see her face when you tell her."

"For the life of me I have no idea what you are talking about, Richard," Andrew told him.

Seeing the seriousness of his friend's face, Richard sat back and stared at him. "You really do not have a new mistress?" he asked in marked disappointment.

Andrew let out a light chuckle, "No, I do not."

"Well, this is rather interesting. Rumor has it that you were seen a few weeks ago kissing a woman and that person was *not* Marian Sanders," Richard told him with a big grin.

"What?" Andrew asked surprised.

"I am telling you, Andrew. Someone claims to have seen you with a woman."

"Impossible!" Andrew interjected.

"That is what I heard," Richard said grinning.

Andrew was shaking his head as he thought back. The only woman he had kissed in months who had not been Marian was Christine Lockhart.

"Impossible, no one was out there to see us," he mumbled.

Richard sat forward in surprised. "What? There is someone else?"

"No, it was just an accident," Andrew said quietly shaking his head. "No, not an accident but it was not planned. I suppose she must have wanted a few moments to herself. I had gone out because I saw her sneak away—but I am sure no one saw us."

"Andrew, who is she?" Richard asked softly. Seeing the look his friend gave him, Richard let out an exasperated sigh and said indignantly, "I am not going to spread any rumors, you know that."

"It was at Peter's, in the garden. That night Elizabeth honored you and Abby over the engagement. I was with—" Andrew hesitated and looked around to be sure that no one was near enough to hear them. Dropping to a whisper, he said, "I was with Christine Lockhart."

Richard's mouth dropped open in surprise and he sat back in his chair to stare at his friend.

"Do not repeat that. I do not want her honor smeared any more than these fools have already done," Andrew said firmly and looked around at the faces.

"My God, I would have never guessed," Richard replied in quiet astonishment. "Do you like her?"

"Of course I like her. I think she is a wonderful person."

"I agree with you on that account," Richard said nodding. He leaned closer to Andrew and asked, "What about Marian?"

"What do you mean, what about Marian?" Andrew shot back. He shook his head and held up a hand to quiet to Richard as he went on, "As you and

Peter may have guessed, I am bored of Marian and her complaints. She repeats useless gossips and I am tired of hearing the nonsense."

Richard looked at his friend and a slow smile appeared on his face. "You are falling for the girl."

Slowly, Andrew turned to look at him as if he had never seen Richard before in his life. "It was just a kiss. Nothing more."

Richard's smile only widened and his eyes twinkled in amusement but he said nothing. Andrew rolled his eyes and looked back the fire.

A moment later, Richard leaned closer and said quietly, "You know, I will say nothing. Not even to Peter though Elizabeth would be delighted to hear of this. But I have to tell you, Andrew, I think this is a step in a better direction. I like her more than I like Marian."

"Richard," Andrew warned.

"Marian is a pampered, selfish witch while Christine is considerate and—"

"I know how the two are different, Richard," Andrew hissed. "You do not have to lay it all out for me."

Richard only laughed and said, "Very well. I guess I do not have to line up the merits of one against the other. But what you might want to do is squelch this rumor and quickly. Should her name get out, well, you know what the Ton would do with that bit of news. On the other hand, dealing with the Ton just may be the easier one to handle. When Marian hears of this—"

"Put it to rest, will you please. Marian will not find out. Hell, I did not even know the rumor was out there," Andrew grumbled.

"Now you have time to think of what to say if this talk of your new mistress reaches Marian."

Before Richard could continue further with his torments, Peter sat in the chair across from them and leaned close to the pair. "So what are you two whispering about over here?"

Richard and Andrew looked at one another and grinned. Peter looked at them and smiled, "You two are always so secretive, just as you were in school. One would think you would have grown out of such behavior."

That same afternoon, Christine was shopping with her mother and cousin. Having put away the black dresses, Christine laughed with Roberta earlier that day as she tried to decide on what to wear. Dressed in a plum-colored gown with a matching cloak, Christine was smiling as she emerged from a store with packages in hand.

"Oh, I think I can forego new shoes, Mother. I have too many as it is. I am sure I can find something to match these," she was saying.

"What do you say we go and have a treat at the bakery?" Caroline suggested.

"I think the baby craves the sweets, cousin," Christine teased.

"Leave Caroline be. I wanted nothing but potatoes while I carried you," Maggie told them.

"We know, Aunt Maggie. Christine was potatoes and with me my mother craved carrots. Uncle Christopher used to say that the only thing missing was the meat and onions," Caroline said, making them laugh.

"Ah yes, a stew to—" Maggie began but stopped in mid-sentence as two constables approached them.

"Lady Lockhart?" one man asked.

Both women acknowledged the name and he smiled before glancing down at his notes. "Lady *Christine* Lockhart?"

"I am Christine Lockhart," she told him and took a step closer.

"We are sorry to interrupt your outing, my lady, but we have been requested to bring you with us. Lady Victoria Sutton states that—"

"I do not know a Lady Victoria Sutton," Christine interrupted.

"It may be that you do not recognize the name. Perhaps when you see her face, you will know who she is. However, she states that some jewelry was taken from her coach last week and she remembered seeing you in the area."

"I did not take any jewelry," Christine interrupted again.

The constables were quick to make assurances as the three women looked at them worriedly. "I apologize, my lady. I meant to say that Lady Sutton thinks you may have seen the man who took her possessions."

"I do not remember the incident," she began.

The constable continued on, "We have several men fitting a description from another witness and we would appreciate it if you would look at these men. Perhaps you may remember then."

"Well, I—"

"Come along, Christine," Maggie began.

"I apologize again, Lady Lockhart, but it will not take long and we will return within the hour."

"Take her without a chaperone?" Maggie asked incredulously.

The constables looked to the smaller coach parked behind the Lockhart coach. There was a constable driver and another constable waiting at the door. "There are four of us, Your Ladyship. Lady Lockhart will be safe with us," the man explained.

The three women looked at the four men for a long moment before Christine said with a smile, "I think it will be fine, Mother. You and Caroline go on home and I will join you within the hour as the Constable has said."

"But alone, Christine?" Maggie questioned.

"I will be fine," she reassured her mother.

Christine turned to the two men and nodded. With a wave of his hand, the constable who did the talking had Christine precede him and his partner. Maggie and Caroline watched as Christine and the three men stepped into the waiting coach. The two women shared a worried look before they stepped toward their own coach.

Christine looked from one man to the next then to the third man. Now that she was alone, she felt uneasy as they stared at her. She looked out the window so that her apprehension was not given away and hoped she looked relaxed in their company.

After a few long minutes in silence, she looked at the one who had approached her outside of the shop and asked, "I suppose this Lady Sutton knows me."

"Yes, my lady, she remembered you quite well. Dressed in black as you were still in mourning over the death of your stepfather," the constable explained.

Christine looked over their faces then asked, "What was taken from her coach?"

"Some packages from 'er day's shopping. Clothes mostly," the third man told her.

Frowning at him, Christine questioned, "I thought she had some jewelry taken?"

"Yes, yes, jewelry as well," the man said almost impatiently.

Wary, Christine eyed the men before slowly turning her gaze back out the window. Her heart skipped a beat as she realized that they were heading for the docks instead of the Inspector's office.

"Where are we?" she was asking as she turned to the constables.

The three men moved into action simultaneously. The third man sitting beside her put a callous hand over her mouth while the other two each grabbed a wrist. She tried to kick but found her movements hindered when one of the men stepped on the hem of her gown. The material ripped under his boot then some more when the two men pressed close so that she could not kick them.

With his free hand, the third man opened her cloak and slipped his hand into her bodice. The hand over her mouth muffled her scream as the material ripped at the sudden moves. The roughness of his hand scratched her as he cupped her breast.

"What are ye doin', Danny? 'is lordship says that she is no' to be 'armed,'" said the second constable.

"I just want to feel 'er is all. So pretty and so soft. Ye are very soft, yer Ladyship," the third man whispered close to her ear.

Christine could smell rum on his breath and felt nauseated from it and her fear.

The other constable looked at her terror-filled eyes. "Leave her be, Danny. She is a lady and you should not—"

"She will not be a lady but 'is whore soon," he said showing a yellow-toothed grin. "And when 'is Lordship 'as 'is back turned away, I think I will 'ave taste of 'er."

Sapphire blue eyes widened at that and, for a moment, Christine drifted back to another place at another time and saw another man's face so close to her own. The man grinned down at her and said in added torment, "I will enjoy me ride on ye, girlie."

The coach stopped and it brought Christine back to the present. The one called Danny lowered his head to run his tongue over the tops of her breasts exposed by the pressure of his hand under the bodice. Christine tried to scream again as she closed her eyes tight. A strangled sound was heard outside and all three men froze to listen.

A shot rang out and one of the men fell back in his seat. Suddenly the doors on both sides of the coach were snatched open at the same time. Hands reached in and pulled the remaining two men out of the coach. With eyes still tightly shut, Christine felt the hand jerk free from her mouth as sounds of a fight ensued.

Opening her eyes and clasping her cloak together, she looked around to find herself alone in the coach with one man slumped in the corner. Putting a hand to her mouth, Christine looked out the window but did not see her other tormentors. She was preparing to run out when a man suddenly appeared in the open doorway next to her.

Christine shrank back into the corner of her seat, taking a deep breath to scream when she realized that it was Richard Pittman peering inside.

"Come quickly," he ordered and put out his hand to assist her out of the coach.

Looking down on the road, she saw the constable who had originally approached her lying face down in the gutter. Taking her hand firmly into his, Richard hurried with her out of the alley and toward a coach that was waiting at a nearby corner.

Hearing footsteps coming up behind them, Christine clutched her cloak together at the bodice and turned to see who was chasing them.

"Andrew," she exclaimed as Richard threw open the door to his coach and nearly tossed her inside.

"Hurry," Richard urged then followed her inside.

"Go," Andrew called up and had barely secured the door before the coach lurched forward.

Christine looked at Richard who sat across from her then to Andrew who sat beside her. Her fear changed to relief and she began to shiver.

"What were you doing going with them?" Andrew asked angrily.

"I was—they said that I—was to identify someone—who stole some jewelry," she stammered in explanation.

"Why did you go with them alone, Christine? That was a foolish thing to do! My God, if Richard and I had not noticed you with your mother and Caroline," Andrew began to scold but Richard broke in softly.

"Not now, Andrew. She is upset."

Glancing up at him and nodding, Andrew took a deep breath to steady his nerves. "I did not mean to scold you, Christine, but that was a foolish thing to do."

"I know," she whispered. "I thought they were constables."

"Did they hurt you?" Richard asked quietly.

Christine shook her head and looked out the window. Seeing that they were heading for the park, she turned to Richard then to Andrew and whispered urgently, "I cannot go home looking like this."

Looking her over, Richard noted her disheveled appearance and had to agree. He looked at Andrew with a raised brow, "Molly?"

"That would be my suggestion," Andrew agreed. With a tap to the small door near the driver, Richard relayed an address and the coach turned down a street.

"We will take you to someone who will help and who will be very discreet," Andrew told her gently. Christine nodded and looked out the window again.

Andrew and Richard looked at each other. Trying not to be obvious, Richard pointed down. Andrew leaned forward slightly and, following the pointed finger, he saw that her gown was ripped near the hem. The two men shared another look then they both turned to look at the woman who stared out the window.

"Are you cold?" Andrew asked noticing her shaking.

Christine shook her head in reply and continued to stare out the window. She could still feel the rough hand touching her and smell the rum on the breath of the one called Danny. But the face wavered from Danny's to that of another man so that, in Christine's mind, the two faces seemed to blur together.

The coach stopped in front of a modest looking townhouse and Christine looked up, becoming aware of her surroundings. Richard gave her a quick reassuring smile then got out. Christine watched as he knocked at the door and was admitted inside. Soon he was coming back and nodded to Andrew.

"Put the hood over your head and keep your head bent so no one will see your face. Do not raise your head until I have told you to do so," Andrew ordered.

When she had done as she was told, he assisted her out of the coach and into the townhouse. From her vantage point under the hood, Christine saw that Andrew stayed to her right with his hand at her elbow. Richard was to her left and a woman was leading the way. There were men's voices followed by women giggling. Their steps over the tiled floor were masked by piano music coming from another room nearby.

A door closed behind them and soon the small group stopped. Christine kept her face concealed as Andrew had told her. The door opened and closed again then she heard the swish of skirts.

"Very well, Lord Richard, what have you and His Grace brought into my home?" a woman's voice asked.

Someone wearing a blue velvet gown stepped before Christine and the hood was pushed back. Christine slowly lifted her head to see a buxom woman around two score years with light brown hair and brown eyes. A shocked expression met Christine's gaze and the woman took a half a step back.

"Lady Christine Lockhart?" the woman exclaimed in a near whisper. The brown eyes roamed over her and the woman asked in amazement, "Dear God, child, what happened to you?"

"We will discuss that in a moment, Molly. Right now, Christine needs to be presentable when we take her home. Can you assist her?" Andrew asked moving to stand beside Molly and having his first good look at Christine's appearance.

Huge sapphire eyes stared back at him. Her face was pale and her carefully pinned hair was falling around her face and down her back. He noticed that she clutched her cloak tightly around herself, so tight that her knuckles were white from her grip.

"Yes, we will make her just as beautiful as ever. Come with me, child," Molly replied and reached for her arm.

Christine stepped back and asked suspiciously, "How do you know me?"

Molly smiled kindly. "I knew your father, dear." With a small shrug as Christine continued to stare at her, the older woman added, "The Captain was—well, that was until he married your mother."

Christine's gaze roamed over the woman's face then she turned her head to stare at the door. Laughter filtered through the closed door from the other rooms as she slowly turned to look at Andrew and Richard accusingly.

"You brought me to a brothel?" she asked incredulously.

The two men smiled then Andrew said with a shrug, "This is the safest place for you at the moment."

"Come along, Lady Christine. Let us see what we can do with your appearance. You gentlemen please stay in here," Molly was saying as she pulled Christine along. They went through another door that did not lead into the large foyer.

The moment they were left alone, Andrew began pacing while Richard made himself a drink. Taking a sip of his drink, Richard decided that his friend needed one as well. Pouring the brandy, a smile played on his face as he thought back to the earlier conversation about Christine and the kiss. Looking at Andrew and seeing the worry mixed with concern on his friend's face, Richard hid the smile as he handed the drink to Andrew.

In the next room, Molly muttered to herself when she saw the torn bodice. "What happened to you, child? Surely Lord Richard or—"

"No, not them," Christine told her quickly.

Molly listened as the story rushed out. By the end of the tale, Christine finally gave into her inner turmoil and broke down in tears. Putting arms around her, Molly gently quieted her.

"Now you dry your eyes, child. I will have this gown mended while Michelle puts your hair back into place. You will look just as you did before and no one will be the wiser," the older woman said soothingly.

Christine looked at Molly through tear-filled eyes and smiled. Following instructions, Christine went behind a dressing screen and removed her gown then slipped into a robe. When she stepped out from behind the screen,

Christine saw that Molly was with a young woman.

"This is Michelle. She will fashion your hair," the woman said sitting Christine down in front of a mirror.

"Thank you," Christine said softly.

Molly gave her a soft smile and left the room with the gown draped over her arm. Stepping into the room where Andrew and Richard waited, Molly walked over to them.

"How is she?" Andrew asked anxiously.

"She will be fine. How did you come to rescue her?" Molly asked.

Richard stepped forward and answered, "I was buying a broach for Abby's birthday and I wanted Andrew's opinion. As we came out of the jewelers, we saw Christine with her mother and Caroline talking with two constables. Then Christine followed them to a waiting coach and got in with them."

Andrew took over telling the story. "I did not like the looks of that so I asked Richard if we could follow them a safe distance behind. Soon we realized that they headed for the docks and I knew something was very wrong. When they stopped in a secluded alley, Richard and I walked up to the driver. We noticed the coach rocking and took it to be a sign of a struggle inside."

"Did she tell you what happened?" Richard asked.

Molly nodded and told them what Christine had said. She lifted the gown and Andrew muttered a curse at the sight of the torn bodice.

"What was she thinking to go alone with them?" Andrew growled angrily.

"They were constables—or rather dressed as constables. She thought that she could trust them," Molly said giving Christine's explanation to the same question.

"Maggie cannot know of this. She was upset enough when Christine left with them," Andrew told Molly.

"No, she will not know. Here is what you two will say to Lady Margaret when you return Lady Christine home and I will instruct Lady Christine on her part. No one else need know of what happened. First, I will give this to Antoinette for mending. I will be back in a moment," Molly told them.

Nearly an hour later, Richard's coach pulled up in front of the Lockhart house. He got out and knocked at the door while Andrew assisted Christine out of the coach. Their eyes met and he said with a smile, "You will do just fine. Come now."

Inside sitting in the parlor, Maggie sat with Andrew and Richard while Christine excused herself.

"It was a surprise to see Christine in the Inspector's office," Richard was telling Maggie. "One of the constables was about to offer her a ride home, but we were more than happy to assist."

"So you saw the man in question?" Maggie asked Andrew.

"Yes. As it so happened on that day, I was picking up the gift I had ordered for Abby and Richard. I remembered the man because I had thought his face was familiar to me at the time. I did not know Christine was in the area," Andrew told her.

"It seems that it is no longer safe to venture out alone. Christine is forever sneaking out to do some errand," Maggie said worriedly.

"I do not sneak out, Mother. I tell you where I am going," Christine said coming into the parlor. She had changed into a silver gray gown and had a lace shawl draped over her shoulders.

"You leave me a note, that is not telling me," Maggie corrected with a smile.

Christine looked at the two men and smiled.

"So did you know Lady Sutton?" Maggie asked her daughter.

"I, ah, did not see her, just the man the constables mentioned," Christine replied.

"Oh," Maggie said with a nod. "I have been trying to place this Lady Sutton myself, but I cannot think of who she is."

"Do not worry over it, Mother. There are times when people say something to me and I have never seen them before," Christine replied thinking of Molly.

When they were back in the coach, Richard looked thoughtfully at Andrew and asked, "Do you suppose that this incident with Christine has anything to do with that wager?"

Andrew had thought of that several times since Molly had mentioned from Christine's tale that a titled lord apparently hired those men to act as constables. With a shake of his head, Andrew looked out the window.

"I certainly hope not, Richard. I hate to think that any man would be so desperate for money as to treat a woman so callously and send unsavory men like those would-be constables."

Nodding, Richard said, "I do not care for the thought myself. To think that someone would be so cruel as to offer such a wager to begin with."

Sometime later, when he entered his home, Andrew was given a note sent from Marian inviting him to her townhouse for dinner. With a tired sigh, he realized that Christine's ordeal had taken up nearly the entire afternoon. He stared at the note for a moment and debated seriously to decline the invitation. He turned to his butler and heard himself say instead, "Parker, send someone to inform Lady Sanders that I will join her for dinner."

"Yes, Your Grace."

Andrew went to his study and sat at his desk. Going through the neatly stacked papers, he let his mind wander. Marian was the last person he wanted to see now. In fact, he had not wanted to be with her since her return from Italy. Though she had not been demanding when he shortened his visits with her, she had tried to entice him into her bed. When he still declined, she had been angry but did not go so far as to throw him out. Her desire to be duchess was always foremost on her mind of proper ladylike actions. But he did not want a wife who cared more for his title and wealth than for him.

Andrew thought back to what had happened with Christine Lockhart a few hours before. He remembered peering inside the coach to see three men holding her down in a corner. The outrage spurred him into action without thinking. With the men occupied by the struggling Christine, he pulled his pistol from his waistcoat and shot the man nearest him. Then he threw open the door and pulled the man sitting next to Christine out the door. He had not realized that Richard had made the same move from the other side of the coach until he followed them and saw the third constable face down in the street.

He wondered at his reaction to her torn bodice. Was Richard correct in his earlier assumption? Was he falling for Christine? The night of Elizabeth's small party, Christine had captivated him as they danced and he could not stop watching her during dinner. She had stirred up his desire when he kissed her. That was something he had not felt even through Marian's attempts to seduce him.

He decided that whatever he was beginning to experience for Christine Lockhart, he needed to talk with Marian. Trying to put both women from his mind, Andrew set to work on the papers on his desk.

Chapter 7

The evening with Marian was not what Andrew had expected. She did not greet him with the overly powerful kiss and caresses. Instead she sat on the sofa in a green velvet gown adorned in diamonds he had more than likely paid for from her trip to Italy.

"How are you, darling?" she asked with a smile.

"I am fine, Marian," Andrew replied as he made himself a drink.

"Marian?" she repeated. "You used to call me your love."

"No, I used to call you, my dear," he corrected conversationally then sipped some of his brandy.

"Come sit with me, darling," she cooed.

Andrew looked at the sofa and, letting out a tired sigh, sat on the other end. Marian's smile did not waver at the subtle rejection to be close to her.

"I wanted to have this evening together before I leave in the morning," she informed him.

"You are leaving? Where to this time?" Andrew asked without emotion.

"I have a friend in York who has been asking that I visit with her and her new husband. I thought that with the weather warming slightly, I would take the time to see her."

"I hope you enjoy yourself as you visit with your friend," he said, not caring that she did not give a name.

"Will you miss me, darling?" she purred.

"Do you have to ask?" he countered.

All pleasantries were tossed aside as Marian huffed and threw herself from the couch. Angrily, she stepped away from him then whirled around to glare at him. "Who is she, Andrew?"

"Who?" he asked sipping his drink coolly.

"You insufferable cad, you spend time with me, though all very casual, then you leave me to go to her. Who is she? This whore you have as a mistress," she demanded.

"There is no one else, Marian," he told her calmly.

"Oh? You certainly have not wanted me," she railed on. "How long have you been seeing her?"

Andrew sighed loudly in annoyance and set his glass on the table beside the sofa. Looking at Marian as she began to pace, he said in a bored tone, "Very well, Marian. Though it is true that I have not wanted you as I once had, I am not—"

Marian let out a screech of fury at his blatant admission. "Oh you bastard! How could you do this to me?" she screamed.

"Do what to you?" Andrew asked as he stood up. "As I recall, your beloved Hayden was barely cold in the grave before you started with your seductions."

Marian strode angrily up to him and threw back her hand to slap him. Andrew caught her wrist then the other when she threw it back as well. "Be still, Marian."

"Let me go!" she yelled.

Andrew did so with a slight shove as he turned her and maneuvered her to fall onto the sofa. He bent to pick up his glass when she launched herself from the sofa.

"You arrogant bastard!" she hissed and gave him a mighty shove.

He caught his step then had to grab for her hands as her nails reached for his face.

"How could you treat me like this?" she shrieked.

He turned her so that she had her back to him then he pulled her up against his body wrapping his arms over hers. She struggled but he held firm. Hissing in her ear as he finally unleashed his own anger, he asked, "Treat you like what, Marian? Like a mistress?" She screeched again and struggled harder but Andrew only tightened his grip on her. "That had been our relationship, or am I wrong?"

"You bastard," she growled.

"Go visit this friend in York for as long as you wish but do not charge anything to me. Do you understand? I will not pay for them, Marian," he told her.

Tired from her struggles, Marian stopped fighting him and began to cry. "How could you be so heartless, Andrew? I have given you so much."

"I did enjoy our time once, but that has passed," he said softly. "I will be leaving now. Have a nice visit."

Andrew released her and she dropped down on the sofa dissolving into pitiful sobs. He looked down at her dispassionately, having no desire to comfort her.

"Goodnight, Marian," he said. She did not acknowledge him or look up. Without a backward glance, Andrew left the townhouse.

* * *

As the men gathered for a session of the House of Lords, Richard looked around and saw Andrew talking with several men. Joining him, he greeted the men.

"Good afternoon, gentlemen." They greeted him back with handshakes. "Walter, I hear you have a new son. Congratulations," Richard proclaimed.

"Thank you. Clara and I wanted a girl this time but a son is always welcome," Lord Walter Reynolds told him. He was a man of their age with brown hair and brown eyes. He was slightly shorter than Richard and Andrew as well as a bit heavier in build.

"Since Henry here has a new son, perhaps you can pass on some words of wisdom," Richard offered with a grin to Lord Batson.

"Patience, Henry, that is all I have to say on that. Learn patience," Walter said with a smile.

Henry chuckled lightly and said clapping the man's back, "I am learning, my friend."

The assembly was called to order and slowly the men dispersed to their seats. As they waited for the other men to resume their places, Richard leaned to Andrew and asked, "You will be at the Lockharts' this evening for Abby's surprise dinner?"

"Of course," Andrew answered looking around.

Richard looked at him and, with a mischievous smile, asked, "So have you heard from Marian since she left last week?" He chuckled as Andrew turned slowly to face him with a look of warning in his green eyes. "I thought as much," Richard said amid his humor.

"You certainly like to live dangerously, Lord Pittman," Andrew teased.

"Do I?" Richard asked with a sudden look of innocence. The look did not last long as he chuckled again.

Andrew smiled at his friend before their attention turned to the session as it began.

That evening as previously planned, Christine had all of the guests arrive an hour before Richard was to appear with Abby. Andrew looked around at the group of guests and noted that most of them were married. Elizabeth had told him earlier that these were the only ones that Christine considered as *'friends allowed in her house.'*

"Goodness, that Christine actually volunteered to have this dinner here is unbelievable," Elizabeth was saying as Christine stepped up to them.

Andrew's gaze seemed to devour the dark haired beauty in a rose-colored gown that made her eyes shine a brilliant blue.

Smiling at Elizabeth, Christine said, "She would not suspect a thing coming here. It is just a quiet dinner with the Lockharts and the Huntingtons." Then turning to glance at the other guests with an innocent look, she added as if muttering under her breath, "Along with about thirty other people."

"Very clever of you, Tee," Peter said coming up behind her. "Women can be so devious, do you not agree, Andrew?"

"Oh I believe I shall pass on answering that question," Andrew replied smiling as he put his hands up in surrender. "I have not had dinner as yet and I am rather hungry this evening."

Christine's soft laughter made Andrew's heart skip a beat. He also felt a quickening in his breathing as he watched her eyes shine with her humor. David stood in the doorway of the small ballroom and announced over the chatter, "They have just arrived."

"This will be fun," Christine said with a laugh then hurried off to greet her dinner guests. Caroline hurried behind her, closing the double doors. Maggie waved to get everyone's attention then put a finger to her lips indicating silence.

"She is having so much fun with this," Elizabeth whispered to Andrew.

"I can see that," Andrew said grinning.

After long moments of silence, voices could be heard before the doors opened and Christine was saying, "…and I cannot even remember when this room was used."

"Surprise!" came a loud chorus of voices as Abby stepped inside with Richard behind her. Startled, she took a step back making everyone laughed.

"Happy birthday, Abby," Christine told her with a delighted laugh.

Behind them, a three-tier cake was wheeled in on a cart. Richard pulled Abby to one side so that the cart could be wheeled into the room for everyone to see. A chorus of 'ahs' came from the collected group of friends.

"Christine Katherine Lockhart!" Abby exclaimed making Christine dissolve into laughter. Then everyone laughed as Abby turned around to face Richard and hit his chest playful, "And you helped her!"

"Guilty as charged, my love," he said as he pulled her to him for a kiss. That brought on another chorus of 'ahs' before everyone laughed again.

Christine clapped her hands together and said loudly, "Now that you are finally here, shall we dine? Someone has already claimed to be starving."

She looked at Andrew who was sipping his drink. Swallowing quickly, he corrected her with a chuckle, "I only said I was hungry!"

Waving away his statement and giving him an impish grin, Christine replied, "Close enough, Your Grace!" Amid the soft laughter, Andrew lifted his glass as if in a toast while grinning at Christine.

With eyes sparkling with the fun, Christine waved towards the dining hall and announced, "Dinner is served, everyone." Then to Abby, she added, "And you cannot have a piece of your cake until you have finished all of your dinner."

Raising a small fist in playful warning in front of Christine's face, Abby told her, "You will find it difficult to eat your dinner with teeth missing, you schemer."

Christine's soft tinkling of laughter reeked havoc on Andrew's emotions.

After dinner, the ballroom was alive with music and dancing. Though the room was smaller in size than other large ballrooms, it was just large enough for the small group to enjoy themselves without feeling crowded.

Andrew claimed several dances with Elizabeth, Caroline, and Abby but his favorite dance partner was Christine. During a rare break that left him without a partner, he leaned against the wall sipping his drink while watching Christine dance with one of the other men.

"How are you, Andrew?" Peter asked. "Tired from all your dancing?"

"Not in the least. I can still match you step for step," the Duke replied with a smile.

Richard stepped up to join them as Abby danced with David Huntington. "Are you ready to admit it now?" he asked as he clapped Andrew on the shoulder.

"Admit to what?" Peter wanted to know.

"He knows what I mean," Richard answered with a nod of his head to Andrew.

"Richard," Andrew began in a warning tone.

"You mean about Christine?" Peter asked looking from one man to the other.

Richard burst into laughter as Andrew turned to Peter with a look of surprise on his face. Peter grinned and gave him a nonchalant shrug as he explained, "It is written all over your face when you dance with her, my friend."

"It is not written all over my face," Andrew argued.

Peter leaned forward and replied with a grin, "Yes, Andrew, it is but if it is to be a secret then I would suggest that you not look at her like you could kiss her at any moment."

Andrew mumbled something under his breath making Peter and Richard grin. Watching the dancers then searching for Christine, the Duke asked quietly, "Is it that noticeable?"

"Yes, and I would consider it a terrible thing," Peter replied.

"It is not a terrible thing," Andrew said firmly. He noticed Peter and Richard grinning at him. With a sigh, he said, "She is the only woman, or shall I clarify that as the only unattached woman I have met who has not tried to lay claim on my title or my money."

Peter snorted in exasperation and said, "And why should she? Christine has her own wealth to deal with. Christopher Lockhart left her with virtually the entire family fortune. I have never known her to yearn for a high title. I think that if she fell in love with a blacksmith, she would be content."

"A blacksmith?" Richard repeated and roared with laughter. Andrew rolled his eyes in annoyance and sipped his drink.

"Well, you know what I mean," Peter said sheepishly.

"Ah, finally," Andrew said in relief as the music died away to another waltz. "This is my dance with her. Kindly refrain from proposing to her until I have had the opportunity to ask her myself."

"Would you really ask her?" Peter questioned with a smile.

"I most certainly would if I thought for a moment that she would accept," Andrew replied with a knowing grin.

"Do not think about it, my friend, just ask," Peter told him.

Andrew waved away Peter's reply as his gaze found the beauty that had crept into his dreams. *Marry her? When had that idea crossed my mind? Perhaps I will ask her,* Andrew thought. *He would be proud to proclaim Christine Lockhart as his Duchess of Kenilworth.* Smiling as he whirled around the dance floor with Christine in his arms, Andrew decided that he would give serious thought to asking Maggie for Christine's hand.

Christine Chandler. Yes, he definitely liked the sound of that.

Chapter 8

Andrew stared up at his father's portrait that hung over the fireplace in his study. His mind had drifted several times to Christine and his feelings for her. He knew that what he felt was more than desire for the beautiful young woman with sapphire eyes. His breathing and his heartbeats seemed to carry on a life of their own when he heard her voice or saw her across the room. He thought of the stolen kiss in Elizabeth's garden and craved for more.

Thinking that Peter and Richard were correct in his behavior of late, Andrew seriously considered the possibility of marrying Christine Lockhart. Over the past week since Abby's surprise party, Andrew had tried several times to talk with Maggie. Yet each time he went to the Lockhart house, he would see their coach out front then see Maggie and Christine leaving for the day.

The chimes of the grandfather clock stirred him from his thoughts. It was time to go to Peter's for an afternoon tea. Peter had talked him into joining them by the mere mentioning of Christine's presence there. Perhaps he could pull Maggie aside and talk with her briefly before approaching Christine. The gardens would be a nice place to ask Christine to marry him for it was where his feelings for her had surfaced.

* * *

Elizabeth ensured that her guests were offered a cup of tea and a choice of the various pastries attractively arranged on the silver serving trays. Peter refreshed his drink and looked around to see if any of the men needed a refill before joining Andrew and Richard by the fireplace.

"Richard, has Abby left for her visit with her grandmother?" Elizabeth asked.

"Yes, she left last week after her birthday surprise at Christine's. Whenever she returns, I will see little of her as she then sits for her wedding portrait. Her gown should be ready then and she cannot wait to sit for the portrait," Richard replied with a smile.

"Abby could sit for hours. I know the artist would find her an absolute pleasure," Caroline said adding a deep tone to mimic a man's voice. Her comment was met with soft laughter.

"Why are you so quiet this afternoon, Christine? Is something the matter? You have not smiled even once since arriving," Elizabeth pointed out.

Christine did not answer immediately so Maggie offered an explanation. "I imagine it has something to do with the visit from the Duke of Whiteford earlier this afternoon."

"Mother, I would rather not discuss it," Christine began in a low voice.

"You have not explained to me why you were so angry and threw him out of the house," Maggie went on to say.

"You threw Whitey out?" Peter asked in a tone of disbelief. "The man is usually insufferable with his candor and you have such a calm way about you when everyone else is ready to call the man out. What on earth happened?"

"Peter, I do not wish to discuss it," Christine stated firmly. With an irritated sigh, she stood up from the plush sofa to stand by the window. She had her back to the occupants in the room as she peered out the window to gaze at the gardens but her mind was back to the conversation earlier that day.

"Aunt Maggie, surely you jest. Christine?" Caroline began.

"Your cousin actually raised her voice in anger, Caroline. I could hear the shouting as I came from the back of the house."

"Mother, please," Christine implored from the window. She now faced them with a look of displeasure that was rarely seen.

"What happened, Christine?" Caroline asked quietly.

Blue eyes moved about the room to look into each person before Christine rolled her own heavenward in exasperation. With a loud unladylike sigh that made Maggie cringe, the young Lady Lockhart said with a measure of ill-suppressed disgust, "Since you must know," she began then paused for a moment to control the anger that threatened to surface. "The Duke of Whiteford asked me to marry him."

"Are you serious?" Peter exclaimed in total disbelief. Andrew and Richard shared a sideways look.

"Yes Peter, I am very serious and, according to His Grace, he is my last hope of ever marrying anyone of importance." Her statement was met with shocked gasps from the women and muttered curses from the men.

"Oh wait, there is more to the drama. According to Whiteford, I am—" Christine stopped in mid-sentence as her anger nearly choked the breath from her. She looked to the high vaulted ceiling and took a deep breath to steady her renewed anger before continuing in slow measured words, "I am after all the daughter of a sea captain. To expect a better station in life, I should not seek beyond his offer for there would be no better offer than himself."

"You have had many offers of marriage in the last few months," Maggie put in. "I was put out that those gentlemen would offer a proposal while you were in still in mourning."

"Apparently, something else has been their motivation," Christine said acidly. "It would seem that an offer of five hundred pounds is more advantageous to the other men than spending a lifetime with me."

Abruptly, Peter downed his drink then whirled from the fireplace swearing under his breath. Looking at Andrew and Richard, Christine thought that they suddenly looked uncomfortable.

Her gaze shifted back to Peter as she asked in a calmer tone, "What did Whiteford mean by that comment about the five hundred pounds, Peter?"

The man's shoulders slumped at the question and he wondered how he could effectively evade the issue. Turning to face her, Peter knew that whatever lie he would use to try and convince her, Christine Lockhart would soon find out the truth. It would be better she found out from a friend who would soften the blow than someone like Whiteford who did not care how much he hurt her feelings.

"Peter, do you know what this is about?" Elizabeth asked.

"Yes, my dear, I am afraid I do. Christine, perhaps you should sit down as I—"

"What is it, Peter?" Christine broke in and stood her ground.

He cleared his throat. "It seems there is a wager circulating the club concerning you."

"I have heard nothing of any wager," David blurted out.

"You are family. No one speaks of it in your presence," Peter explained.

"You are the husband of her friend," David countered.

Peter smiled and nodded, "True, but a gentleman would not speak of this to his wife."

"Speak of what?" Christine asked impatiently.

"The wager is," Peter began uncomfortably, "five hundred pounds to any man who could show that he had bedded you."

There were mutterings of disbelief around the room as Christine stared at Peter who met her gaze. He felt terrible at being the bearer of bad news and in such company. The feeling only intensified when she dropped her gaze from his, her brow knitting into a frown. He looked at Andrew and Richard for some support. Richard was watching him while Andrew held a steady gaze on Christine. Turning his attention back to Christine, Peter saw her biting her bottom lip and knew he had to tell the rest.

"There is more," he began.

"More!" David exclaimed.

"My God, Peter. Is this true?" Elizabeth asked, her voice sounded as though she would burst into tears at any moment.

"What else?" Christine asked quietly.

"One thousand pounds, if a—" Peter began.

"One thousand!" Several voices exclaimed, though not Christine who listened to the rest of what Peter was saying without pause.

"…man could show proof of your," he swallowed hard and said in softer tone, "your lost maidenhood."

Christine's eyes shot up from the floor to look at him incredulously. Her stricken expression hurt Andrew to the core and the urge to gather her in his arms for comfort was strong.

In the shocked silence of the room, Christine announced quietly as she turned her back to her mother and friends. "Well that settles the matter." She shook her head as she stared out the window. "I will never marry now."

Facing away from them, she missed the looks Peter and Richard gave Andrew as the Duke continued to watch her.

"Oh my God! Christine, you promi—" Maggie began.

Whirling around angrily, Christine glared at her mother through tear-filled eyes. "No, I cannot marry. I will not be made a laughing stock for the amusement of the Ton!" Biting her bottom lip and inhaling deeply, Christine refused to allow the tears to fall. "Do you not see the game they are playing? I cannot be sure anymore."

"If a man proposed and you accepted, he would—" Caroline began but Christine interrupted her.

"Show me up as a bride without her groom and in the company of everyone. All of London would be in attendance to watch Christine Lockhart make a fool of herself. The bride waiting at the altar but no groom will be there," Christine said scornfully.

"You cannot know that! How can that be?" Maggie asked in growing hysteria.

"Whiteford told me that everyone would come out for my wedding," Christine said in a harsh tone.

"Whiteford!" David spat in disgust. "I shall call the man out and—"

"You cannot call him out, David," Christine said with a sardonic laugh.

"I most certainly can. As the only male relative—" David began to argue.

"No, you cannot!" Christine stated emphatically. "You are Caroline's husband."

"Caroline is your cousin, that makes me the only man—" David continued to argue.

Christine shook her head and said firmly, "There are only three men who can approach Whiteford for this. My father, my brother and my husband. Unfortunately at the moment, I am without all three."

"This is absolutely outrageous," David hissed angrily and stood up to pace behind Caroline who still sat on the sofa, hugging her quietly sobbing aunt in comfort.

"I cannot believe any proposals now," Christine said calmly though she did not feel it. "I cannot believe any man who would profess his love for me, not after this. '*I love you*' are only words. They no longer have meaning."

"It seems that since Christopher passed away, those sharp tongues have only grown sharper," Peter hissed.

"It is only that they no longer have to whisper among themselves. They can say what they like to my face. I am nothing to them and never will be," Christine said.

"Sometimes I just want to remind them that they are no better, especially when I know just how unfaithful and imperfect these wretches are," Elizabeth grumbled.

Walking slowly to her mother, Christine glanced at Elizabeth and said, "I think we should be leaving now. I apologize for the unpleasant turn of the afternoon, Elizabeth."

"You do not owe me an apology, Christine Lockhart. You are as you have always been—the innocent pawn of someone else's cruel games," Elizabeth said soothingly.

Christine smiled sadly at Elizabeth then hugged her friend. "I am sorry, Elizabeth. I had hoped to be pulled from his hateful words to a more pleasant state of mind."

Elizabeth nodded and said, "Quite understandable. It is far too upsetting and yet it did not happen to me. Do not let such loathsome people like Whiteford make you bitter."

Christine merely smiled as she wondered if it was already too late. Bidding farewell to Peter, Richard, and Andrew, Christine gathered her mother and left the house with Caroline and David following behind them.

It had been nearly three weeks since the day Christine had found out about the wager from Peter. Sitting at his desk in his study staring out the window, Andrew was supposed to be going over some papers on his desk in preparation for the day's session at the House of Lords, but his mind had drifted away yet again. According to Peter and Elizabeth, Christine had been so upset that she decided to go to her country home called the Meadows and escape the hostility of London for a while. Since Chelsea had joined Christine and Maggie, it was thought that they would be away for only a week. Then Peter told him of a message received from Christine requesting that Chelsea stay longer. Andrew wanted to talk to Maggie, needed to talk to Maggie, and perhaps between the two of them, Christine could be approached.

The longer Christine stayed away, the more Andrew missed her. Although she had sounded quite firm in her announcement to never marry, he was just as determined to change her mind. '*There are only three men who can approach Whiteford for this. My father, my brother and my husband. Unfortunately at the moment, I am without all three,*' she had said.

Andrew whispered her name and closed his eyes. Sapphire blue eyes and midnight black hair materialized in his mind. He could almost feel her lips again as he remembered the kiss in Elizabeth's garden. With a sudden realization, Andrew knew without a doubt that he had fallen in love with her. He simply wanted to help her, wanted to protect her. He wanted her and somehow she was going to be his wife. All he had to do was change her mind. Releasing a long sigh as he rubbed his temple, Andrew had no idea how he was going to manage that gigantic feat.

Chapter 9

The April rains brought out the early blooms, letting everyone know that warmer weather was on the way. Each year on the first Friday evening of April, Lady Jacqueline Trenholm prided herself in giving the first ball of the spring. Her gardens were her pride and joy for which she received many compliments. She smiled at the success of her party and the number of guests who accepted her invitation. The music seemed to beckon many couples onto the dance floor. The guests in the ballroom fairly overflowed into the gardens with the number of people enjoying themselves as they talked in small groups or danced to the music.

Her self-satisfied smile faltered slightly as she caught sight of Christine Lockhart dancing with one of the most eligible bachelors at her ball. The Duke of Kenilworth was dressed impeccably in his sapphire blue waistcoat and vest. His presence made many young maidens fairly swoon if he so much as looked in their direction. Yet, he seemed only interested in dancing with Christine Lockhart.

"And how many times does this make now for her to claim the Duke to a dance?" asked Lady Harriet Johnstone.

Lady Trenholm turned with a gasp to face her friend. "So you have noticed that as well? He could be dancing with the other girls but he spends so much time with that one!"

"Oh, that one has no sense of propriety," Lady Johnstone replied firmly. "Why, I heard that she refused the Duke of Whiteford's proposal of marriage. My goodness, she is past the marriageable age and cannot simply choose her husband. Indeed, why any of our well-established families would even cater to her, I ask you?"

Looking around to be sure that no one stood close to be overheard, Lady Johnstone whispered to Lady Trenholm, "And darling, I heard that the Duke cast off Lady Sanders for a new mistress."

"Yes, I have heard that, also," Lady Trenholm replied. "Have you heard whose name is circulating as among his new paramours?"

Both women were nearing three score years, married, and had grown children already married. They whispered with heads together while glaring at Christine's back as she whirled around the dance floor with Andrew. He made some comment that brought out a small smile and he laughed in delight. A sound of disgust emitted from both of the matrons as they watched the couple.

Andrew had been pleasantly surprised to see Christine come in with her mother earlier in the evening. He had not known that she had returned to London and claimed as many dances with her as he could manage to talk her into. He even had some assistance from Maggie who smiled at him conspiratorially as he escorted Christine out onto the dance floor. Yet even as he danced with someone else, he tried to keep Christine within his sights.

The music died away to another waltz but Christine pulled away from him. "Thank you, Andrew. It is rather warm in here and I believe I would like to go outside for a stroll through the gardens."

"Then I will join you. It is beautiful night—"

"No, you will not join me," Christine broke in with a laugh. "You are here as the sacrificial lamb being the most popular bachelor tonight among the throngs of débutantes. I am surprised you are alone."

Andrew pursed his lips at the reminder of his affair with Marian and he certainly did not like it that the reminder came from Christine. He had already decided that whenever she returned from 'visiting friends,' he was going to make the final break in the relationship. His choice was here beside him.

"I most certainly will join you," he said smiling and ignoring her protests. "You think that you are the only one who is warm. The cool night air will be refreshing."

"You should be circulating with—"

"I am not interested in their giggles and silly games of shy smiles and fluttering eyes," he said making Christine laugh lightly again. "I will get us a couple of drinks and we will sit outside on a bench until we catch our breath."

Before she could make any comment against the idea, Andrew had turned and was heading for the refreshment table.

With a sigh, Christine shook her head and started for the open doors to the gardens. Stepping into her path were two young women she recognized from her days at school and whom she disliked. They had married almost immediately after they graduated and now stood before at Christine glaring at her.

"You have no business keeping the Duke for yourself. My sister is eligible for marriage and would like a turn on the dance floor with him," said one girl with the usual coifed blonde hair that was the fashion.

Christine shrugged and said flippantly, "So drag him out there for her. I am not stopping you in your matchmaking schemes."

She made to pass them but the other girl with the same coifed blonde hair grabbed Christine's arm, roughly turning her to face them.

Several people around them noticed the confrontation and stopped to watch. Christine hated to attend these balls for just this reason. If she so much as looked at an eligible bachelor, an older sister would come to the defense of the younger.

"Schemes? You pretentious title seeker," she hissed.

"Title seeker? I am not the one who is trying to marry a sister off to some unsuspecting man for his fortune."

The two girls stood in outraged silence at the remark. Before either one could say another word, Christine added through tightly held anger, "Only you and those like you are foolhardy enough to believe that such marriages are destined. It may bring a nice title and fortune but what of a faithful husband? How many mistresses are your husbands supporting now?"

"How dare you speak to us like this?" one girl exclaimed.

The shrill tone of her outburst carried over the music and caught the attention of many people in the room, including Andrew.

"I dare because I will not stand by and be spoken to in this manner. If you desire to be center of attention, then I believe that you have accomplished your goal. When you wish to discuss this in a more civilized tone, as a well-bred titled lady should, then I will be receptive to that discussion. Now if you will excuse me," Christine told them in a deceptively calm tone.

Rendered speechless by the admonishment, the two women stared at her with mouths agape. Christine decided that this was the perfect opportunity to leave. She walked so briskly between them that the two women had to part or be trampled. Almost immediately, the room buzzed with hushed whispers.

Once outside, Christine did not stop or even slow down until she was at the farthest corner of the gardens. She flounced down on the bench, only to stand again and begin to pace. She released a loud exhale and growled low to let out some of her anger, trying to calm herself.

"Now what?" she hissed when she heard footsteps and turned to face her next attacker.

"Calm down, Christine. I brought you a drink," Andrew said gently as he stepped up to her.

"You need to be inside and away from me," Christine gritted out impatiently. She began pacing again in her irritation that Andrew stepped into her path.

"Stop that," he told her firmly.

She stared at him for a moment before continuing her pacing by stepping around him. Andrew sighed and shook his head as he put the glasses down on the bench.

"You do not understand, Andrew," Christine was saying angrily. "It is the same thing every time. I do not belong. I will *never* belong. I cannot look at, speak to, or be friends with any eligible man that has a good name and high title."

Stopping to whirl around and face him, she growled, "And most definitely not be friends with you. I am tired of it, tired of the whole damn thing. I hate the false faces and the rules and the arrogance of those who are supposed to be better than I am."

"You are better than any of them and they do not dictate who my friends will be," he said softly, trying to soothe.

"Of course not, Andrew. They would not say anything like that to your face nor would any other lady confront another as those two have a few moments ago. Yet because I am only Christine Lockhart and not truly *Lady* Christine Lockhart, it seems to be justification enough to be rude and obnoxious. In other words, all is well, because it is only me and they need not concern themselves with any feelings I may have," she mimicked in a haughty manner.

Andrew took her by the shoulders and held her firmly to stop her pacing. "You do not usually listen to them anyway," he said softly.

She let out an exasperated sigh. "After a time, Andrew, even I get annoyed with the continuous disapproval. I do not care so much for myself, but I care for my mother. She does not deserve to watch this treatment of her only daughter all the time."

Andrew stared down at her wanting to pull her to him and hold her close. He wanted to tell her that she acted more like a lady than any of those inside with their petty grievances and self-righteous attitudes. Smiling gently at her, he whispered her name softly then slowly lowered his head to hers. His lips touched hers and he felt her response. Just as he applied more pressure to the kiss, they heard Maggie's call from somewhere in the gardens.

Andrew was reluctant to release her making Christine pull away. She took a slow deep breath before calling out, "I am here, Mother."

Somewhat surprised to see the Duke when she neared them, Maggie acknowledged, "Hello, Andrew."

"I was trying to offer her some support," he told her.

"You are too kind," Maggie replied.

"I believe I would like to go home now, Mother," Christine informed her quietly.

Her tone made both Maggie and Andrew look at her with concern. Not raising her eyes to meet his, Christine said quietly, "Goodnight, Andrew."

She walked away as Maggie glanced at Andrew then hurried after her daughter. Andrew sighed and shook his head then noticed the drinks he brought out for them. Picking up one, he drained it quickly. Lifting the other glass, he sat down on the bench and wondered how this society he lived in could be so cruel and so blind to someone who could be so generous.

Draining the drink in his hand, his musings was interrupted by talking on the other side of the wall. "Tis an arrangement and only that. Do not think of it as murder," one man was saying. Andrew raised a brow at the word 'murder' and listened further.

"But yer talkin' 'bout killin' a titled leidy," came a second man's voice.

"Titled or not, 'is lordship paid us 'alf of the money and I expect to collect on the rest," the man told the other firmly. "Yer not leavin' all the work fer me to do, do ye understand?"

"Yeah, I 'ear ye just fine. Tis just that she is a pretty one and tis a shame to do 'er in."

"Stop yer blusterin', we only 'ave 'til the end of the week to make sure that Christine Lockhart meets with 'er accident. Pretty or not, she is a dead lady," the first man said.

Their voices were fading as they walked away from Andrew but the moment he heard Christine's name, he stood up and hurried to follow them with the wall between them. The words grew fainter and Andrew realized that the two men were walking away from the house.

He stopped and stared at the wall in disbelief as his mind replayed the conversation in his head. *Paid to kill Christine by a titled lord? To happen before the end of the week? Why and who would do such a thing?*

Suddenly Andrew remembered that she was leaving. Turning back to the house and moving through the clusters of people in the ballroom, he politely declined those who tried to engage him into conversation. At the door, he made inquiries and found out that the Lockharts had already left. Going back to the ballroom and standing at the entrance, Andrew looked at the faces of the men talking, dancing, or standing in small clusters. He wondered if one of these lords paid those men. Studying the faces of each titled lord, he realized that he had little time to come up with a way to save her. Yet one thing he knew was certain, Christine Lockhart would not be dead by the end of the week. He would devise some plan to save her.

* * *

"Christine, have you seen my—" Maggie began then smiled as her daughter held up a pair of white gloves.

It was Sunday morning and dressed for church, Christine waited in the foyer as Maggie slipped on her gloves. As they stood there in quiet conversation, Taylor opened the front door to admit Caroline and David into the house.

Glancing at the clock then grinning at her cousin, Christine said in condescending tone, "Well, you both were almost late."

As if on queue the clock chimed the half-hour and Caroline laughed lightly, "Almost, cousin dear."

"Where is Stephen?" Maggie asked.

"He had not slept well last night and was still sleeping when we left. We decided to let him stay with Mrs. Clarke."

"What was wrong with him?" Maggie asked in concern.

"Nothing except that he ate too many treats yesterday," David informed her while giving Christine a stern look.

"Oh, was that all?" Christine said teasingly.

"Because you tempted him, cousin. Wait until you have your own children," Caroline said laughing but Christine only waved away the words with a laugh.

Taylor reached out and opened the door for the small group preparing to leave. Everyone froze as they faced Jack Hanson whose fist was raised ready to knock.

The first to recover from the initial startled expression, Jack smiled and greeted them. "Good morning, sister and nieces. My, my, you are all certainly very beautiful in your Sunday best."

"Good morning, Jack. We are just leaving so whatever you need, it will have to wait for another time," Maggie said firmly.

"No, I think I will see what this is about, Mother. Go with Caroline and David. I will try not to be late," Christine suggested to her mother.

"Christine, it is Sunday. Jack should go with us, then we will see what this is about," Maggie countered glaring at her brother.

Looking to Caroline and David, Christine managed to convey silently that they should leave without her.

"Come, Aunt Maggie. Christine will be right behind us," Caroline coaxed as she took her aunt's arm and headed out the door.

Taking a step toward her brother, Maggie said, "Whatever trouble you managed to get yourself into should not be a constant concern for Christine to clear up. You know very well what day this is and that we were leaving for church. This could have waited, Jack, I have no doubt of that."

"Maggie, love, I would not burden Christine with anything I could handle myself," Jack said with a smile.

His sister huffed and turned away followed by Caroline and David.

"Goodbye, Jack," David bade knowing that the man did not acknowledge his presence earlier.

Jack watched them get into the coach then leave. Christine had not moved since her uncle's appearance at the door. Now she gained his attention by clearing her throat. "Let us be done with this. Come with me to the study."

"Your welcome could freeze even the coldest of—" Jack grumbled.

"You are catching me on one of my more pleasant days, Uncle," Christine interrupted sweetly and received a glare from him.

At the church, Andrew and Richard stood outside and away from the people as they talked. They had been trying to talk but were interrupted many times to return greetings. Finally moving away, they were able to speak with little interruption.

"No, I have not talked with her but I have made up my mind, Richard. I am certain that once I explain everything to her, she will agree with me," Andrew was saying.

Richard nodded and looked around thoughtfully before he said, "What if she declines, Andrew? Personally, I think your idea has merit. It is well thought out and has the outcome that both of you will find mutually beneficial."

"Mutually beneficial?" Andrew asked.

"You know what I mean," Richard said. "She will have a safe haven—"

Richard halted when he noticed Andrew's attention was drawn away. Looking over his shoulder, he saw the reason for it. The Lockhart coach had just pulled up in front of the church and the two men watched as David stepped out then reached inside to assist Caroline out. A moment later, he was assisting Maggie. The door closed and the trio headed into the church.

Andrew and Richard exchanged a concerned look. "I believe I will forego services today, Richard. I am going to see why Christine did not accompany her family and, if possible, speak with her."

It was not long before Andrew was shown into the drawing room of the Lockhart townhouse and was told that Lady Lockhart would be informed of his presence. Making himself comfortable on the cushioned sofa, he noticed the portrait over the mantelpiece. It was a recent painting of Christine sitting on a marble bench in the midst of rosebushes with blooms in various stages of budding and opening. She was dressed in a cream colored gown and her dark hair hung in soft waves that gently framed her face. Draped over her lap was a bouquet of red roses and her hands were clasped to one side of the bouquet.

As he stared up at the painted face, Andrew thought that the artist captured the mystery that surrounded Christine. Her sapphire blue eyes twinkled, her soft mouth curved at the corners and even the slight tilt of her head hinted at some inner secret that she found humorous.

Loud voices broke into his reverie making Andrew blink as he returned to his surroundings. He realized that the conversation came from the foyer and noticed that the butler had not closed the double doors.

"Damn you, girl! You could be more generous to me. I am your uncle!" Jack bellowed in anger.

"I know you are my uncle but I will not continue to pay fo—" came the calm feminine reply.

Andrew looked around and saw that the French doors to the gardens were opened as well which was where Christine's voice seemed to come from.

"You would dare cut me off? You would rather embarrass your mother?" Jack interrupted.

"These are *your* debts, Uncle, not mine," Christine said more firmly. "If you cared for my mother, *your* sister, as you seem t—"

"Do not speak to me in that tone, girl! I am the Viscount of—"

"You are a drunkard and a gambler, Uncle. You have already wasted your inheritance and I will not have you squander my mother's as well," Christine interrupted, her tone edged with her growing anger.

"You insolent little chit," Jack blustered.

"Call me whatever you like if it makes you feel superior, Uncle Jack, I do not give a bloody damn! Just remember whom it is you seek when you are in dire straits," she hissed through clenched teeth. "Here is your money and I will handle these debts but the damages to your carriage because of your recklessness is your problem to deal with."

"Damn you," he exclaimed. There was the sound of what Andrew thought may have been a fist hitting a table then objects toppling over. "This is not enough," Jack was saying. "How can I show my face at the club to play a decent hand of cards with this paltry sum!"

"You ungrateful bastard!" Christine shouted, her anger full blown. "All you have is your title and that house on the Square. You have no money, Uncle. Think of how you could show your face if that little secret were known. I am the only reason you live so highly."

Andrew raised a brow in interest at that revelation as well as Christine losing her temper.

"Now take this *paltry* sum and get out," Christine said firmly. "I have had my fill of you and your so-called injustice for the day."

A door snapped open and Jack's voice could be heard in the foyer. "Take care, niece, of how you speak to me," he said angrily before stomping away.

Andrew turned slightly to see Jack Hanson walk briskly past the drawing room and then slam out of the house. Turning his attention back to the portrait, he seemed disinterested with his surroundings when the butler returned a few moments later.

"Her Ladyship will see you now, Your Grace," he announced.

Andrew followed the man to the next room. When the door opened, he saw Christine standing stiffly at the French doors, gazing out at the gardens. She turned and smiled though Andrew could still see that the anger had not quite ebbed away.

"Good morning, Andrew. I apologize for your wait," she greeted pleasantly.

"No apologies necessary, I did come unannounced. I should be the one apologizing," he replied. Her smile widened and this time it held more warmth.

"Please sit here," she indicated two winged backed chairs facing the large ornate desk. Taking one of the chairs, she asked, "Care for anything or is it too early?"

"No thank you, I am fine," he answered sitting in the other chair.

Christine looked up at the butler, "Thank you, Taylor."

"Yes, my lady," the butler said and left quietly closing the door.

Andrew glanced over his shoulder to ensure that they were alone before he began. "I truly apologize for this early call. After noting that you had not accompanied your mother and cousins to church, I thought I would take the opportunity to discuss an important matter in private with you."

Christine raised a brow and cocked her head to one side. "Important? Is something wrong?"

Looking at the desk, Andrew answered, "Yes Christine, something is wrong but," he looked up and met her gaze, "I believe it could be prevented."

She smiled somewhat uncertain as her eyes roamed over his face. Andrew had to squelch the urge to stand up, take her into his arms and hold her close. With a sigh to calm his inner desires and fears, he explained, "I came to warn you, Christine, that you are in danger. The other night at the Trenholms, I overheard two men discussing their plans to harm you."

"Harm me?" she repeated.

Andrew nodded and clarified, "Kill you, Christine."

In the following silence, he repeated what he had overheard. He paused as she went pale and her expression was a mixture of surprise, fear, and disbelief.

"Are you sure they meant me?" she asked.

"I am very sure of what I heard."

With an almost apologetic wave of her hand, she slowly stood up. "I did not mean to doubt your hearing." Speaking over her shoulder as she walked to the French doors, she went on to say, "What reason would someone have to see me dead? I know that I am not well liked, but murder?"

"If they talked of their reasoning, then it was before I overheard them or when I could no longer hear them," Andrew replied. "May I ask if there is a significance to the end of next week?"

Christine turned to face him and Andrew's breath caught in his throat. With the sunlight framing her from behind, she was beautiful.

"My birthday is in five days. I will be ten and eight," she told him.

"Is there some stipulation in your inheritance that makes a difference because of your birthday?" he asked.

Christine stared at him again for a long moment leaving Andrew to believe that there was something her birthday would change.

"No, my birthday has no consequences that warrant such actions, Andrew. You mentioned his lordship. Who would that be?"

"Well not wanting to confess this but I did overhear you and your uncle. He is a titled lord."

Christine grunted and muttered, "He is titled in name only."

"True but no one knows of that fact outside of your family. At least, until just a few moments ago."

"Actually no one knows but Uncle Jack, myself, and now you," Christine corrected. "I do not have the heart to tell my mother."

"You do not think that your uncle would consider killing you?"

"Andrew, it would be foolish for him to do so. I am his personal banker. He would be penniless if not for me. If anything happens to me, my money is then passed on to my mother. I doubt she would be as giving as I have been over his debts," Christine explained.

It was quiet for a few moments as Andrew sat back and watched Christine who turned to face the gardens, contemplating this recent news.

"Then perhaps it is someone who hopes to gain the Lockhart fortune," he began. In a quiet tone, he added. "Through your mother."

Christine shook her head as she turned back to him and said, "My mother is not seeing anyone. She is just recently widowed and cared deeply for my stepfather."

"Not seeing anyone *now*," Andrew emphasized.

"What are you saying?" she asked him.

Andrew shrugged and spoke softly, "Let us say that this lord was successful and you met with an unfortunate accident. As you have said, your mother is just recently widowed. Having lost her husband and now her daughter in fairly quick succession, she would be quite vulnerable."

Christine's face drained of color at the thought and, thinking that she would faint, Andrew stood up quickly to help her sit down in the chair.

"My God, Andrew! That someone would be so calculating, so patient," she whispered.

"I am sorry to upset you, Christine," Andrew said pouring a glass of water.

"No, reality is a shocking experience to say the least," she replied. "If this man could be so cold and heartless to plan my murder then what of my mother when he has his hands on the Lockhart fortune? What would he do to her?" Christine was saying when he returned with the glass. She smiled weakly in thanks at his thoughtfulness.

Andrew sat back down in the chair beside her and waited as she sipped at the water. He noticed that the only outward sign now of her distress was her shaking hand. In a carefully worded and gentle tone, he told her, "I may have a solution to this dilemma. I have thought of this all yesterday trying to devise various options for you but I seem to return to one."

"What is your solution?" she asked, her brow furrowing into a frown.

Andrew watched her for a moment then mentally held his breath, "Marry me."

Christine's mouth dropped open in astonishment as she stared at him in wide-eyed amazement. "How does that solve my problem?"

"I know of this plan so if somehow this lord managed to succeed, then I would be able to insist on an investigation and keep it open. I have enough influence at Court and as your husband, I could seek out the King's aid in the investigation. Otherwise, your murder would be deemed an accident because that would be what it would look like. More importantly, and this is why I keep coming back to this solution, you would be the Duchess of Kenilworth. I believe that my name and title could keep you safe. No one would dare harm you as my duchess," Andrew explained without a trace of arrogance.

Neither one spoke nor moved for a long moment. It was Christine who turned away first. She stood up and walked to the fireplace as she mulled over the proposal. She would have said yes to his offer but it was not out of love or companionship for one another. It was only his sense of chivalry for a woman who was on friendly terms with him that made him make the offer. *Nothing more*, her mind told her sadly.

"I appreciate your offer, Andrew," she began as she turned to face him. "However, I cannot accept."

Andrew felt as if he had been dealt a blow to the midsection. "Why not? I want to help you," he heard himself saying in a calmer tone than he felt.

"As I said, I appreciate it but I cannot ruin your life in order to spare mine."

"Ruin my life?" he repeated.

Christine smiled sweetly and took the few steps towards him until she stood just inches away. Taking his hand into hers, she said, "Andrew, a day will come when you will meet a woman that you truly want as your duchess. I cannot be selfish and ruin your chance for true happiness because," she touched his lips with her fingers as he made to speak. "Because of your generosity. I would ultimately be in the way."

"Christine, I—" he began to protest.

"I cannot do this to you. As your friend—"

"Yes, and as your friend, I want to help." She smiled at his insistence and shook her head. Andrew sighed in resignation and said, "Then please consider what I have said. Someone is out there planning your demise and has paid two unsavory men to do the deed. As your friend, I do not want to see you harmed so please think through my offer thoroughly. I will not withdraw it,

Christine."

"I will not make your life miserable because we are married. You will want someone else, have children with her, enjoy growing old with her."

"We can worry over that if the situation comes to pass," Andrew tried again.

Christine laughed softly and said, "No, you are the Duke of Kenilworth. You have a responsibility, Andrew, an obligation to your heritage and it demands heirs."

"It is my title that can save you."

"Please underst—"

This time he touched his fingers to her lips and whispered, "Very well, Christine. Let us just say that you will consider the offer further."

They stared at each other before Christine nodded. He smiled and said softly, "You are a good-hearted woman, Lady Lockhart. There are many women who would do anything to be duchess."

"The title is not important to me, you know that," she said quietly.

"I know and I also know that I would be proud to have you as the new Duchess of Kenilworth. Should you change your mind, please let me know."

Andrew kissed her hand and told her that he would see himself out, leaving Christine speechless.

Chapter 10

When Andrew returned to his townhouse, he went directly to his study and poured himself a brandy. Swallowing a good portion then refilling his snifter, he sat at his desk and stared out the window. He had considered that she would reject his offer but he was sure that he could have gotten her to change her mind. She was not safe and he had to somehow think of a way to get her to marry him. He could hear her voice in his mind. '...*a day will come when you will meet a woman...*' she had said. '...*have children with her, enjoy growing old with her.*'

"You are that woman, Christine," he said aloud in the empty study. "Somehow I will make you see that."

When Andrew had left, Christine slowly headed upstairs to her room, forgetting all about her promise to join her mother and cousins at church. Opening the doors to her balcony, she leaned against the railing with her back to the gardens below and stared down at her feet. She could not believe that Andrew had asked her to marry him. Had it been an actual proposal, she may have accepted. She had been infatuated with him since meeting him at the House of Lords when she was ten and two. Since then, his smile and emerald green eyes had been her sanctuary whenever she needed something to think of that was pleasing. Yet even as her young girl infatuation turned to true friendship then to loving him, she could not accept his proposal. She knew that later he would have resented the fact that he already had a duchess when he found someone else he truly cared for and wanted.

Christine's brows furrowed in thought. When had she changed from friendship to love? She was certain that it was before the kiss in Elizabeth's garden because she had not wanted to stop. She wanted to put her arms around him and hold him as a woman would hold her lover close to her.

With a sad sigh, she headed back into her room and dropped face down across her bed. *Christine Chandler, the Duchess of Kenilworth.* The name played over and over in her mind. Staring down at the floor, she smiled at the thought of being Andrew's wife and bearing his children.

"Wishful thinking, Christine Lockhart," she said aloud. "It would be nice but you will not do it."

She growled in frustration and rolled onto her back to stare up at the ceiling. "Oh be quiet. He has a mistress, remember?" she mumbled aloud.

Lying on the bed, Christine let her mind drift back to his visit. He was so sincere in his reasoning and marriage offer. Could she share him with a mistress? Would she wonder if he had been with Lady Sanders whenever he was not at home? Could she live with that?

Christine sat up and shook her head as she looked around the room. The knowledge of Andrew spending time with his mistress would ultimately be her end. Christine knew that most men had their mistresses and, though they were at most times very discreet, she could never be the docile wife who would turn her head away as if nothing happened. She could not live with that knowledge and, because she did love him, she knew that she could not share him.

Making her mind turn to Andrew's reason for the proposal, Christine wondered again who this man was and why. If someone was going to try and kill her by the end of the week, then she at least had the advantage now because Andrew had overheard the plan and warned her. If she just paid more attention to her surroundings, then the chances of being in an accident would be considerably less.

Her gaze fell on the small music box sitting on her bedside table. The dancing couple stood posed together waiting for the music to begin. She reached out for it and turned the key. The soft tinkling music played and the dancing couple began to move in circles around the top.

"Andrew would keep our secret, I have no doubt of that," Christine muttered aloud to the dancing the couple. "I could trust him with that more than I have ever felt trusting it to someone."

Sadly, Christine placed the music box back on the table then lay down on her bed while staring at the figures turning to the soft music of a waltz.

Later that afternoon, Andrew and Richard were at Hyde Park walking slowly on the grass along the lane for the carriages and horses. It was a beautiful sunny afternoon and the grassy area was filled with laughter as small children ran and squealed in delightful play. At times, Andrew and Richard would acknowledge a greeting from someone as they continued their walk or move apart when children ran between them.

They had met briefly with Peter and Elizabeth as the children played nearby. After the family packed up and headed for home, Andrew and Richard enjoyed the stroll back to Andrew's coach.

"So how is Abby?" Andrew asked.

"She is well. She hopes to return next week." Casting a sideways glance to his friend, Richard said, "Somehow you have managed to avoid the topic, Andrew. What was the outcome of your talk with Christine this morning?"

Andrew looked around the park as he let out a long sigh of defeat and answered quietly, "She refused."

Richard nodded in understanding. "That was a possibility. Perhaps you should have proposed the more traditional way."

"She would surely have refused then. You heard her that night."

"Well, at least you have the advantage of her knowing that you are her friend," Richard said as he looked at two children playing ahead of them.

"Richard, I made my offer as a friend," Andrew said looking down at the ground.

"Then tell her you love her," Richard countered.

"She would not believe that either. You heard that also," Andrew was saying when their attention was drawn to a plain black coach racing down the lane near them.

Stepping further into the grassy area, Richard shook his head and grumbled, "Now that fool could kill someone at that speed."

"Looks like he has lost control of the horses," Andrew observed as the driver tried to pull back the reins in vain but the eyes of the horses were wide and wild, attesting to Andrew's remark.

Richard and Andrew turned to look ahead of the speeding coach and saw people hurrying to move out of its way. Suddenly Richard exclaimed as Andrew saw them at the same time, "My God, it is Christine and Caroline."

Staring in disbelief, Andrew watched Christine on a sleek black mare with Caroline next to her on a roan mare as the two women just entered the park. Neither one of the women was aware of the danger rushing towards them.

"Do you think it is possible?" Richard asked.

In Andrew's mind, he saw the scene as if in slow motion and knew it would be ruled accidental. Taking off into a run with Richard behind him, Andrew called out Christine's name.

She was talking to Caroline when Christine heard her name and lifted her head to search out the caller. Her gaze fell on the approaching coach coming towards them at breakneck speed. Realizing the danger immediately and knowing that there was little time, Christine looked to Caroline then roughly pulled up the reins of her horse making the black mare crowd Caroline's roan mare. In the next instant, Christine's horse reared up and Caroline gasped then jerked the reins to move to the side and away from the startled black mare.

In horror, Caroline watched a black coach hit Christine's horse while her cousin was still astride it and the horse reared up on its hind legs. The impact threw Christine and her horse backwards while the coach sped off without slowing down. For an instant, Caroline's wide-eyed gaze followed the coach's departure then searched for Christine. Her heart leapt into her throat as she found her cousin laying face down on the ground and not moving. Though people were screaming and yelling, all Caroline could hear were the painful cries of Christine's black mare.

Slipping off the sidesaddle and away from her horse, Caroline hurried as quickly as she could to her cousin. Other people were running as well and Caroline had to push her way through them. Andrew and Richard were just behind her and dropped down on their knees beside the still form. Andrew reached out and carefully turned Christine onto her back.

"I am a doctor, please let me through," another man was saying as he pushed through the crowd then knelt down beside them.

Caroline looked up and cried in relief, "Doctor Brownlee! Please, it is Christine!"

"I know, Caroline, I saw what happened. Now let me see how she is," the doctor replied calmly.

Brownlee quickly examined Christine then sighed audibly in relief. "She is alive." Caroline burst into tears at the news. "Damned fool could have killed her," the doctor muttered.

Andrew and Richard exchanged a look, knowing that this was no accident. The attempt Andrew feared had been made and it had looked very convincing.

Suddenly a shot rang out startling everyone. Heads turned to find a man holding a pistol still pointed at Christine's horse. Looking up and seeing all eyes on him, he shrugged and said softly, "The animal was suffering."

Brownlee turned back to his patient and muttered, "I need to get her home. Someone call over my carriage."

"I have my coach here. I will take Lady Christine and Lady Caroline with me while you go ahead of us," Andrew said. "Lady Margaret needs to be warned of what she will see."

The doctor nodded in agreement then looked on with a watchful eye as the Duke carefully lifted the still unconscious Christine in his arms while Richard guided the sobbing Caroline.

The Lockhart house was a flurry of activity. Andrew carried Christine up the grand staircase then followed Florence, the housekeeper, to Christine's bedchamber. Richard followed with Maggie and Caroline as the two women cried into their lace handkerchiefs.

Doctor Brownlee was already in the room with his bag, pulling out various items in preparation for his examination. Florence stood beside him with her hands in her apron and a look of great concern on her face. She put a comforting arm around Maggie as Andrew gently laid Christine down on the bed.

"Oh Florence, look at her," Maggie sobbed. Once Andrew stepped away, Maggie knelt beside the bed and tenderly stroking the side of Christine's face. "Oh baby," she whimpered over and over.

Florence bent down to try to move her from the doctor's way but Maggie shook her off. Caroline sat on the other side of the bed also weeping while Richard and Andrew stepped back and watched the proceedings.

Brownlee put a hand on Maggie's shoulder comfortingly and said softly, "Now Maggie, Christine has been through scrapes before."

Andrew and Richard exchanged wondering looks at the news.

"She has never been brought home unconscious," Maggie said impatiently.

At that moment, David hurried into the open door of the bedchamber, saying, "News is traveling quickly!" Taking Caroline into his arms, he asked softly, "Are you all right?" Caroline nodded then looked back to her cousin. David followed her gaze and asked, "How is Christine?"

"She took a bad fall but she will be fine," Brownlee informed him.

"I heard that she was dead," David told them.

"No, she is not dead. She just had a bad hit but she will come around soon," Brownlee further explained.

Maggie started crying anew and allowed Florence to pull her away. Brownlee bent down to begin his examination when Christine stirred and made a small sound.

"There now, she is coming around," the doctor announced. "Christine?"

Slowly opening her eyes, Christine saw the doctor then her mother standing just over the doctor's shoulder. With worried eyes, Christine called out for Caroline.

"I am here," Caroline answered through her crying. With slow movements, Christine turned her head to peer at her cousin through half-closed eyes.

"The baby?" Christine asked in a whisper.

"We are both fine. You scared Belle and I was out of the way," Caroline replied.

Maggie moved forward and sat on the bed beside her daughter the moment Brownlee was out of the way. Christine turned her head carefully at the movement and smiled weakly at her mother.

"Oh baby, you gave me a fright," Maggie said, her voice trembling with her emotions.

Closing her eyes, Christine said quietly, "You should have seen it from my side."

Doctor Brownlee chuckled and glanced sideways at Andrew and Richard saying, "At least she still has her wits about her. Now I know she will be just fine."

Her mother began crying again as Brownlee stepped up and coaxed gently, "Come now, Maggie, let me examine her. I told you she will be fine."

Maggie ignored him as she whispered, "I have never been so frightened."

"I am fine, Mother," Christine said quietly.

"This is the worst of them all, Christine," her mother said. Christine sighed and tried to smile. Maggie bent down and gently kissed her daughter's cheek then brushed away Christine's dark hair from her temples as she said through her sobs, "Caroline has David now but you are all I have. Oh baby, what would I do without you?"

Maggie smiled down at her as Christine opened her eyes. Snippets of an earlier conversation flashed through Christine's mind as Andrew's scenario became very clear and very real. Closing her eyes and turning to her cousin, she called out quietly, "David?"

"I am here, cousin," came the reply.

"Please find Andrew Chandler," she requested quietly.

Several pairs of eyes turned to Andrew as he stepped forward to the foot of the bed. "I am already here, Christine. I was in the park and witnessed your accident," he told her.

Christine turned at his deep voice and focused on him. After taking a deep breath, she said in a quiet tone, "I have reconsidered." She paused then slowly added as she looked at her mother, "I need you to explain to my mother what you told me."

"I will," Andrew replied and his heart soared. He glanced quickly at Richard who nodded in understanding.

"Take Caroline and David so they will know," Christine went on to say as she closed her eyes.

"I will," Andrew repeated with a nod. He stepped to Maggie and gently tugged at her arm.

"We can talk later. I am not leaving my daughter," Maggie said firmly.

"Come on, Aunt Maggie," Caroline urged, already getting up.

"Not now, I need to be here," Maggie insisted.

Christine opened her eyes and saw her mother jerking her arm free from Andrew's gentle grasp. "Mother, please."

"My place is here," Maggie said firmly.

"I will be here to assist Doctor Brownlee, my lady," Florence offered.

"Mother, I need you to talk to Andrew," Christine said.

"What he needs to tell me can wait," Maggie argued.

"No, Mother. Afterwards I need you to talk to him," Christine argued back.

Maggie was shaking her head and was about to speak again when she suddenly went still and stared down at her daughter. Christine was watching her then nodded in confirmation as her mother realized what needed to be done.

"Let Andrew explain first," Christine said then closed her eyes.

This time when Andrew urged Maggie to her feet, she offered no resistance. Slowly the room emptied with only the doctor and Florence to attend to Christine's injuries. No longer needed, Richard made his excuses and left.

In the drawing room with the doors closed for privacy, Andrew looked up at Christine's portrait then turned to face Maggie, Caroline, and David. He told them of his visit with Christine while they were at church and of his proposal. He was met with shocked faces at the revelation of the plot he had overhead. Finishing his tale, he said, "As she said upstairs, she has reconsidered. She is now accepting my proposal."

"Who could this man be?" Caroline asked in amazement.

"I have no idea but obviously what I had heard was true for we just witnessed an attempt in the park. There is one doubt that if Christine had died, that incident would have been ruled accidental," Andrew told them. Turning to Maggie, he asked, "She has been in other accidents?"

"Well, I was thinking on that," Maggie replied. "They had to have been accidents, Andrew, or this man has made several attempts in the past few months."

It was quiet as Andrew considered this bit of news.

"So what now? When does the marriage ceremony take place?" David asked.

"It must be soon. As you had told us earlier, it is believed that she did not survive the incident today. When this lord realizes that she has survived, he will try again. At least for now, she is safe from other attempts but I will feel much better once she is made Duchess of Kenilworth," Andrew replied.

"This is a generous offer, Andrew," David said. "Even in the name of friendship."

"Over the past few months, David, I have seen a different Christine Lockhart than what is said about her. I am ashamed to say that I too fell in with the gossip but knowing her now, I want to offer what I can."

"Including a marriage of convenience?" David queried.

"No, this will not be a marriage of convenience. Do you think Christine is the type of person who would allow such an arrangement?" Andrew countered.

There was a knock on the door and after Maggie called for entry, Doctor Brownlee stepped inside. "She is resting now. She has refused any medications, as usual," he informed them. "The stubborn girl." He smiled at Maggie and went on in his normal tone, "I will be back some time tomorrow to check on her. Send someone for me if you need me before then."

"I will and thank you so much for your help," Maggie said with relief written clearly upon her face.

"I am only glad that I happened to be at the park this afternoon," Brownlee was saying as Maggie escorted him to the door.

There were a few awkward moments with Caroline and David that Andrew offered to refill drinks while he was standing. When Maggie returned, Andrew informed them, "If you do not mind, Maggie, I will return this evening around seven and the four of us could discuss the arrangements. I need to inform my staff and have preparations made for the arrival of their new duchess."

Turning to David and Caroline, Maggie smiled saying, "I need to discuss a few things with Andrew before he leaves. Could you both return at seven for dinner then we could make plans?"

"Yes, of course, Aunt Maggie," Caroline said then stood up and kissed her aunt's cheek. Turning to Andrew, she added, "Thank you for all that you have done for Christine."

"I am glad to help."

Andrew waited patiently looking up at Christine's portrait while Maggie escorted David and Caroline to the door. Returning a few moments later, she closed the doors then stood beside Andrew. Sensing her nervousness and wondering why, the Duke tried to calm her by saying conversationally, "I like this portrait of Christine. It seems to be recent."

"She had it done for Christopher's last birthday. He had it in his study but she just recently moved it to this room. Christopher loved this portrait of her."

"I like it very much. It captures the playful side of her," Andrew said with a smile.

Maggie looked at him with a small smile of her own and said, "Christopher had said the very same thing. That was what he loved so much about it." She noticed the open admiration on his face as he gazed up at the painting. Indicating the sofa, Maggie said softly, "Please sit down, Andrew, I have a story to tell you. I know you have other matters to deal with so I will not keep you long."

Andrew sat on the sofa and looked up at the painting once again before turning his attention back to Maggie as she began. "You must understand that when Christine insisted on this and Christopher and I agreed, I had always thought that Christopher would do the talking. Then when he died, Christine told me not to worry, that she would tell it when the time came."

She paused and looked at Andrew who sat patiently watching her. Taking a seat on the other end of the sofa, Maggie said firmly, "What you are about to learn must never be repeated, ever. Not even Caroline and David know of this." Andrew raised a brow but Maggie waved a hand dismissively, "You will understand when I have finished."

"Very well, Maggie. No one else will know," Andrew agreed.

Maggie nodded and took a deep breath to calm herself before she began.

"Christopher's first wife, Georgeanna, was very sick when I first met him and he cared for her the best he could. They did not have children mostly because of her illness that befell her shortly after they had married. I only know of this from Christopher." She looked at Andrew who nodded.

"I met Christopher while I was shopping. We quite literally ran into one another. The next time I met him, he was returning to London from visiting a friend near Bath when a storm made it impossible to go further. At the time, I had a small cottage outside of London while Jack lived in our family townhouse." Maggie shrugged and added with a sigh, "Though the house holds fond memories for me, Jack would bring women home and, well, I did not care for the sort."

Andrew nodded in understanding and smiled as Maggie continued. "While we waited on the storm to pass, Christopher and I sat and talked. I found him fascinating and to this day, I believe that was when I fell in love with him. Not wanting to compromise me, Christopher insisted on returning to London when night fell even though the storm had not relented. Since that day, he always stopped whenever he was passing by, leaving and returning to London." Maggie paused then smiled and said philosophically, "Many things happen with innocent beginnings. You never know when something so ordinary could be the turning point of your life."

Andrew smiled at her when she looked up at him. Maggie spoke quietly showing signs of embarrassment. "Before either of us realized it, we became—well, you understand. Sometimes I felt so bad over the affair because his wife was so ill but Christopher always managed to say the right words to comfort me. It was not long before I found myself carrying his child. I panicked. I was sure Christopher would leave me but he took care of me. When I began to show my condition, he sent me away with my maid to stay with a friend who would watch over me. His friend was Jacob Graham, the last Earl of Brasington who also had a love for the sea."

"Captain Graham," Andrew interjected in understanding.

Maggie nodded and said, "Because he stayed mostly to the sea, almost everyone had forgotten that he was an earl." She took a deep breath then returned to her tale, "I feared that Christopher would not be able to return to the Meadows in time for the birth even though he had promised he would. When the pains began, it was during the time that he was burying Georgeanna. Florence and Jacob tried to calm me because we all knew Christopher could not be with me. In the last hour, he was there and helped to bring his firstborn child into the world. He was so proud of his beautiful daughter and I was so happy he was there that I named her after him. Christine." Maggie paused as Andrew stared at her.

"Christopher Lockhart is her father?" he asked in surprise.

"Yes, Andrew. Christine is a true Lockhart. She is a Lady by birth. I was never married to the captain or anyone else before Christopher, but now you see the dilemma we faced. To proclaim her birthright would also announce our affair and me as his mistress. I am a Lady by birth as well and Christopher refused to compromise my status. Not even my family knew of our affair."

Maggie paused again, taking a breath.

"It was Jacob who came up with a solution of which you know. He was very efficient. He made sure my name appeared in the church registry with his and even had papers drawn up. As Christopher waited out the mourning period, we lived in Rome for a time. We were a family there and Christopher loved his daughter so much. It was not until Jacob's sudden death while out at sea that we knew of what he had done. His quartermaster, another friend of Christopher's, found us and explained Jacob's plan. He handed over the papers and a will. To our surprise, Jacob left his home that he called the Meadows and his inheritance to his infant daughter, Christine." Maggie took a deep breath and said with a sad smile, "The rest you already know."

Andrew looked thoughtfully up at the portrait and wondered if the hidden humor was the secret of her birth. She was truly a Lockhart and knew it. The Lockhart fortune that Lady Lucas and the other cronies gossip about as being forfeited because of his second marriage to a widow with a child, rightfully belonged to Christine.

"I understand, Maggie. No one else will know of this," Andrew said tearing his gaze from the portrait.

"Thank you, Andrew. Christine had insisted that the man she agreed to marry should know the truth of her birth but after hearing of that awful wager, she was adamant to never marry. She did not think that she could trust anyone with our secret," Maggie explained.

Andrew nodded, fully understanding now, and said in admiration, "I can well understand, Maggie. It is a wonder that Christine had been able to maintain her wits about her when everyone was being so cruel to her."

"I know, I feared that she would say something but she never did."

"Well, take comfort in knowing that I will make sure those old witches respect her now. I will no longer tolerate the whisperings and storytelling. Christine will be Duchess of Kenilworth and she will receive the respect that is long overdue," Andrew said arrogantly. Maggie smiled at his firm resolve and wondered how much of it would come to pass.

Andrew stood up and offered his hand to assist Maggie to her feet. "I will return by seven so that we can make the arrangements. The sooner she is married to me, the safer she will be."

Returning to his home, Andrew called his housekeeper to inform her of his plans. Mrs. Bailey was a small woman with kind brown eyes and light brown hair that showed streaks of gray. She had been with the family since birth as her mother was a maid in the kitchen and her father was a stable hand.

At the moment, she was staring at her employer after he had given her the news of his new duchess. "Married? When?"

"Perhaps in a day or two."

"To Lady Christine Lockhart?" the housekeeper asked in a mixture of disbelief and dread.

"Bailey, do not listen to the gossips. Christine is not the person you think but then you will see that for yourself," Andrew told her.

"Well then, I should talk with the Lockhart kitchen staff to find out her favorites dishes, her dislikes..." she was saying aloud as she began her mental lists.

Andrew smiled as he watched her brows wrinkle with concentration. Taking her by the shoulders, he gave her a quick kiss on her cheek, "I know you will like her, Bailey."

"Oh Your Grace," she admonished as she pushed him away then laughed softly.

A half an hour earlier than the appointed time, Andrew returned to the Lockhart house. He found Maggie in the drawing room with Caroline, David and their young son, Stephen. The one-year-old was crawling up Caroline's leg and whining for attention. She lifted him onto her lap and jostled him making him laugh.

As the adults made plans, Stephen moved warily around the newcomer. Andrew found out that Christine had her wedding gown made when Caroline was preparing for her own wedding nearly two years before. It turned out that Caroline was a fountain of information of Christine's preferences.

They were all startled when a scream was heard from upstairs before it was abruptly cut off. On the heels of that was the loud clatter of metal hitting tiled floor. Andrew and David raced up the stairs ahead of the women. Another scream was heard just as they turned a corner to see a maid staring in horror into the open doorway that led into Christine's bedchamber. Andrew felt his blood run cold with the fear that something else had happened to Christine. The men were momentarily stunned at the scene before them.

"My God, it is Roberta!" David exclaimed. Lying on the floor with a dagger imbedded in her back was Christine's young maid. A silver tray was on the floor near her head with the food strewn around the area.

Looking up, Andrew found Christine sitting up on the bed coughing and gasping for air while pointing to the open balcony doors.

"He ran out through there," Christine croaked hoarsely.

Andrew ran to the balcony and saw a shadowy figure slip over the wall to the alley beyond. *Gone*, he thought and muttered a curse. Behind him, he heard startled reactions at finding Roberta. Turning, he went directly to the foot of Christine's bed. Maggie was on one side of Christine while Caroline was on the other side with Stephen whining to be on the bed.

"He was already in here," Christine was saying then cleared her throat. Her voice was still hoarse as she spoke. "He had a pillow over my head and held it down over my face so that I could not breathe. I heard Roberta scream then the pillow was loose."

Andrew growled low in his throat as he turned to the footmen who stood nearby. Pointing to the dead body of the maid, he ordered them to take her out.

Glancing around the room, Andrew immediately saw the ploy. An attempted robbery but the lady woke. Startled, the burglar tried to smother the lady.

"A robbery gone awry," Andrew muttered. "Another accident."

"We should call the authorities," David said as he picked up his son and began to walk around the room with the whimpering boy in his arms.

"No," Andrew said firmly. "We tell no one of this."

"But Andrew, a man tried to kill her again," Caroline exclaimed in disbelief.

"I know, which is why Christine and I will marry tonight."

Four pairs of eyes looked up at him in surprise.

"Tonight?" David repeated incredulously, having stopped his pacing.

Andrew nodded and walked to the foot of the bed again. Looking at Christine, he said, "Obviously these men want to finish this so you are not even safe here. Marry me tonight and you will be in my house where I know you will be safe."

Christine stared at him as three other pairs of eyes turned to her. Glancing at the clock on her bedside table, she said with firm resolve, "David, tell the vicar we will begin the ceremony at nine." Looking back at Andrew, she asked, "Is that too soon?"

Andrew smiled and shook his head. In his mind, he thought, *Not too soon at all, my love*.

Chapter 11

Still dressed in her white satin gown, the new Duchess of Kenilworth stared at the fire in the fireplace of her new bedchamber and wondered again if she had done the right thing. Christine had her doubts as she dressed in her wedding gown. She had her doubts as she put on the pearls her mother brought her stating that they were from Andrew. She had her doubts as she stepped out of the vestibule of the small chapel. But when she saw Andrew waiting for her at the altar with the vicar, all her doubts disappeared and she smiled.

Andrew had worn all white except for the waistcoat that was blue. He had told her after the ceremony as they rode the short distance to his townhouse that he had worn the blue jacket because the color matched her eyes.

As she was introduced to his staff, Christine had realized a sudden fear that she would not be accepted until she had felt Andrew's thumb gently caress the top of her hand. He had held her hand through the introductions. When she glanced up at him, his smile was gentle and reassuring.

The dinner that was prepared for the earlier discussion of making plans at the Lockhart house had been carried to his townhouse during the ceremony. The newlywed couple along with Maggie, Caroline, David, and Richard finally sat down to enjoy the meal. Having fallen asleep before they left for chapel, Stephen was left with Florence at the Lockhart house.

A door opened and Christine was pulled from her thoughts as she looked up to find Andrew stepping in through the adjacent door that led from his bedchamber. He held two glasses of wine and offered one to her.

"Welcome to your new home, Your Grace," he said, his deep voice sending a tremor through her.

Christine smiled and raised her glass to his. The soft clink made them both smile as they sipped the wine. Another door opened and Bailey entered from yet another room, Christine's new sitting room.

"Oh I beg your pardon, Your Graces. I will come back," she said apologetically when she saw them.

"No, come in, Bailey," Andrew called out then turned to head back to his room. "Take good care of her."

He smiled at the vision in white satin wearing his mother's pearls then left, closing the door behind them. The housekeeper smiled reassuringly at Christine then assisted her in changing from her wedding gown to a gossamer nightgown and matching robe.

Bailey had no idea why the plans had changed so drastically but she did not question further as the Duke hurried to dress for the ceremony. Now seeing Lady Christine Lockhart, or rather Christine Chandler, the housekeeper could see how the Duke was smitten with the young woman. She was indeed beautiful and that was only where the gossip had been accurate. Bailey was not met with an unfriendly demanding title-seeker. Instead, she was greeted with a shy, soft-spoken young woman. Rumors that Christine never smiled were also false as she presented a soft smile and pleasant 'thank you' whenever she was served her drink or portion of the meal. Her laughter surprised the housekeeper as the talk at the dinner table went from humorous to silly to inane partly due to Richard's antics. Without a reason that she could put her finger on, Bailey realized that she liked this mysterious woman who was now the Duchess of Kenilworth.

"I am sorry to hear of your maid," Bailey began conversationally as she pulled the pins from Christine's hair and the dark waves cascaded down her back. "In the morning, I will introduce you to Mary. She is young and very capable. I think you will be pleased with her."

"Thank you, Bailey. I trust your judgment," Christine said meeting the woman's brown eyes in the mirror.

As Bailey brushed the long dark tresses, she talked of the usual routine of the household. "If you wish to change anything, I will see that it is done."

Christine let out a soft laugh and said with blue eyes twinkling in amusement, "Now why would I change anything? This house has been running quite well before me. My presence here will do no more than cause more clutter."

Bailey stopped and stared at their reflection in surprise then noted the twinkle in the blue eyes. "Oh Your Grace," the housekeeper said with a titter of laughter.

"Do not brush all that gorgeous hair away, Bailey," Andrew said from behind them.

He chuckled as they gasped in surprise and turned quickly to face him. Still dressed in his white shirt, britches, and stockings, he had been watching them while leaning against the wall with his arms and legs crossed casually.

"Do you not knock?" Christine admonished but the smile belied the scolding.

"This is my house," Andrew replied still grinning and adding a shrug.

He straightened and walked over to stand behind them. Taking the brush from the housekeeper, he waved her away in dismissal. Bailey grinned at him then bade them goodnight as she dropped into a respectful curtsy before leaving the room. Somewhere in the house, the chimes from a grandfather clock rang out then tolled twelve times.

"Midnight," Christine whispered.

"Yes, and it has certainly been an interesting day," Andrew replied as he stepped back and took her hand when she stood up. "You awakened in the morning like any other morning never dreaming that so much would happen."

"Having someone try to kill me twice within several hours certainly was not on my schedule for the day," Christine added making him chuckle again.

"Nor was a marriage proposal and a not-so-romantic one at that," Andrew put in. "I am sorry you did not have the wedding you truly deserve."

Christine blinked in astonishment at the soft confession then smiled as she regained her composure. "As you may recall, Andrew, I had not expected to marry at all."

Andrew sighed and a look of sadness flickered in his eyes. "I know but you deserve so much more than that."

He hugged her to him. Knowing that he could, knowing that he had the right to hold her, his arms tightened as he reveled in the feel of her while his heart soared. She was as soft as he had imagined she would be and had the subtle scent of roses.

Parting slightly to look at her, Andrew drew her into a kiss that was slow and deep. He explored her mouth, tasting the wine they had shared and feeling her response to the kiss. Her arms were hesitant as she lifted them to wrap around his neck making him groan with pleasure against her lips. Christine was now his and he wanted her.

Remembering her ordeal in the park, Andrew slowly pulled back and released her lips. Her eyes were still closed as he lifted his head and the urge to carry her to the bed was almost overpowering. When she opened her eyes, the blue was darker from the passion he aroused and Andrew found it difficult to trample the urge to make love to her.

"You should rest now," he said hoarsely. He saw her blink then she frowned in disapproval.

"This is our wedding night," Christine said shyly then blushed.

"There will be other nights," he replied with a smile.

"Yet only one wedding night," she countered.

"You will be sore from your fall," he said.

With a sickening realization, Christine dropped her gaze from his and took a step back. Staring at the floor, she whispered, "You do not want me."

She missed his stunned look of amazement. He reached out and, with two fingers under her chin, he lifted her face so that he could look into her eyes.

"Not want you? My sweet Christine, at this moment, I want you very much. I am only concerned that you do not over exert yourself. You should be resting."

"I can rest tomorrow," she said barely above a whisper. When Andrew only looked at her, she went on quickly to say, "It is just that we have this one night that is truly our wedding night."

Still Andrew said nothing. Uncomfortable under his stare and feeling that she was acting more like a harlot trying to lure her next customer, Christine looked away and turned her gaze back to the fire.

His look had not meant to be intimating but he had been debating with himself. He knew she should be resting and yet, at the same time, he wanted to make love to his bride.

Coming to a decision, Andrew reached out and pulled at the tie of her robe. Opening it, he met her gaze when she turned back to face him. As he slipped the robe off her shoulders, he glanced down at the diaphanous nightgown. Her nipples stood erect against the soft fabric and the sight made his insides pool together centering in his loins.

He gently slipped the nightgown from her shoulders then let it cascade to the floor with a whispered 'whoosh' leaving her naked before him. Slowly his eyes traveled over her body, noting the well-formed breasts, the flat stomach, slim waist, narrow hips and long sleek legs. The triangular patch of dark curls caught his attention a moment longer before his gaze lifted to meet hers.

"You are more beautiful than I could have ever imagined," he whispered thickly then pulled her to him for another slow and passionate kiss.

This time he lifted a hand and reached between them to cup her breast. Again he groaned with pleasure against her mouth. No longer able to resist, Andrew dropped his hand that was between them and bent to tuck it behind her knees. With his mouth still on hers and her arms wrapped around his neck, he lifted her in his arms and carried her to the large four-post bed.

Andrew gently laid her down then undressed quickly as his eyes roamed over her. Christine found it difficult to breathe as she had her first look at a man's hard body. His broad shoulders and chest tapered to a narrow waist and slim hips. Her blue eyes shifted quickly away when she saw him hard and ready for her.

Andrew grinned at her shy innocence as he slipped into bed beside her. He gathered her close again and kissed her, enjoying the feel of her breasts against his bared chest while his hand roamed over her, exploring the soft body.

When his fingers slipped between her slightly parted thighs and touched the soft bud of her womanhood, Christine gasped. She pushed at him and her face was crimson red when he gazed down at her questioningly.

"I know what is said about me, Andrew," she said shyly. "But I have never done this before."

He smiled tenderly as his fingers gently caressed her. "I know, Duchess," he whispered. "Relax and let me show you the pleasures in the art of lovemaking."

He began with kissing her mouth as one hand caressed her breast and the other caressed the softer parts of her. His lips moved to her throat then slowly moved lower until his mouth took a nipple. She gasped at the ripple of desire that coursed through her and she shivered. Understanding the meaning of her tremble, Andrew kissed her throat as he silently beckoned her legs apart with his knees. Christine felt his hard erection against her thigh and willed herself to remain calm.

For a moment, they looked into each other's eyes before Andrew lowered his head to kiss her mouth tenderly. He positioned himself over her then was still for an instant before he plunged into her With his mouth covering hers, the painful gasp over the loss of her maidenhood was nothing more than a moan. He pressed the kiss deeper until she began to relax under him and return his kiss with the same passion he received before. Only then did he slowly move within her.

He released her lips to press kisses over her face. Her soft gasps of pleasure as he drove himself deep inside her stirred his desire and he quickened the pace. His hands moved to her hips encouraging her shy moves to meet his thrusts. He closed his eyes and enjoyed the thrill of feeling her beneath him, moving with him. A low guttural groan escaped him as he held her tighter to him.

Christine began to groan deep in her throat as she moved under him. Suddenly, the desire within her seemed to explode and her body jolted. Her groan was like music to Andrew's ears. He quickened his rhythm and soon he too felt the rapturous pleasure of release as he thrust deep inside her.

Floating back down from the clouds, Andrew held her close and crushed her mouth in a kiss. Rolling off of her, he pulled her with him as he lay on his back and she was draped over him. Now she was kissing him with the same urgent desire.

"Oh sweet Christine," he whispered thickly when she lifted her head to look down at him. Christine smiled and lowered her head to kiss him again.

The soft glow of embers in the fireplace was the only light in the room as Andrew rolled onto his side and reached out for her. He felt only the flatness of the bed and rose up on his elbows to stare down at the empty space beside him. A soft sound from the balcony caught his attention then he saw the edge of the white robe as the breeze buffeted it slightly.

Getting out of the bed and walking naked to join her on the balcony, Andrew smiled as he thought of how often he had made love to her during the night. Neither of them had slept for more than an hour before his caresses led to another session of lovemaking. It seemed as though he could not get his fill of her and even now was becoming aroused again.

The early spring morning was breezy and cool. On the edge of the horizon, the skies were just lightening up though the full moon was still partially visible in the night sky. With the meager light of the dawn, the dark clouds hung low and started to cover the stars and moon.

"Why are you out here?" he whispered from behind her. His arms circled around her waist and he hugged her tightly against him.

Christine leaned back against him and smiled. "I could smell the roses."

His lips touched a spot on her throat just below her ear and she seemed to purr as she tilted her head to give him room. His hands roamed over the front of her as he pressed soft kisses to her throat.

When he untied the robe, Christine began to laugh softly and asked, "What are you doing?"

"I want to see you in the moonlight," he answered thickly and opened the robe.

His hands slipped up her body again to cup each breast. With her back still against him, Christine moaned softly while reaching back until she could thread her fingers through his dark hair. She whispered his name and let her head fall back against his shoulder. His hands continued to gently rub the front of her body as his lips moved from one side of her throat across her shoulders to the other side of her throat.

"Do I please you, Andrew?" she asked him in a whisper.

He turned her to face him and smiled down at her. "Yes, Christine Chandler, you please me very much. I hope that someday soon, I can make you understand just how much you do please me."

His mouth took hers then. They held onto one another before he bent to lift her up in his arms and carry her back into the bedchamber.

Dressed in dark clothing and crouched down behind the well-groomed bushes along the wall, he watched her. As she gazed up at the full moon, he could almost feel his hatred for her course through his veins. *She had no right to be alive, no right to feel joy and happiness!* When the Duke held her close then removed her robe to reveal her pale well-formed breasts to the moonlit dawn, a growl emitted from deep in his throat as he felt a primal tugging in his loins.

Watching the Duke's hands gently caress her breasts, a new vision appeared in his mind and he smiled evilly. The watcher closed his eyes and let his imagination take over. In his mind, he saw her pinned on the bed by the weight of his body and he would plunge savagely into her. Her anguish cries of pain would arouse him as he thrust cruelly. His hands would circle her throat slowly choking her while his mouth crushed hers in a brutal kiss. He would take her last breath as he released his passion deep inside her.

Yes, that would be a much better and more pleasurable ending to Christine Lockhart, he thought as he looked up at the empty balcony. Standing up from his hiding place and as quietly as he had entered the gardens of the Duke's townhouse, he was gone.

Chapter 12

It was raining later that morning as Christine stirred from sleep. She lay on her side facing the balcony doors while the rain tapped against the windows. Sleepily, she had a vague recollection of Andrew kissing her softly as he got out of the bed.

"Sleep as long as you wish, sweet duchess," he had whispered close to her ear before he kissed her again and pulled the covers over her shoulders.

Christine had rolled onto her back and heard him close the balcony doors before she had drifted back to sleep.

Covering herself, she looked around and realized that she had not been dreaming. The room was not her own. *Well, now it is but then I am no longer Christine Lockhart*, she mused as she lifted her left hand to look at the ring Andrew placed on her finger during the ceremony. A large diamond with small rubies encircling it winked at her as it caught the light.

She was now Christine Chandler, the Duchess of Kenilworth, and Andrew's wife. Thinking of him, she took mental inventory of herself and decided that she was a different person for certain. Besides the obvious physical change, she was a wife in truth as she remembered Andrew's attentions throughout the night.

Snuggling back under the covers as she pulled them over bare shoulders, Christine slowly became aware of two women whispering and her eyes snapped open.

"Good morning, Your Grace," Bailey greeted.

Christine pulled the covers to her chin as the two women stepped closer to the bed.

"This is Mary. She will be your new maid," the housekeeper was saying, pretending not to notice Christine's state of undress. The young girl stepped forward and dropped to a curtsy.

"Good morning, Bailey, Mary," Christine greeted then glanced at the clock. She nearly bolted upright in surprise. "It is nearly ten!"

Bailey stepped forward with a bed jacket and held it up discreetly as

Christine slipped it on. As the housekeeper chatted on, Mary adjusted the pillows when Christine sat up.

"Oh yes, Your Grace. We have your breakfast and the water should be here momentarily for your bath."

Once Christine had settled against the pillows, Mary set the breakfast tray over her lap. Looking at the cup of hot chocolate and toast with strawberry jam, Christine looked up in surprise. "How did you know I have this for breakfast?"

Bailey looked at her sheepishly and replied, "I called upon the Lockhart housekeeper for your likes and dislikes as well as your usual schedule."

Christine smiled and, with a twinkle in her blue eyes, she asked, "Florence did not bore you with her chatter, did she? On many occasions, I have had to put a pillow around my ears." She demonstrated with a pillow that was on the bed beside her making Bailey and Mary laugh softly.

"No, Your Grace, she was quite informative and pleasant," Bailey told her.

There was a knock on the door and Bailey hurriedly reached up to let the drapes drop down. The bedside near the fireplace was now concealed while Mary unfastened the drapes at the foot of the bed. Eating her toast, Christine was hidden from view of all doors that led into her room. The only view she had was the balcony doors.

Bailey was heard giving orders as the water was poured into a tub. Mary made sure that Christine was comfortable before assisting Bailey with the preparations for the bath. After some time, Bailey returned with a robe.

"Is the Duke awake?" Christine asked.

"Yes, Your Grace. He has been in his study all morning."

Christine made to move out of the bed then let out a groan. With a sigh, she grumbled, "After that fall yesterday, I am sore this morning."

"I have oils to rub on your aches, Your Grace," Bailey informed her.

"That would be nice," Christine said with a smile then followed the housekeeper to her bathing chamber.

"Tis a wonder you are not covered with bruises," Bailey told her. "Does your head ache this morning?"

"Some but it will go away soon," she answered and Bailey nodded.

A large ornate tub stood in the center of the room with several buckets of hot water nearby for rinsing. Christine let out a delightful sigh as she settled in the steaming bath and felt the soreness ebb away. Bailey showed Mary how to attend to the Duchess' bath but Christine ignored them as she relaxed in the lightly scented water.

Bailey allowed some time for Christine to enjoy her relaxation before they assisted with the rinsing. The water cascaded over her as Mary and Bailey rinsed the scented soap from her hair.

"Such thick hair, just like Her Grace. God rest her soul," Bailey commented. "It used to take extra buckets to rinse her hair thoroughly as well."

Mary slowly poured the water through the dark tresses and marveled at the soft feel of the long hair. "I bet His Grace is proud of your hair," the young girl said in an awed tone.

"Indeed I am," came Andrew's deep voice from behind them.

Startled, Christine gasped and slid further in the water, unaccustomed to a man nearby as she bathed. Bailey and Mary looked around as he stepped further into the room.

"Now Bailey, I thought I told you to let her sleep," he said in feigned admonishment.

"I did, Your Grace," Bailey told him as she stood up. With a pat on his arm, she said shaking her head, "Shame on you for disturbing a lady during her bath. Just like your father, always interrupting your mother's bath." Andrew smiled at the housekeeper who pulled on the young maid's sleeve. "Come along now, Mary."

As the two women left them alone, Andrew's green eyes roamed over the body submerged under the water then up to the sapphire blue eyes. "Good morning, Christine."

"Good morning, Andrew," she greeted in return. A blush appeared on her cheeks and he smiled.

He draped a towel over his shoulder then picked up another. Unfolding it, he beckoned her out of the tub then opened the towel for her. Christine stepped out with his assistance, and then he motioned for her to turn her back to him. She closed her eyes and felt her cheeks warm from embarrassment as Andrew rubbed her dry with the towel.

Rubbing the water from her long hair, he asked softly, "Did you sleep well?"

"Yes, I did. Did you? You were up early this morning," she replied quietly.

"I did. I rose to attend to some business so I can spend the rest of the day with you," he said toweling her hair vigorously.

In truth, he did little work in his study because his mind kept drifting to the woman upstairs and of the wonderful night they had shared. Turning her to face him, he looked into her eyes. He still could not believe that she was here as his wife and now lover.

"You are so beautiful, Christine," he said thickly just before his mouth covered hers.

His clothes were wet instantly from her body since he had not dried the front of her as yet. When he lifted his head, Christine smiled looking at the clinging wet shirt.

"Now your clothes are wet."

"I was going to change anyway," he said with a shrug.

He tossed the wet towel he had just used to the floor then bent to lift her in his arms. "Andrew, please. I can walk," she grumbled playfully.

"Hmm, but I like this mode of travel for you," he replied smiling and making her laugh.

Standing beside the bed with her still in his arms, Andrew smiled at her and said, "I am in a quandary as to what I should give you for a wedding present that could come close to the wondrous gift you have given me."

His smile widened as Christine's brows knitted in confusion. "My gift?"

His green eyes shifted to the bed and Christine turned to follow his gaze. The covers were still rumpled in the same place from when she had gotten out of bed but now she saw the spots of blood, evidence of her lost maidenhood. She knew it would be there yet the sight of it stunned her.

"I thank you for the gift, my sweet," Andrew whispered as he enjoyed seeing her reaction.

He gently laid her on the bed then, with the towel draped over his shoulder, he dried her face with slow purposeful moves. Starting with her face, his lips followed the trail of the towel.

"Close your eyes and feel," he whispered against her cheek.

He smiled when she did as she was told. The towel moved to her throat and so did his lips. When the towel slowly dried the water from her breasts, Christine arched her back slightly anticipating his next move. She gasped as his lips closed over a nipple and he sucked gently. Andrew spent long moments as he enjoyed her breasts. Arching her back, Christine offered him more and he took more.

Moving lower, Andrew followed the towel over her flat stomach and down her thighs. Soon the towel was on the floor and Christine let out a guttural groan as Andrew showed her other pleasures in the art of lovemaking.

Nearly an hour later, Christine sat at the dressing table as Mary put the finishing touches to the styling of her hair. Since Roberta had no other family, Andrew had found out that David took care of making the arrangements to bury the young woman in a well cared for cemetery at Maggie's request.

The funeral services would begin in little more than hour but Christine was beginning to not feel well. Her stomach seemed to be churning within her like the chopping waters of the sea during a storm. The rain and gloom of the day seemed to only intensify Christine's ailment.

Andrew stepped in through the adjacent door from his room and saw Christine still in her chemise. Bailey was at the bed readying the gown for her to slip into while keeping a watchful eye on Mary's handiwork.

"Do you not like it?" Mary asked seeing the look on Christine's face from the mirror's reflection.

Christine pulled herself from her thoughts and surveyed the girl's work. "Oh Mary, you did wonderfully. It is just that with the rain and the funeral, I do not think I am up to going out."

"We can forego this," Andrew told her as he stepped into the mirror's reflection. "You do need to rest and that is more than enough reason."

"I must go, Andrew. If not for her arrival, I could very well be the one who—"

"Thankfully, you are not," he broke in, not wanting to think of how close he had come to losing her.

Christine let out a sigh and stood up. "She was my maid but she was also my friend," she was saying as she turned to face them.

She took a step towards Bailey then cried out in pain as she clutched her midsection. Pain shot through her and Christine could do no more than bend over with the sharp stabs in her belly. Everyone stopped what they were doing and hurried to her. Andrew grabbed her before she toppled forward while Bailey and Mary hurried over to offer some assistance.

"Christine, what is it? What is the matter?" Andrew asked full of concern.

"Oh God, Andrew, it hurts," Christine groaned through painful gasps.

The pain was so intense that Christine could barely catch her breath. Suddenly she went limp in his arms. Horrified, Andrew lifted her and carried her to the bed. "Christine! My God, Christine!"

She did not respond. Looking over his shoulder, he barked out, "Bailey, send someone for Doctor Brownlee! Hurry!"

He shrugged out of his waistcoat and vest, tossing them to the chair at her dressing table. Sitting on the bed beside her, Andrew pulled pins from her hair and dropped them carelessly on the floor. "I am here, Christine," he said softly. "I am here beside you."

Within half an hour, Doctor Brownlee arrived. Andrew explained what had happened since the doctor had seen her the afternoon before. Brownlee examined Christine, nodding intermittently as he listened to Duke's reason for the quick marriage.

"She was fine little more than an hour ago." Andrew said thinking of the lovemaking they shared after her bath.

Perplexed, the doctor looked up at the Duke and Bailey then said quietly, "She has a fever and see this." He lowered the covers to reveal Christine's throat and upper chest. "A rash of some kind. Has she had anything unusual today?"

"No," Bailey answered. "I brought her breakfast just the way the other housekeeper told me yesterday."

"Which was?" Brownlee asked distractedly.

"Hot chocolate and toast with strawberry jam but she barely touched it, sir," Bailey told him. "Since she did not eat much of her breakfast I fixed her a sandwich and cup of tea. She did not drink her hot chocolate so I knew she had not taken her medication. Because of that, I made—"

"What medication?" Doctor Brownlee asked as he suddenly looked at the housekeeper.

"Her medication for her headaches. The stablehand brought it over this morning saying—" Bailey trailed off as the doctor stared at her in disbelief.

"What is it?" Andrew asked seeing the doctor's reaction.

"I did not order any medication," Brownlee replied. "She has always been stubborn about taking them."

Bailey pulled a small brown bottle from the pocket of her apron and showed it to them. "This is for her. It was left behind when everything was changed so quickly last evening."

Brownlee opened it up and sniffed but detected no odor.

"The stablehand said that there would be no smell but to add it to her hot chocolate," Bailey was saying. "It covers the taste which is the only way she would take it."

The doctor looked from Bailey to Andrew and said, "This did not come from me. She would not let me give her so much as a sedative last evening. She just will not take medicines."

Andrew stared at him and asked slowly, "Are you telling me that someone has poisoned her?"

Bailey gasped and put her hand to her heart. "Oh Your Grace, and I poured it into her hot chocolate and then in her tea."

"How much did you give her?" Brownlee asked the housekeeper.

"Only a capful was what the man said. A capful," Bailey said, her voice rising with hysteria.

"Calm yourself, Bailey. You are not responsible for this," Andrew told her.

"I put it in her tea, Your Grace," she argued.

"Did she drink all of her tea?" Brownlee asked breaking into their conversation.

Bailey looked over at the dressing table. Brownlee and Andrew followed her gaze to see the cup sitting in the middle of the table. They hurried to look into the cup. Andrew prayed hard that it would not be empty. The cup looked as though it was barely touched and they sighed in relief.

"Perhaps she only took a sip," Andrew said, a look of hope in his eyes as his gaze met the doctor's.

Brownlee nodded thoughtfully. "I fear of giving her anything for the fever. I am not sure what elements are in here or its potency," the doctor said as he looked at the small brown bottle. He turned back to the bed to retrieve his bag, putting the bottle into the bag. He headed for the door and said, "I will return as quickly as I can. Give her only water. If nothing else, the water may dilute the poison in her body." Looking pointedly at Bailey, he repeated, "Only water."

The housekeeper nodded and they went to the door. Mary stood anxiously outside and Bailey told the girl to show the doctor out. Returning to Andrew's side by the bed as he caressed Christine's forehead with his fingertips, Bailey finally released her grief.

"Oh Your Grace, I am so very sorry." Her voice broke and she began to cry. "I meant her no harm!"

Standing, Andrew put his arm around the sobbing housekeeper and said gently, "Bailey, I know you did not mean to hurt her. If you knew what the bottle contained, you would have never given it to her. I know and so does Christine." He patted her shoulder and added gently, "Now go clean yourself up then call the entire staff together. If she survives this, then those responsible just may try again."

Bailey nodded and, still sniffling, left Andrew with the unconscious Christine. Carefully sitting on the bed next to the still form, Andrew slowly let out a long breath.

"Oh Christine, my love, I have failed you. I gave you my name, my title, and my home. Through my arrogance, I believed that would simply keep you safe. I was wrong," Andrew whispered. He reached out and brushed her cheek with his thumb. "Please do not die, Christine. I love you more than anything in the world. Please do not leave me here alone."

He bent low and pressed his cheek against her warm one, feeling the weight of this failure crush his breaking heart.

Chapter 13

Christine could not feel the ground beneath her although she could see that she stood upon the grass. She looked around and was surprised to see the two children running through the thick grass of the meadow. She knew the children. The boy was barely three years of age and the girl had just turned six. His childish laughter rang out through the crisp summer afternoon as the girl fell onto the soft grassy meadow, making Christine smile.

"You are so slow, Phillip," the young girl scolded playfully.

The boy only laughed as his small legs hurried to catch up with her. When he reached her, he dropped to the grass beside her and the two looked up at the clouds in the sky.

"See that one," the girl said pointing to a large white mass. "That is a horse."

"Hoosey," the boy exclaimed and pointed a small finger to the sky.

"Oh look, there is a turtle," the girl said pointing to another cloud.

"Tuddle."

"No turtle," the girl corrected. "Say it, turtle."

"Tuddle," the boy repeated making the girl laugh.

Christine's smile turned sad as she watched them. "Oh Phillip, you could never really say that 'r' sound, could you?" she whispered.

Suddenly the image changed and it was another warm afternoon as Christine stood under a tree watching the young girl, now ten years old, place a handful of flowers upon the small grave. Tears filled Christine's eyes as she looked at the headstone. *Phillip Charles Lockhart. An angel given to us for only a short time.*

She remembered the autumn afternoon when her brother had fallen into the shallow brook near their home in the country. A few days later, he became ill with a fever. Within a fortnight, he was dead.

When the young girl left wiping away her tears, Christine stepped up to the grave, reading the headstone once again. Her brother had only been seven years old.

"I am sorry, Phillip," she began weeping. "It was supposed to be a shortcut back to the house but that rabbit frightened us and I accidentally knocked you into the water. I am so very sorry."

For a few moments, Christine let out her grief as she remembered the pain of watching her brother being buried on a rainy autumn afternoon. The image changed again and Christine saw herself at the age of ten and two standing next to her father as several men spoke angrily all at once. She recognized the area as the House of Lords where her father had been granted permission allowing her to watch the proceedings for that day.

"My Lords! Please!" the barrister called out.

"This is highly unorthodox! Children have no place here!" one of the men exclaimed.

"Oh, do stop your grumbling, Lord Ferguson," came a voice from behind them.

All chatter ceased at once and the silence seemed to almost crash down upon them as Ferguson turned angrily to face the voice. Christine remembered Ferguson easily and also remembered how she would have dearly loved to slap that smirk from his face.

"So, Your Grace, you find nothing out of place with the child being present?" Ferguson asked snidely.

"If she wants to learn, then let her be. Lord Lockhart was granted permission to have her present so who are you to dispute it," the Duke answered with a nonchalant wave of his hand.

"Given that you are new to the proceedings yourself since your father has turned over his title to you—" Ferguson began.

"Remember your place, George," warned a man beside Ferguson.

Christine turned and stared at a younger Andrew Chandler. She also noticed Lord Richard Pittman standing slightly behind Andrew. The young Duke smiled at Ferguson and shrugged. "True, I am in the learning process as well," Andrew began. Looking at the young girl beside Christopher Lockhart, he winked and added, "So we will all learn together."

Both the younger and the present Christine Lockhart smiled at the unconcerned attitude of the young Duke. Christine remembered thinking that Andrew had the most beautiful green eyes she had ever seen. Glancing back at her younger self, she could see the infatuation in the blue eyes.

"This is business, Kenilworth," Ferguson growled with disdain. "Carry your flirtations elsewhere! The little chit has no—"

"Enough!" Christopher Lockhart bellowed. "You will remember your place, Ferguson, no matter what the age of the one who bears the title and you owe His Grace an apology for your impertinence!"

Many heads nodded in agreement and Ferguson could see that he was quickly losing his support with his show of disrespect toward the young Duke. Not pleased that he had to make an apology, he stated in a monotone voice, "I apologize for my disregard of your position, Your Grace."

Andrew Chandler smiled and nodded in acceptance of the apology. He reached out and pulled the young Christine Lockhart to stand before him. Placing his hands on the girl's slender shoulders, the Duke said with a smile, "Now I believe you owe an apology to Lord Lockhart and to young Lady Lockhart."

Andrew's smile widened as Ferguson's mouth dropped in disbelief. Glancing around, the older man noted the expectant looks before his gaze met the Duke's once again. Taking a deep breath, Ferguson looked to Christopher then to young Christine and said more grudgingly than when he spoke to Andrew, "I extend my apology also to you, Lord and Lady Lockhart."

"Ah, there, now all is well and we can begin what should have started near a half an hour ago," Andrew chirped. Offering a nearby chair with an exaggerated wave of his hand, the Duke turned to the young Christine and said chivalrously, "My Lady, your seat awaits."

Captivated, the young Christine smiled up at him as his green eyes seemed to sparkle with his humor. "Thank you, Your Grace," came the shy reply.

Christine watched the young man who in nearly six years would be her husband and for the first time realized that he had captured her heart at that very moment. "It was your green eyes, Andrew. That was what I remembered for a long time after that day," she said quietly as the men took their seats and did not notice the ghostly figure that watched them.

Once again, her surroundings clouded. When it cleared, Christine found herself standing inside a large foyer with a wide staircase to her right and several closed double doors.

"Oh my God! Lady Bellows School for Girls," she moaned in disbelief.

So many memories assaulted her at once. The pranks she used to play upon the other girls. The long hours of helping Caroline and the other girls with their studies. The late nights when she and the stableboy, Ian, would stay up to prepare the next day's practical joke on a classmate or favorite teacher. The smells from the dining area, the food, the cold nights during the winter. But most of all, she remembered the contempt Lady Bellows had for her.

A door opened interrupting her thoughts and Lady Bellows walked briskly to the foot of the stairs. Dressed in a pale yellow dress, Lady Bellows was a slender woman of nearly two score and five with light brown hair, pale skin, and brown eyes that could be as hard as stone. Her facial expression always seemed to reflect displeasure and Christine could not remember a time when the woman actually smiled. Lady Bellows looked at the grandfather clock beside her then to the top of the stairs.

Soon two lines of girls appeared and came down the staircase. The first girl in each line stopped before Lady Bellows and the remaining girls stepped close behind each other to form tight lines that led all the way up to the second floor.

"I almost had to wait," Lady Bellows said disapprovingly. "A proper lady is expected to be on time. Therefore, we shall stand as we are for the next five minutes and perhaps then you will all remember what time we are to gather for dinner."

No one spoke or even dared to groan although many eyes rolled at the command. Bowing her head and looking down at the spotless tiled floor, Christine's groan was not heard by those images of her past as the girls stood tall on the staircase. Suddenly, she remembered what was going to happen on this day and Christine quickly looked up to the top of the stairs. The last girl in line near the railing stepped over the banister and stared down at the floor below.

"Agatha, get back in your place," Lady Bellows called up.

Heads turned and the girls stared in astonishment as the young girl continued to stare at the floor below.

"Agatha!" Lady Bellows called again.

One girl moved from her place near the bottom of the staircase and ran up to the second floor. Christine recognized herself and put a hand to mouth as she shook her head, knowing what was about to happen.

"Aggie, please," the young Christine screamed up as she lifted her skirts and ran up the steps.

The girls began to scream in panic and Lady Bellows tried to quiet them in harsh tones as she began to climb the steps.

"Christine Lockhart! Return to your place this instant!"

"Aggie! Let me help you! Please!" the young Christine screamed as she reached out for the girl's arm and ignored the order from the head mistress.

Suddenly, screams of terror filled the hall and the girls backed against the wall. Lady Bellows stopped and stared in horror. Just as the young Christine reached for the weeping Agatha's arm, the girl released her hold on the banister and fell to the cold hard floor below.

"Dear God," Lady Bellows murmured, her hand going to her throat.

She hurried down the stairs to the still and crumpled form. She knelt down and touched the dark hair then felt the sticky wetness of blood. Looking up to the second floor, Lady Bellows saw the young Christine leaning over the banister staring down at her with the same horror-stricken look in her eyes.

"Go back to your rooms! All of you! Go!" Lady Bellows ordered still looking at Christine Lockhart.

The girls ran up the stairs and the sounds of doors slamming seemed to echo in the large foyer. Lady Bellows watched as Caroline Pinckney practically pried her cousin from the banister.

The images began to fade and Christine felt a sense of relief that she no longer had to relive that awful day. Looking around, she knew that it was the middle of the night as she watched herself in a nightgown and robe with the stableboy, Ian, in a classroom setting up the next prank.

"Not this night. Please, I do not want to relive this night," Christine pleaded to the shadows of her past.

"Go on, Ian. I can finish here," said the younger Christine to the stableboy.

"Are ye sure, m'lady?"

"Yes, it is getting late and Bill is undoubtedly worried by now. Go on with you," she said and lightly pushed him away.

Laughing quietly, the boy nodded and left her in the room.

Christine watched as her younger self tied the strings for the shades to window latches. With the shades pulled down, the prank was concealed until someone tried to raise it. She was tying the last one when a sound alerted her and the young Christine turned quickly.

"I have been waiting for you, my dear," the man said as he stood in the doorway. The candle in the candlestick holder he held illuminated his face and he smiled. "How can you possibly see what you are doing?"

"Lord Bellows? Why are you here?" the young Christine asked warily. She clutched her robe tightly to her as if it would ward him away.

"As I said, I have been waiting for you," he told her as he stepped into the room and placed the candle on the desk at the front of the classroom. "Many nights I have walked these halls hoping to find you up and about."

"Why?" she asked.

"Why?" he repeated incredulously. "Come, come, my dear. You are very intelligent, more so than any other young girl I have ever had the pleasure to meet."

Sensing danger, the young Christine took a step back as he moved closer to her. Her eyes flickered over him as he was dressed only in a white shirt and dark colored britches. His dark wavy hair framed his face and fell over his eyes. Usually dressed impeccably with a vest, coat and fashionable cravat, his hair tied back with a ribbon, Christine could not understand why he was so informal now.

She watched his hazel eyes roam over her greedily and his smile turned lecherous. His voice was now thick as he said, "You are truly beautiful, Christine Lockhart. Dressed as you are, you look like an angel. Hmm, I will think of you as my angel from now on Does that please you, Angel?"

"Angel?"

"Yes, angels are beautiful. Angels make the mere mortal feel alive and giddy with hope. You do that to me, you know. You give me hope," Bellows said slowly.

"What do you mean? Lord Bellows, you should not be here. Lady Bellows would—" the young Christine was saying as she tried to keep distance between them.

Bellows laughed lightly and gave a short dismissive wave of his hand. "My sister thinks I am away on business," he said. "Finding you here is an answer to my prayers. I have been wanting to find you alone and here you are, my angel."

"Stop calling me your angel," Christine said firmly.

The two had been circling each other around the room. Having kept her eyes on him, the young Christine misjudged her distance from the desk. She bumped against it then scrambled to catch the candlestick as it rocked from side to side. Using her distraction, Bellows lunged forward and grabbed her around the midsection with one hand then covered her mouth with the other.

"Shh, Angel. Let us have some fun before the sun rises. I have been wanting you for a very long time," he whispered against her ear.

The young Christine struggled against him but he only chuckled and pressed his lips to her throat. Her muffled cries excited him as he adjusted his hold so that his hand moved from her midsection to cover one breast.

"You are as soft as I had imagined you to be. Let me introduce you to the many pleasures of the woman's body, Christine."

Her struggles increased and soon she managed to topple him off of her. She heard his curse as she darted away from him hoping to put the desk between them. Bellows anticipated the move and reached for her as she turned. Christine evaded him so that he was only able to grasp her robe. She felt the tug and hurriedly slipped out of the robe then ran from him. Since the room only had the one entrance, Christine felt the panic of being trapped.

Bellows growled and threw the robe to the floor then turned to chase after her. She darted from him several times then once again she was close enough that he caught her clothes. This time there was the sound of ripping material as she spun away from him. He heard her gasp and his hazel eyes gleamed as he watched her run from him clutching the torn nightgown to her breasts. His energy surged at the sight and he lunged for her. Missing her arm, he managed to catch her dark hair instead and he gave a mighty yank.

Her cry of pain was short-lived as she bumped against the desk once more. Trying to steady herself, she tripped over her own feet then felt herself falling. The candlestick toppled over on the desk then rolled across the smooth top and onto the floor. Suddenly the room was enveloped in darkness as the flame went out.

As she fell to the floor, Christine released one hand from her torn nightgown to catch herself. She felt his hand and, with a hard yank, he ripped the nightgown from her body. The floor was unyielding as she hit it and the breath was knocked out of her when Bellows landed on top of her naked body.

His hand covered her mouth as she gathered her breath to scream while his other hand cupped a bared breast. He fairly purred in delight as he felt the soft flesh.

"I want you, Christine, and now I shall have a taste of you."

In a quick move, his mouth replaced his hand as he kissed her hard. His hips moved against hers and she could feel him hard against her bare flesh. Trying to push him off of her, breathing was made difficult as he bore his full weight on her while his hands roamed freely over her naked flesh. He groaned with pleasure and his kiss deepened with his passion.

As he released her lips, he lifted her head with one hand then let it drop hard against the floor. White shards of pain shot through her head and her hands dropped from pushing at him.

Panting from their struggles, he growled, "Now be still, you will enjoy this!"

His other hand moved between their bodies and he worked quickly to get out of his britches. Sheer panic set in as Christine began to lift her arms to push at him again. Her fingers felt cold metal and she closed her hand around it. The candlestick holder! With all the strength she could muster in her tired body, Christine struck his head with the weapon. He let out a grunt then time seemed to stand still as his body froze. She finally felt relief as he went limp over her.

Pushing him off, she rolled away then stood up. Her breathing was unsteady and shallow as she looked around. She grabbed her torn nightgown that lay on the floor at their feet then she saw the pale color of her robe in the darkness. Slipping on the robe, Christine hurried from the room, leaving Bellows behind.

Having watched the terrible scene, the older Christine felt her body shaking as if chilled. She knew that she was feeling the same fear she had experienced that night almost two years before. The images began to change again and Christine felt a sense of dread wondering where she was going to next.

A sparsely furnished room came into view and Lord Bellows stepped in. He lit the lantern on a small table near the door then turned. A look of surprise appeared on his handsome face when he saw the young Christine Lockhart sitting in the only cushioned chair in the room.

"Why, Angel, you startled me? Had I known you were here waiting, I would have—" he began with a smile and took a step towards her.

"Stop," she stated firmly and lifted a pistol from the folds of her shirts.

His smile quickly disappeared. "Now, Angel, last evening was—"

"Be quiet. Now it is your turn to listen." Waving the pistol to the bed, she added, "Have a seat."

Bellows looked from the pistol to the cold blue eyes before he slowly moved to the bed and sat down.

"Very good. Now I have thought through some of the events that had occurred and correct me if anything I say is in error." She paused and waited for an answer. He nodded in understanding. "It seems to me that some of my classmates are leaving school under the cover of darkness. One day she is here then the next she is gone. Before that, some are despondent. Some cry almost incessantly. All these girls have one thing in common if my memory serves me correctly." She paused again as he smiled at her. "They were homesick."

"Very good, Angel. I always knew you were intelligent," Bellows said smiling. "My sister dislikes you because she knows you could leave at anytime but you will not. You will not leave until your cousin, Caroline, leaves and this is your last year here."

"Your sister has tried in many ways to have me expelled."

"True but your stepfather would arrive and manage to strike a deal, much to my heartfelt gratitude," Bellows said. With a smug smile, he added in a seductive tone, "I want you here."

"I know what you want," Christine said with disgust.

Unconcerned with her attitude, Bellows waved a hand to indicate the room and said proudly, "This is my room when I tell my sister I am away on business."

"Yes, I deduced as much. I found the secret passage through that door behind the tapestry. It leads up to the girls dormitory where you and an unsuspecting girl could slip away unnoticed. Then you take from them—"

"I comforted your friends when they longed for home," he interrupted.

"You stole their innocence," she corrected, narrowing her eyes.

"I stole nothing. I showed them that they were desired here and that they should stay. I provide them with comforting arms and gentle caresses. Each one gave to me freely."

"Gave to you! Like Agatha?" Christine sneered. "Oh yes, she was so infinitely grateful to you that she displayed her happiness one afternoon with that fateful leap of joy. You are such an arrogant bastard!"

"Agatha came by this room unannounced. I have a rule about such visits," Bellows told her.

"My God, she found you with someone else. How many others were there like Aggie? How many have ended up with child?" Christine spat.

"I am not sure," Bellows replied with a shrug of indifference. "As a virile man of a score and ten, I enjoy teaching the pure and untouched."

Christine's brows knitted together as she asked in surprise, "How long have you been comforting young girls?"

He smiled and shrugged. "For quite some time. I only take what is offered, Christine, and the girls understand that."

The urge to pull the trigger of the pistol in her hand was almost overpowering as she listened to the arrogant confidence.

"You are ten and six," he went on to say. "I have found that age to be the most pleasurable." His gaze dropped to her bodice where the tops of her breasts tantalized him and he wanted to feel the soft flesh in the palm of his hand again.

"You are a despicable cad, Lord Bellows," Christine hissed.

He shrugged again, unconcerned. "Since your arrival here, however, I was testing a theory."

"A theory?" she repeated incredulously.

"How often do I need to bed a virgin before she came to be with child?" He spoke without remorse that Christine stared at him for a long moment.

Placing a booted foot on the bed, he rested his arm on his bent knee and waved his hand as he went on to explain.

"You see, lately I did not give one whit about them. My only concern was for you. I wanted to get you with child so that I would be made to do the honorable thing and marry you."

"Quiet," she hissed.

"I know that it would not take long. I could have you—"

"I said quiet!"

"I love you, Angel. You are—

"Stop calling me Angel. I am not your angel nor will I ever be your angel," she growled. Glaring at him as he smiled confidently, she added, "My maidenhood is for my husband as a gift on my wedding night and only then. That man, however, will never be you."

The last three words were spoken slowly with much vehemence that Bellows felt himself losing the battle.

"So I am not good enough for you, Lady Mischief?" Bellows questioned sarcastically.

"You are not good enough for any girl who walks these halls," Christine countered. "However, I will make you this promise. If I hear of any girl crying over the loss of her virtue, or hear of any girl leaving in the middle of the night because of her condition, or hear of you trying to comfort another girl, I will see to it that you meet with an unfortunate accident." In a tone that gave Bellows a chill, she added, "Being Lady Mischief that could easily be arranged."

The young Christine almost smiled when Bellow's smile faltered slightly under the threat. He knew well that she could actually make an accident happen and no one would be the wiser. Staring at her beautiful blue eyes that at the moment were as cold as the gemstone, Bellows knew she would make good this promise.

His attention turned back to her words as she went on to say, "Even after I have left these hallowed halls and I hear any of this happening again, I will come back for you. When you see my face, Lord Bellows, it will be the last thing you ever see."

Dropping his gaze to the floor, Bellows smiled at the feistiness this young woman displayed. That had been what attracted her to him from the beginning. Her daring and total disregard for the structured lifestyle his sister had constructed. It had intrigued him and his sense of adventure.

Seeing the smile, Christine said in a calm tone that she did not feel, "Take a long look about this room for it will be the last time you set foot in it. I am barricading it from the inside as well as blocking the passage. I will periodically check for any tampering. Oh, by the by, there will be traps set should you think to venture back here, so do be careful. One wrong move could very well be your last." Waving with the pistol to the door, she said to him, "Now it is time to part company."

The images faded away once again. Feeling exhausted as if she had traveled the long distances of time on foot, Christine felt herself slip off into blissful sleep. The dark abyss surrounded her before she saw him standing before her. His smile lit up the green eyes she so much adored.

"Andrew," she breathed.

He opened his arms to her and she gratefully stepped into his embrace.

"Green eyes," she whispered. With a sigh of contentment, Christine finally felt safe.

Chapter 14

Maggie looked up from her embroidering and smiled as Andrew entered the bedchamber. He stood at the foot of the bed and watched forlornly as Christine slept.

"She has been quiet for over an hour. Though the fever is still upon her, it is not as high. Perhaps the doctor's serum is finally altering the poison," Maggie told him in a whisper.

"Let us hope so," Andrew replied.

"I can stay a while longer, dear. You should rest and take better care of yourself."

"I cannot rest, Maggie," he said then let out a tired sigh. "I have Bailey preparing a tray for me. You may relax in your room with a tray if you like."

"Perhaps I shall. I would like to finish this section before going to sleep this evening," Maggie told him with a smile. "Stubborn design, I cannot imagine why Christine thought this would calm me."

Andrew looked at the needlework and noted the intricate swirls of the colors for the flowery bouquet. He smiled and thought of the flowers that Christine held as she walked down the aisle to him when they were married. A soft knock broke into his remembrance and soon Bailey appeared with the tray carrying his dinner.

"Have the tray for Lady Lockhart taken to her room, Bailey," Andrew ordered.

"Yes, Your Grace," the housekeeper replied with a slight nod.

"Goodnight, Andrew. Do rest, she will be better soon," Maggie said gently and patted his hand before she turned to leave.

The Duke merely smiled and settled himself into the chair she vacated.

At the sound of the door closing, Andrew moved the chair closer to the bed and took Christine's hand into his. He pressed his lips to the back of it and rubbed his thumb over the spot.

"Do not leave me, Christine. Please do not leave me," he whispered close to her face. With a soft kiss to her lips, he added, "One night and one morning with you is not enough. I married you because I love you and I want to spend the rest of my life with you. I have plans for us, Duchess, many plans and I cannot carry them out alone." Andrew stared down at the still form and let out a long sorrowful sigh. "Please, my love, do not leave me behind."

With his elbows on the bed, he pressed his lips to her hand once again then held her hand in both his. Pressing his forehead against the clasped hands, he prayed that she would soon awaken.

From the doorway, Maggie heard his words and smiled sadly. *He loves her*, she thought to herself. For all of Christine's worrying of ever finding the right man to marry, Maggie was relieved that her daughter had one now who loved her. *Oh Christopher, if only you were here to see*, her thoughts went on. *All has worked well for her. Now for the fever to finally leave her, Christine would truly have the life we had all dreamed of her having.*

Stepping back and quietly closing the door, Maggie decided that she would wait until the morning to sew the blue thread into the design.

In his study, Andrew sat at his desk and stared into the fire. Ignoring the mounting letters and other business awaiting his attention, his gaze shifted to the portrait above the mantel. Maggie had given him the portrait of Christine surrounded by roses as a wedding gift since he had praised it so highly. In truth, Andrew would have paid for the painting because it had captured her mischievous look that would make his heart skip a beat. He drank his brandy as he gazed lovingly upon the portrait.

He was jolted from his musings when the door suddenly flew open and Bailey stepped into the study, unbidden.

"Your Grace," she began but a suppressed sob choked her words and she dropped her gaze from his. "Tis Her Grace," she whispered then covered her mouth with her hand.

"No," Andrew breathed with dread.

He threw himself from his chair and dropped his snifter, unmindful of the stain the amber liquid would leave on the expensive carpet.

Bailey moved to one side as the Duke fairly dashed past her and ran up the grand staircase, taking the steps two at a time. She shook her head and buried her face in her hands to cry in earnest.

Andrew ignored all protocol as he ran down the halls and did not slow down until he reached the door leading into Christine's bedchamber. He threw the door open and stepped inside to find the room brightly lit with a multitude of candles and Maggie sitting in the chair beside the bed, crying.

She looked up and when she saw him, cried harder.

Andrew's eyes shifted to the bed where Christine lay in the center. Her dark hair was a drastic contrast against the stark whiteness of the pillows. Her hands were clasped together and rested on her midsection as she held a single long stemmed rose. The red petals of the flower against the white lace of the bedsheets just over her breasts added the only other color beside the dark hair.

"She is gone, Andrew," Maggie sobbed as he slowly moved to the bed.

The Duke stood beside the bed and gazed down at the still form. A deep sadness crept in as he thought that she looked almost as cold as porcelain china instead of the vibrant young woman he had come to know. He reached out and gently brushed his fingers over her forehead.

"I can help you, Andrew," came Marian's voice from behind him. She touched his arm, making him glance back at her. The soft brown eyes looked imploringly up at him as she whispered, "Let me help you to forget her, my love."

"Go away, Marian," he grumbled in annoyance.

"It would not take me long to make you forget this mistake. I can—"

"Christine was not a mistake. Leave me alone," he hissed.

"Andrew, you can have your mourning period then we can begin again as if this ordeal had never happened," Marian cooed as she pressed her body against him.

With a growl deep in his throat, he pushed her away from him. Grasping her arms when he faced her, he hissed angrily, "Get out of here, out of my life! Christine was everything to me and now she is gone! I do not want to forget her!"

With a start, Andrew sat bolt upright in the chair and looked wildly around. Darkness had fallen leaving only the fire in the fireplace to light the room. Taking a deep breath, he raked his fingers through his disheveled hair and looked to the bed. Christine's lips moved but no words came forth as her mind held her captive within the realms of her delirium. Putting out a hand, he felt the warmth of the fever upon her brow and sighed in relief.

"A dream. Thank heavens it was only a bad dream," he whispered.

Andrew moved from the chair to sit on the edge of the bed and bent down to kiss the warm cheek. "I love you, Christine. Please come back to me," he whispered softly.

Christine woke by slow degrees. She remembered the stabbing pain in her midsection but knew that it was not time for her flow. Prying her heavy eyelids open, the first thing she noticed was the bright sunshine coming in from the open balcony doors. She wondered when the rains had stopped. The balcony should still be wet.

The singsong sounds of the birds and the soft warm breeze filtered in from the balcony. The smell of the roses from the gardens below her balcony drifted up and into her room.

She felt groggy and wondered fleetingly if Doctor Brownlee managed to slip some medication into her during the time she had fainted. She moved her head slowly to face into her room and saw Andrew slumped in a chair next to the bed with his head resting on his hand and his eyes were closed.

She must have made some sound for his eyes snapped open and he was alert to her movements. He rose slowly and moved to the bed still watching her. She smiled up at him and he returned the smile with a look of immense relief.

"Welcome back," he greeted with a huge smile as he sat down on the edge of the bed beside her. He reached for a glass of water and helped her to sip some of it.

"Thank you. That feels much better now," she said and cleared her throat.

She took a few more sips before she turned it away. Helping her to sit up, he adjusted the pillows behind her for support.

She glanced at the open balcony doors and said with a smile, "It turned out to be a nice afternoon for the funeral after all. I am sorry we had to miss it."

"The funeral? Oh yes, the funeral." Andrew stood up and pulled the cord to call for the servants. Sitting back down beside her, he told her gently, "Christine, you have been very ill. The funeral was three days ago."

She stared at him and turned slowly to look at the balcony doors again. The sun shone brightly and the shadows were not long denoting that it must have been midday. Trying to understand, she frowned and looked back at Andrew.

"Three days? What happened?"

"What do you last remember?" he asked.

"The pain," she answered. Her hand moved under the covers to her midsection.

Andrew nodded and explained as gently as he could. "You were poisoned, Christine."

She gasped in wide-eyed shock and her mouth dropped open before she repeated in a whisper, "Poisoned?"

There was a quiet knock at the door and Andrew put his finger up, saying,

"I will explain in a moment."

He stood up and opened the door to beckon Bailey inside. With a wave of his hand to indicate the bed, Bailey looked over and found Christine sitting up with a small smile on her face. The housekeeper's chin dropped in surprise then burst into tears.

"Oh Your Grace, tis so good to see you awake!" She buried her face in her apron and sobbed. Andrew smiled at Christine as she looked at him in alarm.

"Bailey, inform Lady Lockhart that her daughter is awake and prepare something for Her Grace. She will want something to eat," Andrew said firmly. Bailey straightened and nodded as she wiped her face with her apron.

"Yes, Your Grace. I apologize for my behavior."

Andrew put his arm around her as they headed for the door and he said in a soft tone, "I am glad she is awake too."

"You barely slept these past three days," the housekeeper said quietly.

"I will rest better now, knowing she is back with us."

Returning to the bed, Andrew resumed his seat in the chair and took Christine's hand into his. "Forgive Bailey, Christine. She was blaming herself for what had happened to you despite my talks with her."

"Andrew, what did happen to me?"

He explained the events of her first morning as Bailey prepared her breakfast and the delivery of the bottle. He told her how he had insisted that her mother stay at the townhouse and how they took turns staying up with her. He was just finishing with his short narrative when the door burst open and Maggie fairly flew into the room.

"Oh baby!" she exclaimed. Andrew just managed to move away from Christine as she rushed over to her daughter. "I had been so worried. You should have awakened long before now."

"Sorry Mother. I had no idea I was asleep for so long," Christine replied with a smile.

"Asleep?" Maggie echoed derisively. "How do you always manage to belittle something so serious?"

Christine shrugged and gave her mother an impish grin. Andrew shook his head at seeing the playful look and stepped forward to announce, "I will send word to Caroline and David. They would most likely desire an audience with Her Grace tomorrow to see for themselves how she is fairing."

Maggie turned to look at him incredulously making Andrew chuckle lightly. Bailey arrived at that moment with a tray of broth and a glass of water.

"Ah, more broth. Just what the doctor ordered," Andrew said with a smile.

"For today. Tomorrow, Her Grace can have something more substantial," Bailey told him as she placed the tray over Christine's lap.

"This broth is too hot, Bailey. Do you think I can soak in a bath for a while?" Christine asked quietly.

"I have the water heating up for you now. I thought you might like to refresh yourself after your illness," the housekeeper replied.

"Now Christine, do not do too much. You have not been out of that bed for three days. You will be weak," Maggie was saying. Christine looked to Andrew for support but he smiled and held out his hands in surrender.

"Do not look at me, my love. I think I will endeavor to stay out of the way for the next several hours."

Christine rolled her eyes at him making him chuckle lightly. "Coward," she grumbled.

Maggie and Bailey looked from one to the other then put their hands on their hips almost in unison. The sight was Andrew's undoing as he burst into laughter. Christine let out a laugh then tried to hide it behind her hand and coughed when Maggie's blue eyes turned on her. Thoroughly delighted and still laughing, Andrew turned away and went to his room. His smiling gaze met Christine's once more before he closed the door.

The sun was setting when Andrew reappeared by her side. Doctor Brownlee had left just over an hour before, pleased with Christine's recovery and her temperament.

Now she was sitting in a chaise near the balcony doors with Andrew who had his arm draped over the top of the chaise near her head. Since her rooms faced more to the east, they watched the changing colors of the skies.

"Your mother and I will have dinner with you this evening. A table will be set up for us so we can keep you company," Andrew was saying.

"Oh? And you both will be having broth for dinner as well?" Christine asked playfully.

Andrew chuckled as he twirled her hair around his fingers. He glanced over to the fireplace and said absentmindedly, "We will light the fire as well and make it rather cozy in here."

"Cozy? With my mother in the same room?" she teased.

"Of course, or you will make me forget that you are recovering from a serious illness and I will end up making love to you all night."

"Again?" she asked in feigned annoyance.

Andrew burst into laughter at the playful look on her face. She smiled as she remembered the first time she noticed Andrew and his smiling green eyes.

He watched how she seemed to be in trance as she stared intently into his eyes. Unable to resist, he pressed his mouth to hers for a kiss.

"Green eyes," she whispered when he released her mouth after a long moment.

He leaned closer and moved his arms around her to pull her into a deeper kiss. Christine moaned softly against his mouth that Andrew tightened his arms around her. As his lips moved to kiss her throat, she let out a soft sigh of contentment. Loosening her robe, he slipped a hand inside and began to caress a soft breast. When he heard her whisper his name, his mouth crushed hers in a hard and passionate kiss.

The robe fell open and he pushed aside the loose satin bodice of the nightgown to expose the soft mound. He caressed her and let his thumb tease the nipple to a hard nub. Releasing her mouth with a soft smack, he dipped his head lower and took the nipple into his mouth. Christine sighed audibly and arched slightly for him. Slowly moving up to her throat then back to her lips, Andrew covered her mouth with his again and was drawn into a soft sweet kiss that made him ache to make love to her.

Suddenly the door from the hall opened and the two newlyweds quickly drew apart. Maggie stepped in looking at her needlework.

"Christine, this design is absolutely—" she was saying before looking up and seeing Andrew covering Christine.

"Oh my! I am so sorry, my dears," Maggie exclaimed.

She whirled around ready to flee in embarrassment then froze in horror when she realized that she had left the door open as well.

"No, Mother, come in. All is," Christine called out then glanced at Andrew who was smiling before she added, "decent once again."

With her back still turned to them, Maggie shook her head and said, "Andrew, my dear, I truly apologize for my indiscretion."

"Do come in, Maggie," he called out. Then to Christine, he leaned close and whispered, "You make me forget."

With a kiss to her temple, he stood up and beckoned for Maggie to join them as she hesitantly looked over her shoulder.

"I must remember that you two have just been married," she said softly.

Andrew drew her into the room just as Bailey arrived with several footmen carrying a small table and chairs. Behind them, serving maids and more footmen held trays that carried covered dishes.

Once Christine was settled comfortably in the bed with a tray over her lap, Andrew sat with Maggie at the table. With her dinner that looked very much like her noonmeal, Christine looked over at the table to take inventory of their delicious smelling meal.

Bailey laughed softly at seeing Christine's inquiring gaze while Andrew and Maggie were served. Leaning close, the housekeeper said with a hint of mischief in her tone, "Do not fret, Your Grace. Though their meal consists of many nourishing foods, they are all dishes you do not truly like but will eat with some tolerance."

Christine stared at the housekeeper and, with a soft chuckle in her voice, asked, "Who told you that?"

"Florence."

"Florence?" Christine repeated in playful shock. "Mother, your housekeeper is gossiping again."

Maggie shook her head and replied, "Do not say such things of Florence. You know very well that she never gossips." With exaggerated tenderness, she added, "Now, Christine darling, you should eat your dinner before I tell Florence of your malice and she will turn you over her knee just as she did when you—"

"I did not ruin her kitchen. That sack of flour slipped from my hands," Christine exclaimed making Andrew smile. Making a face, she said glumly, "Besides, one cannot eat *my* dinner, one drinks it."

As mother and daughter teased one another in their playful bantering, Andrew noticed that the serving maids and the footmen were having a difficult time maintaining an expressionless face. Bailey did not bother to hide her humor as she laughed behind the hem of her apron.

Chapter 15

It was late in the night as Andrew listened to the sounds in the house. After a few moments of wondering what had awakened him, he heard the grandfather clock at the top of the grand staircase chime twice. He sat up in his large four-post bed and looked around. The fire in the fireplace was the only light in his room as it tried to ward off the night's chill.

He looked to Christine's room and saw no light filtering around the adjacent door. He slowly lay back down when he realized that the tinkling sound was what he heard and it was not the remnants of the clock's chimes. The sound was coming from Christine's room. Getting out of bed, he shrugged into his robe and quietly opened the adjacent door.

Andrew stepped in and immediately his heart jumped to his throat. The light from the fire showed that Christine was not in her bed. His eyes quickly looked around, noting the open balcony doors but he did not see her. His gaze fell on the music box on her bedside table as the dancing couple turned with the music on the carousel.

"Christine," he called out softly.

A sound on the balcony caught his attention and he hurried to the open doors. Standing at the open French doors, Andrew looked down as he heard a muffled sob. Christine was sitting in the corner of the cold stone floor dressed only in her nightgown. She was in a tight ball with her knees drawn up to her chest and her forehead on her knees as she tried to silence her crying.

He bent and pulled her to her feet. Her arms were cold from the night air and she was shivering from the chill. "You will make yourself ill," he scolded lightly as he gently pulled her into her room.

He closed the French doors then pulled her with him to stand before the fire. He grabbed a quilt from the stand that was tucked in a nearby corner and wrapped her up in it.

"What is it, Christine? Why are you crying?" he asked in concern as he rubbed the quilt-covered arms to warm her.

She did not answer but Andrew noticed that the crying was subsiding. He continued to rub her arms for a few moments before she leaned into him.

"It is my birthday," she whispered. "I almost lost everything, Andrew." He drew back slightly to look down at her but she did not raise her chin to look up at him. "My father made me agree to it."

"Agree to what?" he asked.

"I had to marry before my birthday, this birthday, or everything I have goes to Caroline and David. The Meadows, my inheritance, everything. I would only have my title."

Andrew gently pulled her with him to a chair facing the fire and sat down with her on his lap. He carefully tucked the quilt around her as he asked softly, "Why would Christopher do that?"

"Because I," Christine bit her bottom lip and turned her head away from him slightly. "I refused to marry anyone. When Caroline and I finished school and we were making all the plans for her wedding, my father thought that I should marry. He started inviting young lords to dinner."

"Fathers will do that, Christine," Andrew said with a smile.

"You will not do so with our children, Andrew Chandler," she told him firmly.

He warmed at the thought of *'our children'* and she had mentioned it with such casualness that it made him smile.

"I will try to curb my fatherly intentions when it comes to our children, sweet duchess." Christine gave him a sideways that made his smile widen. "But I still do not know why you were crying."

She sighed at the reminder and looked at the fire. "My father and I used to play a game. On any given topic, he would argue the opposing side of whatever I was saying. It did not matter that he agreed or disagreed with the side he took. He told me that it would sharpen my wits, make me analyze the discussion, and find a common ground if there was that possibility."

"Interesting game," Andrew said softly.

"One day, I used our game and brought up the agreement papers. I wanted him to take away the agreement and free me of this deadline. Beforehand, I had analyzed each step and tried to anticipate his next words. It escalated into a real argument, Andrew."

Tears filled her eyes as she remembered it. Andrew rubbed her back and whispered reassuringly, "I am sure he knew that, Christine."

She tightly closed her eyes and bit her bottom lip but still she spoke with a tremble in her voice, "*I* will never know. He died that day."

"*That* was the argument?" Andrew asked in complete surprise. He knew the story that circulated the gossips. The two had been arguing and now he knew why Christine blamed herself for her father's death.

"My God, Christine! It was not your fault. You cannot blame yourself for his death!"

"Yes, I can! I did not want to be forced to a deadline and I chose the topic."

"Sweetheart, you cannot blame yourself," Andrew tried to cajole her but she came off his lap in a flash then whirled on him.

"I had over a year to find someone. I was not trapped like a cornered animal, not yet," she told him firmly. Her blue eyes shone bright with the tears and her cheeks glistened from the glow of the fire as the tears ran down cheeks. "I forced the subject, Andrew!"

He rose to his feet as he realized why she felt that she was to blame. He held out his arms to her but she turned away and was walking past the bed. Andrew thought that she was going back out to the chilly night when she turned at the corner of the bed and snatched up the music box.

Heading back to him, Christine was prying at the bottom of the square box until it snapped off. Tossing the music box back on the bed, she held out the hollowed bottom and Andrew saw a folded paper tucked inside. She jerked her hand towards him indicating that he should take it. Pulling out the folded paper, Andrew read the simple terms of the agreement.

On this date, July twentieth, in the year of our Lord, 1727, the following two parties have sworn into the following agreement without duress, coercion, or physical force.

Lady Christine Lockhart hereby agrees that if she is not properly and legally wed by the age of ten and eight which would be by the date of April eleventh, in the year of our Lord 1729, she would forfeit:

1) All properties and holdings held under her name, specifically but limited to the Meadows inherited from Jacob Graham, Earl of Brasington (also known as Captain Jake Graham);

2) All monies from her trust and future inheritance;

3) All ownership of livery stock, namely the mare given the name Midnight and any foals from her line.

All of the aforementioned will then be transferred to Lord David Huntington and Lady Caroline Huntington.

This agreement is so agreed upon by the undersigned and duly witnessed by the undersigned. This agreement can only be made null and void by the consensual agreement of both parties in writing or by the legal marriage of one Lady Christine Lockhart to an esteemed and respected man of England.

Andrew noticed that both Christine and Christopher Lockhart signed the agreement and that the witness was Lord Alfred Renwicke. Andrew knew Lord Alfred as a highly respected banker as well as a good friend.

He lifted his eyes to meet hers as she waited for him to read the agreement. "This is no longer valid, Christine. You have met the criteria placed on you. You are legally and properly wed."

She stared at him for a moment before the tears fell again, she said quietly, "Yes, I know but he is not here to see the outcome. I miss him terribly, Andrew."

This time when he opened his arms to her, she stepped into his embrace. For a moment, Christine sensed as though she had done that before. She felt as if she had let him hold her and with it came the strong sense of feeling safe.

Lifting her chin so that she looked up at him, Andrew used a corner of the quilt to dry her face and said softly, "Dry your tears and have a happy birthday, Duchess."

She presented him with a sad smile then gave into the kiss he bestowed upon her lips.

A few moments later, Andrew was helping her into her bed. As he pulled the covers over her, Christine said in a whisper, "Andrew, when you asked about any significance my birthday had to what you overheard, I had thought of the agreement."

"That is understandable," he replied as he sat on the bed.

"For just an instant, I thought of David but I could not see why he would want to kill me? He did not even know of the agreement," Christine said.

"No, I do not believe David would be the lord who hired those men. We may never know who he was or why he did this, Christine. For whatever reason he may have had to mark your birthday as some sort of deadline, by the end of this day, he would have failed in his quest. Thus far, the only casualty to show for his efforts was your horse."

"I know. Mother told me that Walter Reynolds put Midnight out of her suffering," Christine said sadly. "My father gave me Midnight. She was one of the last of his gifts."

Andrew took her hand and pressed his lips to the top of it. Softly he said, "Though no other can replace the value of Midnight in your heart, I have many beautiful and spirited mares in my stables here as well as at Kenilworth that could endeavor to match the beauty and spirit of her rider."

Christine smiled up at him and whispered, "You are always so charming, Andrew."

He smiled down at her and gently caressed her cheek with his thumb. "I made no plans to leave the house today. You, sweet Duchess, will be forced to stay by my side until the stroke of midnight."

She was still smiling at him and Andrew was relieved to see the mischievous twinkle in her beautiful blue eyes. "I think I can manage through the day, Your Grace," she replied. Andrew chuckled and stood up to head back to his room. Her voice stopped him as he made to turn away. "Andrew?"

"Yes, love."

"If you go back to your bed, then I will not be by your side until the stroke of midnight."

Christine watched the slow smile appear on his face. He turned fully to face her and asked, "And what does Her Grace suggest?"

She moved under the covers leaving the space on the bed nearest him vacant. Andrew looked at the space then back at her. "You will make me forget that you are recovering."

His heart skipped a beat as she slowly smiled up at him and replied, "I will be sleeping, Your Grace."

Andrew chuckled as he shrugged out of his robe and slipped naked into the bed beside her. He put his arm out and Christine snuggled next to his warm body, resting her head on his shoulder. After a moment, Christine felt the deep rumble of his chuckle against her ear and his voice was deep and thick from emotion.

"Sleep will not be possible for me, sweet Christine."

She lifted her head and, with her lips just a breath from his, she whispered, "Then I suggest that you forget."

Her lips covered his, making Andrew groan as he pulled her over him.

Later that day, Christine was in her sitting room with her mother. Caroline and David stopped by for a visit just as Andrew had predicted. Under the watchful eyes of his parents, young Stephen crawled around exploring his new surroundings.

Andrew entered and announced from the door, "Christine, there is something for you downstairs."

"Downstairs?" she echoed.

"Andrew, have it brought up here. Christine is still recovering," Maggie told him.

He looked past her to Christine and the two smiled as they remembered their night together.

"Actually, it is rather large to carry," he told them and smiled as the statement was met with the desired reaction.

David stood and scooped up his son from the floor while Maggie and Caroline helped Christine to her feet. Andrew grinned at Christine as he took her arm and they followed the others who hurried ahead.

When they rounded the corner and Christine could see over the banister to the foyer below, Andrew's broad shoulders effectively blocked her line of vision until he had her positioned at the top of the stairs just the way he wanted her. Stepping to one side, he moved out of the way and the foyer erupted into a jubilant "Happy birthday, Your Grace!"

Christine looked down to find what seemed to be the entire household staff along with her mother and cousins smiling up or laughing at her stunned expression. Before them on a table was a large white frosted cake beautifully decorated with roses.

"Happy birthday, Christine," Andrew whispered and kissed her crimson cheek. She turned her stunned expression on him making him chuckle. "Let me help you down the stairs. The birthday girl must cut her cake," he told her still laughing.

Huge grins greeted her as she slowly made her way down. Eyeing the cake, Stephen whined impatiently in his father's arms wanting to get down.

Bailey was beaming as Christine stood before the cake and stared at its size. "Happy birthday, Your Grace," the housekeeper said again.

"Bailey, when did the cook have time to make this?" Christine asked.

"The moment you woke up yesterday afternoon, we set to work on this monstrosity," Bailey informed her.

"This will be shared with everyone," Christine said firmly. "I do not see the stablehands but they will have some of this as well."

"Oh do not be so modest, cousin," David said with a grin. "You may look as though you eat like a bird but you can certainly store away for the winter."

Laughter greeted his statement as Caroline scolded him. Christine smiled and gave him a look that promised of getting even with him for the remark. Taking the knife from Bailey, Christine made the first slice amid the applause of the staff.

"I will see to serving everyone, Your Grace," one of the maids told her as she stepped next to Christine and held out her hand for the knife.

"Come, we will sit in the drawing room," Andrew said pulling Christine along.

Settling down on the sofa while holding Stephen on her lap, Christine was given the first piece of cake. Stephen greedily grabbed the square and came forth with his small chubby hand covered with icing and cake.

"Stephen!" Caroline scolded but Christine laughed and waved away her cousin.

"Oh, let him have fun. There will be time enough for him to learn proper etiquette." Christine burst into laughter as Stephen decided that he should share his prize and smeared the gooey frosting over Christine's face.

Caroline was horrified and jumped to her feet to rescue her cousin. "He will ruin your clothes, Christine."

"It is only cake and icing. It will wash out, now go back and sit down. Stephen is doing fi—" Her words were cut off as Stephen's small hand tried to cover her mouth. "Oh really!"

Christine playfully taunted and, with a swiftness that belied her recent illness, she grabbed the messy hand and turned so that Stephen lay on the sofa then began tickling the young boy. He squealed in delight at the attention.

The servants who were still around to watch the Duchess play with the child, laughed and shook their heads at the foolishness. Bailey glanced at Andrew and saw the same adoring look his father had bestowed on his mother many times.

After finishing the cake, Christine opened her gifts that were tucked from sight in a corner of the room. Stephen, still sitting on her lap, proceeded to help her by tearing happily at the paper. Caroline's gift was rose-scented stationary paper.

"Smell," Christine told the toddler then held the paper under his nose. He drew in a deep breath then rubbed his nose.

"Men! Always the critic," Christine scoffed then gave the child a hug.

David gave her a music box. "I know how much you love those things. I think that is a different tune," he told her.

She turned the key one full turn then held it up for Stephen to watch the swan make a circle. Smiling at David, Christine gave her thanks then watched the boy's face as he sat enthralled.

Maggie gave her a broach and matching hairpins. "They were given to me when I turned your age by my mother."

"Oh Aunt Maggie, they are the same as mine," Caroline exclaimed.

"Because your mother and I were twins. The only way we could tell which ones were mine and which were hers was the color. Mine are predominately rubies while your mother's were emeralds."

Andrew reached into his waistcoat and pulled out a box that was undoubtedly jewelry. He handed it to her and stepped back, his eyes never leaving her face. Christine opened the box and found nestled within a pair of ruby earrings in the shape of a rose and a matching necklace. Speechless, she lifted her eyes to meet his as Caroline and Maggie gasped in surprise.

"Good choice, Andrew. They match her broach exactly," David complimented as he compared the colors.

"I know," the Duke said still gazing upon Christine's astonished expression.

"Thank you, Andrew," she whispered.

Maggie looked at him in surprise. "You did not leave the house while she was ill."

Smiling, Andrew answered before she asked her question, "I bought it the afternoon she agreed to marry me."

It was over an hour later that David gathered up his son before he and Caroline bade farewell. Maggie followed Andrew and Christine back up to the ducal bedchambers so that Christine could lie down and rest.

"I will be returning home tomorrow," Maggie announced. "Christine is doing well in her recovery and you do not need me under your feet in your house."

"You are welcome to stay as long as you like," Andrew told her.

"I know and I thank you. However, you two have just been married and need to have time to yourselves. Besides you both lost three days together already and I am just a few moments away if you should need me for a time."

"You do not need an invitation to come by."

"Thank you, Andrew," Maggie said smiling as they reached Christine's bedchamber. "I will go now and begin packing before dinner. Christine, baby, I will have Florence arrange to send the rest of your things here."

"Thank you, Mother."

For the next several days, many friends and acquaintances came by to congratulate the newlyweds and bestow a wedding gift. In tones of concerns, many asked of Christine's recovery from the accident in the park. There were only a few of those 'friends' Andrew knew Christine held dear to her. One afternoon, Peter and Elizabeth brought the children while, at the same time, Caroline and David were visiting with Stephen. Having Chelsea and

Jonathon to follow around, Stephen found the world did indeed have small people like himself. By their departure, all three of the children were close to falling asleep where they stood.

During this time, Andrew stayed at home. He had given her a tour of the townhouse, talked of visiting Kenilworth, and took leisurely strolls through the gardens. Whenever Christine napped, he worked in his study. Often times, she insisted that he continue with his work while she grabbed a book from the library and, in companionable silence, sat with him in his study.

The first time she entered the study and saw her portrait hanging over the mantelpiece, she stopped in mid-stride and stared.

"Your mother gave it to me as a wedding gift," Andrew explained.

"With the smell of the roses around me, I could have sat for hours," she told him as she continued to stare up at her likeness. Then with a short laugh, she added, "It did not take long before it was done."

Chapter 16

Nearly two weeks after they had wed, Christine was firm in her resolve that Andrew resume his presence at the House of Lords as well as any other daily routine he had before gaining a wife. Reluctantly and still disgruntled at the thought of leaving her side, he finally agreed. He attended sessions at the House of Lords and met with Richard and Peter at the club. During his visits at the club, he received many congratulations on his marriage and not once did anyone say a derogatory word about Christine. He did notice several men such as Whiteford who kept their distance.

Andrew was thankful that Marian was still piqued with him and had not returned from her travels. He wondered how long it would take for the news of his marriage to reach her. It would certainly make matters easier for him when he broke off their relationship. He had no desire to have a mistress. In fact, each time he made love to Christine, he prayed that his seed would find fertile ground so that he could delight in watching their child grow within her. A child made from the love he felt for his duchess.

Returning early one afternoon after declining an invitation to the horse races, Andrew stepped into the foyer of the townhouse in time to see Christine dash up the grand staircase, taking the steps two at a time and showing a great deal of her ankles. He stared in disbelief at her energy until she disappeared down the hall towards the ducal bedchambers.

Looking questioningly at the butler, the servant merely announced in an even tone, "Lord Alfred Renwicke is in the parlor, Your Grace."

"Thank you, Parker," he replied.

In the parlor, Lord Renwicke was reviewing some papers when Andrew stepped inside the open double doors.

"Good afternoon, Alfred."

Glancing up over the rim of his glasses, Alfred smiled at the Duke. A man over two score and ten years, Alfred Renwicke was still quick of mind and alert. Age had been kind to him, being of lean build, with watchful brown eyes and graying hair.

"Ah, Andrew, my boy," the elder greeted as he stood up to shake hands. "I was pleased to hear that you married Christine Lockhart. Yours is a very good match, to be sure. She is a good girl and has a business mind that was mainly due to Christopher's influence."

"A business mind is your undoing, my friend. For a woman to have beauty and such a mind, I am surprised that you did not vie for her attentions," Andrew told him with a smile.

Alfred chuckled at the banter and tapped playfully at Andrew's arm. "Had I been a score years younger and not already have a wife, you would have had sound competition from me, you young buck "

"You certainly could have tried to win her from me," Andrew countered. Laughing together, he indicated Alfred's drink and asked, "Shall I refresh that for you?"

"Oh yes, thank you."

Refilling the drink, Andrew looked over at the older man to find him back to reviewing the papers. "What do you have there, Alfred?"

"Some rather distressing news from Christine, I fear."

Handing back his drink, Andrew sat down on the sofa across from Alfred as the banker continued, "It seems that one of my employees has been dishonest with Christine's accounts. Perhaps thinking that he was dealing with a woman who had little understanding of banking, he—"

Christine hurried into the room with bundles of papers in her arms and effectively stopped Alfred from further explanation.

Andrew leapt up to relieve her of the burden as he scolded lightly, "Tell me you did not come down those stairs so heavily burdened. You could have stepped on your skirts and fallen, Christine."

"I moved slowly," she tried to cajole but her breathlessness played traitor to her words. Seeing his admonishing look, she took a deep breath trying to steady her breathing and said, "I was careful, Andrew."

Still with a look of disapproval, he pulled her down on the sofa beside him. She slipped to the edge and explained to Alfred her findings. Andrew sat back with his arm laid across the top of the sofa behind her and listened to their conversation. He was highly impressed with her head of business and admired Christopher Lockhart's foresight to teach his daughter to be independent.

"This distresses me greatly, Christine. Thomas Lakely showed initiative that would have made him a partner in the bank in a few years. In light of what you have shown me, I cannot imagine how his other accounts may appear on the surface."

"I truly hope that my account is the only one he has being tampering with."

Alfred shook his head and pursed his lips showing his disapproval. "Even so, his actions will not be tolerated. If he continues to think that he could tamper with your account, how long would it be before he tampers with other accounts? Especially those of widows who do not have the privilege of knowing what you know and understand."

"I am sorry, Alfred, but ten thousand pounds since my stepfather's death just over a year ago is more money than I care to spend to supplement his income."

"You will see that sum returned, Your Grace, I assure you," Alfred stated firmly.

Andrew arched a brow at the banker's use of her formal title. It meant that Alfred was greatly irritated and embarrassed. His reputation was on the line and he needed to repair the damages in order to redeem himself even though neither Andrew nor Christine placed the blame on the banker. The redemption was for Alfred's own self-esteem and peace of mind.

"May I have these for a few days?" Alfred was asking. "I need to discuss this with my partners before we sit down with Lakely."

"Certainly, you may have them for as long as you need. I trust you implicitly," Christine told him. Andrew smiled to himself for he knew she sensed Alfred's need for redemption as well.

"Oh yes, I had nearly forgotten. Since I was coming to see you," Alfred said and reached into his coat. He pulled a folded sheet of paper from a pocket and handed it to Christine with a smile. "I am certainly glad to return this to you. I believe you will find the proper storage place for it."

Unfolding it, Christine and Andrew found themselves looking at a second copy of the agreement between herself and her father. Andrew looked up to smile first at Christine then to Alfred and said, "I know the perfect place to keep the document where we will always know its whereabouts."

Taking the paper from her, Andrew stood up and headed for the fireplace. Tossing it into the fire and watching it burn for a few moments, he looked back at Christine and Alfred. "We have the other one like it stored in the same place but in Christine's room."

Alfred chuckled at the play of the words and looked at Christine who was smiling broadly. "Very good, then. I can be assured that the papers are in good hands," the banker said still chuckling.

Soon the banker was leaving after neatly tucking Christine's papers into his satchel. After seeing him to the door, Andrew returned to the parlor and closed the double doors. Christine looked up from staring at the now empty table as he sat down beside her.

"I hated to do that. I had hoped that I was wrong but I went over the figures three times," Christine said sadly. She moved closer to him and leaned against him as he draped an arm over her shoulder.

"He had to be told and you did a fine job of it. You are quite the diplomat, my sweet," Andrew praised. "When did you go over your books?"

"Just before we married, the night before as a matter of fact. I had been awake nearly the entire night going over the numbers which left me quite tired when I met with my uncle the next morning."

"Ah that would explain why you shouted at him. You are not one to raise your voice," Andrew said smiling.

Christine grunted in disapproval over her behavior that morning. "You overheard me? How unladylike I must have sounded," she fairly moaned.

Andrew chuckled lightly. "How irritated you were with your uncle's demands," he corrected. "Had you been a man, I suspect that a fist to Jack Hanson's chin would have followed."

Christine laughed and turned to face him. "Had I been a man, we would not be married, Your Grace."

He laughed at her observation, his green eyes twinkling with amusement. "Quite true and I would not be so thoroughly enchanted by your charm."

"My charm? Such a rogue you are, Andrew Chandler," Christine teased.

Her blue eyes sparkled brightly and Andrew found himself drawn in by their hypnotic spell. Leaning closer to her, he pressed his lips on hers.

The next afternoon, Andrew surprised Christine with an outing to the park. The footmen spread out a blanket then placed a cloth-covered basket on the corner of it. Andrew nodded in thanks to the footmen as they stepped away to give them privacy. Helping Christine to settle down on the blanket, they enjoyed the food Bailey had packed for them while they talked, laughed, and watched the children play.

From a distance, he watched them. The fools he hired had presented him with disappointment after disappointment. Somehow he needed to finish this quest to see Christine Lockhart dead. With one last baleful glare at the couple laughing and talking close together, he walked away.

After a couple of hours in the sunshine and having been greeted by many who walked by, Andrew decided that Christine had enough excitement for one day.

"We can enjoy another day in the park. Perhaps have Stephen, Jonathon and Chelsea join us for an afternoon," Andrew suggested.

"That would be wonderful. Thank you for this afternoon, Andrew. It was a splendid surprise," she told him as they gathered everything together.

"You are quite welcome. I am glad you enjoyed this. I certainly did."

Returning to the townhouse, Parker announced to the Duke, "A package arrived while you were out, Your Grace. I took the liberty of placing it in your study."

"Thank you, Parker," Andrew said.

Christine followed him to the study where they saw a small bundle wrapped in plain white paper.

Looking at it from all sides, Andrew frowned, "No name."

"Perhaps it is inside," Christine suggested as she poured him a brandy.

With a shrug, Andrew tore the paper and opened the lid from the box. Christine joined him with his drink in hand and was handing it to him when he growled and slammed the box down on his desk.

"What is it?" she asked startled at his reaction.

Before he could comment, she picked up the box and gasped at the number of pound notes found inside. On top was a handwritten note, *payment as agreed – £1,500 — the proof was more than adequate.* Lifting the note, she found a small piece of linen that was stained with what appeared to be droplets of blood.

Andrew muttered a curse then watched in disbelief as Christine slowly lifted her gaze to meet his. The reference to the money and the token proof of her lost maidenhood reminded her of the wager and why she was determined not to marry.

"No, Christine, I would not do such a thing," Andrew exclaimed as the blue eyes turned cold.

Without a word, she turned away but he would not have her thinking that he had any part of the ridiculous wager. Grabbing her arm, Andrew turned her roughly to face him so that he could try and convince her. The slap across his face startled him.

Stunned, he stared at her for a moment. "If you truly believe that I would do something like this to you, then you have learned nothing of me these past weeks," he said in a quiet tone, his anger barely held in check.

"Release me," she hissed through clenched teeth. When he let her go, Christine turned on her heels and stormed from the room.

Andrew stood and stared after her. Turning slowly to glare at the package that had ruined an excellent afternoon, he picked up the scrap of bed linen. It certainly looked like the design from her bed. The muted sound of a door slamming upstairs broke the thoughtful trance. Grabbing the box in the other hand, he walked out of his study and went in search of Bailey.

Christine slammed her door and sat heavily on her bed. *Duped! Is there no one I can trust?* Unable to sit still, she threw herself from the bed and began pacing the floor. She could not believe that Andrew would be a part of this. *Could he be that callous?*

She growled deep in her throat as the circumstances of why they married came to mind. This was not a marriage based on love. Though she was in love with him, she knew that not once had he mentioned anything about love whenever they were alone. He called her sweet, his sweet Christine or his sweet duchess. *What did that mean? Anything? Nothing?* He had a mistress though she was not in London at the moment. Yet, most everyone knew that Lady Sanders could not bear children because of the accident that claimed the life of her late husband. She could give Andrew everything he needed except heirs. Now as his legal wife, that was something Christine was expected to provide. *How could I have forgotten that fact?*

With another growl, Christine threw herself face down on the bed and slammed her fist into the decorative pillow. "I do not know what to think anymore," she hissed to the empty room.

Sometime later, Mary entered with a tray of tea and some cakes. Christine stood at the balcony and did not turn to acknowledge the maid. Quietly, the girl left not sure of what to do. A few hours later, Bailey entered when there was no answer to her knocks to find Christine sitting in the chaise lounge with her eyes closed. Looking at the tray, the housekeeper found it untouched.

"Has His Grace returned?" Christine asked with her eyes still closed.

"Not yet, Your Grace," Bailey answered quietly.

Christine exhaled forcibly and slumped further in her chaise.

"Your Grace, would you like to have dinner in your sitting room or shall I have a tray brought up for you in here?" the housekeeper ventured to ask when there was a long silence.

Without opening her eyes, Christine answered in a tone that held an edge of anger, "When I am hungry, I will call for you or Mary."

"Yes, Your Grace," Bailey acknowledged then turned sadly away. Instead of opening the door, the housekeeper turned to face Christine and said, "That piece of cloth is not a design of any of my linen, Your Grace. I was able to account for all of my linens and none of them are torn or cut away."

Christine opened her eyes and stared at the housekeeper. Meeting the gaze without another word for a moment, Bailey then turned to the door and headed out.

At the club, Andrew found Peter talking with several gentlemen on the far side of one of the rooms. With his irritation and anger riding high, he walked up to Peter and maneuvered him away from the discussion.

"Do you have any idea who the bastard is, or was, that started the damned wager?" Andrew growled.

Peter stared at him in wonder and asked, "Why? What happened?"

Andrew withdrew the note from his pocket and the piece of cloth. Peter's mouth dropped in astonishment and asked, "Did Christine see this?"

"Yes, damn it, she did."

"And?"

"And?" the Duke echoed angrily. "And she thinks I am being paid as requested. What the hell do you think?"

"Christine believed this? That you would do this?" Peter asked in surprise.

"Peter, do you know who he is or not? You were the one who heard of this to begin with."

"No, Andrew, I have no idea who the bastard is. I wish I did. This is going too far."

Annoyed that he could not face the man, Andrew grunted as he glanced around the room and noticed that most of the men in the club were in this room. Taking a deep breath to calm his anger, he called out loudly, "Excuse me, gentlemen. May I have your attention for a moment?"

When the room was silent and more men stepped into the room to see what was going on, Andrew announced, "This afternoon a package was delivered to my home. In it was this."

He withdrew the money from another pocket and heard Peter mutter a curse. Holding up the pound notes, he fanned them out to show that the entire bundle did contain money.

"I do not care who you may be to have sent the fifteen hundred pounds because I bedded Christine Lockhart. She is my wife now, the Duchess of

Kenilworth and I will not tolerate disparaging remarks made about her," Andrew said, his anger evident. "As to this money, I certainly hope that whoever you are, you have enjoyed your fun. However, I do not care to play this pitiful game of yours."

The room burst into muttering discussion as Andrew threw the money into the fireplace. The flames licked at the corners then greedily swallowed up the bits of paper.

Glaring at the crowd and watching for any signs that would reveal the perpetrator, Andrew said over the hushed whisperings, "Nor do I have need of your money."

Turning on his heels, Andrew stormed from the room. Talk broke out at once while Peter watched the Duke angrily leave the club.

The chimes from the grandfather tolled ten as Andrew stood at the foot of her chaise lounge looking down at the sleeping woman. She had not bothered to change into her nightgown or even crawl into her bed. According to Bailey, she had not left her rooms and had refused to eat.

Until a short time ago, Andrew had been with Richard. Since he was not at the club, Andrew had gone to his friend's townhouse and paced like a raging bull as he told Richard about the day. He explained how he was too angry to return home.

"I do not want to take this anger out on Christine. I want the bastard who sent the money," Andrew had told Richard.

"Who could the man be? I was beginning to think that wager was just more malicious talk. I cannot believe that someone would actually send you fifteen hundred pounds," Richard had said in amazement.

Andrew stayed and talked with Richard as the two eliminated only a few people they were sure would not have sent the money. The remaining faces and names were astounding and the two ended up merely shaking their heads that the man could not be discovered.

Now back in his own home, Andrew gazed upon the woman he loved and wondered if he could win her back. The streaks on her face showed signs of crying and he understood the heartache she felt. When she slapped him, his heart sank and it had yet to be revived. With a deep sigh, he quietly walked out of her room then went downstairs to his study where he planned to get drunk.

It was nearly midnight when Christine awakened and decided to dress for bed. She had waited for Andrew, listening for his return. She looked to the adjacent door but no light indicated that anyone was within. She crawled into bed and was about to blow out the candle when she looked to the door once again as a thought struck her. If he had returned and gone to bed, no light would be seen.

Getting out of bed, Christine carefully carried the candle across the room to the door. She knocked then listened for any sound. After a second knock, she slowly opened the door. The room was empty. She leaned against the doorframe and looked dejectedly at the floor.

The rumbling of her empty stomach seemed very loud. She had not eaten since the picnic so she decided that she would sneak into the kitchen to find something to eat. With one last unhappy look into Andrew's room, Christine turned back into her room and slipped on her robe. Carefully shielding the flame of her candle with her cupped hand, she headed down the hall.

Going through the quiet house since everyone had gone to bed, Christine turned at the bottom of grand staircase for the kitchen found at the back of the house. The light under the door to Andrew's study caught her attention, making her slow her pace. Stopping at the double doors to listen, she heard the soft tinkling of glass then the heavy thud of something being placed back down.

Slowly she opened one of the double doors and peeked inside. A fire blazed in the fireplace and the lamp was lit on the desk. Stepping further into the room, Christine found Andrew staring down at the fire with one arm extended out to the mantelpiece. He held a drink in his other hand from which he drank down a good portion. He was devoid of his waistcoat and vest, which she noticed were draped over the chair at his desk.

"Andrew?" she called out quietly as she took another step into the study.

He straightened slightly before he turned slowly to face her. His green eyes flickered over her as she stood before him and he thought that she was poised to run. The look on her face revealed apprehension as she watched him closely.

"Come in, Christine," he said quietly then turned away to look at the fire once again.

Closing the door then moving further into the room, Christine walked to him cautiously. "I was waiting up for you but I fell asleep."

Raising a brow, Andrew turned to her again and asked, "And why would you be waiting up?"

Christine dropped her gaze not wanting to see the suspicious look he gave her. To the floor, she answered softly, "I wanted to apologize for striking you."

The reminder of her slap made his cheek twitch as if the sting was just ebbing away. He resisted the urge to rub the spot and took a drink of his brandy while watching her over the rim.

"I did not give you an opportunity to explain," she was saying.

There was a long silence and she bit her bottom lip before she whispered, "I will leave you alone now."

She turned to leave but he stopped her by saying, "I have no clue who the man is, Christine, or why he chose to send the money other than to play out his silly game. All of London has known for weeks that we have been married."

With her back still to him, she merely nodded and took another step to the door. Andrew went on to say, "I did not keep the money and right now I hope he is in his own home bristling that I would be so callous as to burn fifteen hundred pounds."

Stunned at the news, Christine turned around and asked incredulously, "You burned the money?"

"Yes, at the club where Peter had first heard of that wager. I believe it was someone there who began the ridiculous wager so I wanted to let him see that I did not care for it. I did not marry you or bed you for the damned money," Andrew told her.

"I know. I realized that once my," she paused for an instant, "shock and anger subsided. By then I had struck you and not given you a chance to say anything in your defense." She held up a hand when Andrew started to speak and said, "You have nothing to defend, Andrew. That was a bad choice of words. Again, I apologize."

Placing his drink on the mantel, he smiled slightly. Facing her, the smile was gone as he said quietly, "Come closer." When she was within reach, he pulled her to him and hugged her tightly. "Christine, I want to call him out for being such a cad but I cannot and that angers me all the more."

"Call him out?" she repeated looking up at him with astonishment.

"Yes, call him out. I am one of three men in your life who has that right according to you, as I recall, and I damned well wanted to exercise that right," he told her.

Dropping her gaze to his chest, Christine remembered her words from the day she found out about the wager while at the Hunnicutts. Now she wondered at Andrew's skill with weapons if he had managed to find who the man was and call him out.

As if reading her mind, Andrew lifted her chin so that she was looking up at him again and he said with a smile, "I am a good shot and quite skilled with the sword."

Surprised that he would notice her uncertainty, she opened her mouth to speak but his mouth covered hers in a kiss. Glad that he was back and safe from all harm, she responded to the kiss. Her arms rubbed his back as she held on to him and she could not think of anything else except for the love she felt for him.

Andrew groaned as he deepened the kiss. Her response aroused him but he did not want to take the time to go upstairs. Instead, he reached between them with one hand to untie the robe then he quickly slipped the robe from her shoulders.

She broke from the kiss and, with a muffled laugh, asked, "Andrew? Here?"

He smiled then kissed the tip of her nose. "Yes, here."

She laughed softly then lifted her lips to his. Andrew was elated at her subtle acquiesce and slowly lowered her with him to the floor and the thick carpet before the fire. His hands caressed her over the satin nightgown as she lay beneath him by the warm fire and his kiss seemed to devour her as his tongue explored her mouth.

No longer able to contain himself, Andrew knelt beside her and removed his clothing. He smiled as Christine pulled the hem of her nightgown up her legs then higher until she was pulling it over her head. The pace of his heart quickened as his gaze flickered over her naked body in the firelight. Finished undressing, he moved over her and she opened to receive him. The love they made took their breath away and both soared high in its rapturous spell.

It would be another hour and another blissful trip to euphoria before the Duke led his Duchess upstairs to her bedchambers where he loved her throughout the remainder of the night.

The next morning Christine woke slowly and looked to the empty side of the bed. Andrew had already left her side having awakened several hours before. Smiling, she stretched then felt the familiar aches of her monthly time. With a groan, she sat up in the bed and looked to the adjacent door leading into Andrew's room.

"Now a time for abstinence. For me anyway," she mumbled to herself so that Mary did not hear. Since Andrew had been so attentive and so virile with his new bride, Christine could not dampen the disappointment that he would be like other husbands. Andrew would have his heirs. He would have his mistress to soothe him while his 'sweet Christine' was big with child and unable to take care of his needs adequately.

"Mary, I will soak in the tub for a while longer this morning. Please be sure that enough hot water is available," Christine told her maid while getting out of bed and heading for the bath.

"Yes, Your Grace," the young girl replied and hurried to inform Bailey of the additional water.

Stepping into the warm scented water and sliding down into its soothing depths, Christine closed her eyes and sighed as her mind drifted. Now they have come to the reality of all marriages—husbands, mistresses and all with the turned away glances of society.

"Why the long face, sweet duchess?" came Andrew's voice nearby.

With a startled gasp, Christine opened her eyes to find Andrew crouched down at the foot of the tub with his arms folded over the rim and his chin resting on his arms. He was smiling at her and his green eyes twinkled in merriment.

"Merciful heavens, Andrew! Must you frighten me so?" Christine grumbled but she had to smile in spite of her mood.

"Sorry, my sweet, I was just admiring the view."

She laughed lightly as his gaze dipped down to her breasts. Flinging droplets of water at his face with her fingers, she asked in feigned annoyance, "Must I teach you to knock?"

"Why? It is my house," he replied with a grin. "Actually, it is our house but why waste the energy? I must conserve every ounce to please my duchess."

Christine gasped again but in shock at his obvious reference making Andrew burst into laughter. With a look of pure innocence in her blue eyes, she said with an impish grin, "Then I have the unpleasant task of informing His Grace that he will have ample time to store up such energy over the next week."

For an instant, Andrew looked at her questioningly until the understanding dawned on him. "Ah well, it was definitely fun while it lasted," he said with a sigh as his eyes drifted down to the soft body under the water. Christine felt the pain heavy in her chest and could have screamed.

Unaware of her misgivings, Andrew smiled and lifted his green eyes back up to meet hers. "However, to renew our interludes after a short wait would be glorious to say the least."

Still eyeing her as he stood up, Andrew moved to the side of the tub and crouched next to her. He ran a long finger along her chin causing her to tremble. With a seductive gleam that made his green eyes shine like emeralds, he added softly, "Be warned, Duchess, that when you have finished this monthly calling, you should be well rested for I will have more than enough energy stored to overwhelm you the moment I am given the opportunity."

"You think that you would not be left wanting?" Christine asked somewhat suspiciously.

"During this natural process of womanhood, I would certainly be wanting but having met a certain blue-eyed duchess, I know that I need to just bide my time until I can receive such favors that only she can give me."

"You are a strong man, Andrew Chandler, to have such," Christine paused for an instant before saying, "control of your needs."

Andrew chuckled thoroughly amused with the playful banter and leaned forward to press his lips to hers. Just before he kissed her, he whispered, "You are well worth the wait, sweet Christine."

Pleased for the moment, Christine lifted a wet hand to his cheek and opened her mouth to his urging. Time stood still for the lovers who expressed their love for the other through the kiss. Chattering from Christine's bedchamber prompted the kiss to end. Reluctantly, Andrew moved away and, with a tender look in his eyes, he stood up.

"I will be in my study should you need me." His deep rasping voice was hoarse from the emotions stirred up by the kiss. Christine nodded and watched him as he left the bath chamber.

Nearly an hour later, dressed and ready for the day, Christine sat before her mirror and looked herself over with a critical eye. When Andrew spoke to her earlier, her mood lightened and she felt better. Yet when he left, the doubts crept back in. She could not chase away the thought of him with Marian Sanders whenever he needed the intimacy.

"Is there anything else I can do for you, Your Grace?" Mary asked as she made the bed.

The blue eyes shifted to the young maid in the mirror. "No, Mary, thank you. I will be out of your way in a moment," Christine replied with a smile. The young girl returned the smile and went back to her task.

Greeting each servant as she walked by, Christine went into the dining room for breakfast. Bailey smiled at her as Christine took her seat to the right of Andrew's.

"His Grace has been waiting for you. I will let him know that you have come down."

"Thank you, Bailey."

A few moments later, Andrew joined her for breakfast of mixed fruit, juice, muffins, and hot cereal. Bailey set down a cup of hot tea for the Duke and a cup of hot chocolate for the Duchess.

"Is something wrong, Christine?" Andrew asked when Christine did not contribute much to the conversation.

She shook her head and continued to eat her muffin. Andrew reached out and brushed aside a stray lock of hair as he leaned forward. "Are you feeling the confinement of being inside all day?"

"Some," she replied quietly, looking up at him briefly before returning her attention to her breakfast.

He smiled then remembered their conversation earlier. "Is there something special you require during your monthly times? Something Bailey and Mary needs to be aware of?" Christine looked up when he said teasingly, "Do you snarl like a wild animal and crave raw flesh?"

The remark along with the face he made got a soft laugh from her and Andrew smiled. "There is my sweet duchess."

"No, there is nothing special I need but I suppose I am just tired of being inside all day."

"I think we could go out in the afternoons to the park since you enjoyed being out yesterday."

Her eyes lit up at the possibility making Andrew smile. "Yes I see we have an agreement. Very well, a few hours at the park each day we will do."

"Thank you, Andrew."

"Hmm, you are more than welcome, my sweet. I sent a note out to the Hunnicutts and your cousins to join us this afternoon for tea. Your mother requested to be here so I thought that you might like the company of friends."

Christine's face showed her pleasure at the surprise. "Oh Andrew, really?" she asked smiling happily.

"Oh indeed. You have been a very good patient for the doctor, took your medicine." Leaning forward, he whispered, "Took care of me."

Christine gasped at his lewdness and slapped at his arm playfully. He chuckled in amusement as he sat back and continued with his breakfast. His green eyes twinkled as he watched the blush spread over her cheeks.

Sapphire eyes met emerald ones and, with an impish grin, Christine whispered, "My pleasure, Your Grace."

Andrew burst into laughter.

Chapter 17

That afternoon, Elizabeth and Peter joined Christine and Andrew for tea along with Maggie, Caroline and David. They were surprised to see that Abby had accompanied Richard as well.

Andrew smiled as he watched Christine enjoying herself with her friends and looked for any signs of fatigue since she was still recovering from having been so ill weeks before. After the near fiasco the day before, he was sure he had lost her but her appearance in his study last evening had been like an answer to his prayers. He was falling deeper in love with her as the days went by.

He was jolted from his musings as Abby turned slightly in her seat to look at him.

"To be spirited away in the middle of the night and married in secret! Oh how romantic!" she exclaimed.

"Abby, love, if it is the romance you hope for, then I suggest that we forget our families' wishes and elope as well," Richard told her grinning.

"Oh my God! If only I was sure that my mother would not kill us for the deed! She is making over this whole affair in hopes of outshining Winifred's wedding last fall."

"Well at least the flowers for your wedding will be in bloom," Christine muttered behind her teacup but loud enough for all to hear.

"Oh Christine, that was a cruel remark," Maggie scolded.

Christine merely lifted a brow at her mother but Elizabeth put in with a dismissive wave of her hand, "Not if you knew what Winnie tried to do to outshine Lady Mischief at school."

Christine and Caroline shared a quick and knowing look before the two looked at Maggie. With great effort, the cousins tried to hold down their grins when they saw Maggie slowly closed her eyes. With her loud exhale of exasperation, Maggie nearly caused the two cousins to laugh aloud. Caroline choked slightly on her tea while Christine found a great deal of interest in the fire blazing in the fireplace.

"I had hoped to never hear of that name again! Going to that school changed you and I am sure it was because of your Lady Mischief," Maggie grumbled.

"Lady Mischief made the years bearable, Lady Margaret. Without her, I doubt if I could have survived. I missed her in my last year since she was one year ahead of me," Abby replied looking at Christine who gave her a small smile.

Maggie groaned as if she was feeling some small inner pain. Elizabeth bit her bottom lip to maintain her straight face while Abby carefully looked over the pastries before her.

Though the men could not see the playful grin on her face, Abby's tone held the laughter in check, "I would bet, Andrew, that had you known of Christine's escapades while in school, you would have reconsidered this duchess of yours."

"Oh Abby," Maggie admonished but it was ineffective because she started to laugh lightly. "Please do not bring up those memories of the past."

"It is all right, Mother. What would Andrew do now but lock me away from society," Christine said grinning. She then turned an impish grin on her husband and asked sweetly, "Would you do that, Your Grace?"

Grinning, Andrew opened his mouth to speak as all eyes turned to him but Christine held up her hand and said quickly, "It does not matter now. He is burdened with me and there is nothing to do for it." She shot him a mischievous look that made Andrew's blood stir.

"That you would play instead on concentrating on your studies as you should have," Maggie admonished.

"Oh, Aunt Maggie, Christine did not need to study. After the beginning of our second year, everyone in school knew it."

There were ill-disguised grins and stifled laughter from the women who shared the one year together at the finishing school.

"Do not just sit and laugh! I am just dying to hear. Give over!" Richard exclaimed making the women, except Maggie, laugh aloud in amusement.

"I truly wish you would not encourage her so," Maggie grumbled.

"Christine was dubbed Lady Mischief at school because one never knew when to expect some comical mishap. There would be leaves held by a net over the back stoop and whenever some girl thought to sneak away from a class, the leaves would unceremoniously be dumped from the net," Abby began.

"The opening of the door would loosen the tie that held up the leaves.

Suddenly the girl was showered by them and screamed that the insects were among them and in her clothes," Caroline finished.

"There was another time when Christine covered the knocker in the large clock in the foyer so that it could not be heard to toll the hour. Lady Bellows was very strict of her schedule and if we were late for dinner, we had to stand very straight on the grand staircase for what seemed like an eternity. After one of those lessons, my back would ache so much that it even hurt to finally sit down," Elizabeth said making the men chuckle.

"So you have been a bad girl, Christine?" Richard chided with a grin.

Maggie made a sound that Christine looked up and said, "It is in the past, Mother. I do not do such childish things." She tried to speak without the hint of laughter but the word 'childish' made Elizabeth and Abby nearly choke that Christine almost lost her own battle.

"When you have a daughter in finishing school, you will understand my anxiety over your education," Maggie told her.

"It was Christine who taught Lady Bellows a great deal of things. The most important lesson was to never underestimate a young girl's previous schooling," Elizabeth told her.

"Exactly, remember the time when Christine was found with the answers to the final exam?" Abby asked.

Elizabeth corrected her. "That was not true, Abby. Anne put those answers in my things but somehow Christine found out."

"Oh I know that, Lizzie. You even thought that Christine was about to put the answers in your belongings as a prank," Abby said.

"I know," Elizabeth replied quietly.

Christine reached out and patted Elizabeth's arm. "When are you going to stop berating yourself? I understood what you thought the moment you caught me."

"You did not even try to explain," Elizabeth told her.

Abby and Caroline looked at one another for they had heard this many times before. Christine smiled gently and said, "It would not have made a bit of difference to you then, Elizabeth. You would not have believed me so I had to let you find out on your own."

"Is this the instance you told me of the time Christine saved you from being expelled?" Peter asked.

"I had no idea Anne Lucas was so cruel," Elizabeth said and looked at Christine as she muttered something under her breath. Not wanting to have it repeated, Elizabeth ignored the reaction and answered her husband. "Yes,

Peter, this is the circumstance around it. Anne was angry with me because I received a small shipment of chocolates specially ordered by my mother. It is a tradition from my mother's side of the family that the candy arrive in the last semester before graduation. At any rate, there was not enough to share with everyone so I shared them with my closest friends. Anne thought that because I shared with three of her friends, I should have shared with her. She confronted me one afternoon near the stables when the other teachers were not present but I would not be bullied by her tone and pushed her so hard that she fell in a haystack."

"She should have been grateful that it was only hay," Caroline interjected grinning as she remembered the confrontation.

"In retaliation for what she deemed an embarrassment, she tried to have me expelled from school. Somehow Christine learned of her plans and was pulling the answers from my belongings when I came in and found her. All I saw was Christine with something in her hands and among my things but before I could ask her what she was doing in my room, Lady Bellows came in claiming a surprise inspection."

"Oh Lady Bellows loved to surprise us with inspections. She was sure we had men hiding in our armoires," Abby put in.

"Would you have hidden me away in your closet?" Richard asked with a wink.

"Of course, my darling, but the rule was anything hidden was shared with the other girls in the room," Abby replied sweetly.

Richard put a hand to his heart and said with an air of great sacrifice, "I think I could have survived such an ordeal."

"Careful, Richard, I would not accept so quickly," Christine warned. "You did not see Abby's roommates."

Everyone laughed as Abby swatted at her friend in feigned indignation.

"So it was Christine who was caught with the answers instead of you?" Peter asked going back to the story he had yet to hear in its entirety. "What was Anne's reaction to the spoiled game plan?"

"She was right behind Lady Bellows, of course," Abby said and made a face. "She was more pleased with the outcome. She thought, as we all did, that Christine was done for."

"When Uncle Christopher came for Christine, the three of them were in Lady Bellows' office for over an hour," Caroline began taking up the story. "Mrs. Wright, the strictest and hardest teacher at the school, was strongly urged to join them."

"The end result was that my stepfather made a bargain with Lady Bellows. He affirmed that I was intelligent enough to take the exam right then and knew I would pass it. Keep in mind that I was only in my second year and the exam was difficult enough for one who had studied the full four years," Christine told them.

"And you passed it because you had the answers," Peter tormented.

"I did not take that one because that was Lady Bellows' reasoning. So my stepfather told her to make another exam. That was when Mrs. Wright was called in. Between the two of them, a new exam was made."

"So you passed that one?" Richard asked.

"It was an exam Mrs. Wright gives to the graduating students. Christine passed it in the middle of her second year with only five wrong answers. No one had passed that exam before with less than twenty wrong answers," Elizabeth exclaimed.

Christine looked at her in surprise and Elizabeth went on to explain, "Mrs. Wright took great pleasure in elaborating on that fact. Challenged any girl to do better than you."

"When we received the same challenge, she was still praising you," Abby announced before sipping her tea.

"If I remember correctly, you had another exam to take, did you not?" Elizabeth asked Christine who nodded. "It was the hardest one of all because Lady Bellows called in all the teachers," Elizabeth said looking around at the listeners. "My class was the first to take this new final exam besides Christine, replacing the exam of which Christine had the answers."

"Causing trouble even then, Tee?" Peter asked with a wink.

"Of course," Christine replied with a grin. "How else was I supposed to spend my day?"

"Ah, yes," Richard teased with a finger in the air. "Since you passed the exams, what more was there for you to learn? You could have left early."

"I could have but decided to stay because Caroline was still there," Christine replied. "Because I stayed, Lady Bellows had to make an example of me."

Maggie let out a long sigh and stood up to pace in annoyance. "An example! One I certainly would not have agreed to had Christopher allowed me to accompany him."

"It was not that bad, Mother. Think of what I gleaned from my so-called punishment," Christine said with a grin. Looking at the men, she stated proudly, "Since I did not need the lessons that Lady Bellows' curriculum offered, I had to wake up before all the girls and help in the kitchen. During the meals, I served them."

Peter's mouth dropped open and his eyes widened in horror. "The future Duchess of Kenilworth was a serving maid?" he asked incredulously.

"Did Andrew know then that I was to be his duchess? For that matter, did I know I would have been Duchess of Kenilworth?" Christine asked looking at him. "Besides, Peter, just where did you think I learned to make that crumb bread you like so much?"

"From Maggie," Peter said firmly.

"Me? In the kitchen?" Maggie exclaimed in feigned horror.

"Back away, Peter, while you still have some skin left from challenging the women," Richard whispered loudly.

Catching Christine's grin, Richard winked at her then turned an innocent look to Andrew when he was caught playing with the Duchess.

"I think the best breakfast I had ever experienced while at school was the morning Christine served the pot of porridge over Anne's head for tormenting Caroline. I will never forget the expression on Anne's face when the gooey mix ran down over her eyes," Abby said with a teasing look.

Everyone laughed while Maggie unsuccessfully tried not to smile.

"Christine, you were incorrigible even then," Andrew said jokingly and winked at his wife.

"I am sure Lady Bellows was very glad to see me graduate," Christine said with a grin to him.

"She certainly was," Abby said. "She allowed us an extra hour to settle in after the summer holiday."

The women laughed as they remembered Lady Bellows' stringent time schedule. There was no room for extra time.

"If Lady Mischief made school bearable, then I cannot even imagine how you survived without the pranks and to think that the poor girls after you would never have known such fun could have existed," Caroline said to Abby with a laugh.

"Goodness, how did you not hear?" Abby asked incredulously.

"Hear what?" Christine asked looked at her over the rim of her cup.

"Oh my word, Lizzie, they never heard about what happened!" Abby exclaimed.

"Abby, hear what?" Caroline asked, repeating Christine's question.

"The scandals that disgraced Lady Bellows and closed down her school," Abby told them.

Christine and Caroline stared at her then at each other in surprise. "Scandals?" they repeated almost in unison.

"Yes, the first scandal happened in the middle of the fall after you two graduated. One of the girls claimed that Lord Bellows was the father of her child," Elizabeth began.

Christine choked on her tea and coughed hard. Since Elizabeth was the closest to her sitting on the couch, she pounded lightly on Christine's back. Caroline took the china cup from Christine and carefully placed it on the table before them.

"My goodness, Christine, are you all right?" Elizabeth asked in concern. Christine only nodded and waved away everyone as they moved to help her. Andrew brought her a glass of water and, with watery eyes, she smiled her thanks.

"Christine and Lord Bellows never got along," Abby explained to Elizabeth. "Even in her last year at school, it seemed like Lord Bellows could strangle Christine if she even stepped into a room he happened to be in."

"He used to tutor me with my French when Christine was busy," Caroline put in.

"He helped many girls with their studies," Abby said with a nod.

"What happened to the girl?" Christine asked hoarsely. Clearing her throat again, she sipped at the water.

"My goodness, we might have known her, Christine. Did we know her, Abby?" Caroline asked in astonishment.

Abby nodded and said quietly, "Yes, it was Tilly."

"Tilly?" Caroline asked in complete surprise while Christine stared at Abby.

"Tell the story in order, Abby, just as it happened so they understand it in the end," Elizabeth told the younger woman.

"I remember Tilly. She was always so timid, so quiet," Caroline said almost in a whisper. She drifted back in her mind to a young girl who followed them around like a small puppy, who whispered when called on by the teachers, and seemed as scared as a rabbit. "Tilly would never lie and most certainly not about that."

"Well, Lady Bellows insisted that she was lying because her brother was away on business during the time Tilly was supposed to be with him. When Tilly's family came for her and demanded an investigation, it turned out that Ian was accused of—" Abby was saying.

"*Ian?*" Christine fairly shrieked.

"The stableboy, Ian?" Caroline asked and received a nod from Abby. "My God, Christine, you were up with him all hours of the night setting your pranks up for the next day."

"You were with this boy?" Maggie demanded.

"Yes, Mother."

"My goodness, he could have—" Maggie was saying, starting to get upset.

"No, he could not have," Christine stated angrily.

The rebuke on Maggie's lips froze at the tone from her daughter and the room grew quiet instantly.

Christine closed her eyes and rubbed her forehead in irritation. "Sorry, Mother. Please Abby, what happened next?" she demanded quietly.

Abby looked at Elizabeth then at Maggie before beginning again in a tentative voice, "Well, Lady Bellows had Ian impressed into the British Navy and—" She halted in her tale as Christine opened her eyes and her eyes flashed to a steely blue.

"Impressed?" Christine asked quietly.

When Abby nodded and Christine exhaled angrily, Elizabeth ventured to ask, "What do you know, Christine?"

Turning to Elizabeth, she nearly hissed, "Ian could not swim."

"What does that matter after the misery he caused that poor girl?" Maggie grumbled.

"He did nothing to that girl nor to me or to any other girl," Christine retorted through clenched teeth. "Lady Bellows knows bloody damn well that Ian—"

"Christine, your language!" Maggie scolded firmly.

Ignoring her mother, Christine spoke over the admonishment to say loudly and firmly, "Ian preferred those in britches than skirts!"

Again, the room was silent.

"Lady Bellows knew that?" Caroline asked.

"Yes, she did," Christine growled emphatically. "That was the reason why Ian was allowed to work on the grounds." Looking at Abby, she asked, "What happened to Tilly?"

Again speaking in the hesitant tone, Abby picked up on her tale. "When her family took Tilly home, Lord Reynolds placed her in a convent. He was so upset over the ordeal that he refused to visit her. Walter was the only one to see her. I went once and Walter had to sneak me in then."

"Tilly is in a convent?" Caroline asked herself quietly.

There was a silence before Abby told them, "Tilly is dead."

169

Christine and Caroline stared at her in speechless astonishment. When Abby bent her head and seemed as though she would not continue, Elizabeth explained gently, "She refused to eat. She gave up on living since no one believed her. The pains came early and she died giving birth to a stillborn son."

Christine stared at the table before her, remembering a conversation, a promise made long ago in a small secret room. In her mind, she was back in Bellows' secret room for a moment before she heard Elizabeth continue.

"The irony of it was two days before Tilly died—" She halted when Christine's blue eyes turned slowly to look at her. "Though no one realized it until much later, but the timing of Tilly's death and the final scandal were only two days apart. Tilly died thinking no one believed her but it all came out."

Elizabeth looked around the room at the enthralled listeners that Maggie had to prod her, "What happened to prove the girl right?"

"Lord Bellows was found in a secret room by his sister," Elizabeth replied. "He was with one of the girls and he was—" She stopped not wanting to state the obvious.

"Oh my God," Caroline said, putting a hand to her throat. "A secret room?" She looked at her cousin to find Christine obviously upset over the news. She was rubbing her temple and her eyes were closed.

"Yes. It seems that there was a passageway that led from the dormitory down to this room in the basement of the main house," Abby explained.

"Lord Bellows was arrested and Lady Bellows immediately closed the school," Elizabeth went on to explain. "In his defense, he refused to marry any of the girls. He was waiting for his angel to return."

"His angel?" Maggie echoed.

"Apparently, she was a student at the school who had graduated," Abby said. "He loved her but she spurned him. Yet she had warned him of taking another girl to his bed. If she heard of his misdeeds, she would return for him. His angel was what he called her but everyone else called her the angel of death. At any rate, the authorities decided that they would find this angel and talk with her."

"You jest?" Christine asked in surprise. Abby shook her head.

"No, they talked with every girl who ever attended the school in the last ten years. That is why I am surprised that neither one of you heard of this," Elizabeth told them. "I remember their questions. *'Did he ever call you angel?' 'Do you remember any girl he may have referred to as his angel?'* It was very odd how they pressed on with the name."

"Yes, they asked me the same questions," Abby confirmed.

"When did these scandals happen?" Maggie asked.

"The one involving Tilly was a few months after the summer holiday, after Christine and Caroline graduated," Abby explained.

"Perhaps that was when we went to the Meadows," Maggie said looking at Caroline. Christine turned her gaze to Caroline as well. It was the time when Caroline's parents were killed in a fire and were buried.

"Then the questioning was a short time after the new year. February, I think," Elizabeth said.

"Oh wait, I recall two men and a woman coming by requesting to speak to Christine and Caroline but Christopher had been buried the week before and we were preparing to leave for Rome," Maggie explained.

Christine had to force down a shudder. *The authorities had come by to ask questions. How would I have been able to elude their questions about his angel?*

"Well now, that answers the questions of how the two of you never knew," David observed.

"Yes, that was it. After losing Lord Christopher, I doubt that Christine or Caroline could have withstood those questions. It was quite a stressful session to say the least," Elizabeth stated.

In the silence that followed, Christine asked quietly, "So Lord Bellows is in prison?"

"Actually no," Abby answered. Seeing the incredulous look in the blue eyes, she quickly added, "Walter Reynolds was able to convince the magistrate that Lord Bellows be stripped of his title and holdings then sent to the Colonies to be sold as an indentured slave."

"The Colonies?" Christine repeated without emotion or expression on her face.

"Yes, but he never reached the Colonies," Abby said.

Caroline interrupted in a horrified tone, "Did he escape?"

"In a manner of speaking," Abby replied. "His body was found in the lower decks of the slave ship, battered and beaten."

"How do you know all this? How can you be sure that the discovered body was Lord Bellows?" Christine asked.

"From Walter," Abby replied. "He set sail on the ship because he wanted to ensure that Bellows' life in the Colonies was excruciatingly miserable after the anguish his family had endured over Tilly's ordeal. When it came out that Tilly had been telling the truth, Lord Reynolds went into his study one night and put a pistol to his head. Lady Reynolds lost her mind and was committed to a home where she died some months later. Walter just wanted to be sure the man would suffer."

"I have seen Walter at the club," Peter put in. "Though no one talks of what happened, he has managed to restore his family name by his actions with the magistrate. He is married and has two children, both sons, but his wife prefers to live in the country. He returns to his home for occasional visits."

"There were so many families who were affected by Lord Bellows' callous treatment of the girls. I have to admit that I was surprised when the truth did finally come out. He was such a friendly man who always had a nice word to say or who—" Elizabeth paused when Christine turned to look at her with mild disgust. "You never liked him, Christine, so to you, he will always be repulsive."

Christine shook her head in disbelief and muttered, "I will never understand what everyone else saw in the man."

"Because you did not like him," Abby said with finality.

"I cannot imagine swooning over such an arrogant, self-righteous, pompous—" Christine began but stopped herself.

Elizabeth reached out and patted her friend's hand. "You never were one to swoon over honey-covered words and a handsome smile." Glancing up at Andrew, she added with a hint of a tormenting smile, "So how on earth did you convince her to marry you, Andrew?"

He smiled back at her and replied in a matter-of-fact tone, "I simply told Christine that I could not live without her."

"Well, I am simply amazed," Caroline said with a tone of awe in her voice. "I am just amazed that we had not heard of this before."

"I think that we have given Christine enough excitement for one afternoon." Andrew announced. He had been watching her as her face showed every angry emotion from disdain to total fury.

"I agree with you, Andrew," Abby said as she stood up. "You are nearly fully recovered from your illness and then we bring such distressing news."

"You will need to return on another day and talk of happier times," Christine said.

"Indeed so. Perhaps later in the week, I will bring the children to visit. Chelsea has been asking for you," Elizabeth told her with a grin. "That should give you something to look forward to."

"I thank you for the warning," Christine replied with a tired smile as she stood up to see her visitors to the door.

"No, sit here and rest for a while. I will see them out," Andrew said firmly.

Soon Christine was left in the parlor alone and her mind seemed to reel with the news. *So Bellows wanted me to return, was waiting for me. Did he have some kind of trap set?* Her trap would have caused an accidental death. It was something she had spent the rest of her last year perfecting for just that possibility. She was surprised that, despite her threat, he would actually take those girls' innocence just to lure her back to him.

Christine had not thought that the man would be so devious and underhanded. Would she had suspected a trap? She could not answer that question for certain. Then a thought struck her that made her blood turn cold. She had Bellows that day in his secret room, had the pistol pointed right at his heart. If she had killed him then, Tilly would be alive today, the other girls would be at Lady Bellows Finishing School, and no one else need know the truth of why some of the girls had to leave the school. His death then could have prevented all the pain and suffering experienced now.

Andrew's face loomed before her and Christine backed away in fright. Focusing on him, she noticed that he looked concerned. Only then did she realize that she was crying, the tears streaming down her cheeks.

"Christine?" Andrew was saying as he knelt beside her.

"Oh Andrew, what have I done?" she cried out in anguish as she threw her arms around him.

She needed his comfort, wanted it but could not justify it. When his arms encircled her, she pushed away from him and moved quickly to the other side of the room.

"This is not your fault. None of it," he said firmly as he followed her. "Come to me."

"No, oh God, no!" she wailed mournfully. "Tilly, I am so sorry!"

Andrew reached out for her but she eluded him. Muttering a curse, he quickened his steps and finally grabbed her arm. "You are not at fault, Christine! You could not possibly have known this would happen!"

When she pushed at him again, Andrew was ready. He held onto her and tightened his hold when she squirmed to be free. "Stop this, Christine! There was nothing you could have done. You did the right thing then."

"Kill him! I should have killed him!" she muttered aloud as she fought against the security he represented.

"You are not a murderess. You did the right thing that day," Andrew repeated firmly.

Suddenly Christine stopped her struggles and stared at him through watery eyes. Her face was streaked with tears but her blue eyes were wide with shock.

"You know! My God, you know!" she breathed.

"Yes, I know you are the one he called angel. I know you held a pistol to him and gave him a warning. I know about a girl named Agatha but you called Aggie," Andrew said quietly. He rubbed his thumb over one wet cheek and added, "I know about the night he nearly raped you."

All color drained from Christine's face and she took a step back from him. "But how? No one knows! I never—" Her tone was filled with horror and panic.

"Shh, just calm yourself. During your illness, my sweet, you muttered a great deal during your delirium," Andrew explained.

Christine stared at him as he pulled out his handkerchief and began to gently wipe her face dry. As he did, he spoke in a whisper to calm her fears at being discovered.

"No one will ever know of this. I was the only one to hear the tale of your days at school. I know that Bellows was the reason for the change in you that your mother often speaks of but no one else will know of your secret. No one will know except you and me."

Andrew glanced into her frightened blue eyes and with a gentle smile said, "Now calm your fears and let the past die away. There is nothing you can do now. Bellows is dead and thankfully not by your hand. He cannot hurt anyone anymore and, most importantly, not you."

The fear of his knowing was slowly subsiding from her eyes but they were filling with tears once again as the thought of Tilly's suffering returned. Andrew held her tightly against him while she cried for a girl she once tutored and for all the other girls who trusted in Lord Bellows—until it was too late.

Chapter 18

A few days later, Christine was accompanying Caroline as she was being fitted for her new dresses. Looking at the various fabrics and design drawings, Christine listened to Caroline talking with the seamstress.

"There will be enough material to let out as my time draws near?" Caroline was asking.

"Yes, Your Ladyship," the seamstress answered.

Christine wondered if she would be so meticulous when she was carrying Andrew's child. The thought made her smile for she could not wait to feel the life they would create move within her.

Thinking of Andrew, Christine was still amazed that he would not leave the house except to accompany her to the park in the afternoons. During this monthly flow, she was sure that he would find entertainment elsewhere. Since Marian was still out of town, Christine thought that he might pay a visit to Molly's establishment. Instead, he stayed at home going over papers in his study while she kept him company by reading a book on the sofa.

Another hour passed before the two cousins were leaving the shop and getting into the coach. Caroline sat back with a sigh, making Christine laugh softly.

"Really, Caroline, does having a child exhaust you so much?"

"No, it is the trying on of new clothes. Some of the dresses still had pins in them," Caroline replied closing her eyes.

"Ah yes, cousin, I do believe all of London heard your yelp," Christine teased.

"You lie," Caroline exclaimed opening her eyes. The two laughed at their foolishness as the coach took them to a nearby bakery.

"Hmm, this smells wonderful," Caroline said with a long sniff.

Christine laughed and said teasingly, "In your condition, everything smells wonderful."

"Not everything, cousin," Caroline said with a laugh. Stepping inside the small store, she added, "You are certainly in good spirits today."

"My first day out of the house to do something frivolous and I feel free. I want to go everywhere and do everything right now," Christine told her with a grin.

"Oh no, you are not. Andrew made me promise that you are only going along for the ride. Now order what you want," Caroline fussed. Christine grinned at her then shrugged before turning to the baker and giving him her order.

They sat at a small table with two wrought iron chairs and snacked on the freshly baked pastries. The proprietor of the shop greeted them and served them tea in two delicate teacups.

"Is everything going well for you, Christine? Andrew seems pleased with his decision," Caroline said conversationally when they were able to talk.

"I am happy to be with him. There are so few men I could trust, especially after what the Duke of Whiteford had told me," Christine replied.

"My word, that man must have been mad to say such things to you. At least, Andrew proved him wrong thank goodness. Imagine Whiteford believing that he was the last one to offer marriage," Caroline said angrily.

"Careful, cousin. You are not supposed to get upset over matters that you cannot change," Christine said. Leaning forward, she whispered, "Imagine what Whiteford thinks now that Andrew proved him wrong and I accepted Andrew's offer instead."

Caroline bubbled with laughter at the thought. "Come on, cousin. It has been a fun afternoon but I must get you home before Andrew becomes furious with me."

"Yes, and I will tell him how you made me stay out all afternoon against my will."

After giving their compliments of the treat and saying their farewells, Caroline stepped outside first and turned to Christine saying, "You would do that too. You are so unruly sometimes."

"Just sometimes! Dear me, I am remiss in my torments," Christine teased as she stepped into the coach behind Caroline. For the remark, Christine received a slap on her arm from her cousin and laughed.

Back at the townhouse, the footmen assisted the two cousins out of the coach. The smell of smoke was pungent in the air and the two women looked around questioningly.

"Parker, is there a fire nearby?" Christine asked when the butler opened the door.

Seeing the look on the man's face, she realized that he did not just open the door. He had thrown it open in a hurry and his usual calm demeanor had fallen away to a look of worry and relief.

"Your Grace, at least you are safe," he blurted out.

"Why? What has—"

"Tis a fire, Your Grace! I was told that it is the Lockhart house!"

Christine stared in disbelief for a moment before she asked apprehensively, "What about my mother?"

"I do not—" he was saying but stopped. Christine had turned and quickly got back into the coach with Caroline hurrying inside after her.

The coach rushed down the streets to the Lockhart house several blocks away. A crowd had formed and no one was allowed beyond the corner. Seeing that the coach was not able to get down the last block, Christine was out and running down the street with Caroline calling after her.

The smoke was thick and black as it bellowed into afternoon sky. With fear for her mother's safety, Christine lifted her skirts a little higher as she ran faster to the corner. Turning the corner, she saw the water brigade working feverishly to extinguish the blaze. The crowd made it difficult to see clearly but it seemed to her that the fire was mainly contained to the gardens beside the house. The house was scarred slightly by the flames as they licked greedily at the wall but the house was virtually unharmed.

Staring now, Christine was confused. Her mother's house was not the one threatened. Caroline finally caught up with her and stood beside her cousin staring as well.

"That is not Aunt Maggie's house," Caroline said confirming Christine's thoughts.

"I know," Christine muttered.

He watched the crowd for her. With the fire, he knew that she would come. She had to be sure that her mother was safe. A smile crept over his face when he saw her running around the corner. Slowly, he made his way through the crowd, adjusting the collar to obscure his face as he moved closer. Smiling, he stood behind her as she watched the activity. He was so close to her that the hem of her skirts fluttered around his black boots. Reaching inside the sleeve of his waistcoat, he pulled out the concealed dirk. Without taking his eyes from the dark haired woman before him, he drew his arm back slightly for the strike.

Richard's coach stopped behind Caroline's, not able to move any further.

Getting out, he could see the number of people standing at the corner while waiting for Andrew and David to step down behind him.

"They are already here," David informed them and pointed to his coach.

Andrew muttered a curse and hurried down the street with Richard and David following behind him. Turning the corner, Richard muttered under breath, "Damn, look at the people milling around to gawk."

The three men searched the crowd for the two cousins.

"Ah, there," David said and pointed the two women out.

Pushing their way through the people, the three men were nearly upon them when David was pushed slightly when the crowd shifted.

"Here now," the woman exclaimed when David bumped into her.

"I apologize," David told her shamefaced. With his attention on the woman, David bumped into another person who grunted.

Coming up behind the man David had just bumped into, Andrew felt something hit his boot and looked down. A dirk laid over his boot with the sharp end pointed up at him. He bent down to retrieve the dirk as the cloaked figure moved away.

"Andrew?" Christine asked as he straightened with the dirk in hand.

She looked down at it then back at him. The look in his green eyes frightened her as she watched him search the crowd and a cold chill ran through her.

"Get them away from here," Andrew ordered David and held up the dirk. "That man you bumped into had this."

David nodded in quick understanding then grabbed the women's arms roughly. "Caroline, Christine, come with me. Now!" he commanded.

"David! What is it?" the two women protested as he pulled them through the crowd.

Christine noticed that Andrew and Richard hurried through the crowd in different directions.

"Where are they going?" she asked David while trying to free her arm.

"We will discuss it after you both are safely in the coach," David replied.

Still protesting, the women followed David to his coach. Soon Andrew and Richard were returning and Christine noticed that Andrew was not pleased. Thinking he was angry with her, she went off into explanations.

"Parker was told that my mother's house was on fire and he did not know if she was unharmed. I had to know that she was safe, Andrew."

"Let us go home and get you safe first," Andrew said firmly.

"What? Safe? What do you mean?" Christine asked confused.

178

Without another word, Andrew assisted her into David's coach with Caroline then followed David inside.

When the coach started moving, Christine turned to her husband and asked, "What do you mean get me safe?"

Andrew did not answer but stared out the window and exhaled forcibly. Christine turned her question to David but he too did not answer as he watched Andrew. Luckily the ride to the townhouse was short. Getting out, Andrew glanced behind the coach to see Richard's coach pulling up.

Once inside the townhouse, Parker informed them that Lady Lockhart was in the drawing room awaiting their return.

"Mother, I thought that it was your house on fire," Christine told her the moment she entered the room.

"I had hoped to catch you before you left here. Parker told me that I had just missed you both," Maggie replied as she received a hug from her daughter and niece.

"Aunt Maggie, what happened?" Caroline asked.

"I have no idea. The Stanfords had been gone for months so I cannot imagine how the fire could have started," Maggie was saying.

Richard closed the double doors to the drawing room as Andrew stood before the small group.

"It is possible that it all was a ploy to lure Christine out," Andrew began. Gaining everyone's attention, he went on to say, "We had also heard at the club that the Lockhart house was on fire and hurried back here."

"Parker was told the same thing," Christine informed. "Caroline and I had just returned from shopping and could smell the smoke in the air. That was why we hurried out."

"There was a man standing behind you, Christine. He had this in his hand," Andrew told her and pointed to Richard who held up the dirk.

"Behind me?" she repeated quietly.

"Andrew and I searched for him, but we lost him in the crowd," Richard told them.

Andrew had been staring at Christine, watching her reactions. Releasing a long sigh, he hung his head in remorse and said, "I was wrong, Christine, possibly too arrogant in my thinking. I thought that giving you my name and title would have been enough to deter this man." Looking up, he met her sapphire eyes and added, "Whatever reason this titled lord may have to harm you, he apparently has disregarded his own deadline and no longer cares that your death looks accidental."

David stood up with a thoughtful look on his face. "You know, in that crowd and with the confusion of the fire," he paused as he mulled over his idea in his mind. Lifting a finger in the air, he said, "Given the commotion and the number of people, he may have hoped that all those factors would lend to a scuffle and harm Christine in the fray."

"I would not have allowed an accidental ruling," Andrew replied firmly.

"True, but he does not know that. Or at least, we hope he does not know," David countered back.

"That is a possibility but Christine cannot stay inside all the time," Richard put in.

"I will not have my wife be held prisoner in her own home," Andrew argued. His gaze softened when he met Christine's eyes. "I am proud of my duchess and I intend on showing her off."

Christine blushed slightly at the compliment and smiled at Andrew. The room was quiet for a moment before Maggie suggested, "Perhaps Christine should leave London. She could go to the Meadows—"

"I will not have my wife driven from her home either," Andrew stated arrogantly.

"Andrew, since this man is here, I should leave," Christine began but he was shaking his head.

"No, you should not leave. What you do will not be dictated by the whims of a madman," Andrew stated firmly.

"Then can we not go somewhere that if he followed, he would be noticed?" Christine asked.

"Take her to Kenilworth, Andrew. It is big enough for her to roam yet secluded enough to notice a stranger," Richard suggested. "It will also not look as though Christine was leaving because of him. It is your home after all."

"I will want to accompany my daughter. I will be a stranger though I know we are looking for a man but he could hire a woman to get close to Christine," Maggie advised.

Andrew let out a growl of frustration. Turning, he began to pace as the thoughts tumbled in his mind. *So many damn possibilities to harm Christine. Constables, arranged accidents, and the killer could hire a woman just as easily. But why does this man want to kill her? Good lord, how can she be kept safe?* He could not lose her and most definitely not at the hands of this madman.

A hand touched his arm breaking him from his musings. Christine stood before him with a look of concern of her face. Seeing that his attention had returned, she whispered, "Andrew, we will think of something. We will figure out who this man is. But for now, I think we should go to Kenilworth."

Andrew slumped his shoulders slightly in defeat but Christine continued, "There is too much activity in London that lends to too many opportunities for this man to try something else. You cannot be by my side every moment. If the fire was indeed only to lure me out, then such an opportunity will not be so easily accomplished at Kenilworth."

After a silent pause, Richard had to agree. "Christine is right, Andrew. Go to Kenilworth, take your duchess and introduce her to the village, to your household. Let them see her and Maggie."

He felt like he was running away but Andrew also understood their argument. His gaze tenderly caressed the face of the woman before him whom he adored. Pulling her gently to him, Andrew let out a sigh of resignation as his arms wrapped around her. Resting his cheek against her temple, he said, "Very well, we will go to Kenilworth. Perhaps then I can think more clearly and devise some way to identify this man."

In his home in another part of London, he was livid with rage. Picking up the small objects on his desk, he threw them across the room. With a growl, he cleared the top of his desk with a sweep of his hand. *The idiots started the fire at the wrong house!* Yet she was there and the opportunity was missed.

"Damn it! She was right in front of me," he hissed through clenched teeth.

Breathing heavily, he stared at the mess on the floor but the sight of Christine's unprotected back was all he saw. His fingers moved as if he still held he dirk, rolling it by the hilt. Again, the Duke arrived and thwarted his plans. With a savage animalistic growl from deep in his throat, he could again see his money burning in the fire at the club. He had to clench his jaws tight to keep from shouting out at the Duke.

Taking a deep breath, he knew that once Christine Lockhart had been dealt with, he would seek out the Duke as well. *Perhaps let the Duke see what was left of his precious bride before meeting his own end*, he thought as he tried to calm himself.

A knock at the door jolted him back to the present. Turning he watched the door open slowly and one of the maids peeked inside. She was one of the prettier ones and he had enjoyed the feel of her beneath him many times before. Waving her inside, she smiled timidly and closed the door. As she walked to him, her eyes looked around noticing the mess.

He leaned his backside against the desk and waited until she was close enough to him then he could reach out yank her hard against his body. His mouth crushed down on hers brutally as he turned with her and laid her down over his desk. Lifting his head, he gazed down at the half-reclining maid who smiled up at him. His hands moved roughly over her breasts before he grabbed the collar of her uniform and ripped it open. Her breasts were bared before him and he greedily took a nipple into his mouth.

"Oh yer Lordship," she moaned, used to his roughness.

As he parted her legs, he thought of his alternate plan for Christine Lockhart. *Until then, this one will do*, he thought to himself. Closing his eyes as he freed himself from his britches, he plunged deep into the willing maid, imagining himself ravaging a woman with midnight black hair and sapphire blue eyes.

Chapter 19

The next morning, Andrew sent word of their impending arrival to the staff of Kenilworth. That afternoon, Christine laughingly pushed Andrew out of the house as she and Bailey took care of the packing. With repeated assurances from her that she would not leave the house, Andrew finally left the packing to the women and headed for the club.

"He is nearly as bad as his father when it comes to going to the country," Bailey told Christine with a small laugh.

"You would think we were staying there and never returning to London," Christine put in.

"Yes, Your Grace. Just like his father," the housekeeper replied with a roll of her eyes.

At the club, David and Richard noticed Andrew and waved him over. "Did you get booted from your own home as well?" Andrew grumbled as he sat down.

David chuckled and elbowed Richard in good humor. "No, but then I know the signs of when I am to vacate the area."

Andrew looked at him with some impatience that made David and Richard laugh.

"You are still in the early stages of marriage. You both are still learning about the other," David replied. With a grin, he leaned forward and said in a conspiratorial tone, "This is the fun time."

Andrew finally chuckled at the jest and told him, "Well, we leave in the morning."

"I will be there with my coach ready to follow you. We will take Maggie in our coach so that you can have some privacy with Christine," David said.

"If Maggie wants to do that, then that suits me. I do not mind having her with us," Andrew told him.

David rolled his eyes and let out an exasperated sigh, "Andrew, I am giving you permission to enjoy your bride while on the tedious road trip."

"I may hire you, David, when I want to take Abby away," Richard said through a chuckle.

"No thank you," David said making a face. "Maggie lets me sleep and does not expect me to join in the conversation."

The three men chuckled then settled into light conversation.

With great satisfaction, he stared down at the fresh grave in a wooded area outside of London. The fools he hired were just too trusting in thinking that he would pay for their services. Their attempts had all failed.

They did not kill her in the park with the ruse of the runaway coach. That had been one of his most brilliant ideas and those two fools did not finish her. Following the Kenilworth coach from the park then watching the Lockhart townhouse that night, he had been there when the two inept killers arrived with the plan of killing her in an attempted robbery. When he heard the scream then watched with disappointment as one of the fools hurried off the balcony, he knew that Christine Lockhart had survived. He was sure that the poor judgment in medication would have ended her life. How the idiots managed to convey the wrong instructions was beyond all reason. Yet the final mistake had been the setting of the fire to the wrong house.

"Damn your ineptness," he growled to the shallow grave that covered the two bodies. "I had to watch as the Duke burned my money!" An unpleasant smile appeared on his face as he hissed, "At least, I did not waste any more of it!"

With that, he turned away from the grave and picked up the shovel. In the darkening woods, he hummed to himself as he headed for his tethered horse.

The next morning, Andrew assisted Christine into his coach ready to head northeast for his estate in the country. Behind the coach ready to follow them was David with his family and Maggie. The third coach in the procession was used for the personal maids and valets.

Most of the morning, they dozed. Andrew draped his arm around Christine's shoulders then let her lean against him. The small procession stopped at an inn near a crossroads to rest the horses and have a meal. The toddler was wide-eyed at the new surroundings and was more content to watch the activity than have his meal.

"Better make sure to take plenty for Stephen to snack on later. He will be hungry at the wrong times," Maggie said to Caroline who nodded in agreement.

"Do we need to stop more often for Stephen or Caroline?" Andrew asked.

"No, we are doing well," David replied. "Stephen has surprised me with his behavior. He seems to be happy just looking out the window."

Andrew smiled and watched as Christine tried to coax the young boy to eat more food. Whenever Stephen moved around in his seat to watch the maid in the inn as she went about her duties, his mouth would drop open. Taking advantage of this, Christine would quickly put a morsel of food into the child's mouth. Stephen would chew while watching the maid and it seemed as if he did not know he was eating.

Nearly an hour and half later the small group was once again on the road. Andrew reached out and closed the curtains over the windows.

"What are you doing?" Christine asked watching him.

"Just a little privacy," he replied then pulled her into his arms. She laughed softly then his mouth was covering hers.

Darkness had fallen when they arrived at Kenilworth. Light filtered through the many windows and Christine could tell even through the darkness that the house was enormous.

"The house has a garden to the west that my mother adored when she was in residence. I can see you sitting on one of the benches and reading," Andrew told her. "Rolling meadows surround the estate and there are large oak trees that we can sit under and have picnics."

Christine listened to him describe his birthplace and watched with a smile as his face lit up with pride and excitement at being home.

Soon the coaches stopped in front of the house. Torches were lit in anticipation of their arrival and when the double doors of the house opened, light flooded out. Andrew stepped down first and looked up with a smile at the two figures standing just outside of the opened doors. Raising his hand to the door of the coach, Andrew assisted Christine down. As footmen came out of the house to unload the coaches, Andrew watched her as her gaze first took in the two servants at the top of the stairs before her head tilted back to look at the house up close.

"Those rooms there are for guests. Ours are towards the back," he told her as she looked at the dark windows. "Come, my sweet," he whispered as he took her arm.

Glancing over to make sure that David and his family were being assisted, Christine let him lead her up the granite steps. The two servants had stepped back into the house and Christine felt a pang of nervousness as she noticed the two lines of servants waiting in the large foyer just below the grand staircase.

Andrew first proudly introduced his wife to the masses. Indicating the man and the woman standing rigidly in their finely tailored uniforms, Andrew told Christine, "This is our butler, Dawson, and our housekeeper, Darcy."

Dawson bowed respectfully while Darcy dropped into a curtsy. "Your Grace," they muttered to her.

"Darcy, I will turn over the introduction of the staff to you," Andrew said, pushing Christine forward. With a grin, he watched his wife as she smiled at each servant during the introductions.

Maggie and Caroline entered the house with David carrying Stephen. When Christine returned to his side, Andrew made the introductions of their guests.

"I have some refreshments prepared in the parlor," Darcy told them and waved an arm to point in the direction of the room near the stairs. "All the rooms are prepared upstairs and the other coach arrived about an hour ago." Looking at Stephen, Darcy smiled and offered, "If you would like to put the young lord to bed, I can show you to his room."

"Do you have some warmed milk?" Caroline asked. "That will help to settle him for the night."

"It will take but a moment to prepare, Your Ladyship," Darcy replied.

"Thank you."

"Lead the way, Andrew," Maggie said with a smile as she looked around. "Knowing my daughter, you will be conducting a grand tour of your home first thing in the morning."

"Actually, that was my first order of business tomorrow, Maggie," Andrew replied as he took Christine's hand and placed it within the crook of his arm. Looking at his wife, he playfully tormented, "I should test your memory and see how many names you can correctly attach to the face."

As they stepped into the parlor, Christine replied sweetly, "And if you were to take the same test, Your Grace, how well do you think you would fair?"

Darcy smiled to herself at the remark as she followed behind the group with two maids. In the many letters she received from Bailey, Darcy learned in advance a great deal of the charm of the new Duchess. '*Ignore any nonsense you may have heard of Christine Lockhart. I have noticed none of the arrogance or self-indulgence from the Duchess that are prevalent in most Ladies. She has a fondness to help in the kitchen so pass a warning to the cook. Her Grace especially finds enjoyment in baking,*' Darcy remembered from one of Bailey's letters.

One of the maids assisting with the refreshments tried to step around Stephen as he explored his new surroundings. The child nearly tripped her as he suddenly turned in the same direction she tried to go. In the process, a spoon used to scoop confectionery sugar over some of the pastries slipped from the small plate and fell on Stephen's head. Some sugar still on the spoon left a patch of white on his already blonde hair.

Stephen stopped to inspect the spoon that suddenly appeared before him. It seemed to be more interesting than the slight pain of his head. The maid was horrified that the child was hit with the spoon and that his head was now sprinkled with the confectionery sugar. Her apprehension showed on her face as she put down the tray hastily and took a napkin from the table while looking at the new Duchess.

Christine was grinning as she leaned forward to pick up the child then took the spoon from him before he put it into his mouth. "I think you are sweet enough, little man," she cooed to the child making Stephen giggle.

Glancing up, she noticed the maid's apprehensive expression. "One can never second guess a child," Christine said softly as she took the napkin in exchange for the spoon. "I usually end up stepping on the little beggar."

She smiled at the maid then planted a loud kiss on Stephen's head where the sugar had landed. Stephen giggled again and tilted his head back to look at her as she said to the boy, "Hmm, just as I thought. You are such a sweet boy."

"You are going to spoil him, cousin," David said.

Christine was tickling the child making his giggles louder as she said as if speaking to Stephen, "Of course, I am. Then I will give him to you and Caroline to put to bed."

"Thank you so much for the consideration on my nerves," Caroline grumbled. Christine merely smiled foolishly at her cousin while Andrew chuckled at their play.

The maid and Darcy exchanged a look before they continued serving the refreshments. When the warmed milk appeared, the housekeeper handed the cup to the Duchess who was still holding the child.

Light conversation about the journey picked up as Stephen sipped his milk. It was not long before Christine stood up with a sleeping child in her arms. David stepped forward to collect his son and, taking Stephen's queue for bedtime, the adults decided to retire for the evening as well. Andrew had Darcy show their guests to their rooms while he took Christine to the ducal bedchambers.

Standing at the foot of the large four-post canopy bed, Christine imagined Andrew being born here. With a small smile playing on her lips, she looked around the room.

"You can have the room redecorated, the colors changed, whatever your heart desires," he told her as he stepped towards her.

Christine shook her head as she turned. Looking back at the bed, she said quietly, "Our children will be born here, Andrew, just as you were. That is what my heart desires at the moment. I will decide on the rest of the house later."

Pleased, he took her to the long double French doors that led out to the balcony. "I hope you will like the estate. I miss being here. I do not come home often enough but when I am here, I am reluctant to return to the life in London," Andrew told her.

"I have always liked the quiet of the country. I guess that is why the Meadows is my hiding place when things are too much for me to cope with in London."

"Then we will live here as often as you like," he said.

They stood looking out at the dark open field. Glancing down, Christine could make out the gardens and smell the delightful scent of roses. She looked up at the star-studded sky and made out the shapes of the constellations she used to read about.

Andrew stood behind her and wrapped his arms around her waist, hugging her close. Taking advantage of her stargazing, he pressed his lips to the throat revealed to him.

Christine moaned at his attentions and turned slowly to face him. His mouth took hers immediately and he pulled her close for a deep and passionate kiss. Her arms tightened around his neck and she pressed herself against him. This time Andrew moaned and soon Christine felt herself being lifted up in his arms then carried back into her room.

* * *

Andrew gave the grand tour after breakfast. The first floor consisted of the drawing room, parlor, Andrew's study, a large library, an enormous ballroom, then the kitchens and servants quarters to the back. The grand staircase in the middle of the large foyer led up to a long corridor. On either side of the stairs were more rooms that Andrew stated were guestrooms.

Down the long hall were portraits of past Chandlers. Christine spent a long time gazing at the portrait of Andrew at the age of ten poised on a black steed with his parents standing beside him. She noticed that he had many of his father's features but the emerald green eyes were definitely a gift from his mother.

They passed more guestrooms until they reached a point where the other section of the house intersected with this long portion. Facing the back of the house, Andrew pointed to the right where the ducal bedchambers were located. To the left was the nursery and more guestrooms as well as further down the hall.

"So many bedchambers," Maggie mused aloud.

"Remember that my great-grandfather came from a large family. He was the fourth of nine children but the second of three sons. We have not had a large family since then," Andrew explained.

"Tell me you do not want a large family," Christine said.

"I will take all the children you are willing to have, my dear Duchess," he told her with a smile.

"Humph," Caroline grumbled. "You men always say that! You leave us with the burden of how many. David will grumble later that he really wanted only two children but that is after I have given him three."

"I will love each and every one you bear for me, my darling," David cooed sweetly.

Caroline rolled her eyes making the others laugh. Christine leaned close to David and whispered, "Do not say anything now, it will only be used against you later."

"Christine Chandler! Do not advise my husband on how to save himself."

"Yes, of course, cousin," Christine said in mock servitude. "How silly of me."

"Quickly, Andrew, show us something else about this magnificent house before the girls show us how ridiculous they can be," Maggie advised in a hurried tone.

David and Andrew laughed at the women's antics. After the tour, they went out to the meadow where Caroline let Stephen run to his heart-filled delight.

"We can go into the village if you like," Andrew offered.

Before he could speak further, Caroline shook her head. "I will put Stephen down for a nap soon. After that ride yesterday, I am still tired myself."

"Andrew, take Christine into the village so they can become used to their new Duchess," Maggie suggested.

"A wonderful idea! After that big breakfast, I may lie down myself," David told them.

Andrew looked at Christine with raised brows. She smiled and nodded. Within the hour, the Duke and Duchess of Kenilworth were on horseback heading for the village. While en route, Andrew pointed out several spots where he played as a child or that had some historic event take place. A river flowed nearby and they could hear the water babbling over the rocks.

Coming to a bridge that was wide enough for a wagon to cross Andrew told her, "This is the last bridge before we reach the village. I am surprised that none of the boys are fishing the riverbanks. There were certainly an abundance of us when I was young."

"You are still young, Andrew, and when your sons come along, you can show them all your favorite fishing spots," Christine said smiling.

The sounds of their horses' hooves as they crossed the bridge seemed loud in the quiet serenity of the scene. Birds flew low over their heads as they dove close to the water's surface then they soared up to the sun once again.

The first building they saw was the church and, turning the bend in the road, Christine could see smoke rising in the air through the trees. The village appeared before them as they turned the last bend.

The long narrow road stretched out before them but Andrew stopped at a building to his left near the center of the village. It was the bakery and, knowing her penchant for baking, he thought to treat her with some of the pastries found within.

After the introductions, the baker gladly presented them with slices of freshly baked bread and jam. Andrew smiled as he watched her take in the baker's operation and the artistically arranged displays. They were in conversation about various pastry fillings when the vicar walked by and saw the Duke standing near the door.

A few moments later, Christine looked up and did not see Andrew. She vaguely remembered that he excused himself but she was surprised to find that he was not standing outside the bakery.

"Now where could he be?" she mused aloud.

The baker stepped outside and pointed to the center of the village, saying, "Perhaps he is at the town hall. There was a ruckus earlier and everyone has gone to watch the punishment."

"What punishment? What happened?" she questioned.

"I am not sure, Your Grace. I was taking bread from the ovens and was not paying attention to the talk, I fear."

"That is quite all right, Mr. Summerton. The bread is more important," she replied with a smile. Pointing a finger, she asked, "The town hall is to the right?"

"Yes, Your Grace. You cannot miss it."

"Thank you," she said and mounted her horse.

She frowned as she looked at Andrew's horse still tethered to the post but she turned her mare in the direction of the town hall. Turning the corner, she saw a crowd gathered around a platform where two men stood. As she neared them, she noticed that one man had his hands bound by rope before him and a cloth over his mouth. The other man held him by the arm and had a pistol in the other hand pointed to the prisoner's midsection.

"...and for such an offense, he will be hanged," the unbound man was saying.

Several women from the front of the crowd wailed loudly at the statement and murmurs ran through the rest of the crowd. A man standing at the back of the crowd who was shaking his head looked up to see that Christine was about to dismount and hurried to aid her.

She smiled at him and asked as her feet landed on the ground, "What is happening?"

"The sheriff says that Tinker was found stealin' money from the church's poor box but Tinker ain't ne'er up so early in the morn," the man whispered.

"What does this Tinker say in his defense?"

"Nuthin'. The sheriff ain't let 'im say a word."

Christine's mouth dropped open and she handed the reins of her horse to the man. Walking through the crowd, she heard the sheriff announce, "You are found guilty as charged and the sentencing will commence immediately."

"Hold!" Christine called out loudly.

Heads turned and bodies parted as she purposefully made her way through the crowd. At the steps leading up to the platform, a thick-muscular man put out his hand to aid Christine up since there were no side railings. His brown eyes noted her wedding ring of small rubies and a large diamond as well as the ring on the index finger of her left hand that he held. His eyes widened as he recognized the crest within a circle that was the mark of Kenilworth.

"Who are you?" the sheriff asked in indignation.

"The Duchess of Kenilworth and I presume that you are the sheriff," she stated firmly.

A murmur ran through the crowd at the announcement of her identity and the sheriff took a step back in surprise. As the crowd bowed or dropped into a quick curtsy before the Duchess, the accused man stared in awe at the beauty before him.

The sheriff narrowed his eyes and exclaimed with an air of arrogance, "The Duke is not in residence at this time."

"I had no idea that my husband had to gain prior approval from you before returning home," Christine replied condescendingly.

A ripple of laughter drifted up from the crowd and the sheriff's face turned red.

"When did this man supposedly commit this offense?" she asked curtly, ignoring his reddening face.

"He was found carrying the poor box from the church this morning and—"

"This morning?" Christine interrupted, her tone accusatory. "And so quickly you are about to hang a man without a trial?"

"He was found in the act of stealing," the sheriff told her angrily. "We are all poor people and tis my job to enforce the laws of this land."

"I know very well what your job entails, Sheriff. However, acting as judge and jury does not fall into the realm of such definition," Christine stated heatedly. "This man is due his day in court before a true judge. Do you not have a jail?"

"Of course, but the magistrate is not due here for quite some time and I—"

"You have no authority to pass sentence on anyone at any time," Christine interrupted again.

"These matters are no—" He halted his next words but Christine narrowed her eyes at the implication.

"No concern of mine? I beg to differ as this matter does concern me a great deal. As Duchess of Kenilworth, I have every right to question your actions and require proof of any accusations. It is my position to ensure that everyone living on my husband's land is treated well and fairly."

Christine walked to the stand before the accused man. With her back to the crowd, she studied him. "Take the cloth from his mouth," she ordered.

The sheriff stepped closer to her and hissed in a low voice so as not to be overheard. "You can be some harlot trying to pass as a highly born lady. How do I know that you are the Duchess?"

Her blue eyes met his and he almost flinched with the intensity of the anger he saw there. Without a word, she lifted her left hand and very nearly pressed the Kenilworth ring against his nose. Since Andrew had slipped the ring on her finger the morning after they were quickly wed, she had grown used to the heavy weight of it. Now the weight was truly welcomed as she met her first challenge to her claim as Duchess of Kenilworth.

As the sheriff leaned back slightly and his eyes focused on the ring to note the Kenilworth mark, Christine glared into the sheriff's eyes and repeated in a low menacing tone, "Take off his gag."

The sheriff opened his mouth to make some other retort when a voice pierced through the crowd. "Release the man!"

Heads turned again at the commanding tone of the newcomer and again everyone showed respect as Andrew quickly dismounted his horse. Hurrying to the platform, he repeated loudly, "I said to release him."

When he noticed the crowd, the first thing Andrew saw was the woman in the brown traveling gown and then almost immediately, he noticed her close proximity to the edge of the platform. Once he stepped on the platform, Andrew took Christine's arm and pulled her away from the edge before saying through clenched teeth, "I gave you an order, Sheriff."

Breathlessly, the vicar climbed the steps to the platform with the help of the same muscular man who had aided Christine. As the sheriff released the accused man, Christine stepped closer to the vicar and asked in quiet tones, "Do you accuse this man of stealing?"

"No," the clergyman replied. "His Grace provides me with an allowance each week that is to be distributed in times of need. When His Grace is not in residence, the sheriff raises the taxes then threatens disastrous consequences to family and property if any word reached the Duke."

"Why hang the man?" she asked quietly. Trying to hold her anger in check, she did not trust herself to speak in normal tones.

"I do not know, Your Grace," the vicar whispered in reply.

Andrew stepped before the accused man and asked, "What have you to say in your defense?"

The man's eyes flickered to the sheriff before he shrugged and answered, "I was headed for the church to help the vicar with some repairs when I saw—"

"Liar," the sheriff exclaimed. "This man cannot be trusted in anything he may have seen. He is the town drunk."

Andrew looked to the vicar who nodded slightly in affirmation. Yet it was Christine who persisted in the questioning. "You saw what?"

The man looked at her with wide eyes then to Andrew who nodded for him to answer. Clearing his throat, he began again. "I saw the sheriff comin' out."

"I tell you the man—" the sheriff began but Andrew interjected.

"Sheriff, you will remain quiet while this man has his say." Lifting a finger as the sheriff was about the protest, Andrew warned, "Not a word."

Angrily crossing his arms over his chest, the sheriff glared at Tinker. Seeing the hate-filled eyes, Tinker lowered his gaze and stared at the wooden platform flooring.

"Tell him what you know, my son," the vicar prompted quietly.

Slowly lifting his gaze, Tinker looked directly at the Duke and began again. "The sheriff was leavin' the church and he had the poor box under his arm."

A murmur ran through the crowd as the sheriff laughed scornfully. "He is a liar and drunk. He will tell you whatever the drink tells him to tell you."

Andrew turned to give the sheriff a warning look who slowly understood the message and quieted himself. Facing Tinker, the Duke asked, "Did you drink heavily last eve?"

Tinker looked ashamed then nodded. Andrew let out a sigh and looked at Christine. She was watching the sheriff and the look in her eyes was not friendly.

"Very well," Andrew said loudly. "The credibility of this witness would be questioned severely in court causing him distress and much embarrassment." Turning to the sheriff, he added, "However, for acting beyond your duties as sheriff, I decree that you no longer hold such a position."

"What?" the sheriff protested in disbelief.

"This matter only adds to other discretions I have been told concerning you, Sheriff," Andrew told him. "I would also suggest that you leave the area as soon as possible. Although you have been using the raised rents to your own purposes, you have the rest of today to take what belongings you can. After that, you will not be allowed near your home and other properties and will be arrested for trespassing."

The sheriff glared at the Duke then turned on his heels without a word. The crowd clapped with enthusiasm at the man's sudden dismissal.

Turning to the crowd, Andrew further announced, "The rents have not been raised by my order as you have been led to believe. Because you have been overcharged, I will forego all rents for one month until I—" He had to pause as the crowd cheered loudly at the news. Putting up a hand to quiet them, he went on, "Until I am able to ascertain the correct amounts from each of you. I will send out personal notes at a later date."

The cheering rang out once again and Andrew grinned. Turning to Christine, he saw that she was grinning also. "Does that meet with the

Duchess' approval?" he asked softly.

"You are more than fair, Your Grace," she replied equally as soft.

Turning to the crowd once again, Andrew said loudly, "I fear that I have been remiss in my duties and I apologize to all of you for the treatment of our former sheriff. In talking with our vicar for a recommendation to fill the vacancy, I understand that there is one who can manage the position. Is Mr. James Clarkson among us?"

A joyful cry of happiness was heard from the family that surrounded James Clarkson. From the center of the crowd, a man with light brown hair raised his arm and called out, "Here, Your Grace."

Christine noticed that other villagers expressed their support to the quick decision with claps or cheers.

"Good, come up here, James."

The man stepped through the crowd to join them on the platform as Andrew continued speaking. "Until I have written proclamation from King that states otherwise, Mr. Clarkson will be the new sheriff. I will notify the Crown of the changes within our community immediately. In the meantime, Sheriff Clarkson will assume his new duties as of this moment." Andrew smiled and put out a hand to Clarkson who took it and shook it vigorously.

"Where is your family, Sheriff?" Christine asked with a smile as she emphasized the man's new title.

Clarkson's somber gray eyes beamed and his smile widened as he gazed down at her.

"They should be here to share this moment," she told him.

With a cry of surprise, a stout woman with three young children hurried to the platform. Christine judged the oldest child to be ten years old as the young girl helped her mother with her younger sister and brother. The family huddled together to hug joyfully at the news then the woman turned and dropped to a curtsy before the Duchess.

"Oh, Yer Grace, tis a happy moment fer us," the woman exclaimed through tears of joy.

"I am glad for you, Mrs. Clarkson," Christine said.

The woman turned to Andrew and dropped to another curtsy.

Putting an arm around the wife, Andrew looked at the clergyman and said, "Vicar, I believe that after Sunday services, we should have a picnic to celebrate this man's new duties. What do you think?"

A loud cheer went up from the crowd as the vicar turned to the Duke. Because he would not have been heard over the ruckus, he merely smiled and nodded.

Letting his green eyes drift over to Christine, Andrew realized that she had not been properly introduced to the village. Slipping his hand into hers, he quieted the crowd once again and announced loudly, "I fear that I have been remiss yet again. I am sure that by now you know who this exquisitely beautiful woman is by my side." Then in a playful tone, he dropped his voice down. "Just do not tell my wife." The crowd laughed at the jest.

Proudly he introduced her, "May I present to you the new Duchess of Kenilworth, Christine Lockhart Chandler."

With sapphire blue eyes twinkling merrily, Christine smiled at the crowd as the women once again dropped into a respected curtsy and the men bowed.

"I believe that the halls of Kenilworth have been silent for far too long," Andrew told them. "I am sure you are tired of doing business among yourselves!" The crowd laughed again. "My mother loved to hostess a small ball to welcome the summer to Kenilworth. So next month, guests will fill the rooms of the great manor. They will need to be fed and possibly want to do some shopping. Fill up your stores, good merchants, for we will be buying your wares in preparation of this ball."

Amid another round of cheers, Andrew turned to Christine and whispered, "Buy a new gown from the seamstress. There will not be a copy of it from those of London, I assure you."

For the next several hours, the Duke showed his Duchess around the small village where the merchants gladly presented the best of their wares. No one noticed the former sheriff as he sulked away to the tavern before going home to pack. With the owner of the tavern watching for the Duke and Duchess to near his establishment, the wench who had spent many hours with the sheriff now ignored him. Grabbing her arm, the sheriff roughly took her to the back and up the stairs to a room.

"Since I will be leaving, you will be a good girl and give me a proper farewell," he growled as he pawed at the bountiful bosom.

Chapter 20

"A ball?" Maggie repeated in surprise. "I thought you were going to show her the village?"

"I managed to come away accomplishing both," Andrew said with a chuckle. "Darcy, this house has been closed up long enough. Let us open up the doors and windows. I feel very generous today and I cannot find anyone else to show off my new Duchess."

"When you and the vicar were at the church, Andrew, did you two partake of the sacramental wine?" Christine asked with a raised brow.

Darcy tittered in a laugh as she turned to leave the room. "Your tea is ready, Your Grace," the housekeeper announced.

Andrew smiled and narrowed his eyes at Christine as she merely grinned at him.

The following evening, Christine sent out an invitation to the Clarkson family to join them for dinner. With confirmation of the oldest girl's age of ten and learning that her name was Susan, Christine found out that the younger two, Constance and James Junior, were seven and five.

"I am almost six," the younger James told the Duchess proudly.

"And every bit as tall as a six-year-old should be," Christine told him, making the child beam brightly.

When Stephen made his appearance in the parlor, the three children gravitated to him. They showed him a great deal of attention as they played quietly on the floor near their mother's feet. Caroline sat close to Christine and Maggie as Mrs. Clarkson gave local background information to the new Duchess while the men talked of duties with the new sheriff.

In London, Jack Hanson was in need of money but with his sister at Kenilworth with his nieces, he had no one else to turn to for aid. Since her sudden marriage to the Duke, he had stayed clear of his niece. He had not dared to go near his own family when he learned that Christine had managed to uncover the additional withdrawals from her account, leading to the dismissal of Thomas Lakely.

"Damn you, niece. You have more wealth than anyone thought you would ever have, yet you cannot share a small whit of it with your own uncle," Jack growled as he paced the floor of the sparsely furnished study. "I am selling what I can to make ends meet while you live as the high and mighty Duchess of Kenilworth."

Kicking a small table and watching it topple over gave Jack Hanson little satisfaction. "Daughter of a sea captain made Duchess! You should never have been born, Christine! You should never have stood in my way!"

After a week of relaxing at Kenilworth, Andrew received word from Richard that several merchants with horses of good stock were in London for a grand horse show. He told Christine of the note as they strolled across the soft grass of the meadow with the house behind them.

"Then go, Andrew, your stables here can hold three times the number of horses you have now," she told him. "Yes, I see that look in your eyes. Stop worrying over me. My mother is here along with Caroline and the villagers have grown accustomed to my visits each morning."

"I will worry and it is no use telling me to stop. I do not want anything to happen to you," he said turning her to face him. "I want you to be safe and feel safe."

"Your new sheriff has his new deputies patrolling the area constantly. Nothing will happen," Christine said in a quiet and firm tone. "You and David should go back to London and buy horses. I would love to watch your trainers break them in." When Andrew still looked unconvinced, she added, "You cannot be by my side each second and I will not have you change your entire lifestyle to be a prisoner to me."

He smiled and pulled her into the circle of his arms. With his chin resting on the top of her head, he said softly, "To be your prisoner is my fondest wish, Your Grace."

Christine burst into laughter and backed out of his embrace. "Liar! You will leave if I have to toss you into your coach and slap the horses into a wild gallop back to London."

Grinning, Andrew pulled her back and held her close to his heart. "Then David and I will leave in the morning. We should be back within the week."

"Do not rush through the showing. I forbid it," she said smiling against his fawn-colored jacket.

Andrew closed his eyes and concentrated on the feel of the woman in his arms. The faint scent of roses from her bath water surrounded them and he felt his heart nearly burst with love.

* * *

The first week of June began to show the fruits of their labors as the invitations for the ball were ready for delivery. It was late in the evening when Christine and Darcy finished going over the list of guests and made final decisions of accommodations for those staying overnight. Because of the distance back to London or the surrounding areas, the invited guests would need to stay at least one night. Christine placed a mark beside those who would most likely stay longer by a personal invitation.

The next morning, Christine was still dressing for the day and wondered how much longer Andrew was going to be away. It had been nearly a week since he and David had left for London and she had expected them to return any day.

"A message from London just arrived, Your Grace," the housekeeper informed her when she stepped into the bedchambers

"From London this early in the morning? The messenger must have ridden all night to deliver it now," Christine said taking the note. She read the note then, with a look of alarm, read it again.

Cousin: Unfortunately, we will be delayed in our return. We encountered highwaymen outside of London and shots were fired. Andrew was wounded but it is not serious. All is well and we will return to Kenilworth within the week. —David

Standing, Christine ordered the stunned maid and housekeeper in an urgent tone, "Mary, get my riding clothes. Darcy, have a horse saddled for me—and no sidesaddle. Also, have a coach ready for my mother and Caroline to follow. We have to return to London immediately."

"No sidesaddle?" Darcy repeated.

"I will need speed. I will be going ahead of my mother and Caroline. Have enough food for Stephen—" Christine was saying as she took off her gown then paused in her talking to slip on the riding habit.

"Has something happened?" Darcy asked.

"The Duke has been injured and I must get to London."

"Injured?" Darcy questioned in alarm.

"David says that it was not serious but I have to be sure," Christine replied. "Hurry, Mary, I need to leave."

"You should not ride the English countryside alone, Your Grace," Darcy protested her. "I will have two groomsmen accompany you."

"As long as they ride fast and stay with me, Darcy," Christine said to Darcy's reflection in the mirror. "Give this note to my mother and Caroline."

Darcy nodded and hurried out of the room. Within moments, Christine was downstairs and pacing impatiently in the foyer as she waited on her horse.

"Christine, you have lost your mind to go off like this," Maggie scolded as she came down the stairs.

"I have to go, Mother."

"This note says that the wound is not serious. Wait for us and we will all return together," Maggie said holding up the paper.

Christine was shaking her head before Maggie could finish the sentence. "I cannot wait. I have to see for myself."

"Christine, what if that madman is waiting for you?" Maggie tried to reason.

"Do you think he orchestrated the situation and saw to it that Andrew was injured?" Christine asked.

"David tells us that all is well," Maggie argued.

Turning to face her mother, Christine asked quietly, "Just as he wrote in the note telling us of Caroline's fall?"

Maggie went silent. Christine would remember the note David wrote that misled them to think Caroline was fine from her fall. Instead, Caroline was laid up in bed for weeks for having twisted her ankle. Worse yet was the news that the fall caused her to miscarry the child that was conceived shortly after Stephen's birth.

The sun was low in the sky when Christine arrived in London. Ignoring the surprised looks from the groomsmen and the household staff, she walked with determination upstairs, waving David away as she stepped into her bedchambers. Tossing down her travel cloak on her bed, she heard voices coming from Andrew's bedchamber. Moving closer to the adjacent door, she stared in shocked surprise when she heard a woman's voice speak in anger.

"How could you have married *her*? You knew I wanted to be your duchess, *your* wife," Marian was saying angrily.

Andrew inhaled in irritation. He knew the title was more important to her and the fact that she mentioned it first was only confirmation to him.

"I expected you to marry someone else only because I could not provide you with an heir, but my God! Did you have to marry Christine Lockhart?" Marian wailed.

"No, I did not *have* to marry her or anyone else for that matter," Andrew told her, his anger rising. "I chose Christine."

"*Chose her?* Why would anyone in their right mind choose her?" Marian argued.

"That is enough!" Andrew exploded. "You will not discuss my wife in that tone, Marian!"

She took a step closer to him and growled angrily, "*I* should be your wife. I love you, Andrew, and I know how you feel for me. How do you think I will feel on those nights you are not with me knowing that you are with *her*?"

"Damn it, Marian, she is my wife! This is *her* house."

"This should be *my* house, Andrew!" Marian said raising her voice and stomping her foot angrily.

Growling low in his throat, Andrew said nothing, not trusting himself to speak the words and maintain some civility towards this woman.

The sound enraged Marian and, with an angry wave of her hand, she exclaimed, "And look at you! Injured from an attempted robbery. You could have been killed, my darling! I am here in your time of pain and where is this wife of yours? Your duchess is—"

"Right here," came the calm feminine voice from behind them.

Marian gasped in shock and whirled around, her hand at her throat and her eyes wide in surprise. Andrew looked around Marian who had blocked his view of his door that was adjacent to his wife's bedchamber. He saw Christine standing just inside the door dressed in a black riding gown that was still dusty from her trip.

"Lady Sanders, I appreciate your concern for my husband but your argument must be dealt with at another time. He needs to rest now." Christine's tone was firm and brooked no argument.

Marian looked at Andrew to override the command but he said nothing. The look in his green eyes infuriated Marian for she thought it seemed too tender and lovingly for the likes of Christine Lockhart. Marian resolved that she would never address Christine by her true name, Christine Chandler, nor would she acknowledge her as Duchess of Kenilworth. The situation was only a temporary setback and, when Andrew had sown his seed for an heir, he would return to his senses and come back to where she knew he belonged.

"Very well," Marian replied stiffly. She glanced at Andrew but he did not say any parting words, further distressing her as she looked around for her things.

There was a knock at the door just as Christine opened it to the hall for Lady Marian. Bailey and Henderson stepped aside to allow Marian to pass then Christine nodded for them to enter. Henderson entered first with a tray in hand while Bailey stepped in behind him.

Christine took the housekeeper's arm and gently pulled her out into the hall. "How long has she been here?"

"Possibly half an hour, Your Grace," Bailey replied detecting the hint of anger.

"Does she come here often?"

It was a question that wives did not ask when referring to the indiscretion of their husband's activities. Bailey hesitated for a moment then replied carefully, "Never here, Your Grace."

"That will be all, Bailey. Thank you," came the curt reply before Christine released Bailey's arm abruptly and hurried down the hall in Lady Marian's wake.

In the foyer, Parker was assisting Marian with her cloak as Christine came down the grand staircase. "Lady Sanders, may I have a word with you before you leave?"

With an air of annoyance, Marian looked up at her with no more warmth than a winter's day. Giving the younger woman a haughty nod of her regal head, Marian followed Christine into the drawing room.

Parker watched as they entered the room and raised a brow as Christine did not bother closing the door. A movement at the top of the stairs caught his attention and, looking up, he saw that Bailey had followed Christine and was now watching her as well.

"I am not sure where to begin," Christine said with her rare display of a small smile.

Marian did not return the smile as she stood stiffly regarding this younger woman. She noted that Christine did not offer for her to be seated.

"Well, I suppose I should just get to the crux of the matter," Christine was saying. She took a step closer to the other woman and said in a deceptively sweet tone, "I would greatly appreciate it that in the future you no longer come to my home to see my husband." A slight emphasis on the last words gave Christine pleasure in seeing Marian flinch before continuing, "He has set you up in a townhouse for your dalliances and that is where your affair should be discreetly maintained for as long as Andrew chooses to continue."

"You are rather lenient in his—activities," Marian stated brazenly with a delicate pause for effect.

The fact that Andrew may 'choose' not to continue their affair, after the various arguments they had concerning this very person who was now *his* wife, irked the older woman.

Christine shrugged and said, "They are, after all, his affairs. Mistresses are tolerated in our society as long as the association is carried with a high degree of circumspect. You know that the Ton frowns on such blatant behavior and turns a sympathetic eye on the poor wife, even for someone like me."

Marian's tight-lipped expression revealed to Christine that her use of the word 'mistress' had hit the mark.

"It is only the novelty of being married that he bestows such attentions upon you. Not to mention the fact that I have been out of town," the older woman reminded her.

"Possibly, Lady Sanders, but time will tell of that. Yet should the novelty of being married finally dissolve, the fact that I would still be his wife, still be the mother of his children, and still be the Duchess of Kenilworth will not change."

Marian bristled at the reminder that she could not bear his children. *That* would have ensured her the title of duchess if she had been capable. With brown eyes blazing in anger, Marian hissed through clenched teeth, "I will have his adoration."

Christine's smile worried the older woman. "Adoration, my lady, can be on many varying levels. There are far too many levels to make a comparison. Strangely a man can, with equal adoration, adore his wife, his children, and even his horse."

"*His horse!*" Marian fairly shrieked. A flush of indignant rage turned Marian's face crimson at the comparison.

"Why yes. Many men care more for their horses than family or comfort. Men are so strangely fickle at times," Christine said softly.

She was having a difficult time maintaining an air of indifference as Marian seemed to choke on her own air. Without another word or waiting for a dismissal, Marian turned from her and stormed out of the house. Following at a more leisurely pace, Christine reached the double doors of the drawing room before the front door slammed. The corners of her mouth just would not stay down as her blue-eyed gaze locked to the floor until she heard the coach move away.

Now the smile appeared as Christine looked up and was startled to find David standing at the bottom of the stairs with his arms crossed over his chest in disapproval.

"I do believe that you enjoyed that, Christine Chandler," he said reproachfully.

"David, I know that I should not be but I must confess," she began with a contrite look before her smile reappeared, "I am immensely proud of my speech."

David chuckled as Christine moved towards him to head back up the stairs. When she had taken the several steps up and was even in height with him, he repeated amid his chuckles, "A horse? My God, Christine! It is a wonder the woman did not rear up and strike you with her forelegs."

Christine burst into laughter then pushed at his chest saying, "Go home, David. Caroline and my mother are returning by coach and should arrive in a few hours."

"You should have been with them, cousin. Instead, you hurry on horseback at breakneck speed."

"And you know why," she said with a knowing look.

David huffed in exasperation and called up to her as she headed back up the stairs, "Must you constantly remind me?"

"I have never made reference to that incident since I soundly boxed your ears," Christine replied over her shoulder, "until now."

David mumbled something under his breath but she ignored him as she continued up the stairs.

Returning to Andrew's room, Christine found him in a chair by the fireplace and looking enraged as she stepped inside.

"Where the hell have you been?" he growled when he saw her.

Hearing the tone in his voice, Bailey and Henderson made a hasty and tactful retreat.

"Seeing your guest out," she replied with a shrug.

Andrew snorted in disapproval and grumbled, "She was not my guest. I would never invite her into this house."

"It was my duty to—"

"And why did you travel alone?" Andrew interrupted angrily. "You were to stay at Kenilworth until I returned. It is not safe for you in London with that madman still about and now you gave yourself up as an easy target by coming into the city on horseback."

During his tirade, Christine stood before him very still and let him have his say. When he finished, she shrugged again and said calmly, "My place is here with you after your ordeal."

"I am fine and I told David to tell you so in that note," he grumbled.

"He did," Christine said simply as she turned to stoke the fire with the poker.

"Damn it, Christine, we have servants to do that," Andrew growled as he reached out to grab her arm.

"Well they are not present at the moment because you are raging about like a bloody bear," she countered back without raising her voice.

"Because you are too stubborn to stay where you were told."

"My place is here," she said more heatedly. "David's note stating that all was well had the same type of reassurances to one written before. Caroline slipped and fell but she was not seriously injured. Yet David failed to mention in that damned note how she miscarried because of the fall. He told me later that he used those words so my mother and I would not be upset and shorten our trip from the Meadows!"

Andrew stared at her as her blue eyes flashed with anger. Jerking her arm free from his grasp, she added, "I had no idea what condition you truly were in. Highwaymen are not the sort to be kind to their victims once shots are fired! You are welcome to ask my grandparents, Lord and Lady Hanson."

"Christine," Andrew began, his tone calmer now.

He had forgotten that Maggie's parents had been killed during a robbery and David failed to make any reminders. After a long inhale, he said, "The shots were from the authorities who had been tracking the outlaws. This came from one of the highwaymen who fired when he was startled at their arrival."

"I was supposed to know this?" she retorted angrily. "David mentions a pistol shot that injures you and I am supposed to be assured that it was not more serious."

Ignoring the stabbing pain in his side, Andrew reached out and grabbed her arm to pull her to him. She stood between his knees as his hands rested intimately on her hips.

"I am sorry, Christine. It upset me to know you could have been harmed riding alone as you did."

"I was too upset to notice, Andrew," she replied quietly.

He pulled her closer making her take another step between his legs. He rested his head against her breasts and listened to her heartbeat. She threaded her fingers into his hair, holding him to her.

"I recognized one of the highwaymen," Andrew told her quietly. Her fingers froze in his hair as he went on, "Our former sheriff decided to embark in a new line of employment."

"What happened to him?" she asked.

"He did not escape them, Christine," he simply answered.

The two did not move for a long moment before Christine whispered, "Perhaps you should lie down and rest."

"I am not tired."

"I am," Christine said with a grin as Andrew lifted his head to look up at her.

With a leering grin that made Christine laugh softly, he whispered, "Lead the way, my sweet."

Chapter 21

Afraid that another mishap would lure Christine out of the townhouse, Andrew insisted that they return to Kenilworth. In the early hours of the second morning of Christine's sudden arrival, the small caravan was once again leaving London.

Hidden within the shadows near the Duke's townhouse, he watched as Andrew assisted her into the coach. When the two coaches passed him, he stepped further into the shadows to be sure that he watched undetected. His eyes blazed with fury that she was being whisked out of the city and out of his reach once again.

"Had I known you were back in the city, Your Grace," he began under his breath but he did not finish his statement. Instead, he let out a long sigh of annoyance before turning away and calmly walking down the street.

As the excitement of planning for the ball changed to anxiety with the event only days away, Darcy gently yet firmly began to take charge of the final arrangements. She ordered furniture moved, tables set up and guest rooms prepared. The morning of the ball, the floral arrangements were attractively positioned in rooms on the first floor and each guestroom had a small cheerful bouquet.

Guests began to arrive in the early afternoon. David helped Caroline and Stephen move to rooms closer to the ducal chambers. As Stephen played on the floor of the nursery under his mother's watchful eye, Andrew stepped in.

"All settled again?" he asked.

Smiling up at him, Caroline nodded and said, "It was just where we had left it." Giving her a quizzical gaze, she stood up and explained, "The entire downstairs looked like a different house that I was not sure we were at Kenilworth."

"Ah yes," Andrew said nodding in understanding. "Darcy does not want certain heirlooms to, how shall I put it, disappear." He crouched down to playfully toss a stray wooden block to Stephen. "I had forgotten how chaotic the house becomes when preparing for such a gala event. It has been quite some time since we had one at Kenilworth." Glancing up at Caroline, he shrugged and added, "My mother loved having balls but only twice a year, in the spring and in the fall."

"Well Darcy seemed to remember each and every detail," Caroline put in with a smile.

Nodding, Andrew agreed. "She and Bailey are both irreplaceable. What would Kenilworth and the townhouse in London be like without them? I shudder to even consider." Straightening to his full height and seemingly towering over Caroline, he said, "It is time that I make myself presentable for our guests."

"Please mention to Christine to see Stephen soon. He will go to bed early tonight," Caroline told him.

Andrew nodded absentmindedly as he looked about the nursery. *Someday soon my own children will occupy this very room*, he thought. He could hardly wait.

The house was filled with laughter, music and the aroma of various mouth-watering foods as the Duke and his Duchess welcomed their guests. Andrew was dressed almost entirely in white except for his jacket of sable brown to compliment Christine's gold colored gown. A diamond tiara was nestled upon her black mass of hair that Mary had expertly arranged to show off the slim neckline with the diamond necklace that encircled it and the diamond earrings that twinkled with the light.

After some time, Andrew broke from the receiving line to whisk his wife into the ballroom as a waltz was beginning. Several hours later, the Duke was strolling among his guests, smiling and nodding his greetings as well as stopping occasionally to exchange some remark.

"For the distance, I am rather surprised at the number who traveled," Richard said as he suddenly appeared at Andrew's side.

"So am I," Andrew agreed.

"I am sure Christine is the reason for so many. They want to see how well she fairs as the Duchess of Kenilworth," Richard tormented then smiled at the stern look from his friend. In a quiet tone, he added, "Personally, I hope she gives them a good show."

"Richard," Andrew warned.

"Oh, and there is trouble," Richard said looking over Andrew's shoulder.

Following his friend's gaze, Andrew saw Marian walking slowly towards the room's entrance with a look of determination on her face. Looking ahead, he found Christine with Abby, Elizabeth and Caroline lingering just within the room.

"What in the hell is Marian doing here?" Andrew growled. "I made sure that she was not on the guest list."

"Then someone brought her along. You know how that happens on occasion," Richard tried to explain. With an elbow to Andrew's side, he added, "Looks like the show begins early this evening."

"Damn it, Richard," Andrew snapped and took a step toward the women.

Taking a firm hold on his friend's arm, Richard held him back and whispered, "Let Christine take care of Marian. It will not just be defending herself but she will also be asserting her position as Duchess of Kenilworth."

Andrew turned to face him and argued, "She does not need to assert herself."

"Indeed, she does and not only with Marian but also with the other cronies present. Think of where the loyalties to the Ton gossip mongers will turn if Christine handles this as well as I believe she will," Richard told Andrew. Glancing to the women, he added with a mischievous grin, "That is not to say that we should not prepare to rescue Marian from total annihilation of common sense."

Andrew looked at him incredulously. "Saving face among the Ton for Marian? No one bothered giving Christine such considerations."

Richard shrugged. "Perhaps because Christine had always known when to gracefully step back from an argument."

Turning their attention back to the women, Andrew and Richard breathed a sigh of relief as Marian stopped to talk with someone who had apparently been her destination.

With an exaggerated sigh of annoyance, Richard said in feigned disappointment, "The show must be later in the evening."

Shaking his head as he purposefully bumped his shoulder against his friend to make him stumble slightly, Andrew mumbled, "Total annihilation of your common sense."

Richard chuckled in amusement as he followed Andrew through the crowd.

The evening wore on and everyone seemed to be enjoying the festive atmosphere despite the late hour. Christine stood near the banquet tables with Darcy and evaluated the spread of food with a critical eye.

"They seem to be more hungry than I had thought. We do have enough food for—" Christine was saying.

"Oh yes, Your Grace," Darcy assured her with a firm nod. "The evening may be warm for June, but I remember well how the guests fancy their fine foods."

Christine tried to stifle her amusement but a soft giggle escaped before she straightened in a haughty manner and lightly slapped at the housekeeper's hand. "Really Darcy, such manners."

Grinning, Darcy arched a brow that would have been envied by any one of the titled ladies present in the house. Before the housekeeper could make another comment, a woman cleared her throat. Christine and Darcy turned at the sound and found Marian Sanders at the other end of the long table.

In a tone of marked disapproval, Marian informed them, "I do not care for the sauce served with the goose. Do you have some of the meat without the flavor?"

Christine smiled pleasantly and said, "Yes, Lady Sanders, we do. Darcy, please bring out a tray in case we have other guests who also do not care for the sauce."

"Yes, Your Grace," Darcy replied and gave a respectful nod before retreating to the kitchen. Neither woman noticed the housekeeper's look of recognition at Marian's name which had been mentioned often in Bailey's letters and not in a friendly manner.

"It will be out shortly, Lady Sanders," Christine said as she adjusted several serving spoons.

"I am surprised at how well you present yourself for Andrew's sake. After all, one must keep up with appearances," Marian commented. Christine glanced up at her while idly stirring a sauce and saw her smile. "I mean, once Andrew fulfills his obligations and responsibilities to secure an heir, his eye will wander away from you."

"Do you speak from experience, Lady Sanders?" Christine asked sweetly.

Not wanting to let her know the barb struck home, Marian replied caustically, "He did not leave me. He merely married you because he needed an heir and I could not give that to him."

Standing tall and giving her guest a warm smile, Christine said, "When love is the basis of a relationship between a man and his woman, such obligations and responsibilities do not matter."

Marian let out a harsh laugh. "Ah, idealistic and foolish dreams. As one would expect from low class upstarts like yourself. Even your feeble attempt to exclude me from this weak attempt of entertainment has not worked out well for you. Had it not been for a dear friend, I fear I would have missed this wondrous event." Sipping her wine with a self-satisfied smirk on her lips, Marian's brown eyes met Christine's in triumph when the Duchess stopped and turned to face her.

"Though I am sure Lord Hadley will always be welcome in our home," Christine began sweetly, "we can only hope that his companion is someone of good reputation."

At the veiled insult, Marian choked on her wine. Reaching for a napkin and handing it to her unwelcome guest, Christine added in the same feigned pleasantry, "The wine does have a rather sharp sweetness to it."

Catching her breath, Marian hissed, "You are the most vile of—"

"Careful, Lady Sanders," Christine warned without a hint of pleasantry. "You are here as a guest of a friend. How you managed to convince George Hadley that he needed a companion when he usually comes alone, I do not care one whit. What you will not do is make a spectacle of yourself in my home or embarrass him."

Hearing Darcy's voice as the housekeeper was returning, Christine took a step back from Marian and said in a tone that was once again pleasant, "Enjoy your dinner, Lady Sanders. Be careful not to choke on the humble pie."

Looking over her shoulder to ensure that it was Darcy who entered, Christine smiled at the housekeeper then to Marian before leaving the room. Having overheard the last remark, Darcy squelched a grin as she watched Lady Sanders glare at the Duchess' back.

"The food seems to replenish itself magically, Andrew," Elizabeth was saying as she and Peter stood watching the dancers with the Duke.

"Indeed, it seems as though it has yet to be touched even after my many trips for the venison," Peter confessed.

"Venison? I cannot stay away from the roast pig," Richard remarked with a pat of his firm midsection as he joined them.

"Darcy insisted on a variety of meats. What she and the cook uses to season them is out of my realm," Andrew told them. "Did you try the breads? Christine was in the kitchen until late last evening helping with baking them."

"Hmm," Elizabeth moaned and closed her eyes. "I could always tell Christine's bread from any others. It absolutely melts in your mouth. Andrew, you must find out for me what she uses to make her bread."

Glancing up, Andrew noticed Christine's entrance into the ballroom. He smiled as his gaze roamed over the figure in gold. "Sorry, Elizabeth. I believe on this I will allow Christine to have her small secrets."

Following his gaze, Elizabeth smiled and tapped his arm gently, "You are such a scamp."

"What do you mean?" Andrew asked in feigned surprise. "A moment ago, you would have me sneaking about in my own kitchen."

Friendly chuckles met his statement as Andrew looked again towards the doorway. Christine was still there but his smile froze upon his lips as Marian stepped in. He watched as the two women exchanged a passing look before Marian lifted her chin high and walked away. Andrew did not see the small smile fleetingly cross over Christine's lips.

"I wonder what that barest hint of a smile is about," Peter said aloud as he watched the brief confrontation. He had also watched the two women and now was watching Christine as she made her way towards them.

"Who was smiling?" Richard asked having seen the confrontation as well.

"When you learn to know Christine's expressions, you will learn to see those nearly imperceptible smiles of hers," Peter replied. When Andrew and Richard turned to look at him, he briefly explained, "Having been, on many occasions, the brunt of her humor."

"Oh do stop your nonsense, Peter," Elizabeth admonished with a smile.

Lifting his wife's hand to his lips, he whispered, "Nonsense? It is you who encourages her, my dear."

Smiling as Christine stepped up to them, Andrew gently took her by the elbow and headed for the dance floor. Over his shoulder, he said to Peter, "I see an opportunity to retreat back to the tables for more of that venison."

Christine looked quizzically at Andrew as laughter followed in their wake.

It was a few hours before dawn when Christine blew out the candle beside the bed then, with a thankful sigh, slipped between the cool sheets. Andrew smiled as his arms encircled her and he snuggled closer.

"I am amazed over how cordial everyone had been this evening," she remarked as she made herself comfortable within Andrew's loving arms. Between the soft kisses he was pressing against her bare shoulder, she added, "Some even inquired on my state of health after that incident in the park."

Chuckling softly, Andrew replied, "At long last, the respect you should have always been given."

"Be serious, Andrew," she admonished through a smile.

"Hmm, serious?" he mumbled as he moved and pushed her onto her back. "Yes, Your Grace, it is time to be very serious."

Christine laughed softly as her arms lifted to wrap around his neck and accept his amorous intentions.

Marian turned down the dark corridor and headed for the door she remembered would lead into Andrew's bedchamber. She smiled at how her innocent inquiries to a chambermaid earlier in the evening gave her that important piece of information. She froze in mid-stride as the faint light under the Duchess' door went out. Hearing no other sounds, she quietly resumed her steps to Andrew's door.

Her heart raced as she thought of slipping carefully next to Andrew in his bed. With a smile, she let her hand rest on the knob and was about to open the door when a voice behind her made her jump.

"May I help you, Your Ladyship?"

Whirling around with her hand at her throat, Marian faced the housekeeper. "I, ah, I am just returning to my room," she said quickly.

"These are the ducal bedchambers," Darcy replied calmly.

"Oh my," Marian exclaimed quietly in feigned surprise. To her credit, she even took a step away to look shocked at the door. "I fear that I am turned around in the large house."

"Quite understandable," Darcy replied and, to her credit, sounded sympathetic. "I shall escort to your room, my lady."

Disappointed that her surprise was ruined, Marian had no choice but to follow the housekeeper back down the corridor towards the guestrooms. After seeing that Lady Sanders was safely inside her own room, Darcy set about finding a footman to stand near the ducal bedchambers to deter other intrusions. Though most of the household knew that the Duke spent every night with his Duchess, it was not privileged knowledge to outsiders, and most especially unwelcome ones.

Chapter 22

With only a few hours of sleep, Christine rose when Andrew left for his own room to dress for the day. Her gentle reminder that they had guests when he tried to encourage her to sleep longer only made him smile and shake his head. Having finished his morning routine, Andrew waited for Christine before emerging together from her room. Seeing the footman standing a discreet distance from the door, Andrew met Christine's questioning gaze but merely nodded in greeting to the man.

Hearing voices in the parlor, Andrew and Christine headed for the room instead of the dining room. They found Darcy placing trays of fruits and muffins on a table while David and Caroline tried coaxing Stephen to eat his breakfast. Upon seeing Christine, the toddler let out a squeal of delight and hurried away from his mother.

"Good morning, little man," Christine greeted as she picked him up. She pursed her lips to invite a kiss from the boy and was met with a childish giggle.

"Andrew, I am leaving you," Christine announced. "Stephen had stolen my heart long before your proposal."

"Then why did you accept my offer?" Andrew asked unconcerned.

"I had feared that Stephen had turned away from me," she replied, giving a hug that made the boy laugh. "But as you can see, he has not forsaken me."

"Dear God," Caroline groaned in a tone that made David chuckle.

"Consider it a blessing, my dear," David said to his wife then winked at Christine. "Now someone else will care for him and you are free from the burden."

Darcy entered the room and heard the exchange. She touched the tip of Stephen's nose and cooed to the child, "Do not worry, Lord Stephen, you are not a burden. I will take care of you."

"Wonderful," Andrew exclaimed in feigned annoyance. "The lad can barely run from the women as they fawn all over him."

Sensing that he was the topic of discussion, Stephen offered Andrew his closed fist full of his half-eaten muffin.

It was nearly mid-afternoon when Marian Sanders woke from the long evening. She let out a long exasperated sigh as she remembered how the housekeeper had thwarted her plans to win Andrew back from Christine Lockhart. Laughter from outside made her nearly leap out of the bed. Unmindful of being dressed only in her silken nightgown, she threw back the drapes then squinted her eyes against the sudden brightness of the sunny afternoon. She saw him almost immediately and her heart flipped in her chest.

Andrew stood near a low stonewall and was laughing at something that had his attention from directly below her window. A child's laughter followed then Christine appeared in the path below.

Marian glared at her as Christine approached Andrew who held out his hand. With jealousy seething from every pore of her being, Marian could only watch as he took his wife's hand and the two strolled away from the house. Enraged, Marian turned from the scene below and vented out her anger by flinging the drapes away. A low animalistic growl emitted from her throat before she hissed into the empty room, "I will have him back, Duchess. You can have his children but I will have him."

Nearly an hour later, Marian was at the top of the stairs when she heard Andrew's voice below. "I will take this to the library. Her Grace undoubtedly is ready for me to join them for tea."

"Then I will just put this package on your desk," came Darcy's voice.

Marian stood motionless as Andrew crossed the foyer and headed for the library. Quietly, she descended the stairs after she heard the housekeeper's footsteps retreat to the back of the house. Knowing that Andrew would be alone, Marian hurried down the stairs and followed him to the library.

Slipping into the room, she saw that he had his back turned to her. With a warm smile on her beautiful face, Marian walked slowly and seductively toward him.

Andrew turned at a sound behind him and found her close upon him. Her arms lifted and she had them around his neck in a flash.

"Oh, I have missed you so," she purred.

Andrew did not return the smile as he looked down at her dispassionately. He pried her hands from around his neck and pushed her back a step.

"Andrew?"

"Marian, do not throw yourself like some whore in a brothel," he told her coldly.

She stepped back as if she had been slapped. In wide-eyed disbelief, she stared at him for a moment. Taking advantage of the reaction, Andrew made to pass her but Marian moved into his path.

"Have you lost your mind, Andrew? Do you seriously want me to believe that you would rather have that wife of yours over me?" she snarled.

"That wife, Marian?" he asked, raising a brow. "As I told you before, I chose Christine."

"I know damned well what you said that day. How could you or anyone possibly care for her? She is arrogant, pretentious, conceited—"

Andrew let out a harsh laugh. "All the attributes that better describe yourself."

Her mouth dropped open in shock at his insult. In a swift move, Marian's hand struck his cheek. "You loved me!" she hissed.

"No, you provided a service for me, Marian. You were my mistress, a plaything."

She growled in anger and launched herself at him. Grabbing her wrists, Andrew held her at bay easily. "I no longer need you for those services."

"That whore, that—" Marian spat.

Andrew jerked her roughly closer to him so that he fairly sneered in her face, "Careful, Marian. You happen to be speaking about my wife whom I love dearly."

"You loved *me* first!"

"No, Marian, you are not listening to me. I never loved you but I did grow tired of you long ago," Andrew told her cruelly.

In her desperation to keep him, Marian pressed herself against him and began to rub the length of his body with hers. Growling in disgust, Andrew threw her from him and released her wrists. In his quick action, Marian was nearly dumped unceremoniously to the floor. Staring at him in surprise and breathing hard, she tried to calm down and think of something to make him change his mind.

"I want you out of this house. I do not want you spending another night under my roof or for that matter sleeping in Christine's home. You have nothing here, Marian," Andrew was saying.

"My God, Andrew. How can you possibly enjoy her in bed knowing that other men have—" she tried to reason.

"She had never been with any other men," he growled.

Quickly changing tactics, she purred, "Then she knows nothing of what you like, Andrew."

"I have shown her, Marian, and she learns very quickly."

A pain shot through her heart at the admission. She knew that he would have bedded Christine Lockhart but he looked so pleased when he spoke the words.

"Andrew? What—? How could you—?" she stammered.

"Pack your things, Marian. I will not have you upsetting Christine with your presence here."

Staring at the floor, Marian searched for some way to win him back. Unable to think, unable to reason, Marian looked up into the emerald green eyes she was so fond of and nearly screamed in agony. "I love you, Andrew."

He exhaled loudly and rolled his eyes in exasperation. "Sorry Marian, but I never loved you in return."

They stared at one another for a moment when she suddenly slammed against him. Her hands held his face, pulling him down as she rose up on her toes to kiss him. Andrew's hands grasped her shoulders and pushed her away from him. The room seemed to echo with the loud smack of their lips separating.

Before Andrew could say the scathing remark on the tip of his tongue, he saw a movement out of the corner of his eye. Marian had left the door open when she hurried to follow him inside the library and now Christine stood in the open doorway.

Andrew's heart sank when he saw her standing there and the shock of finding him with Marian in his grasp was just leaving her face. Now he was looking into the stone expression of the other Christine Lockhart as she said acidly, "Sorry to have interrupted. I just wanted to let you know that tea is served."

The cold blue eyes shifted from him to Marian before Christine stepped back and firmly closed the door.

"Damn you, Marian," Andrew hissed and threw her from him.

"Andrew, please!" She grabbed his arm making him whirl angrily around to face her.

Grasping her by the shoulders and painfully digging his fingers into her soft flesh that made Marian wince, Andrew snarled close to her face, "You pack your things and get the hell out of my house and out of my life. Find one of those other wealthy bastards to spread your legs for."

Marian raised her hand to strike him again but he caught the wrist and tossed her away. This time, she did stumble to the floor but he did not care.

Andrew was hurrying out of the room to find Christine and hoped that she would listen to his explanations.

Thinking that she would be too upset to face her guests, Andrew ran up the stairs to the bedchambers. He searched both her room and his then every room in the ducal wing. Rushing down the stairs, he searched the rooms on the first floor then headed for the parlor where he knew everyone else gathered for tea.

"Oh Andrew, there you are," Maggie said with a smile when he entered the room.

"Have you seen Christine?" he asked looking intently at the faces.

"Well, no. She left here looking for you," Caroline replied.

Andrew muttered a curse under his breath and was about to hurry out of the room when a blur of blue out the window caught his eye. Christine was on her horse racing over the hill. With another curse, Andrew hurried out of the room leaving stunned faces in his wake.

Grabbing her cloak as she left the house, Christine headed for the stables. She did not bother to wait to have her horse saddled. She merely slipped the bit into the horse's mouth then pulled herself up on the mare's bare back. With the men staring after her in astonishment, Christine turned the horse and shot out of the stables.

On the meadows, she let her horse take the lead. It was just as well for she could not see through the tears. The sight of Andrew kissing Marian played continuously in her mind. *How could I have been so naïve?* She was sure Andrew was not left wanting. Yet there he was with Marian.

"You are a fool, Christine. He still has a house for her in London," she growled aloud.

The horse ran aimlessly through the meadows but slowed its rapid pace when they entered the woods. Christine was wiping her tear-streaked face with her sleeve and did not see the low branch until the last moment. Ducking her head, the branch caught her at her forehead instead of her throat. Still she was swept easily off her horse. Dazed and breathless for having the wind knocked out of her, she stared up at the afternoon sky while the trees seemed to dance in circles around her. She closed her eyes tight and, after a few moments, she managed to sit up.

Looking around cautiously, she did not see her horse and let out a muttered curse. Using the trunk of a nearby tree, Christine got to her feet, breathing heavily from the exertion and closing her eyes against the sudden wave of nausea. When she was sure she could take a step without falling on her face, Christine started walking.

After searching for nearly an hour without results, Andrew returned to the house with the hope that Christine released her anger and had gone back. The head groomsman met him at the gates but his look of apprehension told Andrew that the Duchess had not returned.

"It will be dark in a few hours. Gather the men together for a search and get me a fresh horse," Andrew said tossing the reins to the man.

"Yes, Yer Grace but it will dark sooner than that," the man replied then pointed to the sky. "There is a storm coming from that direction."

Andrew turned and saw the black cloud looming low in the sky. He growled in frustration then turned to head back to the house. One of the young stableboys called out and pointed to the meadow. Trotting at a leisurely pace across the grassy meadow was Christine's horse. All hopes sank quickly as they noticed that it was without its rider.

"Damn it," Andrew hissed. "Get everyone ready for the search."

Standing at the gates, the Duke stared out at the meadow. His chest felt as heavy as the black cloud behind him.

"Andrew, what the hell happened?" Richard asked from beside him.

Turning at his voice, Andrew found his friend and David standing nearby ready to take up the search. His gaze returned to the meadows as he replied quietly, "A misunderstanding."

Richard and David looked at one another for they both heard the pain in the softly spoken reply. The two men remained quiet as they watched Andrew stare off across the meadows while horses and men moved hurriedly around them. Within moments, a group of men headed back out to search for the Duchess.

Until the storm, Christine had difficulty evading Andrew and the men with him as they searched for her. She finally breathed a sigh of relief when the approaching storm loudly announced its arrival and they reluctantly decided to give up the search. Walking again but staying alert, Christine could hear the sound of water and knew that the river was nearby.

The rain fell hard and heavy through the trees. Trying to step carefully, she still slipped on the wet grass and soon found herself ankle deep in the water.

"Damn," she growled.

Already wet from the downpour of rain, she bent down to scoop up water in her hands. Instantly, her head pounded in objection. Crouching down instead, she used the hem of her wet cloak to dab her forehead. The chilling water helped to lessen the throbbing of her head.

Once she had quenched her thirst, Christine turned to leave. She took no more than two steps before she was halted by a tug on her cloak. Looking back, she noticed that with the current of the river, the hem of her cloak had wrapped around a small stack of driftwood. With a loud sigh of annoyance, she worked to free herself for several moments. Realizing that the driftwood had a firm hold of her cloak, Christine unfastened it and tossed the cloak to the small stack in irritation.

"Very well, you can have the damned thing," she hissed.

Finding her bearings once again, Christine headed away from Kenilworth and in the direction of the road she knew was nearby.

It had been hours since Andrew and the search party returned to the house empty handed. The storm outside unleashed a torrent of rain but the intensity did not match the storm that brewed within the large house. Maggie had demanded to know what happened and received the same brief explanation that David and Richard had heard. Andrew refused to give any other details and insisted on discussing this with Christine first.

As the chimes of the clock tolled two, the storm continued to rage outside in waves of moderate to strong intensity. Andrew sat at his desk in his study and stared out the window hoping to see Christine returning to the house. Peter, Richard, David and Maggie had stayed with him in his vigil.

Not finding Andrew in his bedroom, Marian quietly made her way down the stairs and stood in the shadows as voices were heard from inside the study. She had hoped to find Andrew alone.

"You should rest, Andrew," Maggie was saying.

"How can I, Maggie? Christine is out there somewhere and I am to blame," Andrew replied sounding defeated.

Each time the lightning lit up the sky, his gaze quickly searched the grounds in hopes of seeing Christine making her way back to the house. Still looking out the window, he said, "Do not stay with me. Go on to bed and rest."

"She is my daughter," Maggie reminded him.

The room was silent for a while. Maggie moved to stand behind Andrew and put her hand on his shoulder. He reached up and took it into his, still not looking away from the window.

"I cannot lose her, Maggie," Andrew said forlornly. "She means everything to me."

"I know," Maggie said reassuringly.

Andrew sighed and said, "I will never forgive myself if something happened to her."

"We will find her, Andrew, and when we do, she will be fine. She will be angry with you, probably furious, but she will be fine," Peter tried to reassure him.

Richard leaned close to Peter and said quietly, "No doubt Marian caused this trouble."

At Andrew's growl, the two men smiled. Richard let out a sigh and said, "Then send Marian away, Andrew. Why is she staying another night if—?"

Andrew whirled around in his seat and hissed, "She is still here?"

"I believe she took her meals in her room," Maggie told him.

"Damn her," Andrew snarled as he turned to the face the window once again

Listening, Marian bit her bottom lip to keep from yelling out.

"With the storm, you could not turn her out, Andrew," Maggie said.

"Indeed I can and would have had I known she was still in my house," Andrew replied angrily.

"So Marian did do something—" Richard began.

"Leave it be, Richard," Andrew warned. "Marian is leaving in the morning if I have to toss her worthless hide on a horse myself."

Marian let out a silent huff at the remark. She turned away and soundlessly headed back up to her room.

"I was merely taking back what was rightfully mine, you arrogant ass," she grumbled at the top of the stairs. With an angry glare to the bottom of the stairs, Marian turned and stormed off to her room.

Without her cloak, Christine shivered from the chilling rain and night air. For hours, she dragged herself forward following the river. She was drenched thoroughly from the downpour and, with her clothes clinging heavily to her, she had to force her tired legs to move forward. Whenever she found a tree that had a heavy canopy of branches and leaves, she would stop to rest her aching body and catch her breath.

Relief came in sight when she found the bridge that crossed over the river and led to the village a few miles down the road. Grateful to be out of the rain, Christine slipped under the bridge and used it as shelter. Shivering from the cold, she lifted shaking hands to squeeze the water out of her long hair that fell down her back. Looking around she then slipped out of her dress to squeeze out the excess water. Not daring to take off the chemise, she squeeze the water out the best she could then grudgingly put her wet dress back on. Sitting against a wooden post that helped to support the bridge and, pulling her knees up to her chest, she held herself in a tight ball in hopes of warming up. Tired and hungry, Christine closed her eyes. The vision of Andrew with Marian was the last thing she remembered before she fell into exhausted sleep.

The storm's fury slowly gave away to a light rain. Finally, the first streaks of daylight showed itself on the horizon. The lands seemed to have rejuvenated in the storm's aftermath.

Andrew had already gathered the men together to continue the search. Darcy brought him something to eat and was disappointed to find it untouched.

"You will be no good to the search if you faint from hunger," she scolded lightly.

"For all I know, Darcy, Christine has had nothing to eat. When I find her and get her fed, then I will eat," he retorted.

Her next words were halted when a servant ran into the house and slid to halt in the foyer in front of the Duke and the housekeeper.

"Yer Grace, one of the men found this."

He handed him a thick bundle that Andrew knew instantly was Christine's cloak. Holding it up, he saw that he was right. The cloak was soaked and caked with mud.

"Where was this found?" Andrew asked with dread.

"By the river," the servant answered quietly.

"Dear God, she drowned crossing the river during the storm," Darcy exclaimed in horror. She put a hand to her mouth to hold back the sob.

"Do be quiet," Andrew growled.

His anger was more to himself than the housekeeper. She had only voiced the same conclusion he was thinking. To hear it aloud had made it sound so final.

"Then we start at the river," Andrew said in a tone of impatience. Glancing up at the grand staircase, he saw Marian. Heading for the door, he pointed at her and ordered harshly, "And get her the hell out of my house!"

Chapter 23

In the dimly lit skies of the dawn, Ham Stockwell was making his way to the village with his wife and sons. Though he was born Joseph Stockwell, he was a heavy-set man with thick arms and legs, brown eyes and thin brown hair. Because of his build, he was nicknamed Ham. With his sons, Percy and Jacob, Ham was a builder and had helped build most of the newer homes and businesses in the village. His wife, Jane, worked as a seamstress in a small shop in the village.

His eldest son of ten and six years, Percy, was laying in the wagon trying to steal a few more winks of sleep. Jacob, who was two years younger, lay on his belly and peered over the edge of the wagon watching the road as it appeared from under them.

As they crossed the final bridge that led to the village, Jacob lifted his head to gaze over the bridge to the water below. Suddenly his brows knitted in confusion then his eyes widened in surprise.

"Hey Pa, wait. There is somethin' down there," Jacob called out and was already clamoring out of the wagon.

"Jacob, get back in the wagon or I will leave ye here," Ham yelled over his shoulder.

"Tis a girl, Pa!" the boy cried out with excitement. "I can see 'er 'air."

"Mercy, Ham, stop the wagon," his wife ordered as she reached for the reins herself to pull up the horses.

Percy sat up at the first loud disturbance from his younger brother and was about to scold him when he saw where his brother had gone. He jumped off the wagon and joined Jacob, staring in surprise at their find. Arguing with his wife, Ham grudgingly followed his sons to the side of the road. They all stared at the crumpled form in blue that lay on the grass, half covered by the bridge.

"Is she—dead?" Jane asked hesitantly as she peered down at them from the side of the bridge.

Before either parent could stop them, the boys were bending down and turning the body over. They stared at the pale white face that was partially obscured by strands of wet dark hair.

"Who is she, Ham?" his wife asked.

"Now how would I know that?" the man grumbled as he moved to join his sons.

He stepped closer looking over the body before kneeling down to place a big hand on the woman's midsection then looked up wide-eyed. "She is alive!"

In his closer proximity, Ham glanced over the body and noticed the rings on her left hand. "Oh Christ," he muttered and immediately was scolded for his outburst.

"Ham Stockwell! Not in front of—" Jane started to reprimand but his frantic words stopped her.

"Tis the Duchess!" Ham exclaimed and pointed to the hand with the rings.

Scooping Christine up in his arms amid the excited chatter of his sons and his wife's wails, Ham carried her to the wagon.

"Percy, run to the village and have the doctor go to Kenilworth," Ham ordered his eldest son as he carefully laid Christine down in the wagon.

The young man watched in wide-eyed excitement of finding a body under the bridge that he had not heard his father.

Glancing over his shoulder, Ham noticed that his son had not left and roared angrily, "Get on with ye, boy! The Duchess is injured and tell that to the doctor!"

Ham had to yell the last statement because the boy bolted away. His wife draped a moth-eaten blanket over Christine as Ham jumped back into the driver's seat. Going across the bridge then turning the horses around, the three remaining Stockwells headed for Kenilworth.

The big house was a flurry of activity. Several men were on horses ready to ride while others prepared to mount up. Ham was about to call out when the front door opened and the Duke of Kenilworth hurriedly stepped out. Suddenly Jane was on her feet and yelling out.

"Yer Grace! Please wait! Yer Grace!"

All heads turned in their direction as the wagon continued its careful pace toward them. Andrew was losing patience and growled in annoyance as he mounted his horse.

"Please wait, Yer Grace!" she shouted. "In the wagon!"

A groomsman moved forward to halt the wagon and the uninvited visitors.

"Ye are not—"

"In the wagon! She is in the wagon!" Ham bellowed just as Andrew was about to turn his horse away.

Catching the word '*she*', Andrew turned the horse back to face the new arrivals in the rickety wagon. Ham stopped the wagon as the Duke neared.

"What did you say?" Andrew asked suspiciously.

"In the wagon. We found Her Grace. She is in the wagon," Ham was saying while climbing over the seat to the back.

By that time, Andrew was beside the wagon and looking down into it.

"My God! Christine!" he exclaimed when he saw the rumpled form laying within the wagon and jumped off his horse.

"My eldest, Percy, has gone to the village for the doctor," Ham informed the Duke as he pulled the blanket off of Christine and uncaringly draped it over the edge of the wagon. He then scooped up the limp form as Andrew looked over at the search party.

"Richard, send a coach to the village and bring them back," he ordered.

Stopping at the back of the wagon, Andrew took Christine from Ham and looked down into her pale face. Her lips were blue and he could feel her body shivering in the wet clothes.

"We have to get her warm," he muttered and hurried into the house.

Seeing the housekeeper hurrying from the back of the house, Andrew told her, "Darcy, there is a family in a wagon outside. They deserve a feast for breakfast."

He rushed past her and the rest of the stunned servants who were still in the foyer.

"Yes, Your Grace," the housekeeper replied then turned to the servants.

"We will take care of that, Darcy," Elizabeth said looking at Peter. "Go upstairs and see to the Duchess."

The housekeeper nodded her thanks and hurried to the grand staircase.

At the top of the stairs, Marian stood watching him. When he neared her, she took a step forward and opened her mouth to speak but Andrew growled furiously, "Damn you, I told you to get out! Now move! You are in my way!"

Andrew moved on down the corridor with Maggie and Caroline hurrying after him. David was rushing past Marian but Richard stopped and faced her.

His dislike for the woman showed on his face as he said loudly, "Oh, and Darcy?"

"Yes, your Lordship," the housekeeper answered as she was practically running up the stairs behind him.

"I believe that Lady Sanders will need some assistance with her departure," he said with a smirk.

The housekeeper looked at Marian whose brown eyes had turned cold as she glared at Richard. For a moment, the housekeeper wondered if the woman was somehow responsible for the Duchess' sudden departure the afternoon before.

In a tone that hinted of a smile, Darcy replied, "Yes, I will see to it myself." Marian turned her icy glare to the housekeeper who merely smiled and said with overly exaggerated politeness, "After you, my lady."

Impatiently, Andrew paced in the sitting room. Hiding his smile, David counted the number of times the Duke passed him. Richard leaned against the window and watched as Lady Marian Sanders was assisted into his coach. He was pleased with himself that he could speak to the high and mighty Marian Sanders in the manner he had wanted. With a smile playing on his lips, Richard thought back on his final torment.

"Use my coach, Darcy. Since Lord Hadley left yesterday morning, we would not want to have all of London spreading silly rumors merely because Lady Sanders returned in the Duke's coach," Richard had told the housekeeper as he slowly followed Marian and Darcy down the hall.

"You were always an insufferable bastard, Richard Pittman. Why Andrew considered you as his friend is—" Marian spat.

"He considers me his friend. I am not in the past tense, Marian," he corrected then with a smile added, "unlike yourself."

"He will tire of her, you will see," she said lifting her chin proudly.

"As he tired of you?" Richard countered.

The barb had hit home. Marian halted in mid-stride and turned to face him with eyes narrowed.

"No, Marian, I do not think Andrew will tire of Christine. You see, he loves her, very much in fact. That was something you never had from him," Richard told her.

"You, Lord Pittman, are no gentleman," she said through clenched teeth.

Richard gave her a handsome smile and said, "That may be true, Marian, but then you are no lady."

The coach was now heading down the lane as Richard turned his attention to the proceedings within the house. Still pacing, Andrew was raking his fingers through his already disheveled dark hair while he placed his other hand on his hip.

"What is he doing in there?" Andrew grumbled.

"Shall I fix you a drink, Andrew?" Richard asked.

The Duke shook his head and let out a long sigh. He looked at Richard then to David before dropping down into a nearby chair.

"She will be fine, Andrew," David said just as the door opened and Caroline stepped out. Andrew was back on his feet in an instant.

She held her hand up as if to ward him away and said, "She woke for a few minutes but now she is asleep again."

She stopped when the door opened again and the doctor stepped out behind Maggie.

"She will be fine, Your Grace. She is just very tired. Let her sleep for a day or two then she should be as good as new," the doctor told Andrew.

"She was caught in all that rain last evening and—"

"I am leaving some powders for her that should be mixed in her broth. That should ward off any signs of sniffles or illness. I am sure Darcy has her own remedies as well. However, sleep is what she needs the most."

"I will see to it that she takes her medicine," Andrew said with a nod. "May I see her now?"

"She is asleep, Your Grace," the doctor replied.

"Go on, Andrew, but let her sleep," Maggie said quietly.

Andrew nodded as he headed for the door.

Christine woke feeling warm and dry. With her eyes still closed, she realized that she was lying on a comfortable bed. The warm blankets covered her to her chin and she moved slightly to snuggle down into its cozy depths. Suddenly she realized that she was naked and sat bolt upright with the covers clutched to her body to remain covered.

"You are fine, Christine. You are home now," came Andrew's deep voice from the side of the bed.

She turned to him and noticed immediately the tired face and disheveled appearance. He was wearing the same clothes she had last seen him in and that reminded her of where she had last seen him.

Andrew saw the expression on her face change from fear to uncertainty to anger. Lying back down, she looked away from him in disgust and the look was like a knife in his heart. He reached out to adjust the covers around her but she jerked away from him.

"Leave me alone," she hissed angrily.

Andrew froze at the fury those three words held. He watched her roll onto her side, turning her back on him. Her dark hair fanned out behind her over the paleness of the bed linens and he ached to touch her.

"You have been asleep for most of the day since you were brought home this morning," he told her.

She made no reply and Andrew let out a sigh.

"Christine, what you—" He was about to explain but stopped himself. *Not now,* he thought, *tomorrow will be soon enough to make her understand what really happened.*

"The doctor left some powders for you so that—"

"I am tired, Andrew," she told him, her voice muffled from being snuggled under the covers.

"Very well, sweet Christine, sleep then. I will come back later," he whispered.

He did not move for a long moment as he stared down at her. Closing his eyes, he inhaled deeply and hoped that he had not lost her. With one more look at her unyielding back, he left the room.

Christine heard the soft sound of the door closing and shut her eyes tight. '*Sweet Christine,*' his favorite name for her. She turned her head to bury her face into her pillow and cried.

As the day wore on, the tension in the ducal wing grew. Knowing that there was something wrong between Andrew and Christine, Elizabeth was reluctant to leave. Peter had managed to convince her that it was something Andrew and Christine had to work out on their own. The following morning, Peter and his family left for London.

Maggie had searched for Andrew and found him in his study. He had nearly finished a decanter of brandy and looked as bad to her as he had the night Christine was out in the storm.

"Andrew, what has happened?" Maggie asked. "Christine has never been so inhospitable to anyone before and yet when you come into the room, her whole demeanor changes."

"A misunderstanding," Andrew replied not looking up.

"Yes, I have already heard that from you," she told him as she watched him swallow down the remainder of his brandy in the snifter.

When he reached for the decanter to refill his glass, she put her hand over his and held the ornate glass bottle to the table. Andrew's green eyes were glassy from his drinking but they held a hint of warning as he lifted his gaze to meet Maggie's blue eyes. Staring into eyes the same color as Christine's,

Andrew dropped his gaze.

"It will be cleared up soon," he said quietly.

"Soon?" she echoed in disbelief. "Then tell me this, Andrew. Would this 'misunderstanding' have anything to do with Marian Sanders?"

Andrew let out a loud sigh of exasperation as he tried to raise the decanter once again. Maggie held firm to her grip to hold it down.

"Maggie, may I remind you that you are a guest in my house?" he warned.

"Would you toss me out then? Send me packing as you had Lady Sanders?" Maggie challenged.

Andrew made a low growling sound from deep in his throat as his gaze lifted to meet hers once again.

"I said it will be cleared up soon. Now release the bottle," he hissed through clenched teeth.

Maggie stared at him with wide surprised eyes. She released the decanter and watched him pour the snifter full. Shaking her head, she said quietly, "Drinking yourself to oblivion will not settle the matter with Christine, Andrew."

"It makes *me* feel better," he growled.

Maggie stared at him for some time that Andrew turned to see if she was still in the room. When he saw her, he waved her away in dismissal. Without another word, she turned with a huff and nearly slammed the door in her wake.

Andrew closed his eyes at the sound as it echoed mercilessly in his head. Slowly and somewhat unsteadily he turned to see that he was alone in the study. Lifting his snifter in a toast to the ceiling, he said, "To love and all the pain it brings."

He drank a long swallow of his brandy and thought of how much better he would truly feel if he could wring Marian's neck.

It was the next morning when Andrew had finally reached his wits end. Christine had been in her sitting room with Caroline and young Stephen. He had decided it was time to make her understand what really happened. Her behavior had caused him to toss and turn for the past two nights that he could not stand by any longer.

Christine was laughing with Stephen as she played with him on her lap. Looking up and seeing Andrew step into the sitting room, her laughter stopped abruptly and the hostile look he had been receiving was instantaneous. Caroline noticed the change and turned to look at him.

"Caroline, I wonder if I could impose for a few minutes. I would like to have a word with Christine."

"Certainly, Andrew. Come along, Stephen," Caroline said and took her son from her cousin's lap.

The moment Caroline closed the door behind her, Christine was off the sofa and heading for her room.

"Christine, we need to talk," Andrew said more calmly than he felt.

"No, we do not," she gritted out.

"You cannot continue to ignore me like this," Andrew hissed as he quickened his stride. He had just reached her door to her bedchambers when she nearly slammed it in his face.

"Christine, will you at least listen to me?" he growled as he threw the door open.

She whirled around to face him and he saw pure rage on her face. "Listen to what, Andrew? That I should just turn a blind eye as you and your mistresses make love in my house?" With the fury raging within her that Andrew had now unleashed, Christine stomped her foot angrily and hissed, "This is *my* house!"

"Christine, I know what you think you sa—" he started to explain but Christine interrupted.

"I saw you holding her and kissing her, Andrew. Was I wrong? Did I not see that?"

"It was—" He took a step toward her but she backed away from him.

Through clenched teeth to try and control her anger and humiliation, she said, "Very well, Andrew, I accepted your proposal to save my life from some madman who is still hell-bent to kill me. I had turned your proposal down because I did not want to face this very moment. However, reality is reality. As your wife and duchess, I will be the perfect hostess for you on those occasions we are seen together outside our home. I will also give you the heirs that Marian cannot give you and I will be a good mother to our children. But at this very moment, I do not want you to touch me or be near me."

"You will not even let me explain?" he asked incredulously.

Christine let out a tired sigh and said in a quiet tone, "Go to London, Andrew. Go to Marian, take her to bed, make love to her, and say all those tender words to her as you have done with me."

"The hell with Marian!" he bellowed. "My place is here with you."

"*I do not want you here!*" Christine shouted back. "Go to your mistress, damn it! It has been two months since we married, I am sure you are tired of paying so much attention to me. Go back to London, go to her."

Andrew stared at her in surprise at what she was saying and the tone she was using. The hurt and rejection took over common sense and he heard himself saying, "Very well, Duchess, I will leave you alone. Richard is leaving within the hour and I believe I will accompany him back to London where the air is more—pleasing."

Without another word, Andrew turned and slammed out of her room.

"Although I do not agree of this separation, Andrew, please do not stay away long," Maggie was saying.

They stood in the lane as Richard waited beside the ducal coach. Andrew smiled down at her and said sadly, "She needs time to cool her anger. My presence here seems to only add to the raging fire."

"I have never seen her so angry before, Andrew. She is so furious with you that I cannot even mention your name."

"I know, Maggie. I cannot talk to her, not as she is now. I do not dare take the chance of losing her completely," Andrew said. Taking her hands into his, he added with a smile, "Take care of her for me until I return. I have alerted the household to watch for any strangers."

"She will not leave this house without a small army of escorts," Maggie told him with a small smile.

Smiling sadly, he nodded and turned to the coach. As he neared Richard, he noticed that his friend was looking up towards the house. Glancing over his shoulder, Andrew looked up to find Christine standing at the window of one of the guestrooms watching them. He stopped and turned fully to face her. They stared at one another for a long moment that Maggie turned to see what stopped him. By then Christine was turning away and going back into the room. Andrew closed his eyes and felt the pain in his chest again. Richard looked discreetly away as Andrew turned and stepped into the coach. Smiling at Maggie, Richard turned and got into the coach as well.

As the coach headed down the lane, Andrew's eyes were riveted to the window where Christine had been just moments ago.

"Are you sure this is a good idea?" Richard asked.

"No," Andrew answered still watching the house, "but I have unfinished business in London and it is time I dealt with it."

In the guestroom, Christine leaned against the wall near the window. Tears flowed unheeded down her cheeks as she listened to the coach move down the lane. Slowly sliding down the wall to sit on the floor, she wrapped her arms around her bent knees to hug herself into a tight ball and cried her heart out.

Chapter 24

It was turning hot as summer settled in with the first days of July. The crisp breeze was warm and helped to take the edge off the heat. The soft grass of the meadow swayed with the gentle wind and the various scents of the flowers carried from the gardens to where Christine sat under a large oak tree halfway up the hill from the back of the house. After a refreshing ride on her horse, she would sit in the same spot under the large oak and stare down at the big house. This had been her routine nearly every afternoon over the past two weeks. The house was too empty since David took Caroline and Stephen to their home in the country.

"She is nearing her time and I want her home before the traveling distresses her overly much," David had said a few days after Andrew left for London.

"I would rather stay here with you, cousin, but David is right. Before you know it, I will not be able to travel," Caroline whispered to Christine.

"You should go. Mother will be here with me and I have this big house to run. Everything will be fine," Christine told her.

It did not take long for the emptiness and loneliness to creep in. This was Andrew's house and, though he was not in residence, she felt his presence in every room. Christine could barely stay inside the house, expecting him to walk into the room at any moment.

Her musings were broken as one of the grooms stepped forward and announced quietly, "Tis time for tea, Your Grace. Lady Lockhart is in the doorway looking in this direction."

Christine turned to the direction of the gardens and saw her mother waving. Returning the wave in acknowledgment, she stood up and took the reins of her horse from the groom. With a smile of thanks, she was assisted into her sidesaddle then was followed back to the house by the four groomsmen.

Still dressed in her gray riding habit, Christine walked into the parlor where Maggie waited to serve tea.

"I will go upstairs and lie down instead, Mother," she said in the same sad tone that her mother had heard for two weeks.

"Christine, you have not had tea for nearly a week. Come sit with me."

"I am sorry, Mother, that I am not good company," Christine said in an apologetic tone. "I will see you later at din—"

She was turning away as she spoke to her mother and now froze. With her head bent and staring at the floor when she entered, she had not seen him. She could now only stare in surprise. He looked magnificent in his tan-colored britches and dark green waistcoat.

Her joy that Andrew had returned was short lived as the memory of her hateful words echoed in her mind. Biting her bottom lip, Christine left the room without a word of greeting to him and hurried up the stairs to her room. Andrew and Maggie listened to her hurrying footfalls in the quiet house.

He found her standing on the balcony staring out at the gardens below. His gaze roamed over her and he smiled.

"Christine?" he called softly.

At the sound of his voice, she stiffened then slowly turned to face him. He stood with the door open that led from her sitting room and their eyes met for a moment before Christine dropped her gaze to the floor.

"I had not intended to be away for so long but I had to finish with business that was long overdue," he told her in the same soft tones as he closed the door and stepped further into the room.

"I need to say something to you, Andrew, and I am not sure how to begin," she interjected quickly.

Andrew nodded his head in understanding and waited patiently. Christine took a deep breath and, lifting her gaze up to meet his once again, she let the words tumble out.

"When I agreed to this marriage, it was to thwart some man from killing me. It was a gallant gesture on your part and nothing else." She held up her hand when he opened his mouth to speak. "By agreeing to marry you, I promised to be your wife. As such, I hope you know that I would never embarrass you as a person nor would I willingly place shame on your title. I also agreed to be the mother of your children whenever that comes to pass."

She dropped her gaze to the floor and missed the corners of Andrew's mouth twitch upward.

"I will not make demands of you, Andrew, except for two small requests. First, I ask that you never bring your mistresses to this home or the townhouse in London, especially while I am in residence. Second, I ask that you maintain a great deal of discretion in front of the children. Any sons you may have will know the acceptable behavior of society soon enough. I will carry the responsibility of explaining to your daughters when the time is appropriate."

He watched her face as she spoke and he knew that he was seeing the reserved Christine. This was not the woman he married and made love to their first night together, their wedding night. Her blue eyes lifted up to meet his and he felt the cold wall between them. Now it was his turn to take a deep breath.

"Christine, please listen to me," he began in a soft tone as he slipped out of his waistcoat and draped it on her bed as he spoke. "What you saw in the library was Marian's doing, not mine. In fact, just moments before we were arguing. I no longer desired her, Christine, and she knew it. She also sensed that before I married you."

He paused to gauge her reaction but when she made no comment and looked back down to the floor, he sighed and said, "The truth is I love you, Christine, and have loved you since before we married."

Christine's eyes shot up in surprise and she stared wide-eyed at him. He smiled as he went on, "I made two very big mistakes. The first mistake was to propose to you the way I did. You had mentioned that you would never marry because of that damned wager. That happened to be at a time when I was going to approach your mother with my offer of marriage. Then you had left for the Meadows before I could talk with you. Just when you came back, I overheard the threat on your life and I knew I was running out of time. The second mistake was to never tell you how much I love you. Each time I wanted to tell you my feelings for you, I heard again how you could never believe in those three words."

With his hands out in supplication, Andrew took another tentative step towards her as she stared back at him. "But I need you to believe in those words, Christine. I need you to believe me when I say that I love you more than anything in the world. You are in the center of everything for me. When I saw that coach hit you in the park, I thought I lost you. When I think of how that man nearly suffocated you in your room while I was just downstairs..." Andrew paused and exhaled forcibly. "I cannot begin to explain how I felt. Much like when you were delirious from the fever as you fought that poison or when you were out there somewhere in the storm." He pointed out the window as he shook his head. "I could not rest, could not sleep. I had to know that you were going to be all right before I could think of myself."

"Then why were you kissing Marian?" she asked so quietly that he could barely hear the words.

Shaking his head, he explained, "She threw herself against me when I thought she was leaving. The kiss was barely a touch but unfortunately, it was long enough for you to have seen it. I was pushing Marian away when I saw you standing there and the look on your face told me that my world was about to crash around me if I did not explain. But Marian held me back just long enough that I went after you in the wrong direction."

Christine stared at him trying to believe him but the painful remembrance of seeing them kissing still had a hold on her.

As if reading her thoughts, Andrew told her, "Perhaps I made three very big mistakes. I should have released Marian long ago and I cannot begin to explain why I had not done so. I cannot explain it to myself but I rectified that problem while in London."

Seeing her brow knit in question, Andrew took another step as he continued, "I gave her one week to pack whatever she wanted out of the townhouse. She could have taken every piece of furniture. It did not matter to me. I was selling the townhouse to the first person that made an inquiry. Hell, I would have sold the damn thing for a shilling, I did not care. Until everything was settled and Alfred could handle the rest, I could not leave but I needed to come back here, back to you and explain everything. The longer I was in London, the more I worried that I lost you."

"You look rested," she said looking at his face. "You do not look like you lost sleep."

Andrew gave her a rueful smile before saying, "I very nearly fired Bailey. She is the one to thank for that. She had gotten some sleeping powders from Doctor Brownlee and slipped it in my tea at dinner. I nearly slept through the entire next day. That was two days ago."

Christine showed a small smile that gave Andrew some hope. When he took another step toward her, she took one back. His small wisp of hope dissolved with the move.

"Christine," he began but she held up a hand to stop his words.

"So you would have me believe that you married me out of love and not out of a mutual necessity?"

"Mutual necessity?" he echoed.

"My life for the continuation of your line," she explained.

"Christine, how do I answer that?" he asked. "Yes, it was for love that I married you. In a society where marriages are arranged for profit and gain, I dared to marry the woman I love. Yet in saving your life, it continues my line.

Sweet Christine, there is no other woman in England I want to wake up each morning lying next to but you."

Andrew stood in the middle of the room watching her as she looked at him. His heart quickened as she walked slowly towards him.

"Marian is gone now?" she asked quietly.

"Yes, I have only one townhouse in London. I have Alfred refusing payment for any bills she may try to charge against me," Andrew told her.

She was so close to him that he could just reach out and pull her to him but he remained still. Andrew felt a rush of joy as her arms lifted and wrapped around his neck. Their lips met and he could no longer hold back. His arms were around her and he crushed her to him, deepening the kiss. He whispered his love for her as he lifted her in his arms and carried her to the bed. Sitting down on the bed with Christine across his lap, he reached out for his waistcoat and pulled out a velvet box from the pocket.

"You need only look here to be reminded of my love," he whispered as he handed her the box.

Opening it, Christine found a heart-shaped locket. The heart was a large ruby with sapphires and diamonds encrusted around it. She breathed his name and kissed him but he was impatient for her to read the inscription.

Chuckling, he said, "Read inside."

Opening the locket, she read aloud, *"To Christine, my heart, my love, my wife, Andrew."* She saw his smile through watery eyes.

"Let me put it on you," he said.

He took the necklace from the box and put it around her neck.

He had her stand between his legs and smiled as he gazed at the locket. Slowly he undressed her as she pressed kisses on his face and mouth, sometimes holding her mouth to his.

"Andrew?" she whispered as her riding habit hit the floor around her feet.

"Yes, sweet duchess."

Christine placed her hands on either side of his face and smiled down at him. Her eyes seemed to outshine the sapphires in the locket as his gaze fairly drank in her beauty.

"I love you, Andr—"

She was pulled down across his lap for another crushing kiss. "God, I thought I lost you, Christine," he whispered.

"Perhaps for a while you had," she pulled back and got to her feet once again, "but I have a gift for you, Andrew."

"A gift?" he whispered as he lifted a hand to caress her cheek.

Christine took his hand from her cheek and pressed it to her lips. Still holding his hand, she moved it lower until she pressed it to her belly. Andrew's eyes followed his hand then stared blankly at the spot she pressed for an instant before he understood. His green eyes shot up to meet her face radiating with happiness.

"Your son, Andrew," she informed him gently.

For a moment, Andrew was rendered speechless before he had to remember to breathe. "You are with child?"

Nodding, she laughed softly. "Is that not wonderful?"

She sat on his lap, complete in her joy now that she had his love as well. "I lay in bed thinking of you and the baby. I love you, Andrew Chandler."

"Oh sweet Christine, my love, I am indeed a lucky man," he said then pressed his mouth on hers.

The kiss was slow and deep with passion as he lifted a hand to caress her through the chemise. Pulling away from the kiss, Christine's gaze caressed the face so close to her own.

"I have missed you," she whispered.

"I am sorry I was away for so long," he replied softly and kissed the tip of her nose.

Smiling up at him, her thumb followed the line of his jaw and just before her lips met his again, she whispered, "Make love to me, Andrew."

"I have sorely missed you, my love," he said, his voice deeper from the passion aroused.

News of the Duchess' condition traveled quickly through Kenilworth and the village. The staff was bringing in flowers, vegetables, and other miscellaneous gifts from the townspeople. In appreciation and acknowledgment of the wishes that they had bestowed upon the new Duchess, Andrew arranged for a festival using the large open meadow behind the big estate.

With only a week to prepare for the celebration, Andrew ordered a mountain of food to be prepared. He had Bailey and some of the staff from London join them at Kenilworth to help with the preparations. Some of the townspeople offered their pigs and chickens for the spitfire. Some of the men hunted for deer to be served to the throng.

The festivities began early in the day. Even the heat of the July summer day did not deter the fun and laughter having the pond nearby for the quick dip to cool off. The ponies from the stables were brought out for the children to ride. A puppet show occupied the small children while the adults competed in contests that tested for the strongest man, the best archer, the fastest reflex, and the funniest costume.

The Duke and Duchess of Kenilworth watched a snippet of the puppet show, checked the safety of the children on the pony rides and Andrew was even a judge for several contests.

In a pale blue summer dress with her long dark hair pulled back in a simple braid, Christine walked hand in hand with Andrew. Her first stop was to the makeshift nursery where a few of the older girls and grandmothers preferred to watch over the young toddlers so that the parents could enjoy their day of fun. In the middle of the nursery activities was Maggie who supervised over all. Andrew watched with a smile on his face as Christine cooed over the little ones.

Tents were set up for shade so that children and adults could lie down and take naps in the afternoon. Everyone enjoyed his or her fill of drink and food that seemed to flow continuously. Whenever a disagreement became loud, it was the townspeople who decided the outcome. In the rare occasions that did not work, then the matter was brought before the Duke.

By late afternoon and early evening as the sun dropped low in the sky, the people sat around in small clusters of groups or families and ate their meals while minstrels walked and played among them. Under Christine's favorite large oak, Andrew sat on a blanket with his back against the huge trunk of the tree. Between his legs and reclining leisurely over him with her back against him, Christine listened to the melody of the music and the words of the love song.

"Did you enjoy your day, my sweet?" Andrew asked bending to press his lips to her temple.

"Yes, I did," she said tilting her head back to look up at him. "You made many people happy today, Andrew."

"I am interested in only one person's happiness," he told her.

"And for that, I shall have to think of what I can do to repay you," she replied.

"I can make a suggestion, sweet Duchess," he said close to her ear.

Christine laughed delightedly. "Hmm, I wonder what that could possibly be, Your Grace."

* * *

As Caroline's time drew near, Andrew took Christine and Maggie to be with her. Within a week, the entire household was awakened in the early hours of the morning when the baby decided to make an arrival. Andrew kept David company in the drawing room while Florence and Maggie helped to bring in another Huntington. Christine was only allowed to assist as an extension of arms when towels were needed.

By midday, Maggie was carrying David's infant son into the drawing room. "Mother and son are doing fine, David," she said as she handed the baby over to his father.

"Do you have a name for him?" Christine asked smiling tiredly at him.

"Yes, his name is Michael," David said looking down at his son.

"Michael. Caroline's father's name," Maggie said. Looking with concern at Christine, she added, "Andrew, Christine should rest. She looks tired."

"Yes, Maggie. I will take her back to bed after she has something to eat," Andrew replied. Clapping David on the back, he added, "Congratulations on your new son, David."

"Thank you, Andrew. I hope you are blessed with such fortune," David said with a proud smile.

Grinning, Andrew replied, "Son or daughter, I have no preference. There will be plenty, I hope."

Maggie laughed softly and waved Andrew out with Christine. "David, Caroline is waiting for you. You go on up there."

After the birth of Michael Anton Huntington, Christine and Andrew occupied Stephen's attention so that Caroline and David could enjoy their new son.

"It looks like they are taking Stephen on a picnic," David informed from the window of Caroline's room.

"Again? When they leave for London, Stephen is not going to like having his meals indoors," Caroline said with a smile.

David turned back into the room and smiled as Caroline nursed their one-week-old son. "Now you can tease Christine of her size when her time draws near with this baby of theirs," he told his wife.

Caroline glanced up and, with a mischievous twinkle in her blue eyes, she said, "Oh, I intend to make up for lost time, my dear. I have all the torments she ever directed at me stored right here." She tapped her temple making David chuckle. "And each one is planned to be said at just the right time."

"It would serve you both right if she gives Andrew a girl," Maggie said coming into the room with a tray for Caroline. "Knowing my daughter, she will teach her daughter how to torment your sons until they are the ones running home crying."

David and Caroline laughed. "Aunt Maggie, my sons will have their father's cunning to outwit my cousin," Caroline boasted with a smile.

"Dear Caroline, remember that we are speaking of Christine," Maggie told her with a smile and wink to David. "I would not be surprised if Christine teaches her daughter to merely snap her fingers and your sons suddenly start crying."

"David," Caroline called amid her laughter, "she is speaking of your sons. Will you not defend them?"

"I intend on teaching them to defend themselves," David replied, "even from ruffians like Christine Lockhart Chandler."

"Oh God," Caroline exclaimed with a burst of laughter that startled the baby. As she tried to quiet him, she told her husband, "Ruffian? It is a good thing she is outside with Stephen and Andrew. She would snap her fingers now and have you in tears."

He stared at the invitation on his desk. It would have been the perfect opportunity to get close enough to Christine Lockhart but he had left London when his latest attempt failed. Instead of killing the Duke, he was only wounded and the damned highwaymen were captured. Now returned to London, he had the best opportunity ever to kill Christine Lockhart and he missed his chance.

Pacing the room, he knew that he needed another outlet for his fury. Storming out his study, he called for his coach and paced irritably in the foyer. He would go to the docks and take out his frustration on one of the tavern wenches. When he was through with her, she would never be found just as the others had never been found. He climbed into his coach and gave an address to his driver.

Resting his head back and closing his eyes, he said aloud into the empty coach, "This is your fault, Christine Lockhart. I would not be doing this if you had done what needed to be done in the first place."

Chapter 25

Several weeks later, Andrew took Christine to London while Maggie stayed with Caroline and David. The first item of business was to order new clothes to accommodate her condition in the following months. Andrew shopped with her to choose the colors and styles he liked best. After hours of looking through designs, bolts of cloth, swatches of color, and deciding on the trimmings, the Duke took his Duchess home for a quick nap.

When Christine woke, she found Andrew in his study. Smiling when he looked up and saw her, he held up several invitations for her to see.

"We have one here that will take place tomorrow evening. The Fergusons, I believe," Andrew told her.

"Ferguson? That same pompous lord who tried to have me tossed out of the House of Lords?" Christine asked making Andrew laugh.

"Yes, the very same. I am surprised you remembered him."

"Trust me, green eyes, I could not forget him. He was disrespectful to my father and I remember all those who show such attitudes toward Christopher Lockhart."

"Ferguson was not very friendly to me either, if memory serves me correctly," Andrew said with a grin. "I say we attend and see what he has to say about you now."

Christine let out a sigh of despair and grumbled, "Must we? They will only whisper behind our backs just as they had done when my father was alive. You are not deserving of that."

"You may see a difference in their attitude now, my sweet Christine. None will truly be friends but they will be allies because one never knows when your influence may be needed at Court," he told her with a knowing smile.

"I will not use your title for their petty grievances," she argued.

"Nor would I want you to do so. You have a level head and I trust in you to make the right decisions," Andrew said softly.

Christine looked into his eyes and smiled. "I love you, Andrew."

The kiss she bestowed upon him stirred his desire. As if sensing his arousal, Christine whispered as she tugged on his hand, "Care to help me decide on what outfit would suit me best?"

"For tomorrow's ball or for this afternoon?" he asked with a leering grin.

Smiling seductively, Christine shrugged and said softly, "Let us start with this afternoon and see what comes of that."

"Oh, I certainly do have some ideas," Andrew whispered as they headed for the grand staircase hand in hand.

The coach pulled up to Lord George Ferguson's home in the Square where lights were ablaze in nearly every window. Christine took a deep breath and let it out slowly. Andrew chuckled and pressed a soft kiss to her lips.

"Relax, my sweet. You are not alone to face them anymore," he told her.

"I had not thought of that," she replied with a smile.

He took her hand into his, pressed a kiss upon the top then assisted her out of the coach. He smiled at the vision in sapphires. He had insisted on her wearing the blue gown to match her eyes. Then he surprised her with a sapphire and diamond necklace with matching earrings.

Inside, their titles were announced in loud tones. Christine noticed many heads turn to watch them descend the grand staircase to the main hall. Trying to look unconcerned, she shifted her gaze to notice her surroundings. The Fergusons' choice of décor was far too gaudy for Christine's taste.

"Absolutely garish, do you not agree?" Andrew said leaning close to her so that only she heard him.

"That is not the word I would use," she replied with a pleasant smile. He grinned at her having caught her meaning.

"Ah, Your Graces, I did not realize that you had returned to London," Lord Ferguson proclaimed at the bottom of the staircase where he stood waiting.

"Just yesterday as a matter of fact. We hope that our acceptance was not inconvenient to you," Andrew responded amiably.

"No, of course, Your Grace," Lady Ferguson replied as she came to her husband's side.

Lord Ferguson looked at Christine as Andrew talked with his wife. The Duchess smiled pleasantly but kept silent as they talked.

"It has been some time since I had the pleasure of your company. You have certainly achieved high aspirations from that young girl those many years ago," Lord Ferguson said to Christine while his gaze slid knowingly to Andrew.

Lady Ferguson flushed in embarrassment at her husband's remark. Before Andrew could speak, Christine replied with a smile, "Had I aspired for duchess, my Lord Ferguson, I would have taken Whiteford's offer. However, I must confess that I did have much higher goals in mind."

Glancing at Lady Ferguson then looking in the direction of the ballroom, Christine placed a gentle hand on the woman's arm and said softly, "We would not want to take you from your other guests. If you do not mind, could we—"

"Yes, yes, the dancing is in there and the gardens are available for a stroll. Please help yourself to the banquet table. If there is anything you need, please do not hesitate to ask," Lady Ferguson said returning the smile.

Nodding, Andrew steered Christine to the banquet table. When they were out of earshot, Lady Ferguson turned to her husband and hissed quietly, "Have you lost your mind? We cannot afford to be shut out, George."

Lord Ferguson merely shrugged and watched his wife walk away in irritation.

Andrew shook his head as he and Christine moved to the banquet table. "I cannot believe the man would dare say that to you with me standing right there."

"He has already been drinking, Andrew. Did you not notice the slight slur in his speech?" Christine replied.

"Do not excuse his behavior, my love. Actually, there is no excuse for what he said. Did he think that I would not call him out for offending you?" he asked quietly.

Christine placed her hand on his arm and whispered, "Do not call anyone out, Andrew. I want our child to know his father."

Andrew smiled down at her then kissed the tip of her nose. "I would not miss any moment of our future together, sweet Christine." Spooning potatoes onto his plate, he added with a grin, "Besides I would not call out anyone unless I knew that I could win."

Christine's soft laughter made him chuckle. "Then it would not be fair, Your Grace," she replied in a low tone.

Andrew shrugged and grinned. "Do you want fair or do you want me around for our child to know his father?"

Christine laughed again. "Point well made. Do what needs to be done, my love, to ensure that you return home."

"I thought so," Andrew said with a chuckle.

After they ate their meal, Andrew escorted Christine into the ballroom and straight to the dance floor. Many eyes watched the couple, most having been hopeful mothers looking for a match with their daughters. Whispers among the disappointed mothers and the pouting faces of the dejected young daughters went unnoticed by Andrew who had only his wife in his sight.

Unknown to the couple was one who watched with increased fury. He could not believe that she was back in London. Over the past few weeks, the talk of London had been the dismissal of Lady Marian Sanders as Andrew Chandler's mistress and the selling of the townhouse he had bought for her. The cold eyes searched the crowd for Lady Sanders and he found her near the doors leading to the gardens. She, too, was watching the couple with a mixture of longing and hatred.

He pondered the idea of forming an alliance with the lady and wondered if it would achieve all of his goals. Lady Sanders could become his mistress until he reached Christine Lockhart. Perhaps he would even promise that Marian could have the Duke back if she assisted but that would be impossible. Lady Marian Sanders need not know that part of the game until it was over and then the three of them would be buried together. The thought of the Duke having both women buried with him put a smile on his face. With his mind turning with various possibilities, he continued to watch Marian as she glared at Christine's back.

"Andrew, please, I must sit down for a moment. Three dances are plenty," Christine whispered as the fourth waltz began.

"I want to show you off to those old crones who thought to saddle me with their long-faced daughters," he told her with a smile as he led her off the dance floor.

"I am happy to see you both here," came Richard's voice from behind them.

Turning, Andrew and Christine found Richard with Abby. After pleasant greetings, Abby took Christine to the table for drinks while the men followed behind.

"I missed seeing you come in," Abby was saying.

"We have not been here for very long," Christine replied.

"Well, I am surprised to see you both in London," Peter replied as he stepped up to the small group.

"Just returned yesterday. Caroline and David have a new son. He was born a few weeks ago," Andrew announced with a smile.

"Oh, how nice," Elizabeth said happily as she joined the small group with Connie and Henry Batson.

"Yes, his name is Michael and looks just like Stephen when he was born," Christine told them. Turning to Connie, she asked, "How is your new son?"

"He is wonderful," Connie answered.

Smiling as he put his arm around his wife's shoulders, Henry said, "Spoken like a true mother."

Andrew's arm slipped around Christine's waist and he smiled down at her. "Indeed, Henry. Now I want to be the first one to say this then all of London can hear about it. In the spring, Christine and I will join the ranks of parenthood," Andrew announced.

Elizabeth, Abby and Connie excitedly took turns to hug Christine while the men shook hands with broad grins on their faces.

"A baby? How wonderful!" Abby exclaimed.

"I cannot wait to watch you grow big so I can tease you as badly as you teased me," Elizabeth tormented.

"And me," Connie said smiling.

"Then you will visit us at Kenilworth," Andrew told her. "Before the weather turns cold, I am taking Christine back to the country. I want our child born there."

"When in the spring?" Abby asked looking from Andrew to Christine.

"March," Christine answered. "The middle of the month, I think, although babies have their own time schedule."

Abby looked at Richard who shrugged when he saw her imploring gaze. "Depends on you and if you are expecting then. I see no reason why we cannot bother the Chandlers."

"Indeed not. Andrew will need a strong brace to hold him until the birth. It is one thing to wait patiently while someone else's child is being born. With one's own child, the waiting is interminable," Peter put in.

"Good, then it is settled. Kenilworth will be filled with guests in March," Christine said with some finality as she glanced up at Andrew. He nodded in agreement.

Looking at the women, Christine asked, "Would either of you want to accompany me to the banquet table? I am hungry."

"So it begins," Peter said with a chuckle then ducked away as Christine took a swat at him.

Watching the women leave the ballroom, Richard told Andrew, "I am happy all worked well for you, Andrew. I was not sure what you were heading back to considering her mood when you left."

"I thank you both for listening to me and giving me advice. I especially thank you, Peter, for the advice of just telling her how I felt for her. That, I think, was the catalyst to our reconciliation," Andrew replied. "Not to mention Christine's news of the baby."

"Well everyone has been whispering over the abrupt selling of the townhouse and Marian's change of status," Peter said smiling.

"At least they are talking about someone else for a change," Andrew replied with a grin.

At the banquet table, Christine stared in disbelief at the food she put on her plate. "I ate this much when Andrew and I first arrived. I cannot possibly be this hungry."

"Not you, dear. It is the baby," Connie whispered with a wink to Abby.

"If I eat this much now, how much will it be later?" Christine asked dismally. "Andrew will be pleased to see me grow big with child but when all of me is still there after the birth, he will not be so pleased."

Her friends laughed lightly. "Take heart, Tee. The food tonight will only offset the nausea in the morning," Elizabeth told her.

"I have not had that as yet. I am hoping that I will leap over that symptom," Christine said.

"Whenever I am in the same condition, I will most likely take your share with mine," Abby replied.

"You are welcome to it. My, what wonderful friends I have," Christine teased, making them laugh again.

"I apologize for the interruption, Your Grace," Marian said softly from behind them.

The small group of friends turned to see her smiling sweetly. With a look of embarrassment toward Christine, Marian said, "I meant to write you and ask but since you are here, I was wondering if you happened to find something of mine that I left behind at Kenilworth when I was there."

"There was nothing found that I am aware of, Lady Sanders," Christine answered. "Let me know what it was and where you had last seen it, I will make inquires."

Marian looked at Elizabeth, Abby and Connie with another look of embarrassment. "Well, I would not want to upset you, Your Grace, but it was a silk chemise that," she paused and looked contrite, "Andrew bought for me. I believe I left it in—his room."

Connie's eyes grew wide in surprise. Elizabeth looked quickly at Christine to see her reaction while Abby gasped in shock. Christine stared stonily at Marian until the woman had to look away.

"Lady Sanders, you know as well as I do that you have left nothing in his room," Christine said pleasantly without blinking or smiling.

Marian's gaze shot back and the brown eyes turned icy as she looked at her rival. "Can you be so sure that the silk chemise you wear is not mine? A clever way to hide evidence of infidelity."

Her tone was meant to cause doubt but Christine interrupted her with the same pleasant tone. "You left nothing in his room because he was not there to remove them as you would have me believe. He has not touched you intimately for sometime. That fact is not well known, but I would certainly believe my husband before I believed anything you had to say."

"Then you are a fool, Your Grace," Marian spat. She spoke the title with so much venom and contempt that she could feel her body shake with it.

Looking at the once beautiful face that was now twisted with jealous rage, Christine smiled knowing that it would infuriate Marian more. With a shrug, she said calmly, "I was the fool to believe that scene in the library but Andrew explained everything to me. In the end, Marian, you no longer have the house he bought for you nor do you have my husband in your bed."

Marian stared in shock at the remark. Bristling from the anger that cost her two weeks away from the man she loved, Christine added, "Yet what I find interesting, Lady Sanders, is how your behavior now is no better than what London had expected from me. So what does that say of you? Will the Ton respect a lady who has no decency nor self-respect when facing the wife of the man she is trying to coax back into her bed?"

"I am not a whore," Marian growled angrily, her voice rising slightly.

"The Ton believed me to be a whore and I had never lain with a man before Andrew. If they believed that, Lady Sanders, then what do they believe of a titled lady who had been a man's mistress?"

"*I* should have been his duchess," Marian snarled.

"We have had this discussion before, Lady Sanders. If the title is all that matters to you, there are other men."

"*Your* husband should have been mine," Marian hissed through clenched teeth.

"Lady Sanders, I must speak with you, if you please," Lady Ferguson said quietly as she stepped up to the small group. She took a firm hold of Marian's arm and pulled her away for a private conversation.

Christine looked around and noticed the small gathering that had stopped to listen. Elizabeth took her arm and steered her to a nearby chair.

"Sit here, Christine."

"How dare she say those things to you," Abby hissed in indignation.

"She had no right to speak to you in that manner," Connie said.

"Indeed not! I hope Lucy is being stern with her," said a woman whom Christine knew had not been so kind before.

"Thank you," Christine replied simply with a small smile.

"Christine, are you all right?" Andrew asked in concern when he broke through the crowd.

"Yes, I am fine," she replied smiling at him.

"Where the hell is Marian? She has lost her mind," Andrew growled.

He found Marian standing alone looking around at the women who gazed upon her as if she carried some type of social disease. Lady Ferguson stepped into his line of vision as she approached the small group.

"Your Graces, I truly apologize for the behavior of my guest. I cannot begin to think of how I could make up for such behavior."

"You need not make up for her behavior, Lady Ferguson. I would like for Lady Sanders to apologize to my wife for what happened," Andrew told her. "I want the apology here with these witnesses who watched the earlier confrontation."

"Indeed, Your Grace." Lady Ferguson turned to find one of her friends nearly dragging Marian forward. "Lady Sanders, I had expressed my wish that you apologize to Her Grace. However, now I must insist upon it."

"You will never hear me apologize to the likes of *her*! You and everyone else here are all hypocrites!" Marian shouted out as she turned to face the group that gathered. "You are all the same ones who spoke ill of her yet now that she is a duchess, you would grovel at her feet! She remembers all of you before this supposed kindness and she will remember you when you ask for her assistance! Do you think you will get it? Hypocrites, all of you!"

Turning to Christine who was getting slowly to her feet, she pointed angrily, "And you, *Your Grace*, you will always be the insignificant brat of a sea captain."

"Marian," Andrew hissed in a low warning tone.

"You will never be any better than that, title or no title," Marian finished.

She raised a hand to strike her rival amid the shocked gasps of those surrounding them. Christine tried to take a step back but her leg hit the chair behind her. She was thankful that Elizabeth and Abby were both there to steady her.

Andrew caught Marian's wrist and yanked her close so that he snarled in her face, "That title, Marian, was something you would have never gotten from me! As I have told you before, Christine is my wife by my choosing! I will have no one lay a hand upon her whether she is in her condition or not!"

Marian stared at him for a moment before she looked around him to Christine. "Condition?"

"My wife is carrying our child," Andrew hissed and released Marian's wrist with a slight push.

Straightening his waistcoat, Andrew looked around at the faces and said angrily, "For anyone who dares count the months, the child is expected in March. By then, we will have been married for eleven months! That should squelch those ridiculous rumors that I married Christine Lockhart because she was carrying my child."

With a warning glare to Marian, Andrew took Christine by the elbow and took her plate from her. He led her away from the now quiet gathering and the stunned Lady Marian Sanders.

Connie, Abby and Elizabeth followed him with Peter, Henry and Richard closing the procession. Seating her in a far corner, Andrew handed Christine her plate of food. Pressing a kiss to her brow, he whispered, "This should be quieter for you, my love."

"What rumors?" Christine asked.

"Just as you heard, now put them out of your mind. I had hoped that you would never have known of their existence," Andrew told her with a gentle smile.

"I do not think I can eat this now," Christine said looking at the food.

"Then I will help you," Abby said taking the plate.

"I cannot believe she meant to strike her," Elizabeth whispered to Peter.

Marian turned away from the doting behavior Andrew bestowed on her rival. With her head held high, she walked through the crowd. She looked at them in surprise as they parted and left a wide path while watching her walk by, daring her to speak out again. Quickening her steps, Marian headed towards the ballroom. Lord Ferguson stood in the doorway, his stout frame effectively blocking her entrance.

"Lady Sanders, I believe it would be best if you went home for the evening," Ferguson told her quietly.

"What?" Marian asked in disbelief.

"He wants you to leave," said a woman from the crowd.

"Yes, you are no longer wanted here," another person from the crowd replied loudly.

Marian turned in amazement. "I belong here more than she does." She pointed to the corner where Christine sat picking at her plate with Abby.

"She never called us names," a woman called out from the back of the crowd.

Lady Ferguson stepped up with Marian's cloak, saying softly, "Your coach is waiting."

Marian stared at them for a moment before she snatched her cloak from Lady Ferguson. "You take her side now but she will never lift a finger to help you. *Never!*"

The door slammed in her wake and everyone slowly filed back into the ballroom or picked at the food on the banquet table.

Lord Ferguson brought a glass of water to Christine and said, "I too must apologize for the behavior of my guest as well as my own unthinkable statement when you first entered my home."

Christine looked up at him then accepted the drink. "Apology accepted, my lord," she replied with a small smile.

With a smile of his own, Ferguson said, "Your stepfather would have been proud of you, Your Grace. You are just as patient with disrespect as he was."

A genuine smile appeared on Christine's face as she said, "He was the one who taught me, Lord Ferguson."

Watching from the banquet table as he filled a plate, he pondered the news of Christine's condition. Could an accident still work in his favor? The Duke would certainly be more watchful of his wife. His eyes glanced at the faces of those still hovering around the room. The crowd certainly turned away from one of their own in favor of the Duchess. *Hypocrites, indeed,* he thought. *Marian just might prove to be an effective ally after all.*

* * *

It was a blissful time for Christine as she and Andrew enjoyed being together and knowing of each other's love. Since their declaration of love, it was the first time the Duke and his Duchess were alone. With Maggie still attending to Caroline and the newborn baby, Christine did not have to divide her attention between family and guests. With Andrew beside her each time she left the townhouse, Christine enjoyed shopping and spending afternoons in the park with him.

As they sat in the coach heading for the church to attend the marriage of Abby and Richard, Andrew said to Christine, "You should have had a wedding with your friends and family like Abby. You were deprived of the festivities."

"No, all I wanted was you," Christine replied as she leaned close to him.

"Hmm, very good answer, my love," he said smiling. His arms went around her and he pulled her to him.

Abby's wedding was a modest affair with only family and close friends to witness the exchanging of their vows. As one of her bridesmaids, Christine was dressed in a lavender taffeta gown and wearing the Chandler diamonds.

As the best man, Andrew stood with Richard and watched proudly as Christine walked slowly down the aisle. Memories of his own marriage ceremony flooded his mind.

Leaning close to Richard, Andrew whispered, "The moment you see Abby will be the most memorable time of this day, my friend."

Richard grinned and looked over his shoulder at his long time friend. As Abby made her way down the aisle, Andrew and Christine looked at Richard's beaming face then shared a smile.

The following week while at breakfast, Christine smiled and said sweetly to Andrew, "You know I love you more than I can say, but if you do not return to the House of Lords, everyone will think the worst of me—if that is possible."

Andrew chuckled as he eyed her. Christine shrugged and added, "Besides, I will more than likely continue with my naps. It is a wonder I sleep at night."

"When have I allowed you to sleep at night?" he asked in a low tone.

Andrew burst into laughter when Christine nearly choked on her juice at the soft provocative way he spoke. With her face crimson with embarrassment, she glanced around but the servants were well away from the table and seemingly unaware of the conversation. She shot him a look of warning that he only found amusing.

"All I am saying, Andrew, is that you have always been an active member of the House. You should not change your routine."

"Well, in all seriousness," he began.

"Thank goodness, you are now serious about this," she mumbled.

Grinning at her, he continued, "I thought that I would go in today and see what has been happening. Richard has been keeping me updated but with the wedding and now gone on his honeymoon, I need to go see for myself."

"Good," Christine agreed with a smile. "Do not worry about me. I will take a nap, see what new dish Bailey has heard of, take another nap, have tea with Elizabeth, and take another nap. By then, you should have returned and we will have dinner then go to bed for the night." She laughed with Andrew over her list.

"Just think, that has been your routine for the past couple of weeks," he teased.

She slapped his arm and scolded lightly, "It is your child that makes me sleepy. Look at me, Andrew! I am already beginning to show! Your son will be as tall as you."

His gaze dropped down to the slight bulge but the gown she wore effectively covered the true size of her condition. Earlier that morning when she was still naked in bed with him, the slightly protruding belly had been more pronounced and he marveled at the wonders of a woman's body. That he was responsible for her condition caused him to stir with desire and the love they made had been as it always was—intense and satisfying.

The strong feelings he had for her made him whisper thickly, "I love you, Christine, with all my heart."

The sapphire blue eyes that he could always lose himself into lifted to meet his. She smiled and returned the soft proclamation of love then sealed it with a gentle kiss to his lips.

It was no wonder that Andrew's mind was on his wife as he sat in his seat at the House of Lords later that morning. Though Christine was such a slender woman, the size of her belly at this stage of her pregnancy made him wonder. He made a mental note to talk with Doctor Brownlee about any possible complications with giving birth to a large child. The last thing he wanted now was to lose Christine in childbirth. The thought made his heart thump with fear.

The eyes bore into Andrew's back. If the Duke was here, then she was at home and alone. The idea of foregoing the meeting enticed him but a lure to get her out of the house escaped him. His inquiries from the Duke's friends gave no insight that he would be returning anytime soon. It seemed that the Duke was content to stay at home and dote on Christine Lockhart like a devoted husband.

The thought of Christine living happily with a man who would give into her whims irked him. The woman should have long since been dead. Instead, she was carrying a child. His mind went to another time and another place. It was not fair that she was still alive and now going to have a child. Women die in childbirth every day. Perhaps Christine Lockhart could yet be another statistic and no one would be the wiser. He smiled at the thought and wondered what steps he could take to ensure that happened when the time came.

"You look far too serious, Your Grace," a voice said from behind the Duke.

Turning, Andrew smiled at the man. He stood and shook hands in greeting while saying warmly, "Good morning, Walter. How have you been?"

"Doing well, thank you. And you? I understand that Christine is expecting in the spring," Walter said pleasantly.

"She is and doing well for our first child," Andrew replied with pride.

"Well, married life seems to agree with you. You do not seem to work as hard as before," Walter told him with a light chuckle.

Andrew smiled and nodded. "That was the topic at breakfast this morning as a matter of fact. My wife very sweetly told me to get out of the house for a while." The men chuckled at the remark. "How is your family? Your wife still prefers the country versus life in London?" Andrew asked conversationally.

"Indeed, she does. I miss her as you can well imagine but I must continue business here. I go back to them as often as I can," Walter told him. The call to order was announced breaking into their conversation. "I must go and take my place. It was good to see you here."

"Thank you, Walter, same here," Andrew replied with a nod.

He watched Walter walk away and thought of the tragic end of his sister. He wanted to let Walter know how upset Christine had been over the news, having just heard of it after so long, but decided it was best to leave the past alone. Taking his seat, Andrew thought that Walter had adjusted well and there was no need to drag out the feelings that had been so carefully put away.

Chapter 26

The weather was turning colder as the autumn months soon gave way to winter. Doctor Brownlee visited Christine often to check on her progress since Andrew had spoken to him about his concerns of her giving birth. Keeping the apprehensions to themselves, Brownlee could only reassure him that although her size was larger than expected, everything was going well.

The first time Andrew felt his child move within her was after one of her morning baths. As was his habit, he dismissed Mary and Bailey for a time while he spent a few more intimate moments with Christine. Touching and caressing her naked body, Andrew let his hand move over her protruding belly just as a lump reached out and touched his palm. He laughed and placed both hands over her belly. Several kicks in quick succession made Andrew's green eyes sparkle like emeralds.

Christine smiled at him as he kissed the spot that last revealed a lump. "Your son is very active this morning," she told him.

"Oh sweet Duchess, I cannot begin to tell you how marvelous this is to me," Andrew said as he moved up. Just a breath from her lips, he whispered, "This is *our* child, Christine."

Fully aroused, Andrew carefully positioned himself and made love to her. "My sweet Christine," he said, his voice deeper with the desire that spurred him on.

Maggie visited often as well to make sure that her daughter did not try to over-exert herself with daily activities. Bailey had assured her that the Duchess was not overdoing a thing because she was watched continuously.

"She is a sly one when she has her mind made up," Bailey had said one afternoon as Maggie was preparing to leave.

"Precisely why I come by often." Maggie said with a smile.

"For now, Mary is with her but soon His Grace will take her to the country. I will need to send instructions to Darcy to watch Her Grace with a sharp eye," Bailey replied.

Maggie smiled and nodded in agreement.

The new year was also the beginning of Christine's seventh month. Just two days after Andrew settled Christine at Kenilworth, the first lingering snowfall covered the land in a blanket of white. Sitting in the parlor with a warm fire and wrapped in a thick quilted blanket, Christine listened as Andrew read aloud. His reading would sporadically stop for brief interludes of soft kisses and gentle caresses.

February revealed itself to be the coldest of all the winter months. Though spring was only around the corner, the dreary gray day had a nip in the air that chilled a body to the bone.

As the time drew closer to March and the birth of their child, Andrew noticed how awkward Christine moved about. His worries of complications during birth crept back into his mind mixing with the joy of the baby's impending arrival. Sometimes his worries won over the joyous thoughts and he would ask Darcy to send for the doctor to ensure that everything was going well with Christine and their child.

The arrival of their guests helped to take his mind from his uneasiness. Fires blazed in nearly every room as Christine leaned lightly on Andrew's arm while they stood in the foyer to greet Peter and his family. Chelsea was the first to come into the house and she ran happily to Christine.

"Careful, Chelsea," Elizabeth called out. Chelsea nodded and stopped abruptly in front of Christine.

"Hello, sweetie," Christine greeted her.

"Tee, I missed you so much in London. Oh look, Mother. See how big the baby is now," Chelsea exclaimed and rubbed Christine's belly with a laugh.

"She will exhaust you with her constant chatter, I fear. Are you sure you want company now?" Peter replied as he shook hands with Andrew.

"A welcome change, I assure you. It has been so quiet here that her chatter will just attune us better with the noise of a newborn," Andrew told him.

"Noise?" Christine repeated with a tone of indignation. "Your son would not dare make noise. Demands, yes, but noise!"

They laughed at her remark and Andrew looked to Elizabeth.

"She has been counting down the days until you arrived."

"So has Chelsea. She has become very good at counting down now," Elizabeth replied with a smile.

Chelsea broke out into counting from twenty to one. Praising her, Christine clapped her hands and said, "Now I know you can teach Jonathon then you can teach my son how to count so well."

The young girl broke out into a proud smile and announced, "I already taught Jon to count to three. He just turned three last week."

She pulled her younger brother forward and whispered in his ear. A big grin appeared on his face and he recited the numbers shyly. Everyone clapped and the two children soon became boisterous with their excitement.

"Here now, Chelsea, Jon," Peter called over the din. "Perhaps, we should get settled in our rooms and let them take a nap. It was a long trip for them."

"But I am not sleepy, Papa!" Chelsea exclaimed with a pout.

"No nap!" Jonathon proclaimed stubbornly.

"This is always the fun part of being a parent. I cannot wait to see what you will do to coax your children for a nap," Elizabeth whispered to Christine and Andrew while Peter directed the children to the grand staircase.

"Oh, that will be easy," Christine replied. "A little of Andrew's brandy in their milk and the little dears will be asleep before you know it."

Andrew and Elizabeth burst into laughter as Christine smiled at them with a look of sincerity. "I see you doubt my method."

Laughing harder, Andrew hugged her as Elizabeth patted his shoulder saying, "She is still incorrigible, Andrew."

"She may not be able to stay awake for more than a few hours or sit or stand for long but at least the baby has not taken away her wit," he told her then pressed a kiss to Christine's forehead.

"Wait until the backaches began," Elizabeth said with a grin.

"I have had them before we left London," Christine informed her.

It was late the next afternoon when David arrived with his family and Maggie. The adults were thankful that Chelsea and Jonathon, both down for their afternoon nap, missed the arrival. Dinner was quiet as David and his family took the meal in their rooms then promptly went to bed for the night.

The next morning, Jonathon was beside himself with happiness that Stephen had arrived. After breakfast, the two boys played with their toys on the hardwood floors in the drawing room around the adults. Chelsea sat with a proud grin as Caroline allowed her to hold young Michael in her lap. The seven-month-old boy stared up at the new face and made gurgling sounds that made Chelsea giggle happily.

Andrew stood with Peter and David as they chatted. He was watching Christine as she smiled and looked happy with the children around.

"Oh, it is so chilly these days. Andrew, I cannot believe how warm the house feels," Maggie was saying.

"There are times when I can feel the draft move through the house but for the most part it is kept warm for Christine. She is moving from room to room so much that Darcy decided to keep fires going in all the rooms," Andrew replied.

"Darcy can be so outdone with me because I will not sit still," Christine added with a smile as the housekeeper stepped into the room following the servants with a cart of hot tea, hot chocolate and milk for the children.

"Oh, how well I know that," Maggie exclaimed teasingly. "Do not let Christine see you weary, Darcy. That is only a sign for her to do more."

Darcy smiled at them and said, "Her Grace has been on her best behavior of late, my lady."

"I have?" Christine asked in disbelief, eliciting a few chuckles. "Oh my, this baby has certainly made me fall behind in my usual torments."

"Christine has taken it upon herself to have the furniture rearranged three times in the last month. I believe Darcy has decided to nail the furniture to the floor in order to deter her from any more moves," Andrew teased.

"Not three times, Your Grace," Darcy corrected with a smile. "I can count five times without much effort."

Everyone burst into laughter at the comment. Christine placed her hands over her belly as she laughed. The two young toddlers laughed as well though they had not paid attention to what was said.

As the conversations drifted to other topics, Christine touched her mother's arm and asked, "Mother, could you put that pillow behind me, please?"

Maggie got up and took the throw pillow from the floor then slipped it behind Christine when she leaned forward. Jonathon protested the loss of their pretend building.

"Jon, Tee needs the pillow," Chelsea scolded.

He still protested with Stephen watching curiously until Peter called out his name. Abruptly, the protesting ceased as father and son looked at one another.

In the quiet moment, Christine said softly to Jonathon, "When I am done with it, I will give it back, I promise."

The boy seemed to be content with the gentle promise and settled back down on the floor with Stephen to continue their play.

For the next week, Christine enjoyed playing hostess to her guests.

Though she grew tired early in the evening, she ignored the signs until everyone went to bed.

As he helped her to get into bed, Andrew whispered, "Perhaps you should sleep in a little longer tomorrow morning. You are tiring earlier and earlier each day since everyone arrived."

"Now what kind of hostess would I be to ignore my guests?"

"A hostess about to have a baby," Andrew answered with a grin. "It would be understandable. The women would definitely understand, my sweet."

Christine shrugged and replied without committing, "Let us just see how I feel in the morning."

Andrew slipped into the bed beside her and pulled her close to him. The baby's movements were active as he felt the poking and rolling.

"He is awake this evening. Will you be able to sleep with his movements?"

"Right now, I think I could sleep through a howling storm," Christine said tiredly. "Sometimes it feels as though there are a dozen babies moving about in my belly."

Andrew chuckled and said quietly, "Then you will be quite busy giving birth." He laughed harder when she jabbed his side with a finger.

The next morning, Andrew explained her absence at breakfast to everyone who had indeed understood, as he knew they would. It was after the noonmeal when Christine made an appearance in the parlor, arriving in time to bid the children a good nap. She sat on the sofa and leaned slightly to hug Chelsea. The young boys had to have their share and reached out with small arms for their hugs. Peter helped Jonathon when Stephen slipped off her lap.

"Did you have anything to eat?" David asked when Maggie and Elizabeth slipped out of the room with the children.

"I am not very hungry at the moment. When I am more awake, perhaps I shall have Darcy fix me a plate," Christine said making a face as she arched her back in a stretch.

Suddenly a pain low in her belly caught her and she gasped aloud. All heads turned at the sound and they stared momentarily as her face contorted with the painful wave. Caroline hurried to sit beside her as Andrew moved quickly and knelt before her looking into her pain-etched blue eyes with his worried green ones.

"Christine, tell me what—"

"The baby," she whined. "Something is wrong with the baby!"

"Andrew, take her upstairs and I will have Darcy send for the doctor,"

Caroline told him and hurried from the room.

Christine groaned as Andrew lifted her up in his arms. David and Peter hurried ahead of him calling out orders to the servants. Mary rushed out from the back of the house while Darcy ordered one of the men to get the doctor from the village.

Upstairs, Caroline pulled the covers down while Mary swept the pillows to the floor except for one. Andrew set her gently on her feet just as Christine let out another mournful groan.

"It is too early for the baby, Andrew! Something is wrong, I know it," Christine cried, twin tear trails falling over her cheeks.

"Shh, now my sweet. Everything will be fine, you will see," Andrew tried to soothe though his mind told him otherwise. "I will not let anything happen to you, Christine. Now let us take this dress off and get you more comfortable."

His tone was soft and soothing and Christine felt some of the uneasiness wash away. He had managed to slip her gown off as she took off her slippers when another pain gripped her.

Seeing Maggie and Elizabeth hurrying into the bedchambers, Darcy told the young maid, "Mary, you go and help Townsend put the children down for a nap while we get Her Grace ready."

Suddenly, Christine let out a horrified gasp and everyone looked at her. A gush of water puddled around her stocking feet.

"Maggie?" Andrew began to question but she smiled reassuringly and pushed him to the door.

"Everything will be fine, Andrew. You go downstairs with Peter and David. They have been through this before and will take care of you."

Looking over the housekeeper's shoulder as Darcy escorted him out of the room, he heard Elizabeth explain to Christine as she helped her into bed, "Your water has just broken, Tee. The baby is definitely coming."

"Take care of her for me, Darcy," Andrew told the housekeeper as she was closing the door.

"She will be fine, Your Grace," Darcy said calmly.

Downstairs in the study, David pushed Andrew into a tall wing back chair while Peter handed his friend a drink.

"Here, this will dull your senses slightly," he said with a grin to David who sat in the matching wing back chair.

"Now make it last, Andrew. You will want to be sober when the baby arrives."

"It is too soon," the Duke said quietly. "She is not supposed to feel the pains for another month. Something is wrong."

Peter leaned against Andrew's desk facing them and replied firmly, "Now you know as well I do that no one can accurately judge the birth of babies."

"You do not understand. What if the baby is too large for Christine to birth?" Andrew argued.

"There is no need to consider the worst," David told him calmly. "Nothing will happen to Christine or your child."

"Women die in childbirth every day, David," Andrew retorted glumly.

"Christine is too stubborn to let that happen. I should know," David said in an effort to lighten the mood.

Peter grinned at the attempt. Andrew's shoulders slumped and he turned to glare at the man.

Peter sighed and said, "Tomorrow, we will all be laughing at your behavior, Andrew."

Taking a deep breath then swallowing his drink in one long pull, Andrew hoped that would be the case but all of his worries leapt forward with the sudden events and he could not find a calming peace.

Upstairs, Christine clenched her teeth as another wave of pain hit her. Her fingers clutched the bed linens tightly until the pain subsided.

"Have you felt any pains before that one downstairs?" Caroline asked her cousin.

"There was some tightening all last night and this morning, but I thought that I was just tired and it was a way that the baby was protesting how I let myself get so exhausted," Christine said through tired breaths.

"Hmm, sounds like you began last night and only now the pains are stronger," Maggie told her.

"This cannot be, Mother," Christine argued lightly and shook her head. "This time next month perh—"

She stopped in mid-sentence as another wave of pain hit her. Darcy and Elizabeth looked at one another knowingly.

"The pains are closer together now. It should not be too much longer, Tee," Elizabeth said reassuringly.

"Something is wrong, I know it," Christine sobbed. Looking at Elizabeth, she asked, "Please tell me the truth."

"Do not think of the timing, Tee. The tightening you feel and not being hungry are natural signs of childbirth. Everything is as it should be even though the baby is early," Elizabeth told her.

Sapphire eyes looked up at her pleadingly but Elizabeth smiled down at her and placed a hand on her friend's brow.

"Your baby will be just fine. Do not worry about that anymore. Just concentrate on bringing this new life into the world."

Darcy smiled at the comforting words as she set to work. Soon the doctor arrived from the village and began his careful examination. As the afternoon ticked away with agonizing slowness, everyone seemed to hold their breath as they waited for news from the ducal bedchambers. Even the house seemed quiet from the usual creaks and groans as the waiting continued. Several of the servants entertained the children when they woke from their naps, keeping them in the nursery to play.

One of the maids pushed a cart into the study as tea was served with pastries. Another decanter of brandy, bourbon, and other libations were brought in as well.

"A tray was taken to the children," the maid informed the Duke.

The door opened again and Maggie came into the room with a smile. The men stood up and looked at her expectantly.

"Well, Andrew, you certainly surpassed yourself this time," Maggie said as she walked towards him.

"How is Christine?" he asked fearfully.

"Oh, she is just fine, my boy," she answered. Taking his hands into hers, she announced, "And you are now the proud father of twins."

For a moment, no sound was heard in the study. First, David chuckled followed by Peter.

Andrew stared in astonishment at Maggie and whispered in disbelief, "Twins?"

"Yes, twins," Maggie answered with a laugh. "A boy and a girl."

With the realization of what he heard, a slow smile appeared on Andrew's face before he pulled Maggie to him for a hug.

"My God! Twins!" Pushing Maggie out at arm's length, he said happily, "And that was why she was bigger?"

"Yes, we think so," Maggie said with another laugh. "She was carrying two babies who are both just as loud and healthy as any one baby born."

"Can I see her? Them?" he asked then quickly corrected himself. Turning to Peter and David, he chuckled. "Twins!"

"Yes, she is waiting for you," Maggie told him with a nod.

Andrew was out of the room in a flash. Smiling, Peter and David stepped over to Maggie who dropped into a nearby chair. Peter fixed her a cup of tea while David handed her one of her favorite pastries.

Christine was lying on her side looking at the two small faces from under the covers. Both had wisps of dark hair peeking out from under the small blanket they were wrapped in. She looked up when the door opened and smiled when she saw Andrew.

Looking around the room, Andrew barely registered the faces then he focused on the bed. There was his family and he smiled broadly. He moved to the side of the bed and, for a moment, he stared down at the small forms before shifting his gaze to Christine. Behind him, the doctor and Darcy were quietly pushing everyone from the room.

"Hello, Papa," Christine greeted with a smile.

Still smiling, Andrew moved to the other side of the bed and carefully sat on the edge next to Christine. She rolled onto her back and was shifting slightly when Andrew leaned forward to kiss her. Her arms wrapped around his neck and soon both were caught in the torment of emotions. The kiss deepened and lingered.

"I love you, green eyes," Christine whispered when he lifted his head.

His gaze moved to the newborns and he smiled. "I will never doubt that, sweet Christine."

"Your son is your firstborn," she told him. "Your daughter was just moments behind him."

His smile wavered slightly with concern and his fingertips gently followed the line of her jaw. "And how are you?"

"Just tired," she replied smiling. "I was so worried about it being too early. Elizabeth said that I had exhausted myself too soon."

"Perhaps you should sleep now," he suggested. "I will have Darcy take— our children to the nursery." He had paused slightly and finished his statement with a wide grin.

"You certainly look proud of yourself, Andrew Chandler," Christine teased. "Just remember, Your Grace, you had help."

He chuckled and kissed her lips lightly. "And I enjoyed every moment of your help," he replied lewdly.

One of the babies stretched, jostling the twin. The proud parents watched with a smile until both babies settled back down without waking.

"Simon Christopher and Sarah Margaret," Andrew announced quietly. Christine looked up at him and he asked, "Is that to your liking, my love?"

"Yes, thank you. My father would have been so happy to be remembered and my mother will most likely burst into tears," Christine said.

"You do not mind that my parents' names are first?"

"Why should I? That both sets of parents are remembered is what matters to me." She smiled and looked at him with a mischievous gleam, "But then, when the other children come along, whose names will we draw from?"

Andrew shrugged and suggested, "Names for our sons are from my ancestry, daughters from yours?"

Christine laughed and said, "Agreed, Your Grace. I hope your family ancestry has plenty of names to chose from. I intend on giving you plenty of sons."

"Daughters as beautiful as their mother would be welcomed as well," he told her as he stood up. "Now rest for a while."

Chapter 27

News traveled quickly to the surrounding villages. For the next several days, notes from well-wishers arrived as well as small gifts for the twins. A few days after the birth, Andrew carried Christine to the sofa in her sitting room to receive her guests. Chelsea cooed and talked to the twins when they were awake. The young boys, Stephen and Jonathon, would stop their play whenever the newborns made a sound as if to ensure that the small forms were fine and were going back to sleep.

The chatter did not seem to bother the newborns as they slept in a pair of bassinets. Simon slept in the same bassinet that his father had used long ago but Sarah's bassinet was new. Hearing of the twins, Ham Stockwell and his sons quickly made a bassinet for the second child then had it delivered the day after the birth.

A week later as the weather turned warmer, Peter and his family returned to London. Notes from friends in London had started to arrive before they left Kenilworth but they were surprised that the city was still buzzing with talk of the birth of the Chandler twins. In the men's club, Peter recounted numerous times of Andrew's worries as an expectant father. Elizabeth was questioned of the birth as well in various shops. She had to remember to maintain a cheery disposition as women who once degraded Christine's worth would ask pleasantly of her health and of the twins. Each evening, Elizabeth would write a note to Kenilworth and let Christine know of the inquiries. Each note began with '*I thought that you may enjoy this one*....'

However, not everyone was pleased of the news. It was rumored that Lady Marian Sanders went into such a rage in her home outside of London that several rooms were tossed about in her fury. The worst room to receive the blow of her rage was her bedchamber. Though Andrew had never spent time with her in that house, she snatched the linens from the bed and ripped the sheets in two while cursing his name as well as Christine's. Another fact that did not escape the tongues of the gossips was that half of her servants packed their belongings and left without serving notice.

Another home in London was also caught in the fray of an uncontrolled anger. His study once again felt the blow of his anger as he growled in his madness. *Twins! She should be dead but instead she brought two more lives into the world. There is no justice, no God!* He silently cursed Christine's name as he threw objects about the room. The servants only stared at the closed portal not daring to go near. The animalistic growls that emitted from the room left most of the servants feeling a chill pass through them.

On a warm Sunday in March, Andrew took his family to the church where he had been baptized. Those already seated in the church stood up respectfully when the Duke and his family entered. Walking slowly down the aisle with Maggie and David's family following behind them, Andrew carried his son while Christine held their daughter. Reaching their pew, Andrew and Christine stood to one side allowing David and Caroline to step in first then Maggie.

During the baptismal segment of the service, the twins squirmed as the water was poured over their heads and Simon even balked for a brief moment but soon settled back into the comforting arms of his father. The vicar carefully took a child in each arm then slowly walked down the aisle for all to see.

Left standing at the baptismal font, Andrew put an arm around Christine's waist and felt the ragged intake of breath. Glancing down, he smiled when he saw her watch on with watery eyes.

"Let us welcome the newest of our flock. Simon Christopher and Sarah Margaret," the vicar proclaimed proudly.

Once the twins were returned to their parents and the vicar returned to his pulpit, he announced, "After services, everyone is welcome to stay and celebrate with food and drink courteously provided by their Graces."

A tent was set up for the Duke and his family as well as Maggie and David's gathering. The sides could be dropped to allow privacy when Christine needed to nurse the twins. During that time, young Stephen would join his father and Andrew for some games that were set up to occupy the children. When the sides of the tent were lifted, visitors carefully filed through to get a peek at the newest Chandlers.

April brought on bleak gray days with continuous showers. Having just nursed the twins, Christine had returned to her bedchambers to tidy herself before going downstairs. She smiled as she thought of how the babies looked like their father with the same green eyes and the coal black hair. She glanced at her own midnight black hair and thought that neither one of the children had a chance for any other color.

Andrew stepped into her room from the sitting room and smiled. "Are they asleep?"

"Yes, finally. Simon was fussing today but Sarah went right to sleep once he settled down."

Andrew moved to stand behind her and put his arms around her once again slim waist. "You look as slender as the day I married you," he whispered in her ear.

"Well it is a lie but I thank you all the same," she whispered back with a soft laugh.

Starting at the waist and working up, Andrew unfastened the small buttons of her gown. She smiled at his reflection in the mirror and asked seductively, "What are doing, Your Grace?"

"I want to play with my wife," he answered thickly. "It has been a while since I have been able to truly play."

"Hmm, has your mistress not been satisfactory?"

"You know, there is a funny thing about my mistress," Andrew began with a grin.

"Oh? Is she too demanding?" Christine asked smiling.

"No, not at all. It is that she looks so much like my wife that I decided that I will just play with my wife."

"Oh you poor dear. To be left with so little choices," Christine teased as the gown slipped from her shoulders.

"Not so. What I am left with, when playing with my wife, is exhausted and breathless."

She smiled provocatively in the mirror making Andrew groan as he slipped the chemise from her shoulders. Lifting her in his arms, he carried her to the bed and finished undressing her. Hurriedly, he undressed then rubbed against her body with his.

"I have missed being so intimate with you," he moaned softly as his fingers slipped between them to touch her.

"So have I, green eyes," Christine breathed as she moved under him.

"I had intended to play but I find that I cannot wait," he said as he positioned himself.

Christine gasped as he slipped inside her and began to slowly rock into her. "I have truly missed your lovemaking," she moaned breathlessly.

"No mistress could ever satiate me as you can with such ease," Andrew told her. "Not while you live and breathe. I love you so much, my sweet Christine."

She breathed his name and offered her lips to him. Greedily, Andrew covered her mouth with his and the two were reunited in the waves of passion.

Following the rains of April, the flowers bloomed brightly in May. It was a clear and beautiful spring morning when Christine requested to Darcy that all the windows to the side of house with the gardens be opened so that the smell of the roses could filter in.

Later in the morning, Andrew surprised Christine with a picnic meal under a large shade tree away from the manor. At three months old, the twins lay on the blanket watching the birds fly overheard and the large white puffy clouds float across the blue sky. Though Simon was wont to babble as the birds sang, Sarah found her toes more interesting than the clouds.

While the twins were occupied, Andrew held Christine's attention. She lay on her back with him reclined over her upper body as he plied her with soft kisses. A light fussing drew their attention and Christine moved from under him.

"Time for a feeding," Andrew said with a grin as he picked up his son.

"I knew Simon would call out first. He is always hungry," Christine said, glancing around before unbuttoning her gown.

"Like his father?"

"His father hungers for something else entirely," she told him with an impish grin, taking the fussing boy from his father. Andrew chuckled then picked up Sarah to play on his lap while Christine nursed Simon.

With green eyes shining with pride, Andrew watched his son eagerly fill his belly. Reaching out to tilt her head up with two fingers, Andrew pressed a light kiss to Christine's mouth.

From a hill a safe distance from the estate, Lord Jack Hanson sat under a tree and watched the small family. He smiled but it was not a happy one. Somehow he needed to approach his niece for some money. If he could not persuade her, then he would have no other choice but seek out a loan using his house as collateral. The thought of losing his home because he knew he could not repay the loan riled him.

"What are you doing here, Jack?" came a man's voice from behind him.

Startled, Jack whirled around making the other man chuckle. "Damn! You startled me," Jack told him.

Catching his breath and willing his heart to slow its pace, Jack shielded his eyes from the sun's glare to look up at the man. "What are you doing here?"

"I bought a house nearby," the man told him as he looked up at the blue sky.

Jack slowly got to his feet then pointed towards Kenilworth. "My niece and her family are having a picnic. A rather warming picture, do you not agree?" he asked sarcastically.

The man looked across the field and saw the small family. "And why are you so far away?"

"I need to talk with her but I do not want her husband around. With all of her wealth, you would think she would share some of it with her family."

The man chuckled and looked at Jack Hanson. "Did you run out of the money I loaned you already?"

Jack had the grace to look embarrassed before dropping his gaze to the ground. "I had hoped to talk to Christine and coax her to loan me enough to repay you as well as pay off some other debts."

"You will always have debts, Jack. You cannot stay away from the gaming tables," the man said with another chuckle.

Jack let out a long sigh and shrugged. Looking back to the small family, he asked, "So why did you buy a house around here? It seems rather far from your own lands."

"Well, the house has but one purpose," the man said. "I plan to kill your niece there."

Jack turned in surprise at the statement then felt the sting at his side. His look of surprise became vacant as his death came swift and he never knew that the thin stiletto pierced his heart with its upward slant.

"You were never good at keeping secrets, my friend," the man said softly as he bent down to wipe his blade clean on Jack's clothes. "I cannot have you telling anyone I am here."

Taking out a long glass, he watched the small family. The sight of Christine's exposed breast reminded him of the night he gazed upon her in the moonlight nearly a year ago. He felt a stirring in his loins at the memory of his alternate plan.

He snapped the long glass closed in vexation. "Another year! Too long for someone who should have died from an accident. Too damn long for the likes of you, Christine Lockhart," he grumbled.

The news of Jack Hanson's death was brought to Kenilworth by a message from Richard. Darcy had taken the note to Andrew as he worked in his study. After reading it, he found Christine in the gardens.

"I need to talk with you," Andrew was saying as he approached her.

She looked up and noticed the grave expression on his face. "What is it?"

"Your uncle was found dead, murdered actually, down by the docks in London yesterday," he told her.

"Murdered?" she echoed in a whisper.

"They believe that he was robbed."

Christine sighed and said quietly, "Jack never had enough money to bother robbing him."

Andrew shrugged and replied, "Someone did not know this and apparently killed him. Stabbed him."

"How do you know this? My mother?"

He shook his head and lifted the note up for her to see. "No, Richard sent me a message. I will have Darcy prepare the twins for traveling. I think your mother will need you there."

"Yes, yes, of course. Send a message to her and let her know we are coming. I will need to make the funeral arrangements then—" Christine was saying.

Andrew took her hands in his and said firmly, "No, I will deal with that. You have to calm your mother and take care of the twins. That is plenty for you to worry over."

Darcy appeared with another message. "From Lord Huntington, Your Graces."

"At least David and Caroline are in London," Christine mumbled.

"Darcy, have Townsend prepare the twins for traveling. We are leaving for London as soon as possible," Andrew told the housekeeper. "Lord Hanson, uncle to Her Grace, was found murdered in a robbery. Please hurry."

"Oh dear," Darcy said softly and looked worriedly at Christine.

With a small smile and a dismissive wave of her hand, Christine informed the housekeeper, "We were not close, but I need to see to my mother. He was her brother."

"Yes, Your Graces. I will see to the babies," the housekeeper said then hurried into the house.

In London the next morning, Andrew left his family at the townhouse then sent for Maggie while he began making arrangements for Jack's funeral.

Maggie and Caroline appeared at the townhouse and told Christine all they knew to date amid their sobs.

"His body was floating in the Thames and found by a seaman. His pockets were turned inside out and they tell me that he was stabbed in the heart," Maggie sniffed. "At least, they are certain that he felt no pain."

"A constable came to the house and told David and me," Caroline put in. "I could not believe that they told Aunt Maggie without having someone with her first. I was furious and by the time I got to Aunt Maggie, well, you can imagine."

"Did you call Doctor Brownlee?" Christine asked.

With a nod, Caroline replied, "Florence sent for him but she had already given Aunt Maggie a cup of herbal tea. Thank goodness she was levelheaded."

"Andrew will take care of the arrangements so you need not worry over that. Is there anything he needs to know that Uncle Jack was particularly fond of?" Christine asked her mother.

Maggie shook her head and cleared her throat. "No, Jack never thought that far ahead. It was only what he had to face today or maybe next week."

Christine and Caroline shared a knowing look. Jack Hanson only worried over how he could forestall yet another call for payment of his debts.

* * *

The funeral was not crowded with bereaved friends. Christine recognized many faces as those who loaned money to her uncle. She wondered if they were going to seek her attention to the more important matters at hand soon or wait a space of time. Staring at her uncle's coffin, she glumly puzzled over just how much her uncle's debts amounted to.

After the services, Bailey served a light luncheon then the family went behind closed doors as a barrister and Lord Alfred Renwicke went over the formalities.

"As you can imagine, Lord Hanson did not have a last will and testament drawn out," the barrister began in a quiet and caring tone. His brown eyes looked sympathetically upon Maggie. "Insomuch that you, Lady Lockhart, happen to be the last Hanson, the townhouse and all of Jack's worldly possessions will be turned over to you."

"Yes, I understand," Maggie replied with a nod of her head.

"Ah, yes. Lord Renwicke will go over his financial standings at this time."

Lord Alfred nodded and cleared his throat as he held up some papers that had been sitting primly on his lap. Looking directly at Maggie, he said, "Over the last year, Lord Hanson had to acquire funds to finance his various business dealings with the bank using several antiques in his possession—"

Maggie gasped and put a hand to her throat. "Oh my God, my grandmother's heirlooms?"

Andrew glanced at Christine and saw the disapproving yet almost imperceptible shake of her head. Alfred cleared his throat once again and nodded gravely at the question.

"I am afraid so, Lady Margaret. Even the horses were sold except for those needed to pull a coach."

"What? Why? What happened to his inheritance? Had he gambled all of it away?" Maggie queried. "Katherine and I shared half of the inheritance while Jack had the remaining half along with the house, the lands, the townhouse and—" Alfred cast his gaze to the floor when Maggie let out a sob. "My grandmother's heirlooms," she moaned.

"The heirlooms and anything else that Jack Hanson lost through his gambling are safely stored away in one of my smaller country estates," Andrew told her softly.

Christine turned a surprised look on her husband who merely smiled at her. "Over the last year, I have asked Alfred to seek out the belongings and buy back whatever the winner acquired," he further explained.

"Using what funds, Andrew?" Christine asked but already knew the answer.

"Mine, of course, and before you unleash your anger, my sweet, I will tell you that I also paid whatever debts he had accumulated over the last year."

"Andrew," Christine said softly.

"It was for you and for Maggie, Christine. Jack was a foolish man and did not concern himself with what may lie ahead. Knowing that, I could not have his shortsightedness leave you both in despair. Maggie, you will have the heirlooms to pass down to Caroline or Christine as you see fit."

Alfred began again when Andrew gave him a slight nod to continue. "I must warn you, Lady Margaret, that the townhouse is virtually empty of furniture, paintings, and all that you may remember."

"Oh merciful heavens," Maggie breathed.

As Alfred continued with his accounting of the finances, Andrew watched Christine throughout the remainder of the meeting. Though she offered her mother a great deal of support, the tight-lipped expression spoke volumes to the anger she held within. At the conclusion, Christine politely excused herself to tend to the twins. It was in the nursery as she nursed Sarah that Andrew continued his explanation.

"Christine, when Maggie told me of your birth, she had mentioned that she could not stay in the townhouse because of the company Jack kept. She did mention that there were many fond memories of growing up in that house. Because of that, I could not let her grieve over the loss of precious tangible memories. I knew that would have upset her more than any other loss, other than yourself. The townhouse is virtually barren within its walls but once I have the furniture, antiques, tapestries, and everything I bought over the last year returned, Maggie can spend time putting things back to their proper place."

When she said nothing to him, Andrew turned and picked up Simon from the floor to bounce him slightly upon his knee. "Once you see what he nearly lost, I think you will agree with my decision."

"You should have come to me, Andrew. My inheritance from my father should have paid for all those things, not yours."

"You cut him off, not wanting to continue supporting him," Andrew told her. Glancing at her, he saw the look of wonder on her face. "I overheard some of your conversation with your uncle that day I came to you with my proposal."

"You overheard a great deal," she replied.

"It concerned you, Christine," he said giving her a handsome smile. "Truth be known, until that night I kissed you in Elizabeth's garden, I had not realized how much I was interested when it concerned you."

Several weeks after Jack Hanson's funeral, David arrived at Kenilworth with his family and Maggie. Seeing Christine and Andrew step out of the house, he greeted them while setting Stephen on the ground. The boy bolted for Christine who picked him up and made faces that elicited giggles from the child.

"I thought a quick visit here before going to our country estate would allow Caroline and Christine a chance to catch up on the gossip," David was saying as Andrew tousled Stephen's hair amid the boy's laughter.

"I do not spread gossip," Caroline admonished as she stepped down from the coach.

As Caroline turned to take Michael from Maggie, Christine said while still playing with Stephen, "Oh no, she merely rewords it so that she is not repeating it."

Caroline let out a huff and glared at her cousin as David and Andrew laughed with Stephen following their example.

With the women heading into the house before them, David told Andrew in low tone so that he was not overheard, "Rumor has it that Marian found what is delicately labeled as a new benefactor."

"I am not interested in her exploits, David," Andrew replied.

"Oh I know that. What is interesting is that no one knows who he is. She lives in a nice townhouse near the one you had for her and his visits are very secretive." Seeing Andrew's bored look, David hurried on to say, "Even the servants are not talking which is highly unusually given the fact that servants are a font of information."

Andrew grinned and said with a shrug, "And what do you want me to do? Knock upon her door and demand his name?"

David gave a thoughtful look and said, "That would be helpful." He laughed at the incredulous expression on Andrew's face. "No, that is not necessary but just to warn you that some rumors have it that you are secretly continuing your affair with her."

Andrew let out a harsh laugh then gave the women an apologetic look when they turned their attention to him. Turning David so that they talked away from the women, he asked, "What are the gossip mongers suggesting? That I leave Kenilworth and head for London to spend a few stolen moments with a woman I can barely be civil to let alone make love to then dash back to Kenilworth before Christine realizes I am missing?"

David was having difficulty maintaining an expressionless face but the corners of his mouth just would not stay down. Andrew let out an exasperated sigh and said, "When would I sleep? In my coach as it races across the countryside?"

Trying to sound nonchalant, David said through the laugh that threatened to escape, "I just thought you should know what is being said of you. Even in the country, vicious rumors have the uncanny ability to find the wife of the said unfaithful husband."

"You know Christine better than that and you know that she would never believe such nonsense," Andrew said.

"Oh yes, indeed I do," David said as he tried to suppress his humor behind his hand. "The fun part would be how Christine deals with the one who brings such nonsense to her ears."

Andrew looked at him for a moment then laughed. "David, you may not be related by blood but you are definitely Christine's cousin."

"Ah thank you, Andrew. That is a grand compliment you have given me," David said proudly, making Andrew shake his head.

Chapter 28

As the days turned warmer with the approaching summer, Christine settled herself comfortably in her many roles. As the Duchess of Kenilworth, Darcy and the staff sought her out for opinions that pertained to the daily running of the house. Even the cook had grown accustomed to her presence in the kitchen on those few occasions when she would help in the making of breads.

Christine enjoyed the time spent with the twins. Many times as she nursed them, she would wonder over the miracles of life. Yet oftentimes as she nursed Simon, she would think of her brother, Phillip, and the short time they had together. Andrew found her crying one morning as she nursed Simon and it took most of the day with gentle questioning before she finally explained.

The most pleasurable role that Christine enjoyed was being Andrew's wife. The moments they shared seemed to pass by too quickly that she wished that she had magical powers. If she could, she would halt time so that she and Andrew could relish their time together until they decided to stop. Even the nights seemed to be in a hurry to meet the dawn.

On a clear sunny June afternoon, Christine sat in the garden with a book in her hands. Though the book was open and she stared at the pages, she did not see the words. Instead she was thinking of Andrew and his topic of discussion that morning on the aftermath of lovemaking.

"The twins are growing up so quickly," he began as he played with her dark hair. "I rather miss feeling the movements of our child within you and watching you grow big."

He smiled when she gave him a suspicious look and asked, "Do you know that I have just started wearing my favorite gowns once again?"

His green eyes drifted down to gaze upon the young slender form he held close. With a leering grin, he said, "Indeed. I see beneath me a deliciously supple body that does not look as though it carried and birthed twins. I believe I have been bewitched and was held captive by a beautiful fairy."

Her soft tinkling laugh aroused him though he was sure he was satiated.

Moving over her, he whispered close to her lips, "Do I find fertile ground, sweet Christine?"

Smiling as his lips briefly touched hers, she replied, "Time will tell, green eyes. Until then, we must continue to search."

A throat clearing snapped Christine back to the present. She turned and found a familiar face. Getting to her feet, she smiled warmly at the visitor while setting the now closed book down on the marble bench.

"Walter, it is so nice to see you," she greeted happily. "You are a long way from London."

Lord Walter Reynolds stepped forward to accept the friendly hug. "I hope I was not intruding. You looked as though you were far away from here."

Christine laughed softly as his brown eyes twinkled with amusement. "Well, not too faraway. Come sit with me," she invited and the two moved to the bench.

"Actually, I was passing through the village and ran across the Duke," Walter told her.

"Yes, the new bell for the church's steeple is being installed today. The vicar wants it to ring out its first service on Sunday," Christine replied. "Lightning from one of those terrible late spring storms struck the steeple and nearly burned down the church itself."

"As I saw," he agreed with a nod. "I am stopping by because Andrew had asked if he could impose upon me. The vicar apparently wants to bless the bell today then do the full dedication during Sunday's services," Walter explained.

"Oh?" Christine queried.

"Yes and Andrew wanted you to join him. I told him that I would be happy to bring you to him," Walter told her.

"Well," Christine looked down at her clothes, "I am not properly dressed for the occasion."

"You look fine," Walter assured her. "In fact, you always had that fresh look about you even after your many adventures as Lady Mischief."

"Oh goodness, you remember that?" Christine asked with a laugh.

"Indeed I do. Tilly's letters were filled with the fun of your deeds," Walter told her with a smile.

With a sigh, she looked down at her clothes again and said, "I really should—"

"No time for that," Walter broke in. "I believe that they were nearly finished as I was leaving."

Christine looked at her gown once more then, making a quick decision, smiled at him and touched his arm. "Very well, I will be but a moment."

Stepping to the open French doors leading into the drawing room, Christine saw Darcy dusting within. "I will return shortly, Darcy. Andrew needs me at the church."

"Yes, Your Grace," the housekeeper acknowledged looking up from her work.

Turning to Walter, Christine smiled and asked, "Ready?"

Walter nodded then walked with her to his coach at the front of the house. He assisted her inside then called up to the driver, "Move on."

"Yes, Your Lordship," the driver acknowledged.

Inside the coach, Walter smiled and said, "I had not realized that Kenilworth was so close to me. I just bought a small cottage just south of here."

"Oh, so you must be the one who bought the woodsman's house," Christine said with a smile. "You know, the villagers think that the place is haunted."

Walter laughed and shook his head. "Then that explains why I had difficulty finding someone to do a few repairs."

She nodded in agreement. Walter looked out the window for a moment before he snapped his fingers and reached under his seat. "I almost forgot."

Christine watched curiously as he pulled out a small satchel and set it beside him. "You remember how I used to dream of owning a vineyard so I could make my own wines."

She laughed and said, "I remember teasing you that you would be better off doing that in France."

Walter clicked his tongue and rolled his eyes. "We are not on good terms with France, Christine."

"I know," she said with a soft laugh.

"Here it is," he announced, pulling out a bottle and proudly displaying it to her. Pointing to the label marked only with a large number one, he explained, "This is the first bottle made."

"Really? Here in England?" Christine asked in pleasant surprise.

"Well it has been fermenting for only a couple of years. I have a full crate at home, each one numbered in order to judge the best time for it to set up."

"Well congratulations, Walter. How wonderful," she praised him.

Walter cocked his head to one side and asked, "Care to test it with me?"

"I fear that I must decline. I have twins who are nearly four months old and—"

"Goodness, where are my manners? Congratulations to you and Andrew," Walter told her.

"Thank you. You are most kind," Christine replied. "I am still nursing them and I have found that when I partake of drink, they are unusually fussy."

"Interesting comparison," Walter said thoughtfully. "Can you just have a swallow? It will not be much. A taste sample of English wine."

Christine laughed making him smile. "You always were doing things that did not conform to everyone else."

Walter winked at her. "Spoken like a true conspirator, Christine."

They laughed together as he opened the bottle easily. He frowned and looked at the bottle. "I guess it has not set up long enough to make it difficult."

He sniffed it and nodded with satisfaction. "Ah, I remember the aroma so well. You will like this."

He produced a mug from the satchel and poured a small amount. "It seems more like a drop but I would not want to upset the twins," he told her as he handed the mug over to her.

Christine sniffed and raised a brow. "It has a sweet scent to it." She tilted her head back and drank the small amount. Smiling, she handed it back to him, "Very good, Walter."

"It gets better," he said as he watched her with a smile. He rested the bottle on one thigh and the mug on the other.

Christine looked at him questioningly then smiled. "Are you not going to try it?"

"I will," he said. "I just want to see what happens."

"Happens?" she echoed.

Surprise etched her face as her voice sounded as though she spoke through a tunnel. Her vision blurred then cleared again. Christine looked out the window but the landscape refused to focus for her. The colors melded together without distinction.

"Is something wrong? You do not like the taste?" Walter asked.

Christine turned and stared at him somewhat disoriented. His body seemed to be small and faraway but his face was too large as he peered at her. She heard herself call his name but the sound of her voice seemed foreign and unsure. A strange smile appeared on his overly large face that she stared at it in fascination. It was like a snake stretching out to proudly boast of its length.

"I know you can hear me, Christine," he said still smiling. "I do not want to kill you right away although more than a cupful would certainly achieve that. This will just put you to sleep for now. Unfortunately, when you wake, you will have a terrible headache."

His hands reached out to her, the fingers looking like thin branches of a tree coming for her, and she backed further into the cushion. Walter laughed as he took her by the shoulders and moved her to lie down on the cushioned seat of the coach.

His dark eyes turned cold as he gazed at the figure across from him. "I finally have you, Christine Lockhart."

Percy Stockwell looked up from his repair work on the low stonewall as the coach hurried past him. His brows knitted in confusion that the coach would stop at the back door instead of going to the front of the house. Wiping the beads of perspiration from his brow, he straightened and arched his back to stretch it.

Still watching the coach as he stretched, he saw the man step down then reach inside to pull out a limp form. *A woman?* Percy thought as the man carried the limp form to the house.

The head slowly rolled from the man's shoulder and Percy's chin dropped in surprise. The upside down face revealed to him was none other than the Duchess of Kenilworth. Shocked and confused, Percy turned his back to the house quickly before he was discovered gawking. The Duchess would not be so far from home. He wondered if she was sick then mentally shook his head. *If she was sick, why not take her home?*

He did not know what to do and wished that his father could tell him how to handle this situation. He went back to work on the stonewall but his mind was still churning. If he left now, would the man be suspicious? He remembered the time when the Duchess was caught in the storm and his family found her near the village. His younger brother, Jacob, had told him that the Duke was about to search for her and was relieved when they showed up with her lying in the back of the wagon.

Perhaps the Duke was searching again but this time she was too far away. *He would not think to look for her here*, Percy reasoned in his mind. He glanced around but, as always, he was unnoticed. He decided to test just how unnoticed he was. Dropping his tools, he walked over to the well and turned the crank slowly. No one came out to yell at him for being slow. When the bucket appeared, he dipped the cup into the water and took several very slow sips while looking up at the sky. Still no one came from the house.

His wandering gaze turned to the rundown stable at the side of the house.

The driver of the coach had unhitched the horses and was now tending to them inside the small building. Percy went back to his place at the wall as a plan began formulating in his young mind.

* * *

Andrew returned to Kenilworth with David in time for tea. Going to the nursery first, he smiled at Mary who was rocking one of the cradles.

"Has Her Grace just fed them?" he asked while peering down at Sarah.

"No, Your Grace. She has not been in all afternoon," Mary replied.

Andrew looked sharply at her and asked, "She has not fed the twins? Is she ill?"

"She was not ill when she awoke this morning, Your Grace," the young girl answered. She doubted that he heard her for he had abruptly turned on his heel and left the room.

He hurried down the hall to Christine's rooms and searched. Going back out in the hall, he stopped one of the maids. "Do you know where I might find Her Grace?"

"No, Your Grace," the girl replied.

"Where is Darcy?" he asked.

"Possibly in the parlor serving tea, Your Grace," the girl answered and stared in bemusement as Andrew hurried down the hall towards the stairs.

"Ah, Andrew," Maggie greeted when he entered the room. "Are you not going to change?"

"Where is Christine?" he asked looking around.

"She went out to meet you. You did not see her?" Maggie asked him.

"No, and she has not been back?" he asked looking into the anxious faces.

"We have not seen her all afternoon," Caroline replied. "We just assumed she stayed with you and David."

"Who stayed with us?" David asked coming into the room.

"Christine is missing," Andrew told him. "She has been gone all afternoon."

Turning to the women, he found Maggie standing, Caroline getting to her feet and Darcy behind them putting down the tray. "Darcy, did she say anything to you or anyone before leaving?"

"I saw her talking with a man as she sat in the garden. She appeared to know him," Darcy replied. She took a shaky breath as all eyes turned to her. "She came in and said that she would be back soon. That you needed her at the church."

"Who was the man? Did she call him by name?" Andrew questioned her.

"No, she did not mention a name. He was well dressed and seemed well mannered. A gentleman she seemed to know."

"She did not need her horse?" David asked.

"He had a coach," Darcy replied. "I had thought it odd that there was no insignia. It was just a black coach."

"Oh my God," Caroline whispered. "It was a black coach with no insignia that tried to run her down at the park. Is it the lord who is trying to kill her?"

With a sob, Maggie sat back down on the sofa heavily. Caroline sat down quickly to aid her aunt.

Andrew stepped closer to Darcy and ordered, "Gather the servants. I want to know if anyone else had seen that coach or the man." Turning to David, he added, "We have a few hours of daylight left for a search."

"Andrew, she has been gone for hours," Maggie said fearfully, "and with him."

"I will find her, Maggie," he said kneeling down before her. "I can send for the doctor."

"No," she said quickly. "Do not waste time with me. Go and find her."

Andrew rose then leaned forward to kiss her brow. "I will find her, Maggie," he repeated then hurried from the room.

After a brief questioning, Andrew found that no one else knew any more than Darcy had. Dawson was only able to confirm that the man was a lord because when the man ordered the driver to move on, the driver acknowledged with a respectful, '*Yes, Your Lordship.*'

David gathered men from the household together to begin the search. The riders were mounted and ready to be on their way, when Andrew came out and mounted his horse.

David checked the priming of his pistol as Andrew settled himself quickly. "Where do you want to start?" he asked.

Tucking his own pistol into his waistband, Andrew answered, "Towards town. He had to at least make it look like they were going there because I needed her."

The group of riders hurried in that direction. Andrew knew that at the junction, the coach had to have made a turn but wondered in which direction. He knew that going straight to the village could be ruled out unless the coach turned at the next and only other junction on the road.

When they reached the first junction nearly a few miles from the house, the riders stopped and looked down on the road for any signs. The road was well used so it was impossible to tell if the tracks they were looking at were from the coach or from wagons.

"We will need to split up," David suggested.

"At this junction or the next? He could have turned at the crossroads a half a mile from here," Andrew said in slight annoyance. "Where did he turn?"

"Your Grace, a rider is coming," one of the men announced.

Everyone looked up to watch the horse and rider race across the open field. When the rider was closer, one of the men called out, "Tis Percy Stockwell!"

The boy did not slow down until he was nearly upon them. Pulling hard on the reins, he halted near the Duke and tried to catch his breath.

"She is not—near here!" Percy exclaimed breathlessly.

"The Duchess?" Andrew asked excitedly. Percy gulped air and nodded. "Can you show us?" the Duke asked.

"Tis the cottage—haunted by the old woodsman."

Some of the men looked around at one another in fear when they heard the location.

Percy gulped more air and said, "This horse is tired. I let the other one run free so they would think they ran off."

"Good thinking, Master Stockwell," David praised him.

Reaching out, Andrew pulled Percy behind him on his horse then pointed to the horse and spoke to the men.

"All of you go back to the house and take the horse. Too many of us will spook him and he may harm the Duchess. Collins, tell Lady Lockhart and Lady Huntington that we know where she is."

The one called Collins nodded and the men turned back to Kenilworth. Andrew and David headed in the direction that Percy indicated as the boy told the Duke what he saw. Listening, David looked over and met the cold hard look in Andrew's green eyes.

Chapter 29

Christine stirred as she slowly woke up. Her head was pounding, her vision did not want to focus, and her muscles ached. Even through the blurry gaze, she knew that she was not home. The room had a musty, almost earthen smell to it. The bed beneath her was hard and did not have the canopy overhead. She wondered where she was and how far away it was from Kenilworth. She moved her head and groaned as a wave of nausea hit her.

A sound from the darkening room drew her attention and a large shadowy form moved towards the bed. The face wavered and she had to close her eyes to relieve the ache between them.

"Do wake up, Christine, it has been hours," Walter ordered roughly. The bed creaked with his weight when he sat on the edge beside her.

Slowly she opened her eyes and tried to focus on the face. Her eyelids were heavy and slowly closed again. Suddenly her chin was grasped in a harsh grip.

"I said wake up!" the voice snarled close to her face.

With a gasp, her eyes flew open and she stared into the dark eyes that were framed within a face contorted with rage. She looked up at him in confusion.

"Walter? Why? What is this—?" she mumbled breathlessly.

"Be quiet," he growled as he released his grip on her chin with a shove. With a muttered curse, he shot off of the bed to begin pacing.

Her head snapped in the other direction so quickly that the nausea was overpowering. She rose on her elbows, leaned over the other side of the bed and retched violently. Christine's mind reeled as she tried to break through the fog and pounding headache.

He had barely waited until she was calm before he grabbed her arm and jerked her up off of the bed. She let out another gasp more from pain than fear. In an instant, she remembered the wine and the strange sensation from the drink.

"I have waited a very long time for this moment," he hissed in her face. "Do you have any idea how many times I was so very close to seeing you dead?"

"You are the one who has been trying to kill me?" she asked in astonishment.

His dark eyes narrowed as he studied her. "How did you know of my plans?"

Christine stared at him for a moment realizing her blunder. He shook her hard and she thought that her head would explode as the pounding became more intense.

"How did you know of my plans?" he shouted at her.

Christine moaned as another wave of nausea hit her. Determined not to let him see her sick again, she forced her mind to think of the effects if she told him the truth.

"Your henchmen were braggarts, Walter," she finally answered. "They were overheard and I was warned. Yet there was still the question of who paid them to make my death look like an accident."

She watched with satisfaction as Walter's brown eyes widened slightly in surprise. To ensure that she knew of his plans, she began to list the incidents.

"Let me see, before I knew that my so-called accidents may not have been accidents, there was the loosened straps of my saddle so that I fell from my horse and into the river. I was ill for several weeks. There was a broken wheel on my coach and, of course, there was the matter of the constables who nearly raped me even though you gave them explicit orders not to touch me." Giving him a look of pity, she could not resist the taunt, "They did not seem to mind disobeying you."

His eyes turned hard as he listened to her recount other incidents. "Then there was, of course, the runaway coach in the park. That one was nearly successful but by then, I had been warned of possible attempts. There was the man who tried to suffocate me in my bed that same night and it would have looked like I succumbed to injuries or awoke during an attempted robbery. That was rather ingenious."

Walter's mouth curved up into a smile that Christine did not like. "Then you were taken out of the house by the Duke and moved to his townhouse," he told her. "I thought that perhaps he was taking you on as his new mistress. There was talk then of a new mistress and that Marian Sanders was going to be sent away any day."

"New mistress?" she repeated.

"Well, that was my doing because I saw you and the Duke in Elizabeth Hunnicutt's garden that cold night during the ball she gave honoring Abby's engagement to Lord Pittman. It was very easy to go to someone the next morning and say something so simple as '*Did you hear that the Duke of Kenilworth was seen kissing a woman last evening and it was not Lady Marian?*' Of course, the fools had enjoyed any bit of news just to have something to say," Walter very nearly sneered in contempt.

Christine stared at him as he spoke. His disdain for his own fellow countryman was evident on his face as well as in his tone. Seeing her questioning look, he chuckled lightly. "They do believe anything, even a small wager of say fifteen hundred pounds."

"You sent that money to Andrew," she exclaimed.

"Indeed, I did. I saw you both that afternoon in the park looking every bit the loving couple," Walter said scornfully. "I knew I succeeded in removing the smiles from your faces. The Duke was furious later that day when he appeared at the club. He made a glorious speech on your behalf then to my astonishment as well as everyone else there, he tossed my money in the fire."

Abruptly, Walter thrust her away from him and walked away. Christine had to catch up herself as she bounced on the bed or she would have found herself unceremoniously dumped onto the floor with the next bounce. Standing slowly while watching him warily, she listened to Walter continue with his angry tirade.

"Burned my money! Damn him! He may have plenty of his own but I have a precious inheritance that burning it was not—"

"Did you truly expect him to keep it?" Christine asked in disbelief.

"I expected him to search out the source of the money! I would have led him into a trap, an accident, of course," he told her.

"But why, Walter? What is this about?"

"What is this about?" he repeated in a condescending tone.

He started a slow advance on her as she stood defiantly before him. Christine felt the prickles of fear rise within her as she watched his features twist with his building fury.

"What is this about?" he repeated again, his voice rising with each word. "Then I shall explain it to you, Your Grace."

The door opened suddenly and Christine stared as Marian Sanders entered the room. Smiling unpleasantly, Marian crossed her arms and walked over to Christine.

"Well, look at you." Waving about the room, Marian sneered, "Such adequate surroundings befitting the daughter of a sea captain."

"What are you doing up here?" Walter asked angrily.

"I just wanted to see the high and mighty Duchess of Kenilworth returned to her rightful place in society," Marian replied with a smile.

"You still believe that Andrew would turn to you after I am dead?" Christine asked with just enough doubt to irk the other woman.

The taunt worked for Marian let out a low growl and lunged at her rival. In a swift move, Christine was struck with the back of Marian's hand and fell to the floor.

"You took him from me! He would have married *me*!" Marian shouted.

"I took nothing from you, Marian," Christine replied calmly as she slowly got to her feet. "If he wanted to marry you, then he would have swept you off your feet so quickly that you would have ended up breathless from the romance of it." With a self-satisfied smile and out of pure vindictiveness, Christine added sweetly, "Instead, he swept me off my feet. As a reward for his amorous attentions, I gave him two children instead of one. You cannot even give him the one."

The enraged howl that emitted from the other woman made Christine's blood run cold. Marian's brown eyes were almost black with rage and her long slender fingers were like long talons reaching out for her nemesis. "I will kill you myself, you whore. Then I will raise your children so that they would hate their mother with such intensity they will spit on your grave. Andrew will forget you after I—"

Suddenly her words were cut off as Walter stepped behind her and grabbed her by the neck. "Be quiet!"

Christine thought that he was going to snap her neck but he tossed her away so roughly that her body fairly flew across the room hitting the wall with a loud thud that left Marian dazed for a few moments.

"Get out of here and stay out! I will deal with you when I have finished with her!" Walter snarled and savagely pulled Marian to her feet.

He opened the door and practically threw her out of the room then slammed the door closed. Christine heard Marian hit the wall with another thud. Blue eyes watched warily as Walter leaned against the door glaring at her.

"You are a poison," he said in quiet fury. "You reek havoc everywhere you go. Because of you, Tilly is dead, my parents are dead and you are the key to the whole ordeal!"

Christine felt a cold hand grip her heart and she found it difficult to breathe. "I did not know what happened to Tilly until last year, Walter. It was Lord Bellows who—"

"*I know it was Bellows! I was there!*" he shouted. "Before the fool died, he told me about you!"

Christine stared at him, stunned and full of apprehension. "He told you what about me?" she dared to ask saying the words slowly.

Walter let out an evil laugh that made Christine shiver. "What about you?" he repeated sardonically.

He began to pace with a thoughtful look on his face and his hands clasped behind his back. He was like a teacher before the class giving instructions while speaking slowly and reverently. "He killed Lady Anne Lucas for you! Did you know that?"

With wide blue eyes, Christine shook her head when he glanced at her for an answer. "Because she had dared to upset you, he went after her in the woods. When he caught up with her, he twisted her neck. He was the one who sent your horse back to the stables and no one had been the wiser. Just a low branch and a dead foolish girl," Walter told her.

He paused in his narrative as he continued to pace. Then with a nod of his head as if he came to some kind of conclusion, he asked, "But who was the one Bellows so loved that he took innocent young girls into his bed because she dared him to disobey her commands? Who was it that Bellows called his Angel? Who left my sister behind unprotected, knowing what kind of man Bellows was?"

Christine's eyes widened in shock and she opened her mouth to speak but no words would come out. Walter pointed at her accusingly and said in a tone that was far too composed, "You had the opportunity to kill him, to shoot him but you did not. You planted the idea in his head that you would return if he disobeyed your orders. Because of your ultimatum, Tilly suffered the consequences. She fought him when he raped her but no one believed her when she tried to explain how she came to be with child. And for what?"

The calm demeanor dropped away suddenly as he yelled at her, "She died as she gave birth to their dead son. Tilly died because of you! My father killed himself when the truth came out but by then, we had buried Tilly! My mother went mad because in her tormented mind, she could hear Tilly calling for her in every room of our house! All because of you!"

Walter glared at her as he paused to catch his breath. "Bellows was waiting for you to come back. He was waiting so that you both could have died together. He had a trap set for you, too," he told her in a disquieting calm.

In a few quick strides, Walter was standing before her and he grasped her shoulders in vice grip. "You destroyed my family, Christine Lockhart. You are responsible for their deaths. You have no right to be happy, living the life of a duchess, having a family. *No right!*" he was shouting again.

"Walter, please! I can explain," Christine pleaded.

He did not seem to hear her as he said once again in a calm tone, "So that you will know the pain and humiliation my sister endured, I will inflict the same upon you!"

Before she realized what his intentions were, he gave a mighty yank and her gown ripped from her shoulders. Driven more from self-preservation than fear, Christine fought back. She shoved him with all her might. He stumbled backwards but his hands still held her gown and the material ripped further as he fell to the floor.

Trying to step past him but hindered by her gown, Christine quickly shed the torn dress and rushed for the door. She could hear him behind her but she refused the urge to turn around. She could not waste such precious seconds.

Grabbing the knob, she opened the door but a hand shot out from behind her and slammed the door closed again.

"No!" she cried out in desperation. She bucked her body backwards to knock him off balance while pulling at the door.

Strong arms grabbed her around the waist from behind and lifted her off the floor. Christine turned into a hissing hellcat as she fought savagely to get free. She was thrown to the bed where she bounced once and turned to fight him off. When she turned, a balled up fist filled her line of vision and connected solidly against her cheek. Hot white pain exploded on that side of her head.

Dazed and nearly unconscious from the blow, Christine felt herself fall backwards upon the bed. As she slowly regained her senses, she heard the sound of ripping material and felt her body jolting with the sudden jerks. She no longer felt clothes on her body as the cold air touched her skin. Then hands were painfully kneading her breasts that were filled with milk since she missed the twins' feeding. She winced with the pain and heard a laugh.

"I will enjoy this," Walter said as he eyed the woman before him. In Christine's mind, she heard Bellows again hiss, *'Now be still, you will enjoy this!'*

Walter's hands moved lower down her body as his eyes fastened to the triangular patch of dark hair at the apex of her legs. One hand touched her knee to part her legs while the other hand slowly moved to savor the feel of her.

Abruptly, Christine's knee shot up but was too high to hit her target.

Instead her knee struck his midsection and the air went out of him in a 'whoosh.' Walter stumbled backwards gasping for air and, in a flash, Christine was off the bed.

He glared at her seeing that she had a duped him with her feigned injury. His lips curled in a snarl as he told her menacingly, "For that, I will not only let the Duke see what is left of you but he will also see what would be left of those brats you brought into the world. Then I will kill him, too."

"Try to kill me then, Walter!" Christine screamed. "I will escape from you just as I escaped from Bellows!"

"I *will* kill you, Christine," he replied with a smile.

With that, he lunged for her. The room was small and though Christine had been able to twist her body from being captured by the outstretched arms, Walter managed to put out a booted foot that effectively tripped her. She muttered a curse as she fell to one knee before catching herself but that lost moment was enough for Walter to turn and grab her from behind.

Kicking and snarling obscenities, Christine fought him as he turned to the wall. In a swift move, he hit the wall with her sandwiched between them. She grunted and barely caught her breath before he slammed her against the wall again. Her hands went up to ward off the next assault but Walter turned and tossed her down on the bed.

Gasping for air, Christine turned to roll off but he caught her shoulder and turned her back. His other hand went to her throat and he squeezed slowly. Realizing what he intended to do, Christine took a deep breath as her hands lifted to fight him. He leaned back as her hands sought his face, her nails ready to claw at him. A surge of pleasure much like a sexual encounter filled him as he watched her face turn red.

"Fight me, Your Grace," he said with a hint of laughter as both of his hands encircled her throat. "Will you not fight me?"

Christine's body squirmed under him and he remembered his vision of taking his pleasure on her. Releasing one hand, he parted her thighs and laughed as she fought harder against him.

"Do you want me, Duchess?" he hissed as his fingers painfully entered her.

Christine gasped but it was abruptly cut off as his fingers dug deeper into the sides of her throat. Her eyes closed against the pain and she felt herself slipping away.

"No, you are not ready but I will take you anyway," he told her.

His voice sounded so far away to Christine and her arms were slowing their fight against him. She could not get away and her mind went to Andrew and the twins. Walter had made so many attempts to kill her and she knew that he would go through with his threat to kill the twins then Andrew.

Grinning with anticipation, Walter was growing hard with rampant desire as he stared down at her. Her body was slender and nearly unmarred from carrying the twins that he wondered why his wife could not look so attractive after giving birth. She had carried only one child each time and yet she had not tried to fully regain her own figure.

Christine's struggles started to slow and he knew that he would lose her soon. Fumbling to open his britches, he wanted to be inside her when she died beneath him. Licking his lips in excitement, his gaze shifted from her face to the softness between her legs. He thought of the feel of her as his fingers probed and he stopped from freeing his hard erection to reach out to touch her again.

Chapter 30

Darkness had fallen by the time the three riders approached the cottage. Looking around, they spotted only one window with light filtering through the drawn curtains. They dismounted and Andrew ordered Percy to stay with the horses.

"If anything happens to us, you get on that horse and go home," Andrew told the boy.

"Do not go into that cottage, no matter what you hear," David added sternly.

Percy nodded and grasped the reins tightly in his fist. As Andrew and David turned, Percy reached out and touched the Duke's arm. "There is a driver, the man and a lady."

"There are two women inside?" Andrew asked for clarity. "The Duchess and someone else?"

"Yes," Percy said, his head bobbing up and down.

"Good lad, thank you," Andrew said smiling as he patted the boy's shoulder. "Now stay here and out of sight."

Quietly, Andrew and David headed for the rundown stables. Inside, they found the driver lying on a pile of straw, a near empty bottle was cradled in the crook of his arm.

Examining the still form, David whispered to Andrew, "He is dead."

Nodding, Andrew turned to look at the house. Carefully and as quietly as they could, they crept up to the room where there was light. The shadowy figure of a woman passed the window. Pointing to the back of house, Andrew directed David to turn and move on.

The back door opened easily and without creaks, a sign of a recent oiling. Stealthily, the two crept inside the house. David closed the door then stepped further into the kitchen behind Andrew. Something on the floor crunched under David's boot and the two men froze.

"You little beggar, you better not have your filthy hands on another bottle," the woman called out.

The uncertainty of what to do next was quickly replaced with rage as Andrew recognized the voice. Motioning for David to stay still, Andrew hurried to the wall beside the door leading into the next room. The woman appeared in the doorway and her hands went to her hips.

"Why are you just standing there? Get out of—"

Her words were abruptly halted as a hand covered her mouth and another hand crept around the front of her to circle her throat. She struggled against the hands that held her and pressed her back against a hard body.

"Where is she, Marian?" Andrew hissed in her ears.

Shocked at the voice, Marian was still instantly and cried out his name but it was muffled with his hand covering her mouth. Squeezing his fingers around her throat, Andrew repeated the question barely controlling his anger, "Where is she?"

She pointed up to the ceiling indicating the second floor. Whirling around, Marian found herself being slammed against the wall, the air rushing out of her lungs. At that same moment, a loud thud was heard above as something hit the floor.

With his hand still clutching her throat and the other hand grasping her arm in a vice grip, Andrew leaned close into her so that she could not fight him easily. "I should kill you now for your part in this!"

"Andrew, please," Marian implored as she gazed into his green eyes. "You have your heirs. I can love them as my own."

He stared at her in disbelief. "You actually believe that I would let him kill her and take you back?"

"She is dead already," Marian sneered.

"If she is then I am coming back down here to kill you," Andrew told her.

"I can help you to forget she ever existed, my love," she purred, moving her body seductively against his. Instead of the flare of passion she had hoped to receive, she felt his fingers dig into her throat.

A vague memory of a frightening dream from long ago crept into Andrew's mind. Christine had died and Marian was consoling him, saying the same words.

"Damn it! Do you have any idea what you have done?" he growled. "I love her, Marian. She is the mother of my children. How can you possibly think that I would let you near the twins and replace her?"

"We had so much together," she squeaked. His grip on her throat was becoming more painful.

"It was nothing to me," he hissed. "You were nothing but a high-priced tavern wench without the diseases."

"You bastard," Marian spat. "Nothing? That was all I meant to you?"

"You could never have been my duchess. You did not have the qualities required for the title," he told her cruelly.

The rage exploded within her from his insults, distorting her beautiful features. With a low hiss, her hands came up and shoved Andrew's chin upward. He released his grip to her throat and took a step back.

With the weight of his body away from her, Marian groped around for some kind of weapon. Her fingers closed around a broom handle and she swung out but Andrew's arm shot up to block the blow. With his other hand balled into a fist, he hit her chin. Marian's mouth closed with a loud 'clomp' before she slid slowly down the wall to the floor.

Enraged that she had a part in the kidnapping in order to rid herself of her enemy, Andrew merely gave her a cursory glance before he headed for the stairs. David stopped only to ensure that Marian was unconscious and would not call out the alarm before he followed Andrew.

Listening at the door for a brief instant, Andrew took a step back then lifted a leg. With a mighty kick, the door crashed open sending pieces of wood and splinters into the room. Walter's head shot up and fury replaced passion almost instantly. His hand hovered just over the softness he was about to touch when he glared at the Duke.

Charging into the room, Andrew took in the scene immediately. His heart stopped when he saw Walter's hand around Christine's throat and, at that moment, her arms fell limp to her side.

Laughing, Walter straightened and announced gleefully, "You are too late!"

With a savage growl, Andrew launched himself upon the man. The two crashed against the wall away from the bed. With his face just inches from Walter's, Andrew snarled, "I will tear you apart with my bare hands!"

Behind them, David entered the room and saw Christine lying on the bed. "Dear God," he exclaimed and rushed to her side.

He lifted a corner of the moth-eaten bedspread and covered her. Seeing the ashen color of her face and the red marks on her neck left by Walter's fingers, David shook her hard. "Damn it, breathe," he growled as he shook her again.

Christine was floating in the darkness when everything started to shake. She gasped in surprise then coughed as air whooshed through her sore throat. Each time she tried to fill her lungs, she coughed. Her lungs burned as the air slowly filled them making her cough harder.

Relieved, David made sure that she was covered then glanced over his shoulder at the fight. The two combatants stopped for an instant and turned to the bed at the sound of Christine's coughing. Walter muttered a curse then braced himself as Andrew turned again to face him while his fist shot forward with the momentum of the turn.

Walter fell backwards against the wall, hitting his head. Andrew stepped forward and pulled him up by the front of his shirt as the man started to slump. The move was only a trick as Walter's arms shot up to break Andrew's hold. With a shove, Walter pushed Andrew away from him.

Stumbling slightly, it took Andrew a few long seconds to catch his footing. When he straightened, Andrew froze then felt around his waistband for his pistol. With the shove, Walter was able to get his hand around the butt of the pistol and pull it free as Andrew stumbled backwards. Now he pointed Andrew's own pistol at him and grinned.

David's attention turned away from the fight as Christine, still coughing, tried to sit up. He tried to gently push her back down but she fought against him. David moved away slightly as she turned to her side thinking that she was going to be sick.

"No, Walter," she managed to say then in a swift move, David's pistol was free.

The loud report of the shot echoed in the room. Andrew dropped to the floor and rolled towards Walter, not able to understand how the man could have missed. Then wonderment was replaced with surprise as Walter looked to the bed then dropped forward like a falling tree, the pistol falling harmlessly to Andrew's side.

Andrew's gaze shifted to the bed in time to see Christine drop the pistol and roll off the bed. David caught her and gently laid her down on the floor. She had held her breath for just a moment to shoot and now was coughing again. Crawling over the torn material that had been Christine's gown, Andrew made his way to her on the floor.

"Christine! My sweet Christine!" he called out in relief as he touched her face. She turned her head to him and he pressed a kiss on her cheek.

David got up and picked up his spent pistol from the floor. Giving the couple on the floor a moment of privacy, he went over to check on Walter's still form. He picked up Andrew's pistol then kicked Walter over onto his back. Instantly, David saw the blood covering the front of Walter's shirt. The shot Christine fired hit Walter in the middle of his chest. David was shaking his head at the lucky shot when an animalistic growl came from behind him.

At the sound, Andrew turned his head and tried to tuck Christine under him. Marian rushed at them with a large knife in her hands. Raising her arms over her head, she snarled, "Now watch her die!"

Andrew rolled away, taking Christine with him. He shielded her with his body then tensed as he expected to feel the cold steel slice into his back. Instead, another pistol shot echoed in the room then the sound of metal clattered behind him. Andrew looked over his shoulder and found that Marian had fallen onto the bed. Looking around, he found David standing near Walter's body with his arm extended as he held the still smoking pistol towards Marian.

Christine shivered as her mind registered on how close she had come to death. Thinking that she was cold, Andrew pulled more of the bedspread around her. Helping her to her feet, Andrew closed his eyes and enjoyed the feel of her as he hugged her tightly. When he opened his eyes, he looked over her shoulder to the bed. Marian lay still, her sightless brown eyes staring at the wall.

Turning away from the body while shielding Christine from the sight, he waved for David to join them and said tiredly, "Come, David. Let us go home."

While Andrew and David had been in the house, Percy had busied himself with the task of hitching the horses to the coach as quietly as he could. He was not sure who would be the winner, but he remembered that the Duchess looked ill as the man carried her into the house.

The shots from the cottage frightened the boy and he quickly unhitched one of the horses in case he needed to escape as the Duke had directed. When a lantern appeared from the back door of the cottage, he saw several figures walking slowly towards him. Percy froze and stared wide-eyed with the reins held firmly in his hands. If it was the man and the other woman, he had no explanation to offer for his actions.

The boy released his breath as he heard the Duke call out, "Good thinking, Master Stockwell."

"Thank you, Your Grace," the boy muttered, somewhat surprised yet glad to see them.

Percy finished with the horses while David opened the door of the coach and Andrew helped Christine into it. Wrapped in another thick quilt that David had found in another room, Christine lifted a bare foot then froze. In the middle of the floorboards was the satchel that held the bottle of wine. As

Andrew pulled out the satchel, Christine explained about the bottle and that it was laced with some kind of drug.

Looking inside the bag, Andrew and David found the satchel empty. Remembering that the driver had a bottle, David went back into the stables to check the bottle cradled in the crook of driver's arm and noticed the label marked as Christine had described it.

"Too much would kill, he had said," came Christine's voice from the entrance.

David turned to see Andrew beside his wife. Percy was peering inside from around her shoulder.

"It is time for you to be home," David said to her as he walked towards them.

Sitting with Percy in the driver's seat, David drove the coach while inside Andrew held tight to his wife. He had nearly lost her to the madman, to the titled lord who had hired men to kill her and ordered it to look like an accident.

"I was Lady Mischief," Christine was saying as she lay across Andrew's lap. "I made accidents happen, Andrew, funny incidences to relieve the boredom."

"You are not to blame for any of this," Andrew told her.

"Walter was the one who tortured Bellows on that ship and Bellows told him everything," Christine went on to say. "Walter knew everything. He knew I was the one Bellows called his angel. He knew about my promise to kill Bellows if he harmed another girl."

"Christine, stop blaming yourself. Walter had lost all reasoning. You cannot blame yourself for what happened after you left that school."

"Oh Andrew, so many people suffered. Ian, Tilly—" she began.

"Lady Bellows allowed the blame to fall on Ian. You said it yourself. She knew the type of person that Ian was and allowed the blame to fall on him rather than seek the truth of Tilly's accusations towards her brother," Andrew tried to reason. "Tilly was another who fell victim to Bellows' callous treatment of young women but what eventually happened to her was of her father's doing, not yours. He refused to believe his daughter and, when it all came to light, he realized his mistake but it was too late."

When Christine only stared at him, Andrew added, "Tilly was a lonely girl. Bellows preyed upon that loneliness for his own pleasure. He preyed on the young girls before you even enrolled in the school. That is all it ever was, Christine. Do not let him or Walter shift their wrongs to you."

Finally, he saw a flicker of a reaction in her eyes and she nodded slightly, giving him a small smile.

"Good," he said softly. "Let the past go back to the past. I will not lose you, Christine. Not to the past, to Bellows or to Walter."

She rested her head upon his shoulder but almost immediately sat up again. "Andrew, Lady Reynolds should not face the humiliation of Walter's deeds," Christine told him. "Walter had restored his family's honor. Revealing all of this would serve no purpose."

"I have no intention of revealing this. It would implicate you as well and everyone would know who Bellows' angel was," Andrew said softly.

"Then how will the bodies be explained?" she asked.

"I am not sure at the moment but by morning I may have a plan," he told her then kissed her lightly. He lifted her chin so that he could examine the bruised neck in the wavering light of the lantern. "Darcy may have something for you because your throat will be sore for a while."

Christine winced slightly and said with a smile, "I am sore now but not my throat. The moment we are home, I am feeding the twins." Adjusting the blankets around her, she mumbled, "I certainly hope they will be hungry."

Tragic news usually spreads like wildfire and it traveled quickly back to London of how Lord Walter Reynolds and Lady Marian Sanders, while en route to Kenilworth, were attacked by highwaymen. Lord Reynolds was to speak to Andrew concerning a business venture. Though it was said that Marian had accompanied him because she was planning to visit some friends living on a small estate outside of London, the gossips believed that she was going to make another attempt to win back the Duke.

A crowd had gathered for Walter's funeral to pay their condolences to his widow and young sons. Crying by the graveside, Lady Clara Reynolds was comforted by the Duke and Duchess of Kenilworth. After the services, Andrew walked slowly with Clara back to her coach while Christine stepped over to another grave.

Standing with Caroline and Elizabeth, Andrew watched as Christine knelt down and ran her fingers across the name on the headstone. *Matilda Ford Reynolds.*

"I am sorry, Tilly," she whispered softly. "I should have killed him that day then your family would not have suffered so much."

Bowing her head, Christine let the tears fall.

Epilogue

The grounds of Kenilworth were covered with a blanket of fresh snow over the night. Andrew smiled as he pressed soft kisses to his wife's bare shoulder.

"Time to wake up, sweet Christine. Your children are awake and want to start the day," he whispered.

Christine rolled onto her back and the tops of her breasts drew his attention immediately. Lazily opening her eyes, she grinned up at him. "I was up half the night with them. Be a good father and play with them for a while."

Andrew chuckled lightly. "I have been a good father. I have played with them for hours but they grow impatient waiting on their mother."

Unable to resist, he dipped his head to kiss the exposed flesh before him. Christine moaned and lifted her arms up to thread her fingers through his thick hair. "This would only make them wait that much longer, Your Grace," she whispered seductively.

Andrew grunted then shrugged in unconcern. "So they wait a little longer."

She laughed as he used his face to lower the covers and touch a nipple with his tongue. He lifted his head and, with a smile, gazed down into her sapphire eyes. "I could stay right here and love you all day."

"You have and all night too, as I recall," Christine replied with a radiant smile.

Andrew inhaled deeply and rolled his eyes as he rose, taking her with him. She stood naked before him and his emerald eyes roamed over her. "I can never have enough of you," he whispered then pulled her to him for a long deep kiss. When he released her lips, he sighed and said, "If you do not emerge from this room soon." He paused for effect and shrugged. "Well, I cannot be held responsible."

"I would be out much sooner if you were not responsible for detaining me."

Andrew smiled as he turned her towards the bath chamber. "Then go make yourself presentable, my love."

Christine was coming down the staircase when Darcy looked up and let out a sigh of relief. With a soft laugh, she asked the housekeeper, "Have they been unruly?"

"Excited is more like it. They cannot be still," Darcy replied with a grin. "One would think that as late as they were up last evening, they could have slept longer this morning."

Following Christine into the parlor and standing together in the doorway, the two women took in the scene with loving smiles. Andrew sat on the sofa with two-year old Robert while ten-year-old Sarah made faces to make the toddler chuckle happily. Four-year-old Katherine, lovingly called Katie, and her six-year-old sister, Victoria, lay on the carpet near their father's feet coloring pictures. Nine-year-old Phillip was having a quiet argument with his ten-year-old brother, Simon.

"Mama!" Katie called out announcing Christine's arrival.

"Good morning," Christine greeted in a singsong tone as she stepped into the room. "And why is everyone awake so early this morning?"

She sat on the sofa next to Andrew and Robert deserted his father by reaching out with small arms to his mother. Taking him onto her lap, Katie took the toddler's place as she climbed up onto Andrew's lap. He smiled down into his daughter's face as she hugged his neck.

"To open the presents!" Victoria answered with excitement. She tossed back the thick wavy black mass of hair and pleaded with wide emerald eyes. "May we open the presents now?"

"Now Lady Victoria, your mother just came in. Let her catch her breath first," Darcy scolded lightly.

Christine gave Andrew a sideways glance that made him chuckle. "I thought that we were going to wait until Grandmother arrived later this morning."

The reminder was met with a chorus of groans that Christine was hard-pressed not to smile. "Stephen, Michael, and Matthew will be coming with her along with Caroline and David."

Simon and Phillip shared a smile at the thought of their cousins coming to visit.

Victoria was not about to be distracted from her quest. "Please, Mama, can we open just one? Papa, can we?" she begged with a pitiful look.

"Yes, just one," Phillip put in.

"Well," Christine said then paused to ponder the thought. Looking at Andrew, she raised a brow. "What do you think?"

"Hmm, what do you think?" Andrew turned the question to Katie.

Her sapphire eyes sparkled as she let out a giggle. "Open presents," she nearly shouted.

"Very well then," Christine said and the room echoed with loud cheers of '*hoorays*' as the children scrambled for the stack of decoratively wrapped gifts.

"However!" Christine added loudly that the children stopped in their tracks and turned to face her.

Darcy nearly laughed aloud as the children's groans echoed in the room.

Christine smiled and said quietly yet firmly, "Simon and Sarah will find one gift for each of us while we sit and wait patiently."

Darcy hid her smile as she turned to idly rearrange the figurines on the nearby table. *The Duchess certainly has each one of her children and the Duke wrapped around her finger*, she thought.

As Simon searched the nametags so that Sarah could pass out the gifts, Victoria and Phillip hurriedly sat on the opposite sofa facing their parents and young Robert. From Andrew's lap, Katie clapped happily making Robert clap.

Smiling, Christine's gaze roamed over the faces of each child. The children had hers and Andrew's thick wavy black hair and, with the exception of the two youngest, Katie and Robert, who had her sapphire blue eyes, the older children had Andrew's emerald green eyes.

My family, she thought with a smile. She had not stopped with only two, three, or even four children. Christine enjoyed feeling the new life within her and even the pains of childbirth did not deter her from the joy of bearing Andrew another heir to the Chandler name. When the news circulated that she was carrying her fifth child, London had been buzzing with gossip of how there seemed to be enough Chandler heirs. She had merely shrugged and told Andrew that she was going to have her children, however many, and no crone was going tell her when to stop. He had laughed at that remark and kissed her slightly protruding belly.

Looking at Robert, she saw a small likeness of Christopher Lockhart whenever he smiled. The corners of his eyes would crinkle up like her father's had when something struck him as funny. Christopher Lockhart would have enjoyed the large number of grandchildren to spoil. Thinking of her father, her gaze drifted to Phillip. Andrew had surprised her by breaking their bargain of how the children would be named and he named their next son after her younger brother who had died in childhood.

Andrew was having his own thoughts of how his life had turned out. Christine had given him more than he had ever hoped for or thought he would ever receive. She had never cared for his title or his wealth, only his friendship at first. Now their love grew by leaps and bounds.

Draping his arm over her shoulders, Andrew pulled Christine close for a soft kiss. "I love you," he whispered.

Christine smiled up at him and touched his cheek with gentle tips of her fingers. "That love is returned wholeheartedly, Your Grace," she whispered as she kissed his lips once more.

Excited gasps and exclamations came from each child as the gifts were opened. Victoria held up her new slippers to go with a dress she had yet to open. Phillip clapped his hands together with glee as he thumbed through the blank pages of his new journal. Katie let out a giggle as she saw the many colors of ribbons she now had to decorate her dark hair. Christine helped Robert open his gift and the young toddler's eyes grew wide in pleasant surprise as he reached out greedily for his new wooden horse.

"A present for you, Father," Sarah said quietly and held out a box.

Andrew smiled up at his eldest daughter and took the gift. He watched as Sarah handed Christine a long slender box of the diamond bracelet he had bought for her. Still not opening his gift, he waited for each child to open his or her gift. Simon and Sarah were the only ones left to see what surprise awaited them. He and Christine smiled as Simon let out a soft yell of surprise to see that he had his own copy of Shakespeare's plays while Sarah happily draped her new lace shawl about her shoulders.

Andrew smiled as Christine sat Robert down on the floor to play with his new toy before she opened her gift. The diamonds sparkled in the light of the fire. Leaning to him for a kiss, Christine whispered, "Very beautiful, Andrew."

"Not nearly as beautiful as you, my love."

Smiling, Christine's gaze dropped to his unopened box. "Now it is your turn."

He shrugged and made a face at his wife as he opened the box then stared at the contents for a moment before he lifted it up.

Katie glanced up from her gift of new ribbons and saw her father's gift. Her giggles attracted everyone else's attention.

"Oh Papa, that shirt is too small to fit you!" she exclaimed loudly.

Darcy gasped and clapped her hands together in excitement. "Oh, Your Grace!"

Andrew turned to stare at Christine who was smiling at him. "Number seven?"

"Mother, are you with child?" Sarah asked happily.

"Yes, my darlings. We will have another one before the summer," Christine told the children who then started to chatter at once. She faced Andrew and, with a smile, she whispered, "You have three sons and three daughters. Which would you like next?"

Andrew gently urged Katie off his lap and she slid down to the floor to color once again. Putting his hands on each side of his wife's face, Andrew's countenance lit up with happiness. *Our love is still growing by leaps and bounds*, he thought happily.

"Why not make it an even four and four, sweet Christine?" he whispered.

Christine laughed softly making his insides melt as it always did. "I will see what I can do for you, green eyes."

The End

Other Books by C.C. Colee

The RB Trilogy:

RB: The Widow Maker, 1-58851-378-5

RB: The Enchantress, 1-59129-065-1

RB: The Game, 1-59286-135-0

Printed in the United States
18805LVS00003B/13-48